Whatever Happened to
FREDERICK G?

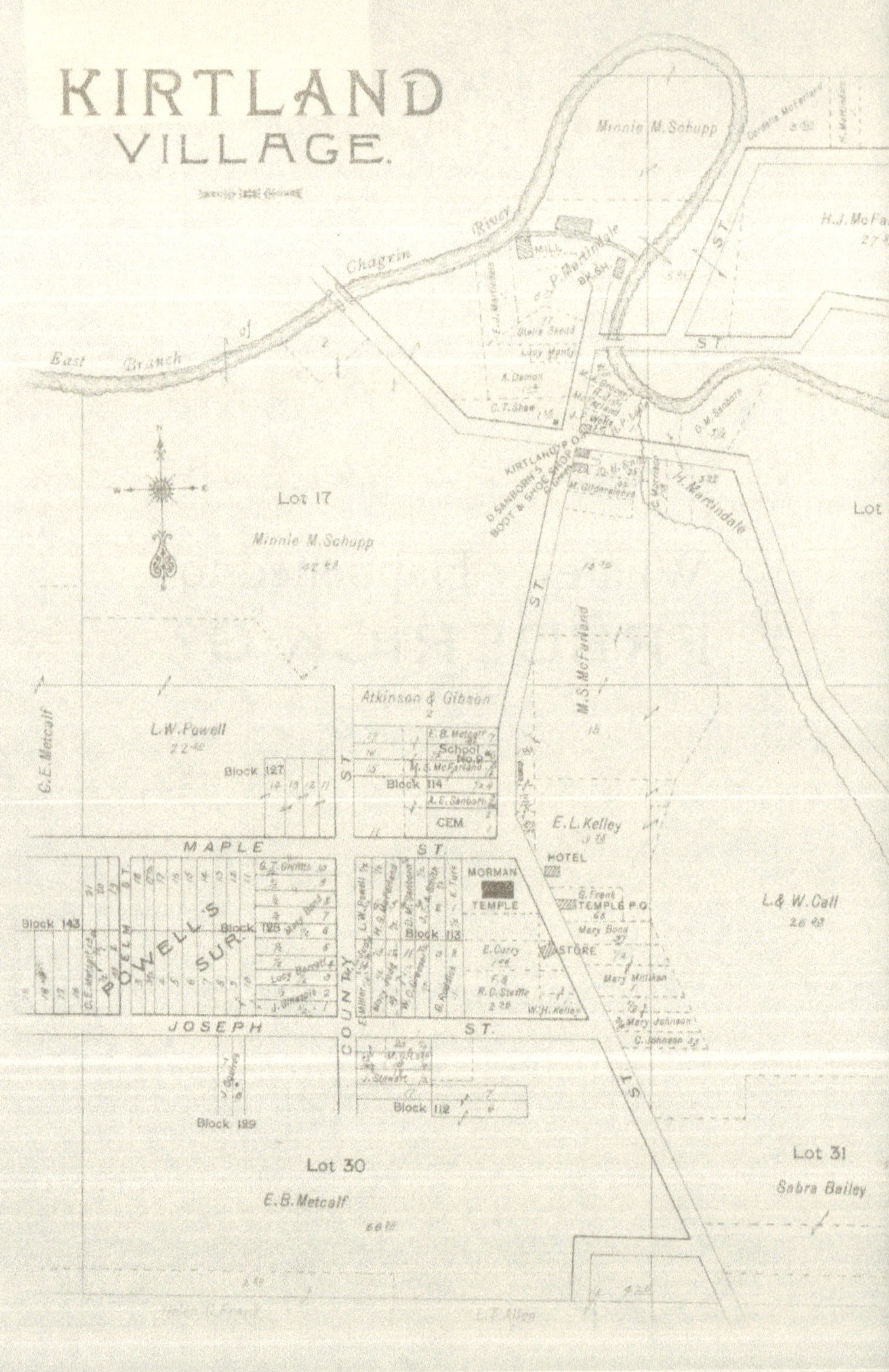

KIRTLAND
VILLAGE.
Minnie M. Schupp
H. J. McFarland
Chagrin
River
MILL
E. P. Martindale
BK. SH.
ST.
ST.
East Branch of
Stella Snead
Lily Young
A. Damon
C. T. Shaw
J. F. Weeks
KIRTLAND P. O.
O. SANBORN'S
BOOT & SHOE SHOP
M. Gildersleeve
H. Martindale
Lot
Lot 17
Minnie M. Schupp
M. S. McFarland
N
W E
S
Atkinson & Gibson
C. E. Metcalf
L. W. Powell
E. B. Metcalf
School No. 9
M. S. McFarland
Block 127
Block 114
A. E. Sanborn
CEM.
E. L. Kelley
MAPLE ST.
HOTEL
S. T. Griffith
MORMAN
TEMPLE
G. Frank
TEMPLE P. O.
L. & W. Call
Block 143
POWELL'S SUR.
Block 125
L. W. Powell
Block 113
STORE
Mary Bond
Mary Millikan
E. Curry
F. S.
R. O. Steele
W. H. Kelley
Mary Johnson
C. Johnson
JOSEPH
COUNTRY ST.
ST.
M. G. Fish
J. Stewart
Block 112
Block 129
ST.
Lot 30
Lot 31
E. B. Metcalf
Sabra Bailey
Helen G. Frost
L. F. Allen

Whatever Happened to
FREDERICK G?

SHERRIE FARR DUNFORD

TABLE OF CONTENTS

IOWA
WINTER QUARTERS
KANESVILLE
MISSISSIPPI RIVER
MISSOURI RIVER
MISSOURI
SPRING HILL
(ADAM-ONDI-AHMAN)
GALLATIN
HAUN'S MILL
FAR WEST
LIBERTY
INDEPENDENCE
JEFFERSON CITY
ILLINOIS
NAUVOO
CARTHAGE
QUINCY
SPRINGFIELD
ST LOUIS
INDIANA
INDIANAPOLIS
OHIO
CLEVELAND
KIRTLAND
LAKE ERIE
COLUMBUS
REFERENCE MAP

Author's Note

The idea of writing the history of Kirtland through the eyes of the children came to my sister and me after attending a Williams Family Reunion there around 1997. Julie and I worked on many Williams Family projects for the next few years, along with our cousin Velma Williams Skidmore, and we had great plans for many good things, including turning our idea into a play. But alas, the best plans often go awry, and when Julie passed away in 2003, it wasn't fun for me anymore.

I thought about turning the play into a book from time to time but never acted on it until twenty years later when I was prompted to record the lessons of Dr. Williams' life, lessons that everyone can learn from if they will. And so I began to put these chapters down in writing, as seen through the eyes of Frederick's son, Ezra. The words came to me easily, as if someone were telling me what to write. I have to believe that Julie, Ezra, Frederick and Rebecca, and many other family members on the other side of the veil have helped me through this process.

I could not have done any of this, however, without the aid of the excellent comprehensive history of Dr. F. G. Williams by my cousin Dr. Frederick G. Williams III, who spent years gathering every scrap of information he could find on our ancestor's life. Although President Williams spent untold hours scribing revelations and much more for the Prophet Joseph Smith and creating histories of events in early Church History, he did not leave us any writings about himself.

I have used authentic names wherever I could, and where no name was known, I substituted the names of people I know, trying my best to make all the characters represent real people.

Although this powerful story is based in fact, I do not claim that the history is totally accurate. With the exception of some excerpts from the journals of Henrietta C. Williams and Ezra G. Williams, the dialogue is the result of my imagination. I have used my own poetic license in many events, imagining how Ezra as a young child, and then a young man, would have seen things. Nor is it a comprehensive history, as I tried to remain faithful only to events that Ezra would have had first-hand knowledge of, and how he might have experienced them. If you want a more accurate and complete history of these events, go to the many histories kept by the Church of Jesus Christ of Latter-day Saints, other books by many authors and historians who have put together accurate histories of the time, and to the excellent volume entitled *The Life of Dr. Frederick G. Williams, Counselor to the Prophet Joseph Smith,* by Frederick G. Williams III. It is easily obtained as an e-book on the Deseret Book site, and also as a Kindle e-book from Amazon.

Although no list of people to thank is ever complete, I would be amiss if I did not name a few. My sincere thanks to my husband, Craig R. Dunford, who untiringly read and listened to me read to him; to Richard Paul Evans who I came to know through a chance meeting, and who set me on the path to publication; to my editors, Debbie Ihler Rasmussen and Kim Autry; to Bethany Dunford Robbins who designed the cover, and Francine Platt who designed the interior; to my many friends who were willing to read and critique portions of the manuscript; to my faithful cousin, Dr. Frederick G. Williams III for his willingness to share his knowledge with me; to the man, President Frederick G. Williams, for living a quiet but amazing life, and for setting the example of staying true to the principles of the Gospel of Jesus Christ despite his many trials and his own weaknesses; and for my Father in Heaven for allowing me the privilege of writing this book.

PERTINENT WILLIAMS GENEALOGY

Names in **bold** type are key characters in this book

Frederick Granger Williams, son of William Wheeler Willliams and Ruth Granger

Born:	28 Oct 1787
Married:	25 Dec 1815 to Rebecca Swain
Died:	10 Oct 1842

Rebecca Swain, daughter of Isaac Swain and Elizabeth Hall

Born:	3 Aug 1798
Died:	25 Sept 1861

Children of Frederick and Rebecca:

Lovina Susan Williams   1816–1847, m. 1836 to Burr Riggs
Joseph Swain Williams   1819–1838
Lucy Eliza Williams   1821–1845, m. 1842 to Nathan Pinkham
Ezra Granger Williams 1823–1905, m. 1847 (1) **Henrietta Elizabeth Crombie** (1827–1922)
m. 1857 to (2) Electa Jane Barney (1840–1883)

Children of Ezra and Henrietta who attained adulthood:

Lucy Ellen Williams   1848–1942, m. 1867 to William Reeves Godfrey
Mary Elizabeth Williams   1852–1934, m. 1869 to Joseph Smith Gardner
Frederick Granger Williams II 1853–1918, m. 1876 to (1) Amanda Burns
m. 8 Apr 1889 to (2) Nancy Abigail Clement
Ezra Henry Granger Williams 1855–1929, m. 1874 to Sarah Ann Hickenlooper
Francis Henrietta Maria Williams 1864–1890, m. 1880 to Thomas Budge

Child of Ezra and Electa:

Hyrum Royal Williams   1858–1927

Two of the 13 children of Frederick II and Amanda:

1. Amanda Elizabeth Williams Farr (oldest child)
   Oswald Woodrow Farr (Twelfth of her 12 children)
      Sherrie Farr Dunford (Third of his four children)—author
2. **Joseph Frederick Williams** (first of nine sons to live to adulthood)

CHAPTER ONE

OGDEN, UTAH 1904

House Guests from Mexico

I'm dying. It's a fact.

But then, we all are. It is an inevitable part of life. I've been a doctor long enough to know the smell of death, and I am dying. I've saved many lives and have failed to save many others. But in the end, they all die, and now I'm dying. Right now, I have a very hard time walking, and so I spend most of my time in this prison of a bed. And my poor sweet Henrietta takes care of my every need. How I wish I could get up and help her instead of lying here day in and day out. My death will be a blessing for both of us.

In an attempt to make the time pass faster, Ezra Williams sat propped up on pillows in his bed, writing a few things in his journal to leave for his posterity.

This was a big day for Ezra. His son, Frederick Granger Williams II, was on his way from Mexico. Fred had moved his family there after narrowly escaping prosecution for plural marriage, a practice that many members of the Church of Jesus Christ of Latter-day Saints were asked to live in the late 1800s.

Ezra could hardly contain his excitement.

I was born in Warrensville, Ohio, on November 17, 1823, which makes me—

He stopped to make a calculation.

Let's see, it is 1904, so that makes me 80 years old, turning 81 this fall. That is a pretty long life for someone like me, someone who has been exposed to every imaginable disease from cholera to whooping cough to—well, I've treated them all.

I wanted to become a doctor at first because my father was a doctor, and I wanted to be just like him. When he helplessly witnessed his sister-in-law, Lovina Dibble Williams, and her newborn baby, die in childbirth back in March of 1816, he decided to pursue in earnest his lifelong dream of practicing medicine. His hope was that someday he would be able to prevent things like this from happening, and the inevitable sadness and despair that this kind of loss brings to a family.

My father was Frederick Granger Williams. He became second counselor to the Prophet Joseph Smith in 1833.

His father, William Wheeler Williams, commonly known as Wheeler, took possession of some land in what is now Ohio, but what was then called the Western Reserve. It was a part of the Connecticut land grant, reserved for citizens of that state who wanted to go west. Their hope was to start anew in a wild country that seemed to offer untold opportunities.

Wheeler jumped at the chance. He packed up his wife and five children and moved west to Ohio. Turns out Wheeler became one of the founders of Cleveland, right there on the shores of Lake Erie. Because he was willing to run a mill on a nearby waterfall, he got the land for very little money.

When my father was old enough to go out on his own, the sea beckoned him, and he gained the experience needed to be a ship pilot on Lake Erie, near where he was raised. He came to know that lake well, and his expertise earned him the position of pilot for Commodore Perry during the War of 1812.[1]

Lake Erie can be treacherous, and without a good pilot, a ship can easily get into trouble. There are sunken reefs, rocky coasts, and many small islands that present problems for sailing vessels, especially when a storm suddenly comes up, but Father had learned to navigate all of these pitfalls. After the war, it seemed a simple choice for him to pilot a commercial ship on the lake, taking people and goods from one end of it to the other.

Ezra looked up from his writing. "Henrietta! Henrietta, can you see them coming?" Although his voice was not as strong as it once was, he was still able to make himself heard.

She yelled back from the front porch. "No, Doctor. I promise I will let you know as soon as I see them."

The Williamses lived on Washington Boulevard, the long, straight main street through town. Their house was quite far north, so Henrietta would be able to see the buggy a long way off as it came from the railway station.

One day, a beautiful girl named Rebecca Swain boarded the ship in Buffalo, New York. She was going to visit her sister Sarah in Michigan. She was making the long journey by way of the ship piloted by the handsome young Frederick Williams.

Sarah lived with her husband, John Clark, in Wyandotte, Michigan, at the opposite end of Lake Erie from her sister. Rebecca lived with their father and brothers in Youngstown, New York, very close to Niagara Falls.

When Frederick saw her, it was love at first sight.

The two must have talked the whole way to Michigan and back. Even with a favorable wind, the two hundred and forty-mile one way trip would take all day and part of another.

Perhaps Rebecca often found excuses to go see her sister because soon, Frederick and Rebecca decided to spend their lives together.

After an acceptable length of courtship, they were married on Christmas Day, 1815. Rebecca was expecting their first child when Lovina Williams and her baby died the following March. His wife's pregnancy hastened Frederick's resolve to learn the art and science of medicine.

That September, Rebecca delivered a baby girl, both she and Mother coming through the ordeal healthy and strong. They named the baby Lovina Susan for my father's ill-fated sister-in-law, and my mother's older sister Susan who had also died young.

The family grew to include three more children. The second, Joseph Swain, was born three years after Lovina, in 1819. Then two years later, my sister Lucy Eliza came along on September 27, 1821. I was the fourth and last child, born two years after Lucy, in 1823.

They named me Ezra Graves Williams, as a tribute to Dr. Ezra Graves of Bedford, Ohio, who had helped my father with his medical research and training. Bedford was very near Warrensville where Father had purchased one hundred and sixty-one acres of land.

My father and I were alike in so many ways, and I was his shadow until the day he died. One thing we didn't share is the gift of gab. Father was a quiet, pensive person who liked to go about his business behind the scenes, so to speak, and who did not like to be the center of attention. Me, I like to talk.

Henrietta quietly came into the room, took a peek at what Ezra was writing, and pulled the journal from his hands. "And talk and talk," she said as she wrote.

"Wait, Henny, what are you doing? Give that back!"

"I just had to write two cents' worth of truth, Doctor." She laughed as she returned the journal to Ezra and then left the room.

Oh Henrietta! She can be a stinker sometimes, but I have to admit, she is the delight of my life.

"Now, where was I?" he mumbled. "She has messed me all up, and I can't remember what I was trying to say.

"Father was a quiet, pensive person … go about his business behind the scenes … did not like … center of attention. Me, I like to talk. Oh yes. Now I remember."

I wrote to our son, Frederick—named for my father—, in Mexico, and asked him to come here to Ogden, Utah, where we live, to help me tie up the loose ends of my life, and to write down some of the history of our family before I pass to the other side. He is on his way and should be here today. And here is the bonus: he is bringing my fifteen-year-old grandson with him. I haven't seen young Joseph since he was two years old, when the family left for Mexico, and haven't seen my son for nearly that long as well. I cannot wait to see them. My grandson was named for two of the greatest men I ever knew, the Prophet Joseph Smith, and my father, Frederick G. Williams.

Now I am putting this journal away but expect to have Fred continue writing things in it that I think my posterity needs to know. I hope the youngster finds some interest in what I want to say as well. You never know what a teenager will find to his liking!

Henrietta came screeching into the room. "Ezra! Ezra! I think they are here!" She untied her apron and threw it down. "I can see a buggy coming down the street! It must be them."

Henrietta left the room, ran out the front door, and into the street. She waited as the buggy pulled up. Out jumped her son Fred, who swept his mother up into his arms, swung her around, and hugged the daylights out of her.

"Oh, Mother! I have needed to see you for so long."

Still handsome at age fifty-one; just under six feet tall with dark brown hair and big eyes, he set her down and held her back at arms' length, looking into her face. "You are even more beautiful than I remember."

"Oh, stop it, Frederick. I am an old woman."

"Well, you have the face of an angel to me."

She hugged him back as hard as she could, as if she couldn't believe he was really there. Parted in the middle, her long gray hair was tied back in a bun. She had a pleasing face that seemed to always be ready to smile.

Henrietta hadn't noticed Joseph take their bags out of the buggy until she saw him awkwardly standing nearby, a muscular fifteen-year-old with sandy blond hair and a smattering of freckles strewn across his nose and cheeks.

"And who is your traveling companion, Frederick?" she asked.

"Oh, Mother, forgive me."

Joseph stepped up and introduced himself. "Hello, Grandmother. I am your grandson, Joseph."

It had been thirteen years since Henrietta had seen the boy. "Oh, my little Joseph. Look at you, just look at you. You are big and strong enough to shoulder some responsibilities, no doubt."

"I do what I can, Grandmother."

She smiled and pulled him into a quick hug.

"He is a good son, Mother, and my right-hand man. He is a great example for his younger brothers and sisters. I wish I could have brought them all with me."

Henrietta, admiring the man-child her grandson had become, asked, "How is it that you were the lucky one to get to come with your father, Joseph?"

"Mother insisted that someone come to take care of him, and since I'm the oldest son, I was chosen for the job."

They all laughed.

Hesitantly, Joseph asked, "Where's Grandfather? I have been so eager to meet him as well."

"Oh, my stars! Let's get you in here where you can make a house call on the Doctor. He is probably crawling out of his skin with anticipation to see you both." She linked her arm in Joseph's and pulled him through the house and into Ezra's room.

"Dr. Williams, here are our guests for the next little while."

Ezra, with his full head of white hair and long, well-trimmed white beard, had pulled himself upright and smoothed the bed clothes. Even in his weakened condition, he retained his look of distinction.

Fred hurried to his father and threw his arms around him.

"Papa, how are you? I have been looking forward to our time together for so long."

"Well, it's a good thing you are here now, because I don't think I'll last very much longer."

"Mercy! That reminds me, Ezra. It's time for your medicine. I'll be right back." Henrietta disappeared into the hall.

Frederick watched her leave, and then turned to his father and presented his son. "This young man is your grandson, Joseph Frederick Williams. He has been eager to meet you."

Ezra took a long look at the boy and said, "You know, Joseph, you are named for two of the best men who ever lived on this earth, the Prophet Joseph Smith, and my father, Frederick G. Williams."

Joseph managed a sideways grimace at his father. "So, I hear, Grandfather. I only hope I do their names justice."

"Papa, Joseph and I have thought of a lot of things we would like to talk to you about. Would it be all right if we do that, maybe tomorrow after a good night's rest?"

Henrietta had come back into the room with Ezra's medicine. "Son, have you forgotten how your father likes to talk? Of course he will answer your questions, won't you, Doctor?" She turned to her grandson. "Here, Joseph, hold this glass of water, and give it to your grandfather after he swallows this medicine."

Ezra obediently opened his mouth as Henrietta uncorked a glass bottle, poured a big spoonful of some horrible smelling liquid, and brought the spoon toward his mouth. He made a terrible grimace as she shoved the big spoon in, hurriedly swallowed, then gulped down the glass of water that Joseph handed him.

"Blegh! That is a nasty tasting concoction! What is it?"

"I have no idea, Doctor, you are the one who made it."

"Well then, if it doesn't kill me," he said slowly, "it just might cure me." Ezra shuddered, looked at Fred, and crossed his eyes. He took a long breath, settled back into his pillows, and turned his gaze toward Joseph. "Tell me about your trip to Utah, Grandson. Was it a grand adventure?"

"It was a very long trip, Grandfather. I wondered if we would travel right off the edge of the earth sometimes. How could there be that much road in the whole world?"

Ezra let out a long and hardy laugh. "I have been on a few of those trips myself!"

"Really, Grandfather? Could you tell me about them sometime?"

"I expect to get around to those stories, Joseph. All in good time, though. And as far as your questions are concerned, the reason I sent for your father was to tell him many things about our heritage, things I want all my posterity to know, so I'm very happy to learn that you have questions. I just hope I have all the answers. But it's getting late tonight, and we could all use a good meal and some sleep." He took a deep breath and yelled, "Henrietta."

The peppy little septuagenarian came bustling into the room. "What is it now, Dear?"

"How is dinner coming along? Is there anything these two boys can do to help you?

"Give me five minutes and it will be on the table." She left the room again.

"Great," said Ezra. "That is just enough time for Joseph to finish telling me about his adventure." Ezra turned to Joseph. "Well? What happened."

"I don't think there is that much to tell, Grandfather. We drove our buggy from our home in Dublan up to Deming, New Mexico. Northern Mexico is a very barren land, but pretty in a way. I had never really seen it before that I can remember."

"I certainly enjoyed the ride," said Fred. "Joseph took the reins, and I sat back and relaxed. It gave me a chance to be with my son one-on-one, which is a luxury I don't have very often, and yet here I am with him and you, and Mother, for a while. With so many children, it is rare to get time alone with any one of them."

"I would think so," said Ezra. "How are the children doing, Son? I certainly wish I could see them more often."

"Well, let's see. My two oldest, Elizabeth and Josie, are married ladies now. Lizzy is expecting her sixth child already, next month."

"What? Are you sure? She can't be that old!" Ezra must have been remembering her as a child before the family moved to Mexico.

"You're right. She can't be that old. It doesn't seem so to me either, but she married young. There wasn't much to do in Dublan when she was a girl. She couldn't go to school because there wasn't one, although she would have loved to have an education. She found a great young man, Heber Farr is his name, the Bishop's son. They fell in love and could see no reason to wait to get married."

"By the way," Joseph eyed his father. "Lizzy does not like to be called *Lizzy*. She told me that herself. She likes to be called Elizabeth."

"Is that right? I wonder why she never mentioned that to me. We have always called her Lizzy." Fred pondered that new information for a minute, then said, "You know, now that you mention it, her mother always calls her Elizabeth. I just thought it was because Amanda likes that name."

Ezra, chuckling a little at his son's revelation, queried, "And what about Josie?"

"We call her Josie, even though her name is Sarah Josephine." Then he looked at Joseph. "Does she like to be called Josie?"

Joseph laughed and nodded his head. "Well, Papa, I think so. She never told me any different. But it is easy to get our names mixed up, you know. When Mama calls one of us, we sometimes have a hard time telling if she wants Josie or Joseph, so Mama usually calls me Joe."

"It is pretty much the same story with Josie, Father. She and her husband, Frank Johnson, have two little children, a girl and a boy," Fred said with evident pride.

"I guess that makes me a great-granddaddy then, doesn't it."

Henrietta popped into the room again. "Oh, Ezra, you have been a great-grandfather for quite some time. You know our children all have grandchildren of their own. Now come and get up to the table because dinner is ready," she said over her shoulder as she left the room.

Ezra, clearly embarrassed by his forgetfulness, whispered to Fred, "I must get out more."

Fred and Joseph lifted Ezra into his wheelchair, and the boy pushed his grandfather up to the table. As they went, Fred continued, "Then there is Flora May, Hazel, Leonard, Vernal, and Rolla," he said, ticking each one off on his fingers as he said their names. "And Joseph of course. How many is that? Eight? Those are Amanda's children. Nancy has Orlando who we call O. C., then Henrietta, named after Mother of course, then Orin, and my baby girl, Naoma, who just had her first birthday not long ago. That is four more, making a total of twelve. Of course, I didn't count the babies who died. It's hard to think about them."

As they all took their places at the nicely set table, Henrietta added, brushing at her eyes, "Yes, we all know that story, don't we, Son."

"My good grief, Fred. How do you keep them all straight?" asked his father.

"It's not hard when you love each one, Papa, you know that."

Henrietta then took Ezra's hand on one side, and Joseph's hand on the other. Fred completed the circle by taking Ezra's and Joseph's hands, one in each of his.

Ezra bowed his head and gave thanks. "Our dear Father in Heaven, how grateful we are for the safe arrival of our son, Frederick, and his son Joseph. How grateful we are for Thy loving care of us, for our health, or what is left of it, and of course for the Gospel of Jesus Christ that binds us together forever. And we thank Thee for this beautiful food, prepared by the willing hands of my precious Henrietta. Please bless it to the nourishment of our bodies and minds. Bless our family, Dear Lord, and I say all of these things in the name of Jesus Christ, amen."

They ate the meal with joy, a glorious beef stew with thick gravy and lighter-than-air biscuits, and Joseph couldn't seem to get enough. "May I have seconds, Grandmother? This is the best food I've ever eaten."

"Oh, now Joseph, I'm sure your mother is a great cook," said Henrietta.

"She does the best she can with what we can get, Mother," Fred offered. "Dublan is an entirely different place than Ogden, Utah."

"I would love to give my mother plates and knives and forks and spoons like yours, Grandmother." The table was set with nice china, crystal glasses, real silver utensils, and a cloth napkin at each plate.

"But she probably wouldn't know what to do with them." He looked around the dining room as if he had just noticed it. "This is one of the most beautiful rooms I have ever seen!"

The room was tastefully decorated with floral wallpaper, a large dining table with eight chairs, and a fairly elaborate chandelier that held ten candles, although oil lamps were used in preference to candles in these days. At the windows were ruffled white curtains, held back with ties. A large stone fireplace, on leave from its duties for the summer, could surely keep the room well heated during colder weather.

"I'm glad you like it, Joseph," Henrietta responded. "The Doctor has worked hard to provide for his family since we have been here in the west. We do enjoy a few nice things, but really, this room is quite modest compared to some people's homes around here."

"Well, it is amazing to me. Can I have another biscuit, please?"

Henrietta laughed at Joseph's outsized appetite. "Of course you may. You remind me of someone else I know, who just might be sitting in this room with us." She glanced up at Fred who gave her a sly wink.

"Grandfather?" asked Joseph.

"*Your* father. That boy nearly ate us out of house and home. I guess he knew he would need all the strength he could get to face this world."

"That's funny, Grandmother," laughed Joseph. "It's hard to think of my dad as a young boy."

After the dinner was mostly eaten, Henrietta went to the kitchen and came back with a beautiful cherry pie.

Joseph's eyes widened as big and round as the pie itself.

Henrietta cut a healthy serving, put it on a small plate, and handed it to him.

"Is this all for me, Grandmother?"

Henrietta laughed. "Yes, my boy, it is all for you. You are growing fast and need the energy that it will give you."

Joseph eyed his father as if for approval.

Fred nodded, and Joseph dug in, seeming to savor every mouthful.

Ezra asked, "Is there any whipped cream for the pie, Henny?"

"Sorry, my love, but there was no fresh cream on hand. You will have to eat it plain."

"Oh." Obviously disappointed, he turned to his grandson. "Have you ever had whipped cream, Joseph?"

"No, Grandfather, but it sounds interesting."

"Well, it is absolutely heavenly!"

"Don't worry, Doctor, I will make some soon," said his wife. "I think you will like it too, Joseph."

After a few quiet moments of chewing, swallowing, and murmured compliments on Henrietta's baking skills, Ezra said, "So, Joseph, you didn't tell me about the train ride. Did you enjoy it?" Ezra seemed determined to get more information out of Joseph.

"It was long." Joseph swallowed another bite of pie. "In Deming, we were able to get on the train that brought us the rest of the way to Ogden. It was long, hot, and bumpy, Grandfather. When we finally arrived, we hired a horse and buggy to bring us here to your house. The best thing about that train ride was that my dad and I had a chance to talk about many things, and I got to ask many questions."

"Oh, so many questions." Fred rolled his eyes.

"Then you are a man after my own heart and mind, Joseph. I like to question everything," said Ezra.

Joseph went on. "My dad told me that you knew the Prophet Joseph Smith, Grandfather. Is that really true?"

Ezra looked at Henrietta, then Fred, and finally back at young Joseph. "Yes, I did, Joseph. He and my father were as close as brothers. He even named a son after my father, Frederick Granger Williams Smith. What do you think of that?"

Joseph swallowed the last bite of pie and said, "I didn't know that, Grandfather. What was he like?"

"Who? My father, or the Prophet?"

"Well, I guess…both of them."

Ezra studied his grandson for several minutes, and then said, "I have much to tell you about them both. In fact, I couldn't tell you our family story without telling you so many things about them. But now I am tired and need to rest, and it is a long story, so we will start it tomorrow."

CHAPTER TWO

Ogden, Utah 1904

Ezra's Story Begins

The next day dawned a bright and clear August morning. Well into the previous night, Joseph and his father had talked about many things, but mostly about what they wanted Ezra to tell them. It seemed this gift of gab that Ezra possessed skipped a generation because it was Joseph who wanted to know so much. Or maybe it had something to do with the name. Ezra's father Frederick G. had been a man of few words, and his son Frederick G. tended toward the quiet side as well. He didn't possess the gift that Ezra had, but Joseph seemed to have it in abundance.

At the end of a hearty breakfast of ham, eggs, buttermilk biscuits, and homemade jam, Joseph turned to his grandfather. "Well, we're ready, Grandfather."

"Ready for what?" asked Ezra.

"For you to answer our questions. We came up with several more last night."

Ezra heaved a sigh. "Help me get into that rocking chair there in the parlor, then. I need to be comfortable for this, and I would rather stay out of that dreaded bedroom as long as I can."

Fred and Joseph pushed Ezra's chair into the parlor, then lifted him into the rocking chair. They helped him get as comfortable as they could, putting his feet up on an ottoman, making sure he had pillows everywhere, and throwing a light blanket over his legs, even though it was August. "I seem to remember you asking me last night if I really knew the Prophet Joseph."

"Yes, yes!" both father and son said in unison. They were eager to hear everything about this subject.

Ezra cleared his throat. "Joseph, go in my bedroom and bring my journal. It is on the table next to the bed."

Joseph left and returned with a thick book with leather covers and handed it to his grandfather.

Ezra said, "I can't really tell you about the relationship between the Prophet and my father until I tell you more about him. My father, that is. I started writing a few things down about him and our family that I want you to know. It's a good place to start answering your question too, I think." He handed Fred his journal, then asked, "Will you please read the entry I made yesterday, Son? I thought perhaps you would add to what I have started by writing down the things I will tell you. Would you be willing to do that?"

"Of course, Papa. I would be happy to." Fred pulled a chair up closer to Ezra on one side, and Joseph made himself comfortable by moving his chair near his grandfather on the other side.

Fred read aloud the things Ezra had written the day before. "I'm dying," he read. Then with a thickness in his voice, he read on. "It's a fact. But then, we all are..." After reading a few more lines about the state of Ezra's health, Fred looked up at his father and said, "Papa, this is very hard for me to read. I just got here, and you are writing about leaving permanently!"

"I know it is hard, Son. A lot of the things I have to tell you are hard. But let's move on for now."

Fred continued reading about how Ezra's father became a doctor, and how the family happened to live on the shores of Lake Erie in Ohio in the early part of the 19th century.

He read the part about Frederick Williams being a pilot for Commodore Perry in the War of 1812.

"Wait, Grandpa, did your father really fight in that war?"

"What I wrote there is exactly what my father told me many years ago. The fact that Father could pilot a ship on that treacherous lake after the war tells me he spoke the truth. The Great Lakes are known for their terrible storms, especially ice storms in the winter. They only had sailing vessels in those days, you know. Can you imagine how hard it would be to fight a war in a sailing vessel under those conditions? It would take someone who knew that lake well to be able to get through it at all. Besides, I never knew my father to lie, or even stretch the truth."

Fred asked, "Is there a question about his being a pilot? Surely there are records that would attest to his being there with Perry."

"Father was a hired pilot, and the government kept no record of the hired pilots. But he and Perry were good friends, and after the Battle of Lake Erie in, I think it was 1813, my father hastened him to General Harrison, and on up the river into the Tecumseh War. They were both still very young."

"That is amazing, Grandfather," said Joseph. "My great-grandfather was a famous war hero."

"Well, let's not go so far as to say that, Joseph, but he did his part. That was the way he did everything. He never liked being the center of attention, in fact, he didn't like attention at all. He liked doing what he was supposed to do, and if people didn't notice him, he was happy. You might say he took that idea to the extreme, because he left us virtually no written record of himself, even though he wrote plenty about others as a scribe for Joseph Smith."

Fred continued reading in the journal about how Frederick and Rebecca met, fell in love, and got married. "Let's see, Father, this is a little hard to read." They all looked up at a sound in the hallway and glimpsed Henrietta folding some laundry just outside the room.

Fred looked up at Ezra and in a whisper, questioned, "Love at first sight?"

Ezra chuckled and nodded. They both knew she did not think there was such a thing.

Fred read a little louder, purposely distorting the words for his mother's benefit. "That girl's noun, uh, name were, was, Rebecca Swim—oh it must be Swain." Fred corrected himself and winked at Joseph. "And when Frederick sawed her, no that can't be right, oh, saw her, it has, no, *was...*"

Henrietta looked puzzled.

Fred spoke a little louder still. "Live at frost sigh. Uh, no, it's live at first sigh. Father, what does this say?"

"It's *love,* Fred, *love* at first *sight!*"

"Oh, of course it is." Fred glanced again at his mother, then shook his head and snickered. "How could I miss that?"

"Was it really love at first sight, Grandfather?" Fifteen-year-old Joseph's eyes widened.

At this, Henrietta came purposefully into the room. "Oh posh, Doctor. You know there is no such thing as love at first sight. Love takes time to develop and deepen to become meaningful. You can't just do all of that in an instant."

This was the response Fred seemed to hope for.

Ezra grinned. "Now, Henny, you know I fell in love with you the first time I laid eyes on you."

"Well, I admit I was a sight for sore eyes," Henrietta said, with a sly smile at the corners of her mouth. She started tidying up the room a bit, obviously trying to hide her blush. "I guess I could have had you a bit stirred up, but I don't think you could call it *love.* And I did not get all in a tizzy when I first laid eyes on you, that's for sure. Of course, I was very sick."

Henrietta left the room with an armful of items. Ezra leaned toward Joseph with hand to mouth as if to tell him a secret, gave him a wink, and said *sotto voce,* "She fell in love with me the first time she saw me." They both laughed a low-pitched, conspiratorial laugh.

"Are you sure about that, Grandfather?" whispered Joseph.

"Of course I am," answered Ezra, softly. "How could she not fall head over heels for someone so strong, handsome and smart ..." His voice trailed off as he seemed to lose himself in thoughts about his beautiful young bride. Coming to himself, he went on, "Now, where were we? Oh yes, Fred was reading my journal. Continue, Son."

Fred looked from one to the other as if trying to figure out what was going on between them, then picked up where he had left off, suddenly not having any problem reading Ezra's writing.

He read about the children that were born to Frederick and Rebecca, and when he got to the part about Ezra's birth, Joseph stopped him once again.

"Wait, Grandfather. I thought your middle name was Granger, not Graves. Did your parents really name you Ezra Graves?"

"Yes, they really did, Joseph. Dr. Ezra Graves was a tremendous help to my father in getting his medical practice off the ground, sharing his formulas for medicines, giving him tips on what he might do in certain circumstances, and warning him of things to avoid. He took Father with him on many visits to his patients, which gave Father his practical education. You might say Dr. Graves provided my father with the bulk of his medical training. That was the best and fastest way to gain the needed knowledge and skills in those days, and it also gave him the experience and confidence he needed to treat patients on his own. My parents thought it only right to name a child after him. But as I got a little older and my respect for my father grew, I became his shadow, you might say."

Fred looked in Joseph's direction and gave him a slight nod.

Ezra went on. "I admired and loved him so much that I begged him to change my name to match his. Father finally consented to change my middle name if I would keep the first name of Ezra. I consented to that. Since my first name would still be Ezra, and since the first three letters of my middle name, which would now be Granger like my father's, would still match the first three letters of Graves, surely the good doctor would be satisfied with my having a good part of his name, or so was my reasoning, and I was very happy to finally have Granger as my middle name, which, by the way, was my Grandmother Williams' maiden name. And somewhere in my young mind I thought about the likelihood of naming a son after my father and using all of his name."

Frederick looked up. "Thank you, Papa. I am honored to bear his name."

"Me too," said Joseph, "even though I only bear his first name. And his last, of course."

"I never knew Dr. Graves, but I did know my father, and I wanted to be just like him. I worked on the farm by his side as early as I can remember. I don't know how much help I was, but I tried, and he seemed to like me being around."

"That sounds a lot like my Joseph, Papa. This boy has been able to hammer a nail straight into a board since he was ten years old," Fred said with obvious pride.

"Hey, wait a minute!" Joseph protested. "I've been hammering nails since I was younger than that, Dad, you know that."

"Yes, I do," said his father with a little snicker in his voice, "but I had to pull out most of them and straighten them so they could be properly used."

Joseph winced a bit, but relaxed when Ezra, with a wrinkly nose, added his own snicker and said, "He's just like his father, I guess."

"What?" said Frederick. "I never hammered a crooked nail, did I?"

Henrietta had returned, and her observation calmed everyone down, as she put some clean tablecloths and napkins away in a parlor cupboard. "Now, Fred, you know we all have to start somewhere. None of us was born knowing how to hammer a nail. I still can't do it. But I understand that this young man has already developed a skill at driving a wagon. Is that true?" She glanced at Joseph.

"Yes, Mother, it is true. I'm very proud of the way he can handle a team and wagon. He has worked for me for several years now… How many, Joe?"

"Six years," he responded quickly.

"I've witnessed him driving loads of timber and other things through some pretty rough places with much confidence."

Joseph asked Ezra another question that quickly diverted the attention away from himself, "But what about your brother? He was older than you, wasn't he? Didn't he help your father too?"

"My brother Joseph Swain did not develop properly before he was born. There was something very wrong with him. He was small and didn't walk or talk too well so he wasn't able to help, in fact, we had to take care of him all the time. But that little boy was so full of love." Ezra had a faraway look in his eyes as he talked about his brother.

"What happened to him, Grandfather?"

Joseph's continuing curiosity was contagious, and it was evident already that the two of them would become very good friends.

"Well, Grandson, that is a story for another day, but I promise I will get to it. Right now, though, I want to tell you about my earliest memories of living in Kirtland, Ohio. Fred, do your best to write this all down."

"I'm getting it, Papa. Don't you worry."

CHAPTER THREE

OHIO 1820

Early Life in Kirtland...
Through Ezra's Eyes

Grandfather Williams moved to Ohio around 1800 because of the Western Reserve land that Connecticut had received and was selling at a very low price to anyone who wanted to go west and settle that wild territory. In order to receive his land, Grandpa had to find a river on which to build a mill. He found one in Newburgh, just five miles east of Cleveland, that he appropriately called Mill Creek, and built two mills, one for sawing timber into boards, and one for grinding wheat and other grains into flour. In return, he received eleven thousand, three hundred and six acres of land at a reduced rate. I can only imagine how valuable that land would be today. It seems funny to think of it now, but there was almost nothing in Cleveland when Grandpa Williams arrived, just one home. He built the second one in the area, and he and Grandmother Ruth proceeded to raise their family of five children there, Father being twelve years of age at the time.

Father often told me how different life was in Ohio from how it had been in Connecticut. There was no school for him to go to for a few years after they arrived, and no church either. He had left all of his friends behind, and everything else that was familiar. Luckily, his mother was able to teach her children many of the things they would have learned in school, as well as spiritual things from the Bible. And perhaps most importantly, they had each other. Father and his two younger brothers, Joseph and William Wheeler Jr., grew to be very close during those years, and helped in every way they could.

Even at the age of twelve, Father was a hard worker on the farm, and Grandpa came to rely on him. He helped clear the land, helped plant and care for a large apple orchard, and worked at the mills. He also helped construct their new home on a tree-covered bluff over-looking the bay. It was hard work, but the things he learned stayed with him throughout his life. As the community started to grow, barn or cabin raisings for new neighbors were always a lot of work, but also a lot of fun and a chance for young Frederick and the rest of the family to socialize with their neighbors.

Tragedy struck the family when their mother Ruth began losing her eyesight. Now in addition to all the rest of his responsibilities, Frederick started taking over more of his mother's household duties and caring for the younger children. Ruth's sight became worse until she was totally blind. In a way, it was a blessing for my father to care for her because it gave him a gentleness and sensitivity he would not likely have otherwise acquired growing up on the frontier. Serving his mother in any way possible set him in good stead for his treat-ment of others in his medical practice.

As the children grew up and his younger sisters were able to help their mother, Frederick was able to find time for more recreational activities. There was dancing, boating, swimming at the falls, fishing, and bear trapping and other forms of hunting. There were plenty of places in and around Cleveland in 1810 for a young man to explore and conquer. But the sea called loudly to Frederick, and he spent quite a bit of time with sailors onboard their vessels learning the secrets of sailing ships, and of navigating Lake Erie. What a great life for a teenaged boy. It was this that prepared him for his time with Commodore Perry in the War of 1812. And the time he spent pilot-ing ships for Perry prepared him for his navigating up and down the lake after the war, which in turn prepared him to meet the beautiful Miss Rebecca Swain.

When he was just twenty-three, Father bought some land from his father, one hundred and sixty-one acres in a little nearby place called Warrensville for four hundred and two dollars, and it turned out to be a very good investment. After the War of 1812, and his marriage to my mother, he built a house on that land, and that is where the two of them lived for quite a while, and where all of us children were born.

Dr. Graves, it turns out, lived very nearby in a little place called Bedford. It was the perfect time, and the conditions were just right for Frederick to start his career as a physician. Dr. Graves convinced him to become a botanical doctor, a practice as old as civilization, but which seemed like a radical idea at the time compared to the more popular orthodox practices of using toxic chemicals and blood-letting. Dr. Graves urged him to get literature on the Thompsonian Method of healing through the use of herbs and clean, healthy living, which Father did. That more natural way of healing appealed to him, which is a good thing because it turns out those orthodox practices were not such good ideas. They did more harm than good.

Father soon took out ads in the local newspapers, announcing his medical skills to help with childbirth, setting broken bones, stitching wounds, treating burns, and treating cholera and other diseases. His medical practice began to grow, and he soon became a sought-after physician.

By 1828, Father had sold nice chunks of the Warrensville land to three different men which enabled him to buy a nice home in nearby Chardon. We enjoyed the newer, bigger home in Chardon for a couple of years. Looking back on that time, I see the Lord's hand in it because in late 1829, Father made a trade with the rest of his land in Warrensville for a large farm owned jointly by Isaac More and Peter French in Kirtland. Although Father had paid both French and More for the Kirtland farm, Peter French did not follow through with the recording of his half of the sale. However, on the 1830 Kirtland tax map, Father's name is on two large Kirtland lots, 29 and 30. Each of the two lots contained one hundred and five choice acres. Father continued to pay the taxes on the land, and assumed French had had the sale recorded, until he tried to sell it.

CHAPTER FOUR

Ogden, Utah 1904

A Case of the "What ifs"

Henrietta bustled into the room, then abruptly stopped as she noticed both Fred and Joseph had nodded off. "I think you have lost your audience, Doctor," she whispered.

"What?" Ezra glanced around at his son and grandson. "Oh goodness, I didn't know I was boring them to death."

Henrietta edged closer to Ezra, and then in a low voice said, "I have something I want to do, Ezra. I was thinking that since Joseph is so good at driving a horse and wagon that maybe he could take me up to Smithfield. I would really like to visit the babies' graves before the snow falls."

Joseph came fully awake when Henrietta said *snow*.

"Snow? Is it going to snow? Grandmother, am I going to get to see snow?"

"Of course you'll get to see snow, young man. This is Utah. It snows all winter!"

"I never thought about getting to see snow. I've never seen it before, you know. Oh, I am so excited!"

"No, not since you were two years old. I'm sure you wouldn't remember it. And Joseph, there is something I would like you to do for me, if your father consents. I would like you to take me to Smithfield before the weather gets cold. Smithfield is where three of our babies are buried, and I want to visit their graves. Your great-grandmother Rebecca is buried by the boys as well."

By now Fred had revived and looked at them quizzically. "What is it you want to do, Mother?"

"Well, Son, I guess what I want to do depends in a good part on you. I want Joseph to take me up to Smithfield in the buggy before the weather gets bad. You know we would have to go through Sardine Canyon. It is steep and can be pretty nasty, but if you think Joseph could handle it, I would so dearly love to visit the graves of Rebecca and the babies. What do you think? Could Joseph handle that?"

Fred took a deep breath. "I don't know, Mama. I had a pretty awful experience going up that canyon as a youngster at about his age. Do you remember that?"

"What happened, Dad? Did you run off the road?"

Fred nodded. "Yes, I did, Joseph. We were moving to Smithfield in the early spring, and the roads were muddy. I was taking a load of household items up in a big wagon. There was a sharp turn onto a bridge, I misjudged how soon to turn the horses, and the wheels of the wagon slid off the muddy edge of the bridge, dumping all of our household belongings into the river."

"Oh no! That must have been terrifying."

"It was very frightening, Joseph, but the bridge has been widened since then, and this is August, not early spring," said Henrietta. "And we won't be pulling a heavy load, just our little buggy." She turned to Fred. "What do you think? Do you think Joseph could take me there?"

Fred leaned toward her. "Mother dear. It's not that I don't trust him. It's that so many things could go wrong. Joseph is an excellent horseman and driver. He has hauled heavy loads through some remarkably difficult terrain since he was very young. Still, this is Sardine Canyon we are talking about."

Joseph, obviously excited at the prospect, said, "I would love to take Grandmother up to Smithfield if you think I can handle it, Dad."

Fred smiled at his son. "Let me think about it for a minute, then."

"All right. That's fair." Then turning to his grandmother, he asked, "Where is Smithfield, and why are the babies buried there?"

Henrietta slid a chair next to her grandson and sat down. "Dr.

Williams was called by Brigham Young to go to Cache Valley, about fifty or sixty miles north of here, to help colonize it. President Young sent groups of people all around the Utah territory, north and south, and into Idaho and Arizona, and probably other places, to settle and strengthen those areas. Your grandfather was excited about the prospects of constructing a sawmill, much like his grandfather had done in Ohio many years before. Ezra being a doctor was a big part of the reason President Young sent him north because there were no doctors up that way at the time. While we lived in Smithfield, there were some terrible outbreaks of whooping cough, and our three boys had the misfortune of dying from it."

While Henrietta was telling Joseph about Smithfield, Fred had been pondering his mother's request. Then he took his son into the hallway, pulled him close, and spoke in a low voice so his parents could not hear their conversation. "What do you feel in your gut and in your heart about taking your grandmother to Smithfield? Does it scare you, or do you think you could handle it?"

"I know she wants to go so badly, Dad, and I'm willing to do it if you think I can. I think we will be all right."

"I really believe you can do it, especially if you go slowly and are cautious, and I want to say yes to her for the same reason. Losing all those babies was so hard on her. I trust you completely, but at the same time, I have a bad case of the *What ifs.*"

"*What ifs*, Father? What is that?"

"It means my brain keeps running away with what if this happened, or what if that happened? What if you lost control and the buggy overturned, what if it rained so hard you could not get up the canyon? It makes me worry."

Joseph quietly thought that over for a moment, then he softly replied, "I just won't let that happen, Dad. I'll pray and I'll go, and God will answer my prayers. Don't you remember when I asked you a couple of years ago how you had the courage to just up and leave Ogden for Mexico, a place you didn't even know anything about? You said, 'We pray, and we go.' Isn't that what we did before we left home to come here? We prayed, and we left. It's what you have always taught me."

Fred sighed. "You're right, Son. I guess I have underestimated your faith. I suppose it would be hard for me not to give you permission now. I trust you, and I know you can do it. I have to remember that just because I had a bad experience going up there doesn't mean you will. I will add my faith and prayers to yours."

"Thank you, Dad. I will make you proud."

He put his arm around his father's neck and gave him a quick hug. They re-entered the parlor, then speaking to his grandmother, Joseph asked loudly, "Can I take the horse out a few times and let him get used to me before we go to Smithfield?"

Henrietta turned to her son and asked, "Does this mean you give your consent, Fred?"

"I suppose it does, Mother."

She turned back to Joseph and said with happiness in her voice, "Of course you can take the horse out, Joseph. But there is one more thing. Fred, it hinges on whether or not you would be willing to stay here with the Doctor and take care of him. You would have to fix his meals and get him dressed and in and out of bed, bring him the newspaper, you know, take care of all his needs and wants. Are you good with that?"

"I would consider it my greatest privilege, Mother." He squeezed his father's hand. "I know how to cook, at least well enough to keep us both alive. And I can handle everything else about taking care of him. You know, I'm practically a doctor myself after all I learned about medicine from watching Father. I still have the book of cures that he gave me before we left for Mexico, and I have put it to good use. In fact, I've nearly worn it out. I've treated just about everything you can imagine, and I don't know how many babies I've delivered. I'm the closest thing to a doctor there is in Dublan."

"Well, I don't think you will have to deliver a baby while we are gone, and I know you are a good doctor in your own right." Then giving him a sly smile, she said, "But are you a good nurse?"

Before Fred could answer, Joseph jumped in and asked, "How long will we be gone, Grandmother?"

"I imagine it would be a good week, maybe more. It will take us at least two days to get up there, then we will spend three or four days visiting the graves and seeing old friends, and then two days to get back." It was impossible to miss the excitement in her voice. "You know, Joseph. There is one other complicating item. There are a lot of automobiles on the roads these days, and being in a buggy, we will really have to watch out for them. They go maddeningly fast." She turned to Ezra. "How fast did you say those automobiles can go these days?"

"I read in the newspaper that they are going to impose a fifteen mile per hour speed limit out on the open road. It will be a little slower than that around town of course, maybe twelve miles per hour. Some cars can go a lot faster than that, but it's just not safe on the public roads."

"Maybe someday I'll have a car, Grandpa. Wouldn't that be great?"

"Like a dream come true, Joseph."

Joseph asked his grandmother, "Do you really think it will take two days to get there? I bet I could get us there faster than that."

Fred said, "Joe, if everything goes right, you will make it in two days. There are so many unpredictable things that can happen on a road like that one. I know you would like to move the horse along, but this can be a tough fifty-five-mile journey. You would have to run the horse ragged to make it any sooner. As it is, making it in two days will take all your skills as a horseman."

"And we don't want to feel rushed, Joseph," she added. "As long as your father is here with the Doctor, we can afford to take a little extra time. I want to be able to enjoy every minute of it."

"All right. We can take our time. When do you want to leave, Grandma? I am so excited now that I don't think I can wait very long."

"Let's see, come in here and we will look at the calendar together." Henrietta took Joseph's arm as they both walked out of the room.

"Well," said Ezra, looking at Fred with dismay. "She certainly stole my thunder."

"Uh, Papa, um, I'm sorry I fell asleep while you were talking about …"

"I was talking about the places we had lived in Ohio. I know it wasn't the most interesting part of the story, but you will need to know some of that a little bit later on. I want to turn all of my papers, histories, everything that is important to me over to you before you go home, and you need to know how they tie into this family legacy. That includes everything my father left, Fred. Anyway, I can tell you what you need to know as we get to those parts of the story."

Henrietta and Joseph came back into the room, beaming as if they had witnessed a magic show.

Henrietta was breathless. "I think we can leave the first week of September. That will give us two weeks to get ready, and I will have time to write to some friends to see if we can stay with them in Smithfield. And I'll write to my friend Abigail who lives in Brigham City to see if we can stay with her on the way up and back. Brigham City is about halfway to Smithfield."

She turned to Ezra and said in a much more conciliatory tone, "You are starting to look weary, Doctor. I think it is time for you to lie down for a nap."

✦

The next morning, Fred and Joseph helped Henrietta pick all the ripe produce out of the garden, and then they fixed a few things around the house that had been annoying her. There was a chair that had a loose leg, something that Joseph was able to fix. A towel rack had come loose in the bathroom, and after fixing that, Fred made sure all of the faucets and handles were in working order, and all of the drains were clear and free flowing. Because of Ezra's insistence on cleanliness and sanitation, the Williams house was one of the first in the area to have indoor plumbing, although it sometimes created more problems than it solved. Clogged drains were common, and broken pipes were not unheard of.

When they were finally able to sit down after lunch, Fred asked, "How are you doing, Father? Are you feeling well enough to tell us more of your history, or would you like a nap first?"

"No, Son," he said. "I've had enough rest for now, and I am eager to tell you many more things before I forget them."

Fred quickly pulled out the journal, ready to write whatever it was

Ezra would tell them that day. Joseph helped him get comfortable in the rocker, then once again pulled a chair up close to Ezra.

"Grandfather, did you know your Grandfather Williams?"

"Oh yes, Joseph. I knew him and Grandmother very well. They only lived a few miles from Kirtland, in what was then called Newburgh. My grandmother had gone blind, you know, but Grandpa and my aunts took great care of her. It was a blessing to have my grandparents so close. In fact, I got to stay with them a few times just for fun."

"Did they get to meet Joseph Smith? Did they join the Church?" asked the ever-questioning Joseph.

"Yes, they did meet Joseph Smith and liked him and the other Church leaders very much. In fact, the brethren occasionally stayed at the Williams home on their way to other places," said Ezra. "But sadly, my grandparents never quite saw the vision of the restored gospel and never joined the Church, in this life at least. In spite of that, I was lucky to live close enough to see them frequently."

"I wish I lived closer to you, Grandpa. I love it here. How about your Swain grandparents? Did you know them?"

Ezra looked down at his hands. "No, Joseph. I never even met them. Grandmother Swain had passed away before my father met my mother. And Grandfather—well, he disowned Mother when she refused to leave the Church."

"That is heartbreaking, Papa," said Fred. "I can't imagine not wanting to stay in contact with my children no matter what they had done that displeased me."

"I feel the same way, Son. I guess someday we will understand his reasoning. I just know it broke my mother's heart."

"Did he live close to you in Kirtland?" asked Joseph.

"Have you heard of the great Niagara Falls, Joseph? He lived very close to those falls, in Youngstown, New York, right on Lake Ontario. Mother used to say you could hear the roar of the falls from their home. I guess they are very loud. When Father was piloting on Lake Erie, he would go from very near those falls to Detroit, Michigan. You might recall from my journal that that is how he met Rebecca. How I would have loved to go up there and see those falls! And I wish I could have met old Isaac Swain, maybe talk some sense into him, and tell him how much his daughter loved him! When Rebecca wrote to him and told him all about meeting and marrying Frederick, and later about learning of the restored gospel of Jesus Christ and the Prophet Joseph Smith, he sent a letter back to her begging her to 'leave those crazy ideas behind and come back to him.' She wrote back and told him that she couldn't deny the truthfulness of the Gospel of Jesus Christ. She begged him to listen to her, but he would not. He never wrote to her again. After he passed away, Rebecca's brother wrote and told her that when her father had received that letter, he cried and said, 'she has not repented one bit.' That was the end of their relationship. She continued to write, but he refused even to open the letters."

"That is so sad, Grandpa. I'm very glad you are not like that!" Joseph patted Ezra's arm, then he leaned his head over toward Ezra's, and seemed a little surprised when Ezra leaned toward him in a mutual gesture of admiration.

"So am I," added Fred. "Where would any of us be without our knowledge of the restoration of the true Gospel of Jesus Christ? All of our lives would have turned out very different."

They all sat for a few minutes contemplating the blessings—and hardships—that knowledge had brought them.

"So, as I was saying," Ezra began again, "we moved to Kirtland around 1829. Is that what I was saying, Fred?"

"You were saying something like that, Papa, but that was yesterday."

Ezra chuckled, and then so did the other two.

"Getting old is not for sissies, boys," quipped Ezra. "It is a lot of hard work trying to remember things and keeping things straight, and of course," he looked down at his legs, "not being able to do whatever I want to do."

"Well, you are doing what we want you to do, just by being here and telling us your story," said Joseph.

"Then let's get to it!"

CHAPTER FIVE

KIRTLAND, OHIO 1830

Spunk Skew and a Mission Call...
Through Ezra's Eyes

I was only five, going on six, when we moved to Kirtland around 1829, but I had soon made many new friends. The Chagrin River was nearby, and we children loved playing in it when it wasn't running too high. Even when it did, we played near its banks. It was kind of a lazy river, and just had a way of drawing us to it. Our house was quite nice, with three bedrooms upstairs. Swain and I slept in one room; Lovina and Lucy in another, and the biggest and nicest room was for Mama and Papa.

We had plenty of land to plant any crop we wanted. Near the back door, Mother kept a kitchen garden, where she grew things that were handy for making meals, things like squash, onions, peppers, potatoes, beans, those sorts of things.

Father's medical practice continued to grow, and as it did, so did his prestige in the community. One night when Father came home rather late from attending to a patient, he found my mother sitting on the table. We children had all gone to bed some time before, so Mother was there alone in the kitchen. She had drawn her knees up to her chin, holding them close to her with trembling arms. She had pulled the hem of her nightgown down around her feet, tucking it in all the way around her.

"What on earth are you doing on that table?" Father asked incredulously.

"Oh, Frederick, I saw a mouse!" she cried out, with all the disgust and repulsion she could muster. "You know how I feel about mice, so when I saw one run behind the cupboard, I…I panicked. I couldn't find the broom to defend myself, so I climbed up here where I could keep watch all the way around and make sure that mouse didn't run up my leg." Her voice had gotten increasingly higher in pitch as she talked.

Well, my father began to laugh, and he laughed so hard that my mother started to cry. "Frederick, I'll thank you to stop laughing."

Father tried, but he couldn't stop completely. "Oh, my dear sweetheart, I will save you from the big bad mouse," he said, still trying to stifle the laughter.

"Frederick, it is not funny!" And she started to cry again.

"Now, Rebecca, you have to admit it looks pretty funny, you up there on that table with your nightgown tucked around your feet. Come here and I'll escort you up to bed, and then I will find that offensive critter and put an end to him."

Mother put her head down on his shoulder as he helped her off the table, and then let all of her emotions out. Papa just held her and let her cry.

"How long have you been up there, Love?"

She tried to tell him, despite the involuntary sobs that continued for a while. "Since I put the…children to bed. Then I came…back down here to sit and do…some mending while I…waited up for you."

"Good grief, woman, that must have been two hours ago." Father walked her upstairs to their bedroom, turned down the covers of the bed for her, and then said, "Tell you what. Tomorrow I will ask the children to keep their eyes open for a kitten that we can keep around here as a mouser." He kissed her on the forehead and pulled the covers up under her chin.

"Thank you, Freddy," she choked. "You are my hero."

Papa just smiled at her as he turned to go look for the mouse, chuckling softly all the way down the stairs.

•

He finally heard it scratching behind the corner cupboard. He found the broom, then gingerly pulled the cupboard out so he could see the culprit. He quickly swept it into the corner and held it there with the broom until he could catch it. "There you are you little wretch," he said as he quickly grabbed hold of it. "I will teach you to frighten my woman!"

Papa took it outside to put an end to it, but he looked at the poor little thing's face and decided he couldn't kill it. It was only doing what nature had taught it to do and was probably much more afraid than Mama was. So, Papa took it quite far away from the house into the trees, and let it go. That thing took off as fast as it could go, to be seen no more by womankind.

The next day at breakfast, we children heard all about the exploits of the night before. "So, if you hear of a family whose cat has had kittens, see if they will let us have one," said Father.

"Oh, a kitten!" exclaimed Lucy. "I am going to take such good care of it."

"Me too!" echoed Swain. "I wio wuv it to pieces."

"Well, don't love it too hard, Swainy," Papa said, "or it will go to pieces. It needs to be able to breathe to learn how to catch mice."

"Otay, Bapa, I wio be bewy tarefo."

Swain had an inborn sense of love for all of God's creations, but sometimes that love went a little overboard. John Rigdon and I found some baby ducks a few weeks before, and we brought them home to put in our pond. Swain got hold of them by the neck and didn't know how to let go, and, well, you can probably guess the outcome.

I was excited to look for kittens, and so was my friend Horace Whitney, and wouldn't you know it. We found just the thing while we were out in the woods not too far from home.

"Ezra, Ezra," yelled Horace. "Look what I found!"

I went running to see a nest of the cutest kittens you ever saw. They were all black with a beautiful white stripe running down their backs to the tips of their fluffy tails. There were five, and their mother seemed to have abandoned them. At least she was nowhere to be seen, and the babies seemed to be hungry.

"My mother is going to be so happy to see this kitten," I said as I picked one up and started toward home.

Horace took one too, and we ran home as fast as our little seven-year-old legs would carry us.

Meanwhile, Mother was just getting dinner on the table when Father walked in. He hung up his jacket and hat and said, "Umm, umm, that smells so good, Rebecca. I am so hungry I could eat the whole potful and leave none for the children." Lucy and Lovina looked at him in disbelief.

"Papa, you will leave us a little, won't you? We're hungry too." Lucy informed him with a very panicked look on her face.

Swain, who was playing with a toy on the floor, looked up and said, "I'm weely hungwy, Bapa."

"All right, I'll leave a little bit for you children. But you better hurry and get washed up or I might change my mind."

Taking him at his word, the girls took Swain and hurried to get washed up and back to the table before Father had a chance to eat the whole pot of stew.

Then looking around, he said, "Where is Ezra?"

"He and Horace were playing over in the edge of the trees just a minute ago, Frederick. Please go out and call him home."

"Well, he better hurry or I will eat his share," said Father, as he left the house to find me.

Just as Father stepped outside the house, he saw me running toward him with my precious kitten in hand. "Ezra, what have you got there?"

"I found a kitten for Mother." I held the little thing out in front of me for him to see. Just then that kitten did something I had never known a kitten to do before. He raised his beautiful tail and sprayed me with something that smelled to high heaven.

I looked at Papa in dismay. I didn't want to put it down but was unable to hold onto it.

Father started to laugh, and my eyes started to burn.

Mother came running out of the house screaming at me. "Ezra, you get that blesséd creature out of here right now. That odor will taint the stew."

She came at me with a spoon. I thought she was going to swat me with it.

Father, still laughing, took the kitten and booted it over the fence.

"That isn't a kitten, Ezra, it's a skunk!"

"Oh no!" My eyes were already burning from the skunk spray, so it was easy for me to let go and cry. "I knew Mama wanted a kitten, and I was so excited to bring it to her," I sobbed.

Father grabbed me and ripped my clothes off, then put me under the water pump and washed me off in ice cold water. Mother had gone into the house and came back out with a big blanket to wrap around me, and Father took my clothes and buried them. Then my parents, one on either side of me, took me into the house, and we all sat down to the beautiful stew that Mother had been working over all day.

Mama took one bite and cried, "I knew it. It has been tainted with skunk spray." She couldn't eat a bite of it, and neither could the girls. They all wretched and left the table. But my father took a big spoonful and said, "Umm, umm, this is the best skunk stew I have ever tasted." I gingerly put a spoonful in my mouth and soon realized I was so hungry that it tasted delicious to me as well.

Swain took a bite and said, "Dis is da bes spunk skew I evvo ate."

And there the three of us sat, laughing at each other, me wrapped up like a papoose in a blanket, Swain with his endearing way of speaking, Papa showing us what true love really means, and all of us savoring what would forever be called *spunk skew.*

◆

A few days later, we noticed a stray cat hanging around our garden. Lucy set out some milk for her, and that was all it took. She seemed to want to stay with us Williamses. We decided to call her Bill Williams. Somehow the name "Bill" fit her. She wasn't the most beautiful cat in the world, but she was an excellent mouser. She would sit in the garden and wait and wait so patiently, then suddenly pounce on a mouse. She had one bad habit, though. She would often bring her dead prey and leave it on the kitchen doorstep as a gift for my mother. When she saw it, Mother would go to pieces all over again. On the other hand, she was so grateful to have an ally against mice that she put up with Bill's little gifts. And she soon found a simple way of getting rid of them.

"Ezra," she would yell. "Come get rid of the gift. Quickly."

I would go rescue the damsel in distress, take the dead mouse out into the trees, and throw it as far as I could. She would give me a hug and tell me I was her knight in shining armor. I didn't know what that meant at the time, but I sure liked her needing my help and her extra attention.

A few weeks after the skunk incident, four strange men came to town. They wanted to find Sidney Rigdon, a nearby preacher with a large congregation. Our family had attended his church a number of times, and he and Father were very good friends. His children, Sydney A. and John, were friends of mine, and their sister Eliza was good friends with my sister Lucy.

One of the men, Parley P. Pratt by name, said he knew Sidney Rigdon, Newel Whitney, and several other people in Kirtland, including my father. He wanted to tell everyone about a new religion he had joined, and the four of them were on a mission to spread the word. They invited everyone to hear what they had to say and said they would be preaching that evening in the bowery down by the river. Mother and the girls attended that meeting, taking Swain with them. I was not quite seven at the time, and I stayed with my father, trying to help him in some way or another. He was a busy man, what with taking care of all of his patients and trying to run a farm as well, so I figured he needed my help. But when Mama and the girls came home, they were breathless.

"Frederick, these men have something important to teach us." The words tumbled out of Mother's mouth as fast as she could say them. "They say that the original Gospel of Jesus Christ, the way he taught it when he was on earth, has been restored through a living prophet. It is marvelous news, Freddy. I want you to come listen to them. I had the chills running up and down my spine the whole time they were talking."

Mother commenced to tell us everything she could remember that these men had said. Mr. Pratt was selling a new bible called the Book of Mormon. He said it was translated from golden plates by the power of God, and that it contained God's word to ancient Americans, and the fullness of Christ's gospel. I thought it all sounded exciting, but Papa was very skeptical.

"Where did he get these *golden plates*, Rebecca?" He had a puzzled look on his face.

Lovina, who had just turned fourteen, was quick to tell Father. "Papa, they were revealed to a young boy named Joseph Smith, who then became a prophet."

"Revealed?" asked Father. "What does that even mean?"

"He was shown where the plates were buried, and after a few years, he took them home and translated them into English."

"Hold on there, girl. That sounds made-up and far-fetched. Who showed him these plates, and why did he wait a few years to take them home?"

Lucy jumped in. "An angel appeared to him and told him where to find them. He went to that place, and sure enough, there they were. But the angel wouldn't let him take them for four years."

"He had to grow up a little first," Lovina added.

I soon had that same tingling in my spine that they had described.

"Look, Frederick, one of the missionaries let me borrow his copy of the book. Let's read it together, and then we can decide if we believe what it says." Mother handed the book to Father.

He opened the cover and saw that someone had written the name *Oliver Cowdery*. "Is this the owner of the book?"

"Yes, he is the missionary who loaned it to me."

Father's reluctance to take any of this seriously was easy to read on his face. "Why don't you read it and tell me about it, and then we can discuss it further," he said, handing it back to her. Mother's disappointment at Father's easy dismissal of the whole matter was hard for me to see.

"All right, Frederick, but if it turns out to be as amazing as I think it is going to be, will you read it then?"

Father sighed a deep sigh. "We shall see, my dear wife. Just keep me informed on what you find of value in it, and I will decide from there."

Mother and the girls continued to go to the meetings, and I occasionally went with them. I liked what I heard very much because it gave me a peaceful, hopeful feeling that I began to desire. Even Swain seemed to understand at least some of what he was hearing, or at least the spirit of it, and would put his head down on the shoulder of whoever he was sitting by and actually listen, or at least keep still.

A few days later, Mother called my father to her.

"Freddy," Mama said in a calm voice, "please just read this book. You will be surprised at what you find in its pages." Mama had been reading the borrowed copy every second that she was not busy with something else.

Papa rolled his eyes. "Really, Rebecca, a gold bible? Angels? Found in an ancient stone box on the side of a hill? Living prophets? Do you know how ridiculous it all sounds? I just can't believe such nonsense."

"If you will just give it a chance, Frederick, I think you will see it is not nonsense."

"But I like the way Sidney preaches, Rebecca. He tries to get as close to the teachings of Jesus as possible, and I can understand him. Why is that not good enough?" Papa reasoned.

Mother agreed. "You know I think Sidney is a wonderful preacher, too. Freddy, but where did he get his authority? This new religion claims they have authority that came from God himself. That must mean something. And anyway, Sidney is starting to believe what these men are teaching. Doesn't that tell you something?"

They went back and forth like this for what seemed like a week. Finally, Papa said he would read it for her sake, but not to expect him to believe it.

It wasn't long before Mother and the girls announced that they had decided to be baptized into this new church that believed in living prophets and a restoration of Christ's true gospel. I had the inclination to be baptized, too, but Mama said maybe I was too young. I hadn't yet had my seventh birthday, and besides, I thought, if my father wasn't going to be baptized, then maybe I would stand by him.

But Father was far from finished with this whole affair. I noticed him picking up the book from time to time, and then throwing it down again, leaving it mostly unread. Then a few days later, he picked it up again, and this time he didn't put it down for a long time. He paced back and forth, reading, pondering, sitting, then standing, as if he were in an argument with himself. He would pick up the family Bible, holding it in one hand and the Book of Mormon in the other, like he was weighing them to see which was heavier. Then I saw him fall to his knees. I left, because even at age seven, I knew he would not want his prayer to be interrupted, and anyway, I needed to do my chores.

While I was out feeding the chickens, I saw Father leave in our little buggy. I assumed he was going to see some patients because he had his doctor's bag with him. Later that evening when Mother was preparing supper, Father came in. We all ran to him, calling "Papa, Papa," and each trying to be the one to win his attention. Swain was pulling on his pant leg, calling "Bapa, Bapa" until my father finally acknowledged him, too.

"Children, children, let your father have a little peace," my mother instructed. "Go get washed up for supper."

"It's all right, Rebecca. These children are this doctor's best medicine, and how I need these hugs right now." He hugged and kissed us all as we ran off to wash up.

I was the first to get washed up, then as the girls took their turn and helped Swain with his, I went back to the kitchen. I don't think my parents knew I was there because I saw Mama step up behind Papa and put her arms around his neck. I heard her say, "And what about my hugs, Frederick?"

He turned around and embraced her. "If these children's hugs are my medicine, yours are my life's blood." He gave her a kiss, then went to the little room he used for his medical practice and shut the door.

When the girls and Swain were back, Mother put the food into serving dishes, and Lovina set the table, letting Swain help by putting a spoon at each place.

"Wook Mama, I am heoping," he called out, and grinned up at her as she put the food on the table.

We were just sitting down when Mother said, "Lucy, go tell Father that supper is ready." She got up from the table, then quickly came back. She had an oddly sweet look on her face

"What did he say, Lucy?" asked Mother.

"I went to his office and knocked softly on the door. I stuck my head in and told him it was time for supper and to wash up. He said, 'Oh, sweet Lucy, tell Mama I am not hungry tonight. I have something on my mind, something I must do.' I said, 'All right, Papa, I'll tell her' and shut the door. Then I stuck my head back in and said, 'I love you, Papa.'"

Lucy sat still a moment, and I could see tears start to fill her eyes. "Go on, Lucy," Mother gently urged.

"He said, 'I love you, too, angel.' There was a good feeling in that room, Mama."

"What was he doing?" asked Lovina.

"He was writing something."

"Do you think he is all right?" I asked Mama.

"He is more than all right, Ezra. He is struggling in the Spirit, and he is going to come out on top, I know he will."

I had no idea what Mama meant by that, but her faith in my father gave me the courage to believe that whatever was going on was a good thing.

After Mama put us children to bed, I didn't fall right asleep as I usually did. I was thinking about *struggling in the Spirit* and hoping my father really would *come out on top*. I needed him to be all right.

Just then I heard Papa's footsteps coming up the stairs. I heard Mama say, "Is everything well, Frederick?" I was suddenly wide awake. I was not about to miss his answer. They went into their bedroom but didn't shut the door. I crept out into the dark hallway, sat outside their door, and eavesdropped on my parents' conversation.

Yes, I know it wasn't my business, but I just had to listen.

Papa started talking. "I didn't want to read it, Rebecca. I threw it down a hundred times, only to pick it back up. My eye caught a passage that Oliver Cowdery had underlined, 'I will go and do the things which the Lord hath commanded.' I don't remember the exact words, but something like, I know God won't ask us to do something that He hasn't prepared a way for us to do, even if it is a really hard thing. Those words sang to my soul, and I knew He had prepared a way for me to read this book and know if it is really true.

"I decided then that I would keep reading until I came to something that I couldn't believe. I read all day, Rebecca. I pondered every word that I read. I paced back and forth as I sat on the line between belief and disbelief. Finally, I fell to my knees, and I prayed and prayed. I talked to God, Rebecca, like I have never talked to Him before. I begged Him to let me know without a doubt if what I was reading was true. The words came to me, *keep reading*. And so, I did. I read so many amazing things, words that taught me things I have wondered about all my life. Then I thought of this young twenty-four-year-old so-called prophet. How could a lad, really, a very young man with no schooling to speak of, write such an incredible book, such truths, such, such, … well I was unable to reconcile the whole thing. I am at a loss to know where he got it. And that is when I stopped reading."

I tried to peek in, but I couldn't see them. Then I heard Mother say, "Frederick, look at me." I dared to poke my head a little further around the doorframe and saw her put her hands on his shoulders and look deep into his eyes. "Joseph couldn't have written that book any more than I could have."

When his eyes met hers, he asked, "Well then, who did? Do any of his friends have the education or talent or, or, or gift to write such a thing?"

"My sweet man," she spoke softly, "I love you so much and admire your sense of right and wrong more than you will ever know, your sense of what is and what could or should be, and your determination to do God's will no matter what. That is why I fell in love with you. But listen carefully. That book came forth exactly as Parley P. Pratt and the other missionaries said it did. Joseph was directed to those plates that were buried in a hillside for hundreds of years and translated them by the gift and power of God himself."

I was hopeful that she was convincing him, but then he said, "Do you know that, Rebecca? I mean do you really, really know it. I have to know it without a doubt if I am to be baptized."

"When you get to the last page you will read this, Frederick." They sat down on the bed with the Book of Mormon in hand. She turned to the very last page. "Listen to this, Freddy." She read, "And when ye shall receive these things, I would exhort you that ye would ask God, the Eternal Father, in the name of Christ, if these things are not true; and if ye shall ask with a sincere heart, with real intent, having faith in Christ, he will manifest the truth of it unto you, by the power of the Holy Ghost."

My father broke down into tears and hugged my mother. "Is this what you did, my love?"

"Yes!" my mother exclaimed. "I have no doubt whatsoever about the truth contained in that book."

Father held her close to his heart in a loving embrace. "It has come so easily for you, Rebecca. It is not coming so easily for me. But if it is true, …" He let the silence finish his sentence.

"There is more," said my mother, picking the book up again. "This is the very next line: And by the power of the Holy Ghost ye may know the truth of all things."

She emphasized those last two words, *all things.* "Do you know what that means, Frederick? God has given us a gift that can guide us through this life in light and love. We don't have to wander through darkness, wondering if this is true."

After a few moments of careful contemplation, my father said, "I have more work to do, my love. I will go and do these things…" Again, he let the silence finish his thought.

— ◆ —

The next day my mother and sisters were baptized. As we got ready to go to the services, it was obvious that they were very excited about what was going to happen. But Papa did not go. He told us he had important things to do, and also that he had to see many patients who needed him badly.

As we left for the baptisms, I saw Papa walk through the field to a nearby grove of trees. *He's just like the Prophet Joseph Smith, going to pray in a grove of trees*, I thought.

I didn't follow him, although I really wanted to because I was sure he would have a heavenly manifestation, just as the Prophet had.

Although the Indian summer we were experiencing that November made for mild autumn weather, it was a little too chilly to think about getting down in the river to be baptized, at least for me. All of us children wore coats and had blankets to put over our laps, and we all sat together with my mother on the log bench. Before the baptisms took place, each of the four missionaries gave short talks. I have to admit I wasn't paying much attention until that man named Oliver Cowdery, the one who had loaned his book to my mother, said, "and so you see, brothers and sisters, the true gospel of Jesus Christ has again been restored to earth. God once more talks to his prophets. Of this I bear solemn and firsthand testimony in the name of Jesus Christ, Amen." I suddenly felt like lightning had run through my body. I didn't understand what it was, but it was much stronger than the tingling I had felt before, and my heart was burning. I felt love for everyone, maybe even for Henry Jones. He was the town bully.

There were several people being baptized that day, and I waited with anticipation for the Williams' names to be called. Finally, it was Mama's turn. Brother Pratt took her down into the waters of the river, raised his arm to the square, said a kind of prayer, and put my mother down in the water. She had to be covered completely, which made me a little nervous. I didn't want her to drown. When she came up, dripping wet, she was smiling the most beautiful smile I've ever seen. Again, I had that feeling of love overcome me and my heart wanted to sing. Then my sisters were called up in turn, and they each likewise came up out of the water with beautiful, radiant smiles. Mother had brought some extra blankets especially for this occasion, and she and the girls wrapped themselves up in them.

Brother Pratt hurried toward us at the end of the meeting. He shook Mama's cold hand, and then he shook my sisters' hands. "Sister Rebecca, congratulations on making perhaps the most important decision of your life. Lovina, Lucy, congratulations to you as well. I know the Lord is pleased with you today." Brother Pratt then shook my hand and asked, "When will it be your turn, Ezra? Soon, I hope." Brother Pratt tried to shake Swain's hand, but he was hiding in Mama's blanket. Suddenly he stuck his head out and gave Brother Pratt one of his trademark goofy smiles. Then he extended his little hand, which Parley took in his big one, and Swain gave it a big shake.

Parley asked, "How is Frederick doing? Is he still reading the book?"

"He is a very busy man, Brother Pratt," Mother answered, "but yes, he has made time to read a lot of it. In fact, he is not here with us because he said he needed to put the scripture at the end of the book to the test. You know, the one about asking with a sincere heart? I read it to him last night."

"I am very glad to hear that. You know and I know that when he opens his heart to the truth, it is only a matter of time until he accepts it. He is a good man, Rebecca." Then he added, "And an excellent physician."

"And don't forget *farmer*," I chimed in.

Chuckling, Brother Pratt tousled my hair, and then said, "You are right, Ezra. When your father decides to join the Church, he will be a force to be reckoned with. The Lord has big plans for Dr. Frederick G. Williams."

Mother said, "Well, children, speaking of your father, we better get home and put supper on so that he doesn't starve to death. Goodbye, Brother Parley."

"Goodbye, Sister Rebecca." We had started walking home when we heard Brother Parley yell, "Just keep him reading that book!"

When we got home, Papa was not there. I guessed he was out making house calls on his patients. I took the opportunity to go into Father's office to see if I could see what he was writing the night before. "Curiosity killed the cat," so the saying goes, but I was compelled to be curious and couldn't seem to help myself. What I found on Papa's desk was a kind of poem. I tried to read it, but I couldn't read cursive writing yet, so I just left.

Soon I saw Papa coming toward home across the field. I ran to him as fast as I could and excitedly asked, "Papa, did you see them? Did they answer your prayers? What did they look like?"

"Hold on, Ezra. What do you mean, did I see them? Who?"

"God and Jesus. I saw you walking toward a grove of trees, just like the Prophet Joseph did. I just knew you were going to have a vision, too. Did you?"

Father laughed a soft but kind little laugh, and said, "No, Son, I did not see God or Jesus." My face fell. He lifted my chin and said, "But I heard their voices."

"You did?" I was incredulous. "You really did?" He opened the door to our house, sat down in the parlor, and pulled me down beside him.

"I guess I should say that I felt God near me, so near me that I couldn't help but know He was there." He started speaking more quickly. "His spirit whispered to me, *Frederick, the book is true.*" Papa's voice was getting stronger and stronger. "*It is right for you to be baptized and join this Church, for it is my Church. You will help my Prophet Joseph in every way you can in spreading this gospel.* I felt the words in my heart, and I knew then that my feet had been set on a path back to him."

Mother came over to us and asked, "Frederick, is it true? You got your answer?"

"Yes! Yes, oh yes," he nearly yelled. He stood up and took hold of my mother and swung her around in a kind of dance. "It came so strong that I can never deny it. I know this work is true, and the Book of Mormon is true, and Joseph Smith is truly a prophet, and …" Father exclaimed breathlessly. Then acting as if he had used up all of his energy telling us these things, he sat back down and went on more slowly and quietly. "And a huge weight is lifted off my shoulders." Suddenly he stood back up, and in a re-energized, almost frenzied state, said, "I need to go find this Oliver Cowdery right now, return his book, and buy my own copy. And I'll find out when I can be baptized."

He was heading out the door when Mother yelled, "Wait, Frederick. Have your supper first. You will need your strength." My mother and father laughed together, and then cried together, and I have to admit I sort of cried right along with them, and so did my sisters. Swain began turning in circles, yelling, "It's twoo, it's twoo," until he fell to the ground in a dizzy heap.

Father was baptized just a few days later, two days before my seventh birthday. When I saw him come up out of the water with that glorious smile on his face, I had that same wonderful tingling throughout my body that I received at my mother's baptism a few days earlier. I ran and put my arms around my soaking wet father, and my mother quickly wrapped a warm blanket around his shoulders. He wrapped me right up with him, encasing me in a cocoon of love. It was the safest place I could possibly be, right there so close to my father. Looking back from a different vantage point, I could see that the Lord was bearing witness to me of the truthfulness of the gospel of Christ, but right at that moment, all I knew was the happiness and safety of being in my father's arms.

The four missionaries surprised us by telling everyone who was at the baptism that they would be leaving soon. They needed to be on their way in a few days and would be heading west to preach to the Indians. As we were leaving to go home, Oliver Cowdery stopped us and asked to speak with Father in private, so the rest of us went on home, wondering all the way what Oliver might be telling him.

When Father finally came home, we all ran to him, asking at once what Brother Cowdery had said. "Everybody be patient," he said. "I need to change out of these wet clothes and then I will tell you."

"Then hurry, Papa," said Lucy. "I don't think we can wait too long."

When Father came back and we were all seated and quiet, he said, "Oliver Cowdery has called me on a mission."

Mother didn't hide her surprise. "A mission, Frederick? What exactly does that mean?"

"Elder Cowdery—that is how they address each other, as elders," Father paused. "Elder Cowdery has asked me to go west with them, to preach to the Indians, only he called them *Lamanites*. He said they are the descendants of the Lamanites in the Book of Mormon."

"But Frederick, you are so new to all of this. How will you be able to teach it to others?" Mother's face was full of apprehension.

"I share your concern, my dear. I asked Oliver that very question. How would I ever be able to do it? He told me he would teach me as we go. He said he and I and the other missionaries will study the Book of Mormon together every day. This is an unimaginable opportunity, Rebecca, to study this book with the one who wrote it down as it fell from the lips of the Prophet, the one who shared so many miraculous events with Joseph. I want to go, Rebecca. I need to go. This is a calling from God himself, but I don't know how to make it work."

Mother hesitated before saying, "We shall make it work somehow. I will go and do the things…"

" … which the Lord commands," finished my father.

Later that evening, he and Mother sat down together and tried to figure out what they would have to do so that Father could leave. "How long will you be gone, Frederick?" Mother asked.

"I don't know for sure, dear. All I know is that the Lord has called me to this mission, and I won't be returning until He calls me back." Although this showed a lot of faith on my father's part, it made my mother nervous.

"What if it is six months, or a year, Frederick? What if it is two years, or three? What am I supposed to do without you?"

"Is your faith wavering, my strong girl?" Father took both of her hands in his and looked deep into her eyes. "I would not consider leaving you at this time if I didn't know with all of my being that this call is from the Lord." Mother sighed a big sigh and relaxed into Father's arms. "I will do as the Lord commands, Rebecca. That is the truth that you first introduced me to and repeated just minutes ago. Now I am asking you to live by it as well, only I guess in your case you will say, 'I will stay and do the things…' That is just as valid, my love. This is your mission as much as it is mine. I could not do it without your support."

Mother agreed, and despite the hardship it would place on her, having to take care of everything at home without him, she knew it was the right thing to do. She looked at my sisters and said, "Lovina and Lucy, this means you will have to help me as much as you can, even more than you already do. You will have to make sacrifices to do that. Are you willing to give up some things so your father can serve the Lord as he has been called to do?"

They looked at each other and nodded their heads. "Oh yes, Mother," said Lucy.

"Can this be our mission, too?" asked Lovina.

"Absolutely," Father assured them both. "We are all in this together. And Ezra," he looked at me and continued. "You will now be the man of the house. Are you willing to do that?"

"I wio be a man, too, Bapa," Swain piped in as he stood up.

I went over and stood next to Swain. "We will be the men of the house together," then looking at him, "won't we, my brother?"

Swain's face beamed with delight at being recognized as being a man, and my equal. I put my arm around his shoulder; he put his arm around mine, and we stood there like two little soldiers, ready to do whatever we were called to do.

Father knelt in front of us and smiled. "You are soldiers for the Lord. How could I ever fail when I know you are taking care of things here and fighting for what is right?" He wrapped us up in his arms and whispered, "I am so proud of my sons."

He released his embrace, and Swain said, "We aw shodos fow Jesus," and smiled his goofy smile at us.

We all laughed, and then Father reached for his daughters, and with his arms around them, said, "I am just as proud of my girls. You will be your own kind of soldiers. You fill me with love."

My parents spent the next few days figuring out exactly how it would all work. Several of our neighbors said they would help with clearing the fields and preparing them for winter and planting them in the spring if Father was not back in time. And a lot of Mother's friends promised to help her with things around the house and taking care of Swain. The Whitneys, the Rigdons, the Cahoons, and the Kimballs as well as other good neighbors promised Father they would not let his family go hungry. My Uncle Wheeler Williams, who lived nearby in Painsville, promised to help us as well, and for that I was most excited as I loved him dearly and always looked forward to his visits to our farm.

We had already chopped enough wood for the winter, Mother and the girls had dried quite a bit of fruit the previous summer, and Mother and Father had dried a lot of meat in our smoke house. We had chickens for eggs and for eating, and a cow for milking. We had a few steers that we were raising for beef. As they made this list of our assets, my parents knew we would be all right.

Father assembled everything he thought he would need to take, including his medical bag and a lot of the medicinal herbs he had previously prepared. Luckily, or perhaps not by luck at all, Father had put a little money aside over the last several years, so he had enough to take with him, and still be able to leave us with a way to get what we needed. In fact, he was able to help finance the whole mission for all five of the missionaries. He contributed his best horse, and someone else from Kirtland donated another horse and a wagon. They put as many provisions in the wagon as they could.

And so, they left on a chilly, snowy November morning in 1830. We all choked up when we saw them go down the road and out of Kirtland, leaving the tracks of the wagon in the newly fallen snow, but they went on their way rejoicing.[2] I have since come to realize what a leap of faith it was for my father to do that. When his testimony of the Gospel of Jesus Christ came, it came full force, like a landslide, and he never doubted again.

CHAPTER SIX

Ogden, Utah 1904

A Poem and a Poet

Ezra looked up at his son and then his grandson and asked, "Now, have I answered any questions for you, or have I made you think of more?"

"You haven't even come close to answering mine," said Fred. "But I trust you will answer them in your own time, Papa."

Joseph asked, "When did you meet the Prophet? I thought you said you knew him."

"I'm getting to that, Grandson."

"Oh. All right, Grandfather. I'll try to be patient. I was wondering what was on the paper, you know, the poem? Did you ever figure it out?"

"That is a great question, Joseph. Not only did I figure it out, but I have the actual paper that he wrote. It somehow fell into my hands, as did most of Father's papers. Your grandmother put it in a book with some other precious things. Go ask her if she will find that book for us and we can read the poem together."

Joseph returned with the book, and Henrietta followed him into the room.

"Give it to your father, Joseph. Fred, you read it, please."

Joseph handed the book to his father, who read:

Is it true? Could this thing be true?
Can my mind believe the thing my heart is crying out for?
Is it real? Would God talk to men?
Can I trust this feeling that my spirit seems to shout for?

If I ask, will He hear my prayer?
How can I know these things are true without misgiving?
It exhorts me, "Ask the Father now."
Can He erase the doubt I feel, while I am living?

Does He love me? Will He answer me
These things that other men seem to accept so easily?
Does He care? Can He know my mind?
Does He have work for me to do, this man called Frederick G?

The Bible says if you lack wisdom
Ask of God and He will give you knowledge liberally.
This new book says if I ask with faith
In Christ, with true intent, then I can know it literally.

Do I? Can I? Will I have that kind of faith?

Fred turned the page over and found there was more. At the top of the page was written Moroni 10:4. "What scripture is this?" he asked no one in particular.

"Look it up and read it." Ezra motioned to Joseph. "Could you get my Book of Mormon from off the shelf right there, please."

Joseph found the well-worn volume, and his grandfather had him look up the scripture, which he found at the very end of the book. "Read it out loud, Joseph."

He read, "And when ye shall receive these things, I would exhort you that ye would ask God, the Eternal Father, in the name of Christ, if these things are not true; and if ye shall ask with a sincere heart, with real intent, having faith in Christ, he will manifest the truth of it unto you, by the power of the Holy Ghost."

Looking at his grandfather, he said, "That is the scripture that Rebecca read to Frederick that night, isn't it!"

"Yes, it is, Joseph." Ezra motioned to Fred to finish reading the poem.

I will ask. I will trust in Him.
I will have the faith in God that now my heart demands.
As I pray, I'll give my heart to Him,
Then I will go and do the thing that I know God commands.

Fred slowly closed the book and said with trembling lips, "I have always wondered how this great man who was my grandfather received such a strong testimony in such a short time. Now I know. What incredible faith he showed." Fred stopped to brush at his eye, then said, "I have often wondered if I was anything like him, or if we could have had a relationship. Now I know that as well. He expressed his deepest thoughts through poetry, and Papa, so do I."

Joseph, noticing that his father seemed to be very emotional over this poem, said, "Dad, I wish we had known him."

"I do, too, Son, but I feel closer to him right now than I ever have before."

Henrietta took her son's hand in hers and kissed it. "I had forgotten that you are quite the poet yourself."

Fred pulled his mother closer to him and gave her a hug. Then they were all quiet for several minutes until Henrietta said, "Ezra, it's time for your medicine."

CHAPTER SEVEN

KIRTLAND, OHIO 1831

Fun in the Snow and a Living Prophet...
Through Ezra's Eyes

It was a long, snowy winter after Father left. We all missed him and longed for any message from him. Occasionally, we got word about him from letters written to other people in Kirtland by one of the other missionaries, but Father never sent a letter of his own.

We got through the worst of the winter fairly well, and by February of 1831, I started to have hope that the weather would begin to clear up, and that Father would soon return. On this particular day, though, there was no sign of spring. A big storm had moved through the town, and snow had fallen throughout the night. My friends and I dressed up warmly and went outside to play. The snow was piled nearly up to our knees. We had built a snowman by the Whitney home, just west of their store, and now the play had deteriorated into a snowball fight.

The two brothers, Andrew and Daniel Cahoon, were siding against Horace Whitney and I in what we thought was a snowball fight for the ages. The Cahoons had both hit Horace in the face, and I was going after them with all my strength when Sister Gates came out of her house across the street and called to us from the front door.

We stopped and turned toward her. "Boys, boys," she yelled. "Come here a minute." We thought we were in trouble. "Boys," she continued as we got closer, "I will give you a penny if you clear this snow away from the walkway so that we can get out of our house."

Far from being in trouble, we were offered the chance to earn a penny which would buy us each a piece of candy at the Whitney store. It would be a rare treat. And besides, clearing the snow sounded like fun.

With thoughts of candy in our heads, we consented to help her, and she told us that in the shed out back we would find a shovel or two. She said her husband Thomas was not feeling well, and anyway, they were both pretty old. We felt valiant to be able to help them. So, we took our pride in our hands and began to clear her walkway. We took turns with the shovels, and when it was not our turn, we took a board we had found in the shed, and one boy on each end, we used it as a kind of snowplow. The snow was light and fluffy, and had not yet been packed down, so it was easy to move. We did her walkway, and then we did the road in front of her house. We cleared a path to the shed and the outhouse, and everywhere else we thought might need to be cleared, with childlike energy.

Finally, we knocked on her door to ask for her approval. When she answered, I said, "We are finished clearing your walkway, Sister Gates."

She looked at the job we had done, then back at our red faces and runny noses, and exclaimed, "Why, you have done a great job clearing this walkway, and much more than that! What good workers you are!"

Despite our frozen cheeks, we all smiled at her for recognizing our hard work. "I'll be right back." She returned a few minutes later, and at her request, we each held out a mittened hand. She dropped a penny into every one of them. This was unheard of! We instantly knew where we were going next.

"Thank you, Sister Gates," we yelled as we ran across the road to the Whitney store. She stood on the porch and watched us run away, and I waved back over my shoulder.

Once we were inside the store, we took off our frozen mittens and blew warm breath into our cold hands. We rubbed them together to get the feeling back. Our cheeks were burning from the cold, but our eyes were seeing everything in that store with new sight because we had purchasing power.

Newell Whitney, Horace's father, smiled broadly as he watched us try to decide just what we should spend our newly acquired fortunes on.

We finally made up our minds and were just putting the candy we had purchased into our pockets when the door of the store was thrown open, and a man strode in.

He pointed at Brother Whitney, and in a strong voice, said, "Newel K. Whitney, thou art the man!"

We quickly moved out of the way and ducked behind some nearby barrels.

The man extended his hand toward Brother Whitney, who took it with much less energy than the one that had been offered him. "Stranger, you have the advantage of me; I could not call you by name as you have me."

This was getting intriguing.

The man stood up straight and said, "I am Joseph the Prophet. You have prayed me here. Now what do you want of me?"

We all gasped. The Prophet had come to Kirtland!

Brother Whitney's mouth dropped open. "Brother Joseph! How did you know me without an introduction?"

We stayed motionless and silent, waiting to hear the answer.

"Brother Newel," the Prophet went on, "I have seen you in my mind's eye, kneeling in fervent prayer. The Lord has answered your prayer and has sent me here to Kirtland for a grand and glorious purpose. And *you* are to be involved in this great work."

Brother Whitney, overcome with emotion and hardly able to speak, squeaked out, "I will do whatever the Lord asks of me, Brother Joseph."

"I know you will, and so does the Lord." He hugged Brother Whitney as if he had found a long, lost friend. Then, while looking over Brother Whitney's shoulder, he noticed the four of us behind the barrels.

We were all staring at him with our mouths open.

He strode toward us. "And who are these fine young men?"

We slowly stood and came out from behind the barrels, not able to take our eyes off him.

Andrew, being the oldest among us at age nine, started the introduction. "I am Andrew Cahoon, and this is my brother Daniel."

Joseph shook their hands and said, "It is so nice to meet you. And who is your father?"

Daniel stammered out, "H-he is R-r-renolds C-c-c-cahoon, sir."

"Ah, yes, I have heard of him. I believe I can say you have a faithful father."

The two boys were obviously pleased that he knew what a good man their father was.

Then Horace, holding out his hand to the Prophet, said, "I am Horace Whitney, sir. I am the son of Newel K. Whitney. You are standing in his store."

"I know your father better than you can imagine, young Horace." He took hold of Horace's hand and shook it vigorously. Then extending his hand to me, he asked, "And this lad?"

"I am Ezra Williams," I managed to squeak out as he shook my hand, also with that same vigor. "My father and mother have joined your church."

The Prophet seemed amused. "My church, eh?"

"Yes sir. My father was very anxious to meet you, but as soon as he was baptized, he left with four other missionaries to go west and preach to the Indians."

"You don't say. When was he baptized?"

"Last November, two days before my birthday, just a few days before he left with the missionaries."

"A few days?" Then rubbing his chin in thought, he said, more to himself than to us, "What manner of man has the faith to just leave his work and his family only a few days after being baptized, and …"

He looked at me again. "What kind of work does your father do?"

"He is a doctor, sir, and he also has a large farm."

"Where do you live, young Ezra? I should like to meet your mother."

After explaining to him where we lived, I ran home as fast as I could and breathlessly told Mother what had happened.

"He's coming here?" she squealed, half with joy and half with trepidation. "Quick, Ezra, help me put these dishes away."

No sooner had we finished, than the Prophet and Emma Smith came to call on my mother. I answered their knock while Mother removed her apron and smoothed her hair back, and I let them in.

With that same booming voice and vitality I had witnessed in the Whitney store, the Prophet said, "Hello, young Ezra. Is your mother at home?"

My mother was now standing behind me, so I introduced them. "Mother, this is the Prophet, Joseph Smith, and this is Rebecca Swain Williams, my mother."

I felt awkward, but when all was said, I did a pretty good job at the introduction. I had seen my father do it enough times that I felt fairly confident about how to do it.

Brother Joseph turned to his wife and put his arm around her shoulder. "And this is the person who keeps me going, my wife, Emma Smith."

Emma smiled and gave Mother a little hug. "It's so nice to meet you, Sister Williams. I hope that we can become great friends."

"I would like that very much." Mother offered to take their hats and coats. "Come and sit down here in the parlor where it is warm, and we can chat."

We had just sat down when Swain, who had been hiding in Mother's skirts, stuck out his hand toward the Prophet and said, "I am Swain Wioyums."

"Williams" was a hard word for Swain to say, but I had been working on it with him.

Joseph stood, took his hand, and shook it, then he bowed to my brother and said, "It is a privilege to meet you, Master Swain."

Swain blushed, then grabbed Mother's skirts again. He peeked up at Joseph and said, "Ah you da pwofet?"

Joseph chuckled at this straight-forward question. "Yes, I am, sir."

Swain just grinned his goofy grin and grabbed at Mother's skirts again. On a silent cue from her, I took Swain by the hand.

"Come on, Swain, let's play with your blocks." I got the blocks out that Father had made him, and the two of us sat on the floor building tower after tower with them, then knocking them down. Swain loved to knock them down and giggled every time he did. I made sure we were sitting close enough to the grown-ups to hear what they were talking about, but far enough away not to be too big of a distraction.

The chatting went on for quite a long while as the Smiths told about their journey to Kirtland and many other things. Then they asked about my father. Mother told them all about Father's struggle to gain a testimony of the truth, but when he did, he was all in. "That's the way he does everything," she said. Then she offered, "Why don't the two of you stay here with us tonight? Then tomorrow you can make more permanent arrangements."

The Prophet looked at his tired wife. "What do you think, Emma? Shall we stay here tonight?"

"I would be so grateful," was her sleepy reply.[3] That night, Lucy slept with Lovina so Mother could have her bed, then Mother gave her room to the Prophet and his wife. The next morning, I got up a little earlier than usual and fed the chickens, gathered the eggs, fed the pigs, made sure the horses and cattle had hay and water, and then milked the cow, all the time thinking about a true prophet of God being right there in our house. I took the eggs and fresh milk to Mother, and she and my sisters fixed our breakfast of bacon, eggs, hot cracked wheat cereal with honey and fresh cream.

"Is there anything I can do to help you, Sister Williams?" came a voice from behind Mama.

"Good morning, Sister Smith," she said as she turned to greet her house guest. "And please call me Rebecca."

"And you must call me Emma."

"Breakfast is almost ready. Please sit down and enjoy the morning while we finish up."

My sisters set the dishes on the table while I kept Swain occupied. "I hope you slept well, Emma. How did you find the bed?"

"It felt like heaven, Rebecca, after the less than restful nights we spent on our way here to Ohio."

"Sister Emma, I want you to know you are welcome to stay with us as long as you like. I don't know when Frederick will be back, but I am sure he will agree with me that you are welcome here."

"Oh, Sister Rebecca, thank you so much for the offer, but Joseph has already made some arrangements to stay with the Whitneys. It was so kind of you to allow us to stay here last night, but Brother Newell said we could use a spare room in his house while he fixes up the second floor of his store for us."

"That will be nice. And at least we will be neighbors."

Mama and the girls set the food on the table, while Swain and I got washed up and ready to eat.

The Prophet came down and joined us. "Good morning, everyone," he said with exuberance, rubbing his hands together as if in anticipation of something good. "How are you all this fine morning?"

He went over, stood behind Emma, and put his hands on her shoulders. She looked up at him, and he leaned over and gave her a kiss.

"Good morning," we all said in turn, and took our seats around the table.

While we ate, Brother Joseph talked to us about many things, including seeing God the Father and his Son Jesus Christ in the Sacred Grove, learning about the gold plates and his experience translating them, and the decision to come to Kirtland. We listened without making a sound.

He then asked us about Father, and we each told him our favorite things about him. I said, "I love to help him on the farm, and sometimes he lets me go with him to visit his patients."

"I love how strong he is," offered Lovina, "and that he can fix anything."

Lucy said, "I love him for saving me from spiders."

"I love him for saving me from mice!" declared Mother.

We children laughed at that, and then realizing the Smiths were not in on the family tale, we all took turns telling them parts of Mother's traumatic mouse experience. We all had a good laugh, and by now, Mother was at least able to smile about it. She still hated mice.

Then Joseph turned to Swain, who had not said one word since the Prophet came in, and asked, "What do you like about your father, Swain?"

Swain's face beamed at being noticed, and I could see him thinking hard about what to say. "Mmmm, I wuv him to call me *witto man*," said Swain. "He is my *hewo*."

I had been talking to Swain about what a hero was just last night. Then he surprised us all by saying, "You aw my hewo, too." But it was no surprise when he stood up and went over to Brother Joseph, put his little arms around him as far as they would reach, and laid his head on the Prophet's chest. It was just his way. "I wuv you," he added.

I think the Prophet was surprised by Swain's response because he didn't seem to know what to do. After a thoughtful moment, he hugged Swain back. "You are a special child of God who loves you *very* much. Keep being your father's little man, Master Swain. That is exactly what God wants you to do."

Swain looked at Joseph and then, seeming to remember what he and I would say together every night before bed, he said, "We aw shodos fow Jesus!"

He turned and motioned for me to come stand by him. We both stood tall and saluted the Prophet Joseph Smith.

———◆———

Spring finally came, but Father did not. Nor did he come that summer. True to their words, our neighbors helped by plowing the fields and getting them planted and preserving the pork and beef from our livestock in our little smoke house. It seemed like one of our neighbors was over at our place all the time. One or two of the men were always outside helping with the animals, weeding the vegetable garden, or pruning the fruit trees. Their wives, who were all friends of Mother's, could often be found inside helping Mother with the housework, drying fruits and vegetables, and taking care of Swain.

To my delight, my Uncle Wheeler often came to help. He would ask Mother what needed to be done, she would give him a list, and he would take care of it. He let me work beside him just as Father did, and he was funny and kept me laughing all the time. He was also very caring toward me. He must have known how much I missed my father, and his presence at our farm went a long way toward filling that hole in my life.

"Wheeler," my mother said to him one day as he was ready to leave, "I can't tell you how much I appreciate your help."

"Ah, it's nothing, Rebecca," he said as he tousled my hair.

"It is more than nothing, Wheeler, it is everything. It means everything to us, especially because you have your own family to take care of." She handed him two fresh loaves of homemade bread she had wrapped in a towel and put into a sack so he could hang them from his saddle horn as he rode home. "Give our love to Nancy and the children."

"She will be very grateful for the bread, Rebecca." He rode off toward home. Mama told me later that Uncle Wheeler's first wife, Lovina, had died giving birth to their first baby, who also died, and that his second wife, Nancy, had been such a blessing in his life. Together they had about nine children or so.

Mother, in fact, all of us were very grateful for the help of everyone who came day after day while Father was gone. The girls had always been willing to help Mother, but while Father was gone, they were by her side so much of the time. They even helped me with the farm chores sometimes, although it was not their favorite thing to do. We were getting along just fine, but I longed for my father to come down that road and home again.

Then one day in September it happened. It actually happened! The missionaries came into town, looking worn-out, but beaming with joy. I didn't know what to do first, run to Papa and welcome him home, or run to Mama and tell her he was home.

I couldn't help myself. I ran to Papa. I threw my arms around him and cried with relief and joy at being with him again. Mama soon came running as well, and when Papa got close enough, he scooped her up in his arms and swung her around. What a happy day!

Swain had followed Mama out of the house and was coming as fast as his little legs would let him. Papa ran toward him and picked him up. "My goodness, Swain. You have grown so much that I can hardly lift you anymore."

Swain answered, "I am a shodow fow Jesus, Bapa. Wemembow?"

Papa laughed a hearty laugh as he set Swain down on the ground. "Of course I do, Swain. We are all soldiers for Jesus, aren't we." Father held Swain by the hand, with his other arm around my mother's waist. Mother held onto me with her free hand, and we all marched into the house together.

News travels fast in a small town, and it was only a matter of minutes before the girls came bursting into the house. Papa stood and grabbed them up, an arm around each one, and they kissed and hugged him, tears coursing down their cheeks.

We were all together again.

CHAPTER EIGHT

Ogden, Utah 1904

A Trial Run to Ogden Cemetery

"Grandfather," said Joseph, "what a happy day that must have been!"

"Oh, yes it was, Joseph. I had imagined so hard and long about the day that he would come home that I had to keep pinching myself to believe I wasn't dreaming and that my father was really there. He had been gone for ten long months, nearly a year, and how I had missed him."

"Sometimes my father goes away for a long time, and that is exactly how I feel when he finally comes home," Joseph said as he looked at his father with affection.

Fred still held the journal, ready to write whatever Ezra would tell them next. He asked, "How was it when he finally got to meet the Prophet Joseph? That must have been a happy event as well."

"It was, indeed, Son," said Ezra. "Joseph traveled to Missouri in the spring of 1831 with about seven other people, while Father and the other missionaries were still there, so he got to meet the Prophet in Missouri, before he returned to Kirtland. I will tell you all about it tomorrow. It is getting late now, and I think we are tired of all this talk."

"I could never get tired of your stories, Grandpa, but I know it is wearing you out."

Joseph and Fred hugged Ezra in turn, then they helped Henrietta get him into his bed and ready for a good night's sleep.

But Ezra did not have a good night's sleep and wasn't up to talking the next day. It seemed that stirring up all the memories of long ago was having its effect on him, so they let him rest most of the day, and Fred and Joseph took the opportunity to help Henrietta.

"What would you like us to do for you today, Mother? We are here to do whatever you need."

"That's an offer I must take advantage of. I was thinking it would be a nice day for a buggy ride."

At this, Joseph looked at her. "Can I drive, Grandma? It would be a perfect way for Woodrow to get used to me."

She looked at Fred. "What do you think, Son? Is this a good idea or not to let this young lad take the reins?"

Fred seemed to be thinking things over for a few minutes. "Why don't the two of you go out for a ride, and I will stay here with Papa. I'll help Joseph hitch up the buggy, and he can take it for a dry run for a few minutes, then come back and get you."

"Oh, yes. Where would you like to go, Grandmother?"

"Since this is sort of a practice run for our trip to the Smithfield cemetery, I think I would like to go up to the cemetery here in Ogden and take some flowers to put on the graves of family members there. The summer flowers are perfect for cutting right now, and the cemetery isn't very far from here. It might just be a perfect trip for us to make with the buggy. What do you think, Joseph?"

"That is a great idea, Grandma. Let's go."

He went out to the barn and brought Woodrow, the carriage horse, into the yard. Joseph had been out there every day feeding and brushing him, so the horse was already familiar with him.

Fred brought the buggy around, and the two of them hitched up the horse. They climbed up into the buggy and, with Joseph at the reins, took it around the yard, then out onto the road.

"Remember, Son, you have to watch for automobiles here," Fred warned.

"I will, Dad. This is going to be so fun."

The two of them went off down the road. It wasn't long before a car drove by, but Woodrow hardly seemed to notice.

Joseph looked at his father. "That was a good sign, right, Dad?"

Fred nodded, and Joseph drove the horse down the streets of Ogden for a quarter of an hour or so, and then went back home.

"What do you think, Son? It seems to me that you can handle the buggy just fine. Of course, it is exactly what I expected."

Joseph looked at his father and grinned. "I knew I could do it. Woodrow is a good horse, Dad, and the buggy is light and easy to maneuver. I don't think I'll have any problems with it." They climbed down out of the buggy, and Fred went to get his mother.

Henrietta came out, holding a basket in each hand. Fred took the baskets, one of them full of flowers in every beautiful color, and put them in the back of the buggy.

Joseph helped his grandmother up into the buggy and then took his seat beside her.

"Freddy dear, please hand me my parasol out of the basket."

Fred found the parasol and gave it to his mother. She opened it to shade herself from the sun, and Joseph pulled the buggy out onto Washington Boulevard.

"Just tell me where the cemetery is, and I'll get us there safe and sound," said Joseph once they were on the road.

"Turn east up this street right here, Twentieth Street."

As they approached the cemetery, Henrietta showed Joseph where to find the graves. "There, down this little road marked Fourth Avenue. We are right over there in the middle."

She pointed to the right, to some tall grave markers of family members who were buried there, and Joseph pulled Woodrow to a stop. He got down from the buggy and then helped his grandmother down. He lifted the big basketful of flowers out of the buggy and carried it for her as she walked rather slowly, Joseph thought, toward the headstones. She stood for a long time in front of one marked "John Albert Williams, April 13, 1860, to November 20, 1870."

"Your son?" he asked softly.

"He was only ten years old." Henrietta did not look up and spoke slowly and softly. "He had appendicitis, a ruptured appendix, as Ezra called it, and there was nothing anyone could do to save him.

I suppose I should be grateful that we had him for ten years. The others were only babies."

She sat down on the ground and put her hand on the headstone, as if she were caressing her child.

"Such a good boy," she said seemingly to the headstone as she brushed dead grass and leaves away. Joseph thought she might be thinking about that little boy whom she would never hug or kiss or scold again, not in this mortal life. Or perhaps she was thinking of what a fine man he could have become, or of the grandchildren that would never be.

Joseph stayed quiet until his grandmother looked up at him and with a sigh, said, "Help me up, Joseph."

He took both of her hands and easily pulled her to her feet. She was a spry seventy-seven-year-old, and rarely needed help getting around, but today was a little different. She seemed lost in thought and was more than a little emotional.

She had always been the steadfast caretaker of her family through health and sickness, and in death, too much death, and now taking care of Ezra was her full-time job. She seemed to be feeling the weight of it all today.

Joseph put his arms around her and gave her a warm and lengthy hug. He let her cry her soft tears, and as she did, he silently wondered how this woman could have such strong emotions for a child she had lost thirty-four years before. Perhaps he would find out one day, he thought. This family seemed to lose a lot of baby boys. He hoped he would never have to go through the pain of losing a child, boy or girl.

Henrietta arranged a big bouquet of flowers by John Albert's head stone, then took Joseph's hand and led him to another grave marker. It read, "Electa Jane Barney Williams, August 29, 1840, to January 25, 1883." Henrietta said softly, "She was forty-two years old, Joseph. Much too young to leave her family."

"Who was she, Grandma? I don't think I've ever heard that name."

"She was our wife."

"Your wife?" Joseph was startled at the revelation.

"Well, that is what I always called her. When your grandfather was called to take a second wife, we chose Electa Jane. She was actually my choice for him. If I hadn't loved her, Ezra would have never gone through with it. She only had one child, Hyrum Royal. He grew into a fine man with a large family. He became a doctor, like his father." She arranged a bouquet of flowers on Electa Jane's headstone.

"Does he live around here?" Joseph asked hopefully.

"No, he lives in Idaho. Pocatello, I think."

"Pocatello?" exclaimed Joseph, laughing in amazement. "That is a funny name for a city."

Grandma smiled. "I'm sure it is an Indian name. A lot of places here in the west are named for Indian words." She placed the rest of the flowers on other family members' graves.

"Pocatello. Maybe he was a great chief. Chief Pocatello," he mimed. Then a thought suddenly occurred to him. "Will I ever be able to meet my cousins?"

Henrietta looked at Joseph for a long moment, then asked, "Did your father ever tell you that he had a younger sister?"

"No, Grandma. I only know of Uncle Henry, Aunt Mary, and Aunt Lucy. And now Uncle Hyrum."

"Her name was Francis, my youngest child. Francis Henrietta. Your grandfather insisted on naming her after me. She was a young mother, only twenty-five when she passed away, having already given birth to five children. She died three weeks after her last child was born."

Joseph could read the pain in her eyes as she thought about her little girl who had grown into a beautiful woman and mother, and then was gone.

"Your grandfather tried so hard to save her, but I guess it was her time to go," she said slowly. Then brightening, she said, "Her two youngest boys, Thomas and Louis, are around your age. They don't live too far from here. Perhaps we could take another trip to meet them sometime."

"Oh, Grandma, I would love that. I have never had any cousins around me at all. It will be so great to know them."

"No cousins at all, not even on your mother's side?"

"I have a lot of cousins on the Burns side, Grandma, just none near me. I live in Mexico, you know, far away from everyone," he said a little wistfully. Then eyeing the buggy, he asked, "By the way, Grandma, what is in the other basket?

"Oh mercy! I nearly forgot. That is our picnic lunch. Go get it, Joseph, and we will spread it out right here on the blanket and have lunch by our people."

The next day, Ezra seemed bright and chipper after a day of mostly napping and eating Henrietta's good food, and he was eager to resume his story. Fred and Joseph helped him into the parlor where they could all be more comfortable, and Henrietta covered his legs with an Afghan that she had knitted a few years before. Fred got the journal and the pen as they all prepared for the next part of the story.

"Now, where were we?" Ezra asked.

"You were telling us about your father coming home from the mission," Fred reminded him.

"Yes, now I remember."

CHAPTER NINE

KIRTLAND, OHIO 1831

Papa Recounts His Mission...
Through Ezra's Eyes

We were so happy to have Papa home with us and could hardly wait to hear all about his experiences. Mother helped him unpack his things and put them away, as the water heated for him to have a bath in the big wash tub. After he was dry and dressed in clean clothing, we all begged him to tell us about the frontier and the Indians, and whatever else he saw and did while he was gone.

"I'm awfully tired today, children. Maybe we better wait until tomorrow." He looked at me and winked.

"No, no, Papa," we all begged at once. "Tell us now, tell us now."

"Oh, all right. I'll try to stay awake." His eyes sparkled as he tried to suppress the smile that was playing at the corners of his mouth. I knew he wanted to talk about it as much as we wanted to hear.

We all got comfy in the parlor and waited for Father to tell his story. "Let's see, ummm, now what was it you want to hear?" he teased. "Oh, that's right. My adventures as a missionary. Well, fine, I'll start at the beginning.

"One of the first things I noticed when we left on that cold, snowy day back in November was that I was the oldest one of the five of us. In fact, I was nearly twice as old as any of the others. Oliver Cowdery was twenty-four, Parley was twenty-three, Peter Whitmer was twenty-one, and Ziba Peterson was about that age as well. So, I was the old man at forty-three. They looked to me for leadership. I knew my fair share about driving a wagon and surviving off the land, but I knew less about the gospel than any of them.

"Since we were heading west, I asked if we could stop in Newburgh and tell my parents of the restored gospel. The others were more than happy to oblige, and we, or I guess I should say they, taught my parents. Mother and Father listened politely and treated us with kindness, but they were not ready to receive the good news at that time. Having struggled with my own reservations for a short while, I completely understood their reluctance to jump right in.

"My father had become a pretty good cook since Mother had lost her sight, and he made us a great dinner of tender steaks, potatoes, and carrots. He even made a nice gravy. We didn't know it would be the last hot meal we would have for a long time.

"As you know, we took my best horse, Dodger, and someone from Kirtland gave us another good horse and a wagon. With our provisions stowed in the wagon, we left that snowy day, heading for Cincinnati, almost three hundred miles away. And the snow just got deeper and deeper until we had to give up on the horses and wagon."

Lovina looked upset. "Papa, what became of Dodger? You didn't just leave him out in the snow, did you?"

"No, you know I would never do that, my dear Lovey. We didn't want to, but we sold both horses and the wagon as well. We didn't have much choice."

"That is so sad, Papa. We loved Dodger."

Both of my sisters had a soft spot for the horse.

"Can't you find him and get him back?" sobbed Lovina.

"How I wish I could. But I don't even know who might have him or where he is now."

Lucy wailed, "Oh no, Papa! Then what did you do without the horses?"

"We were almost to Cincinnati by then, so we thought we could take a steamer to St. Louis, but the ice at the mouth of the Ohio River prevented us from taking advantage of that luxury."

"Then what did you do?" I asked, hoping for some exciting and exotic circumstance to magically transport them.

Father sighed, then smiled. "We walked. We trudged three hundred miles through snow often up to our knees."

"Walked? You just walked, Papa? Why didn't an angel come and save you?" I was disappointed that they had to walk. After all, weren't they on the Lord's errand?

"Who says they didn't?"

"But wouldn't an angel have just picked you up and flown you to Missouri?" asked Lucy.

"That is not the way they usually work, my dear children. More often, they work undercover. We usually don't know they are helping us until we look back and think about how impossible the task was that we just accomplished, and then we realize the only way we could have done it was with divine help."

"But ..." said Lovina.

"But what, Lovey?"

"But if God truly loved you and what you were doing, wouldn't he have taken care of you? Wouldn't he have made it so you didn't have to sell Dodger? Wouldn't he have opened a way on the road so the horses and wagon could continue to take you?"

"Here is the great lesson, children. The Lord lets us experience those hardships and disappointments exactly because He loves us."

Lucy scowled. "But that doesn't make sense, Papa."

"Let me put it this way, sweet child, and maybe it will start to make sense. When you were a baby, Mother fed you and took care of your every need, right?"

"Yes, I know she did," said Lovina. "I watched her take care of these three when they were babies."

"That's true," said Father. "But what if she was so concerned about you that she didn't let you learn? Lovey, do you remember when Ezra was learning to walk? How often did he fall?"

"All the time, at first."

"That is right. We had to let him fall, although we were nearby in case we could see that he might get hurt, right?"

"Yes, and he learned to get back up."

"That is precisely the point. He learned to walk by falling and getting back up, then falling again and getting back up. Soon, he was walking without falling very often at all. And now he hardly ever falls." He looked at me and winked.

"Papa …" I responded to his teasing with mock sadness.

"The point of all this is that we learn from experience. A loving Heavenly Father lets us experience all kinds of problems, because that is how we learn the best."

As I was thinking about all this, and particularly about Father walking three hundred miles in the snow, I remembered how cold I could get just playing outside in the snow for an hour. "How did you stay warm, Papa?"

"We didn't. We put on all of our clothes at once. That helped a little, but the wind blew so cold in our faces that it felt like our skin was being ripped off. It blew right through our coats. We were always cold. Gratefully, we had good boots and warm socks, but often it was so cold that by the time we found places to stay at night, we had to rub the feeling back into our feet, our hands, and faces. It took us six weeks to walk much of the nearly one thousand miles to Independence. So many times, I wished I still had my horse. We were able to get a stagecoach or a wagon some of the time, and what a blessing that was. But we walked a lot of the way in the deep snow, carrying bundles of Book of Mormons on our backs along with our food and bedrolls."

"What did you find to eat, Frederick? I hope you at least had good food." The concern and love for my father was written all over Mother's face.

"If you want to call frozen cornbread and raw pork good food, then yes. Sometimes it was so frozen that all we could do was bite the crust off the outside of the bread."

"Did you ever just want to give up and come home, Papa?" asked my older sister.

"Oh yes, Lovey! When we couldn't find people to preach to, a decent place to stay, or good food to eat, or when we were cold and tired after a hard day of walking mile after mile in the snow, it was easy to get discouraged. We had to rely completely on the Lord for guidance, and for our very lives. There were no roads, only obscure trails to hopefully lead us in the right direction, and very few houses where we could stay. There were many days that we didn't see a house at all or were not able to find wood to build a fire. That is when thoughts of all of you here in a warm, cozy house eating three hot meals a day would run through my mind, and I would long to be with you. But then I remembered that I was called of God to go on this mission, and the blessings I was imparting to others and receiving myself made it all worth it. I realized that those hardships, as difficult as it was to bear them, were minimal compared to the importance of the work we were doing, and I knew the hard times would eventually be over."

"Poor Papa!" said Lucy.

"No, my dear. I was not poor at all. I was with these men of God, day and night for ten months. I talked to, prayed with, and studied the Book of Mormon with Oliver Cowdery, the Second Elder of this dispensation, this man who is a firsthand witness of the restoration, and he taught us the restored gospel of Jesus Christ in great detail. How I admire him! Not too many people get such an opportunity, and I wouldn't trade it for warm days with no snow, or a horse, or anything else. I knew that this sacrifice of time away from home would be worth it. I came to love my companions for many things, but especially for what they were able to teach me about the 'marvelous work and a wonder' that the Lord is bringing forth right now."

"But we prayed so hard for you every night, Papa," said Lucy. "It seems like God would have made things easier for you."

"When I look back on that time, Lucy, it doesn't seem hard at all. We made it through and did what we were sent to do. When the four of them were called by Joseph Smith to the mission while in New York, they were promised in a revelation that the Lord would go with them and be in their midst.[4] When I was called to go with them, that same blessing was extended to me. I knew the Lord was with me, and day after day, even in the bitter cold with a growling stomach, I felt his Spirit with me so strong that I could never deny it. And the experiences we had!"

He paused a moment to take a deep breath. "Well, I'm not sure I can convey to you so many of the miraculous things that happened to us. They are sacred experiences never to be forgotten. We had great success teaching many people who immediately recognized the truth, and we were able to organize several large groups of newly baptized saints into branches of the Church. I pray for them every day in hopes that they will stay true to the faith and remember what a valuable thing they have been blessed with."

Mother took his hand in hers and leaned in close to him. "It was all worth it, Freddy. Every lonely hour without you, every day spent worrying about how you were, if you were warm enough, if you were well, and if you had enough to eat, and wondering when you would be home. It was worth it to know you were doing the Lord's will spreading this glorious news." She lay her head on his shoulder.

Lovina was sitting near Father on the floor, and with her head on his knee, she hugged his leg. "I missed you so much, Papa."

Father patted her cheek and caressed her hair.

Lucy wedged herself in by Father opposite Mother and put her head on his other shoulder. They made quite the scene.

I had had enough of this mushy stuff and wanted to get to the really important things. "Did you see any Indians, Papa?"

He laughed and sat up so that the girls and Mama had to sit up, too. "Oh yes, Son." He was immediately back into his missionary experiences.

"We were able to get to Independence, Missouri, the farthest civilized place west before nothing but frontier. As the weather began to warm up a bit, we were able to go by boat part of the way, and even secured a wagon for a fairly long distance. But when we couldn't get some kind of conveyance, we walked, no matter the weather, freezing cold or boiling hot. But as he had promised, God was with us all the way. Now, I can see that we really wanted for nothing. He led us to places to stay, food to eat, and people to preach to most of the time. And we always gave thanks for his bounty. Most of the people we met had never heard anything like our message, and they were astonished by it."

"What exactly did you tell them?" asked Mother

"We bore testimony of God, and that he had restored the gospel the way the Savior had established it, through a living prophet whose name is Joseph Smith. We said that this prophet had seen an angel who directed him to buried scriptures engraved on gold plates. We told them that he had translated the plates through the power of

God, and we had copies of the resulting book which was called the Book of Mormon. Then we would lend them a copy of the book to read. Oliver would show them where his name was in the front of the book, bearing witness to the authenticity of it. He would tell them that he had been a scribe for Joseph as he dictated the words from the plates, that he had also seen angels and had held the gold plates himself. Peter Whitmer also testified that he had seen the plates and that he had inspected them thoroughly. We then told them that we were ordained ministers who had the authority to baptize, given us of God. Oliver would tell how he and Joseph had received that authority from John the Baptist himself, as a resurrected being. We told them that the Indians were descended from the people in the Book of Mormon, and that was why we were sent to preach to them, but that this new book and the knowledge of the restored gospel of Jesus Christ was for everyone who would read it and willingly ask God if it was true. Then we all bore testimony that we knew through the power of the Holy Ghost that this book was true."

Mother asked, "But, what did *you* say to them? They probably wanted to know how you could believe everything when you had not even met Joseph Smith."

"You are right about that. I would tell them that I knew it was true the same way they could know it is true—through the power of the Holy Ghost. I used that scripture on the last page of the book, where Moroni challenged anyone reading the book to put it to the test, the one you showed me the night I was struggling to accept everything, Rebecca. I bore witness to them that I did not have to meet Joseph face-to-face to know he was a prophet, and that they could know the same way. I only had to read that book, and then ask in faith. That is the way most people on this earth will learn that it is true."

"Papa, I am worried that I haven't read the Book of Mormon, and yet I am a member of this Church. Don't you think I should read it?" asked Lucy.

"I have been having those same thoughts," said Lovina. "It seems wrong that you have been out urging everyone you meet to read the book, but I haven't read it myself. Do you have a book that we could read?"

Father was obviously taken aback by these comments. "Well, why don't we read it together? That way we can discuss the things we read. And I can tell you some pretty incredible things that Oliver and the Prophet disclosed to me."

Mother's eyes brightened. "That sounds wonderful, Freddy. Can we start right away?"

"Let's read it around the table at dinnertime when we are all together," suggested Lovina.

We all agreed.

"That sounds perfect." Father lifted Mother's hand and kissed it. Then he continued with his missionary experiences.

"When we were finally in Independence, Peter and Ziba were able to secure jobs as tailors in order to procure funds for us to proceed, while the rest of us, Oliver, Parley, and I, crossed the frozen Kansas River and walked to the Delaware Indian village, about twelve miles west of Missouri. We preached the restored gospel to these people."

"Did they wear feathered head bands and shoot with bows and arrows and live in teepees and paint their faces and ..." I asked, all in one breath.

Father laughed. "Hold on, Son. I can only answer one question at a time."

I sighed but sat back to listen as patiently as I could.

"Yes, they did wear feathers but not in head bands. The men and women all had long hair, tied back with a strip of leather. Then they stuck the feathers in those leather strips, or if there were a lot of feathers, they tied them together first and then tied the bundle to their hair. The feathers did not stick up, but rather, hung down. It was actually very becoming. Some wore many feathers, and they fluffed out like an eagle's when perched in the wind. They didn't live in teepees, but rather hogans, which are like little round houses made out of straight sticks tied closely together. They were roomy and warm, and more permanent than teepees. They hung blankets on the walls all around the inside of the hogans to help keep out the wind and cold. None of these Indians had painted faces. They saved the face painting mostly for when they were at war, and we were there in peace. I did see many bows and arrows, but I did not see any Indian use one while I was with the Delaware Indians."

"Oh." I was disappointed.

"More importantly, though, was their reaction to our preaching. They received it with great joy. More than one Indian man told me that what we were telling them seemed familiar, that it reminded them of some of the stories their ancestors told, as if they had heard this all before. Some of them spoke fairly good English and were easy to understand, but we had a translator with us most of the time. The Delaware called themselves 'Kasa' or 'Kansa,' and from that, the name Kansas emerged.

"Sadly, we had to stop preaching to them because a man named Richard W. Cummins, who was a government agent over the Indians, would not allow it. So, we left the Delaware Indians and began preaching to people in and around Independence."

"Aw, I wish you could've stayed longer with the Indians, Papa, so you could watch them shoot something with their bows."

"Well, I did get to see Indians shoot with their bows later on. When we could no longer preach to the Delaware, we turned our efforts to the Independence area, and there was a tribe of Kaw Indians nearby that we were able to teach."

I perked up. "Did they wear headbands with feathers?"

"As a matter of fact, they did. I saw many of them wearing wide headbands with one long feather stuck upward in the very back."

"And what about teepees?" I was trying very hard to ask only one question at a time.

"No," he replied, "they live in little huts much like the Delaware hogans. They like to wear bright colors and decorate their clothing with colored beads that they trade the white men for."

I continued to probe. "What about face paint?"

"Many of the men painted their faces red, but it wasn't a bright red. It was more like the rouge you see some women wearing on their cheeks these days. The Kaw men put it on their faces, but also in streaks across their necks and upper bodies. It makes them fierce looking, but not mean or terrible as the bright, bold Indian war paint can do."

"Which tribe did you like best, Papa?"

"That is a good question, Lovey. I made many friends in both tribes, but I spent more time with the Kaw Indians. Many of their tribe were ill, and I was able to relieve a lot of pain and sickness there, which endeared me to those people. It also gave me the opportunity to teach them the gospel and talk about the Book of Mormon while treating them."

"It's a good thing you took all your medicines with you, Papa," said Lucy.

"Yes, it was. They were put to good use, and I ran out of some of them before we came home."

Always seemed to be worried about his physical needs, Mother asked, "Did you run out of money?"

"Yes, we did, Rebecca. But Elder Cowdery and I taught school there in Independence, for which we were paid enough to support ourselves. We also held meetings on Sundays in the school room, which worked out very well for all of us."

"Papa, tell us about shooting the bows," I said impatiently. "Did they kill each other?" My eagerness to hear about the Indian exploits got a little out of hand.

"No, I don't think they shot each other." Father laughed. "They mostly shot wild game for food. One day, a flock of geese flew overhead, and before I knew it, those young braves had their bows and arrows in hand, and were tracking those birds across the sky, and shooting them. Many of the arrows hit their marks, and several families had roast goose that night."

"I yike gooses," Swain piped in, making us laugh as he grinned at us.

"How did they cook the geese, Father?" asked Lovina. "They didn't eat them raw, did they?

Father smiled and patted her hand and said, "Oh no, my dear. They put them on a spit, a long stick that they put right through the goose, and that was supported at both ends, then they roasted them over a fire. The women were responsible for turning the spit to make sure the meat cooked through and didn't burn."

"Did you get to eat some?" asked Lucy

"Yes, I did, and it was very tasty." Father seemed to be thinking of that good meat, because he paused for quite a while, then he suddenly became very serious.

"Now, I have something to tell you that will affect all of us. As you know, Joseph Smith joined us in Missouri in the middle of July. All of my missionary companions knew the Prophet Joseph personally, but I did not. What a thrill it was for me to meet him. The two of us became close friends almost immediately. It felt as if I had known him all my life. He came to Independence to dedicate a parcel of land for a temple."[5]

Mother looked puzzled. "A temple? What kind of temple, and what will it be used for?"

"Joseph told me that we were to become a temple-building people. There will one day be many of them, even one right here in Kirtland. They are to be houses of the Lord, places where He can come to give guidance and direction to his children. The building in Independence will be something special, a little different than any other temple we will build, because it will be the center of activity when the Savior comes again."

Everyone gasped at that revelation.

"Is he coming soon, Frederick?" asked Mother with trepidation. "I'm not ready for that!"

"None of us are, my love, but having this temple site dedicated is a big step toward his return, and the many glorious things that will come to pass leading up to that. I don't know when we will actually build it. We certainly don't have enough money right now."

"When you say *we*, Frederick, who does that include?" Mother asked.

"I mean the Church of Jesus Christ that Joseph was called to establish. All of us. Great things are coming, more than I can even describe to you at this time."

He paused again, as if he might be thinking about how to say what was coming next. "Joseph had something else to tell me personally. Before he had even met me, when I was a thousand miles away from Kirtland, the Lord gave him a revelation about us. Our family, our home, and our property. He said that we are to remain here because the Lord needs our property.[6] I don't know all that it will entail, but it could mean that we are to give everything to him, all of our property, all that we have. Rebecca, I am ready and willing to give everything to the Lord. Are you with me in that?"

Mother seemed uncomfortable. "I don't really know how to answer that, Frederick. I promised to do whatever the Lord asks us to do, but that seems like it is asking a lot."

"We made that promise to each other and to Him long ago, do you remember?"

"Yes, of course I remember, but ..."

"But it seems like more than you bargained for. Am I right?"

"Yes."

"It seems that way to me, too. But when I read the revelation that Joseph had received before he even knew us, it started to make sense. Of course, I won't do anything unless you and I are united in the decision, and we don't have to do anything just yet. But whatever we do, we will do it as a team. That means all of us."

He turned to look at us, and said, "This isn't just me. You children are an important part of this as well. It can mean making some big sacrifices. We are all yoked together in this as a team, and we must pull our weight together. Will you team up with me?"

We all in turn asserted our desire to do whatever our father asked of us, especially when he was following his Father, the one in Heaven. I was not quite eight years old at the time and didn't understand the full implications of what he was asking me to do, but I trusted my father implicitly, and if he said we needed to do something, I accepted it.

I guess Swain felt the same way, because he said, "I wio be a team too, Bapa."

It seemed we all needed to let everything sink in for a few minutes, then Lucy, ever the worrier, shifted our attention back to Father's mission. "How did you get home, Father? Did you have to walk home, too? Did your feet hurt? Did you get tired and hungry? Where did you sleep at night?"

"Hold on, sister." Father chuckled. "Let me answer your first question before you ask the second and third and so on. You remind me of your brother," he teased, looking in my direction.

"Yes, we did walk a good part of the way, and since my boots had long ago worn out, my feet did hurt by the end of the day. But we also traveled by boat as much as possible, and since it was summer and the weather was warm, there was no ice to freeze us in. Did I tell you that Joseph returned with our party? There were seven other people who had come west with him and who then returned home with us, and because one of them was Elizabeth Gilbert, the wife of Sidney Gilbert, we did our best to accommodate her, so she did not have to walk so much. I must say, she was willing to do whatever we had to do. Gratefully, we were usually able to secure lodging at inns at night, but sometimes we had to ask people if they would let us bed down in a barn or on a porch. Brother Gilbert made sure his wife was comfortable, and we helped by offering extra blankets for her to use, or anything else that would help her feel respected and cared for."

"Did you get cold sleeping outside, Papa? Did you find enough to eat?" asked Lovina.

"Happily, since it was summer, it was much easier to find warm, dry places to sleep at night than it had been on our way west. Occasionally, it was cold at night even then, but we were so grateful that it wasn't raining or snowing that we didn't seem to mind. We did get hungry, sometimes very hungry, from time to time, but we usually found enough to eat before we starved. I don't think I remember any of these things as being hardships I had to endure, because I was in the company of a prophet of God."

Father seemed to glow as he went on. "I could not believe how blessed I had been to go on this mission with Oliver and the others who knew so much about the gospel. But the return trip with Joseph was ..." Father choked up and tears welled up in his eyes. "It's hard to express how much I learned and how strongly I felt the Spirit of the Lord with us. Every day was a feast of truths and revelations, and I treasure every moment of it," he said softly

Suddenly, Mother stood up with a start. "Oh, my goodness, it is late, and dinner is not even started. You are probably all starving. I'm sorry, but I couldn't stop listening to your story, Frederick."

Father laughed. "We will all live, Rebecca. I haven't died of starvation yet, and it doesn't look like the children have either. I don't feel any protruding bones," he said as he felt our ribs and under our arms, tickling us mercilessly. We all convulsed in laughter until he said, "Come on, team, let's help Mama get something fixed for dinner."

Two days after his return, my father received an urgent message summoning him to Newburgh, where his parents lived. His father's health was failing and perhaps he was near death, so Father left to be with him and his mother. This sad news cast a dreary feeling over our previous joy. When Father returned, he told us that his father had passed away, and that they had buried him in the Harvard Grove Cemetery, near where they lived.

I felt sad to realize there would be no more visits to my grandfather, and my heart was broken for myself, but also for Grandma Ruth. I wondered how, being blind, she would ever get along without him. I also wept for Papa, who no longer had his father with him, and I thought how broken I would be if that happened to me. I secretly went out to the barn where the hay was stored, crawled up on the haystack, and wept. I don't know how long I was there because I eventually cried myself to sleep. I felt I had lost a friend and ally in my grandfather and knew I would miss him very much.

The next day when I saw Father coming home from seeing his patients, I ran to him and as soon as he dismounted from the horse, I threw my arms around his waist and sobbed.

"What's the matter, Son?" He put his arms around my shoulders.

I couldn't say anything for a few minutes. I just wanted him to hold me tight. He must have sensed what I was feeling, because he just hugged me and rubbed my back and head while I held onto him. He finally took my face in his hands and looked into my eyes.

"I miss Grandpa," I was finally able to say, and then cried again.

Papa kneeled next to me. "I miss him, too, but remember that through Christ's atonement, we will be able to live with him again someday."

"But Papa," I cried, "he hasn't been baptized."

"Was Grandpa a good man, Ezra?"

"The best, Papa. He loved us all so much."

"Do you think Jesus loves him?"

"Well, if Jesus loves me, he must certainly love Grandpa."

"That is correct. He loves Grandpa one hundred percent, just as he loves you and me the same."

I wasn't that great at math at age seven-and-a-half, but I knew what one hundred percent meant. "Even if he wasn't baptized?"

"Ezra, if the Savior only loved people who were baptized, he wouldn't have very many people to love, would he? His job is to bring as many people to him as he possibly can, but way more than half of this world doesn't even know who he is."

"I didn't know Jesus had a job."

"Of course, he has a job. What do you think he does all day?" My father smiled at me. "He continues to bless his children, which is every single person on this earth."

"Then why do we need to be baptized?"

Father stood and removed the saddle and bridal from his horse. "It's like this, Son. He loves all of us one hundred percent, but do you think everyone loves him that much. How much do you love him?"

"I love him a lot, Papa."

"But can you say you love him with every fiber of your being? With your whole heart, might, mind, and strength? Do you think about him all day long? Are you willing to do anything he asks you to do?"

Now it was getting personal.

I hung my head. "I'm trying, Papa, but I do a lot of dumb things, so I guess I can't say I love him one hundred percent."

He put the horse in his stall. "And neither can I, but I'm trying, also. The more we try, the more he asks of us. Then we have more responsibility to do what he asks us to do. Do you see how that works, Ezra? He gives us blessings, and we try to be obedient to what he asks of us, and when we do that, he gives us more blessings. So, then we continue to obey, and when we succeed at doing better, he gives us more blessings. We can never get ahead of him."

We started walking toward the house. "Was Grandpa trying to obey?"

"Yes, I think he was. But he wasn't ready to accept the blessings of the restored gospel while he was on earth. Now that he is in heaven, I feel sure that he will have the chance to be taught, and that our loving Father in Heaven will make a way for him to be baptized."

"How can that happen?"

"I don't know, Ezra, but I have become pretty close to Joseph the Prophet, you know, and he has hinted at some marvelous things yet to come from Heavenly Father. According to Joseph, the complete restoration of all things is far from over."

We went into the house and sat down together at the table, and Father said, "I have had a strong feeling ever since Grandpa passed away, that we are about to learn how those who have died without baptism can still have that ordinance performed." I thought I could see tears forming in his eyes.

"Really, Papa?" I felt hopeful.

"Yes, Son. Baptism by someone who holds the true priesthood of God is so important to us that Heavenly Father can't just ignore people who have died without it. He would be losing billions of people if he did that. That is my opinion, anyway, and I'm pretty sure Joseph Smith feels that way, too."

"But why is it so important?"

"It is one of the things God has asked of us. Through baptism, our sins can be forgiven, and we can claim the blessings that come from being a member of the Church of Jesus Christ. After all, Jesus himself was baptized, and he was perfect. It only makes sense, then, that those of us who are not perfect take advantage of this ordinance. It puts us on the pathway back to him, you might say. When we are baptized, we promise Jesus that we will take his name upon us."

"What does that mean, Papa? How do we take his name upon us?"

"When you were born, Mama and I gave you a name. We named you Ezra, but your last name automatically became Williams. That is because my father's last name was Williams and so I became Frederick Williams. I took my father's name, and now you have taken your father's name, and someday your children will take your name as well."

"Hmmm, that makes sense, but how do I add Jesus's name to mine? Will I be Ezra Granger Williams Jesus?"

Father laughed gently at that. "Ezra, when you are baptized you promise that if anyone asks you if you believe in Jesus, what do you suppose you should say?"

"Yes."

"That is right. And how do you show others, but particularly Jesus, that you believe in him?"

I thought for several moments, then answered rather tentatively, "Do what he asks me to do?"

"Yes. I have tried to live my life in such a way that I bring honor to the name of Williams. When people found out who my father was, I wanted them to know how proud I was to be his son. I wanted them to tell him that I have honored his name. How would he have felt if I had done something mean or dishonest? It would not have pleased him, would it?"

"No, it would have made him very sad."

"It is the same with our Father in Heaven. When we are baptized, we make a promise to act like we are sons and daughters of Jesus. We try to do every single thing he asks us to do, and when we do, guess what he does?"

I knew this answer now. "He blesses us with more blessings."

"That is right, my boy. You are learning. We also promise to help bring others to a knowledge of Jesus. That is one of the most important things we can do in this life."

"Is that why you went on a mission?"

"That is exactly right. And even though I am home from the mission, I need to live in such a way that I can continue to bring souls unto Jesus."

"How do I know what he wants me to do, Papa?"

"Where do you think you can learn God's will? Where would you look?"

I thought I had this one in the bag, too. "The Book of Mormon?"

"Yes," he said, "and the Bible. These two holy books bear witness of one another, and each has recorded the words of prophets. God gives us prophets to help us understand the words he gives to us. That's why those books are so important."

"Oh," I said as a dawning came over me. "That's why we read from them all the time."

"Yes. But remember, we have also been blessed in these days with a living prophet. How important do you think it is to also heed his words?"

"I would say very important, Papa." Then remembering my original concern, I asked, "Do you think Grandpa is all right then?"

"There is one way you can know for sure, Son. Get down on your knees and ask Heavenly Father. Then listen very carefully to the very next thing that comes into your mind. That is how the Holy Ghost works. He will tell you the truth."

"Will the Holy Ghost teach me even though I haven't been baptized?"

"It is true that we are given the gift of the Holy Ghost as a companion at baptism, but all people on earth have access to his witness if they ask for it. You just have to listen because his voice is very soft. I believe with all my heart that if you ask Heavenly Father about Grandpa, he will answer you by the power of the Holy Ghost. And if I am right and you listen carefully, I believe he will whisper to you that Jesus Christ will take care of Grandpa. One day we will be with him again, and somehow or other, I know he will be baptized."

CHAPTER TEN

KIRTLAND, OHIO 1831

Weak Things Made Strong ...
Through Ezra's Eyes

True to their commitment, my parents made sure we read the Book of Mormon every evening around the supper table. We each took a turn reading from the book, and I, being seven-going-on-eight, was only given a verse or two to read at first, but I soon learned to be a good reader because of it.

What wonderful discussions we had, and I looked forward to that special family time every day. The exploits of Nephi, Alma, Helaman, Moroni and the 2000 stripling warriors, and all the other heroes in the book were exciting to a young boy, but the spiritual things spoke equally to my young heart. I determined I would be like them, and always keep my promise to take the Savior's name upon me, to keep the commandments and love the Lord. I guess I am still trying to be like them in that way.

As time went on, Father fell more and more into his routine of working on the farm and treating people who were ill. Many patients started coming to our house for help so that he didn't have to drive to see them. That was very helpful because he began spending a lot of time with his old missionary companions, and with the Prophet. Brother Joseph had asked him to scribe for him, to write down things that he needed to remember. As he saw what a fine penman Father was, how good he was with the language, and especially how thorough and dependable he was, Joseph had him scribe more sacred things, revelations that the Lord gave him, as well as personal thoughts.

It wasn't long before Father had given the Prophet the use of our farm, including our home.[7] When Joseph's parents came to Kirtland, they had nowhere to live, so they moved in with us. Even though it was crowded, I liked having them there. I came to know Father Smith while working with him on our farm. He said funny things that made me laugh.

One day, he said to me, "Ezra, did you hear about the doctor who moved his office near the graveyard?"

"No. Why did he do that?"

"To better accommodate his patients," he answered, and laughed out loud.

I just looked at him with astonishment until I had it figured out. The doctor was not a very good one, and many of his patients died, so being near the graveyard made it easy for them to be buried. I laughed a belated laugh.

Another time he told me this one:

"A little boy asked a preacher if he had a lamp he could borrow.

"No, child," he said, "I am one of the lights of the world and need no other lights."

"I wish then," said the child, "that I could hang you up at the end of our alley. It is devilishly dark there."

I caught on to that one right away, and we both laughed together.

In addition to making me laugh, Father Smith was always kind and thoughtful to all of us. And it was nice to have an adult to share the work that daily became more burdensome since Father was occupied elsewhere most of the time. And another good thing about having the Smiths live with us was that Joseph and Emma, either together or separately, often came to visit them, which meant we got to know them better as well. Emma was expecting a child, and she took comfort and advice from Mother, who was a bit older and more experienced with having babies. Emma had already buried a baby boy a couple of years before coming to Ohio, so that made her all the more anxious about this one.

We had a large barn on our property that the Church started holding meetings in. It was about forty feet square, and it became the central gathering place in the town. I helped Father and a couple of other men including Father Smith clean it up and make some wooden benches for everyone to sit on.

When another family needed to move in with us, things just got too crowded. But several of the men in the community helped Father fix up a little cabin on our property that was near our house so that Joseph's parents could move into it. And it was nicer for all of us to have a little extra room to move about. The Smiths stayed there in that little cabin until their house was built nearby.

We were supposed to be given a new house, a "comfortable dwelling," as the Lord had commanded the Prophet, but that didn't happen for quite a while.

As always, Father stayed very busy between the farm and his medical practice. He worked the farm with Father Smith when he could, helping to cut and store the hay, and also riding the horse to plow the fields to prepare them for planting corn and potatoes, and the two became great friends. But he was also spending more time assisting the Prophet.

As more and more people joined the Church and moved into Kirtland, things changed almost daily. Many of the new families and even some of the older ones were building houses on our property. There were plans for a schoolhouse and a printing office as well, and Father even hinted of a temple being built on our land. The other family that had moved in with us was still there, but they had plans to build their own house soon. However, our housemates were not taking very fast steps to procure their own dwelling and trying to survive with two families in our small house was very difficult for all of us.

Before too long, we moved to a place about a mile and a half away.

I didn't like being further away from my friends, but Father promised we would soon move back into town. I have to admit it was nice having plenty of room, but it changed things. It seemed that Father was gone more of the time, and I didn't like that. He often did not make it home in time for dinner. Mother did her best to keep us reading the Book of Mormon, but it just wasn't the same without him. That was the thing I started missing the most.

Despite the growth of the Church, or maybe because of it, some of the members, some of whom had been very strong in the faith, began criticizing Joseph Smith. I had seen the Prophet up close enough times that I knew he was not perfect. Sometimes, I would ask my father about little things that bothered me, and he was quick to say, "Ezra, just because the Lord chose Joseph to be the Prophet of the Restoration does not make him perfect. Joseph Smith is a man. He is not a god, nor does he claim to be one. He is full of flaws, just like the rest of us. But the Lord has promised us that he will never let the prophet, be it Joseph or someone else, lead this Church astray. That is what we have to keep sight of."

Those words calmed my worries, and I started to see the Prophet in a true light, an imperfect man who was called to do perfect things.

Father went on. "That's the way the Lord works with people. It has to be. We humans are all he has to work with, and until he comes to earth and runs everything himself, that's the way it will be. Because we are imperfect humans, we learn and grow by doing, and that includes making mistakes, in fact, we tend to learn the best lessons in the process of correcting our mistakes. Haven't you found that to be true yourself, Son?"

I had to admit that I had.

He continued. "When Joseph first became the prophet, he could barely read and write. He has me write so many of the things he needs written down because it is still hard for him to spell correctly and put words together coherently. The Lord chose him in part because of that very thing. He wanted someone who was uneducated and did not hold a position of prominence so that the rest of us would realize that Joseph could have done none of this without complete reliance on the Lord who teaches and guides him. In fact, in a revelation I wrote down for him just the other day, it says, *The weak things of the world shall come forth and break down the mighty and strong ones, and that the gospel might be proclaimed by the weak and simple before kings and rulers.*[8] God reveals truth through prophets despite their weakness and imperfections, but He does not make choices for them in their everyday life, not even for Joseph. He must do that himself and learn from his mistakes just like the rest of us."

That helped me understand why God called Joseph, but I still did not understand why people, especially those that I thought were such good people, were getting so angry with him. I knew that Joseph had experienced opposition right from the day he received the plates, but to have it come from within the Church was heartbreaking.

Ezra Booth was one of those who was in Missouri with Joseph, my father, and other missionaries. In October, after their return, he began publishing letters criticizing the Prophet and the Church. Father told me that Brother Booth had once witnessed the Prophet heal a broken arm, and that he went with Joseph to Independence hoping to see more of that. When that didn't happen, and he actually had to experience hardships on the journey, his faith wavered, and he soon abandoned the Church completely. Father guessed he thought that being a member of the true Church would mean living a perfect life. The whole mess shook a lot of people's faith. Even Bishop Partridge became critical of the Prophet, and some men even quarreled with Joseph.

People started leaving the Church for ridiculous reasons. One man left because the Prophet misspelled his name on a Church document. I guess he didn't know that Joseph was always a horrible speller. Another one left because his horse died while traveling to join the Saints in Missouri. Another man left after seeing Joseph playing with children. He thought that was beneath the dignity of what a prophet should be. That one made me sad because the Prophet had played all kinds of games with us boys many times, creating some of my fondest memories of him.

Some people left because the Prophet could not solve their financial problems. Some left because others in the Church had offended them. Perhaps that was the hardest thing to see happen. For people to turn their backs on the truth because someone outside of their control said or did something they didn't agree with is crazy to me.[9]

It seems that a lot of people have certain high expectations of what the Church or a prophet should be, and if it turns out not to fit their ideas, instead of finding out what the truth really is and how things really were or should be, they just abandon their faith. How sad for them.

I could go on and on, but I will tell you a good thing and a bad thing that resulted from all this nonsense. First the good thing. As the Church leaders counseled together, they decided to publish all the revelations that Joseph had received. Some people thought he was keeping them secret so that he could tell the Church members whatever he wanted to. That was never the case. Father told me that it just never occurred to the leaders to publish the revelations. Those revelations became what we now call the Doctrine and Covenants, and they are canonized, meaning we Church members are bound by what they say, just as we are bound by the teachings of all scripture. And how that book has blessed our lives! It contains revelations given directly to us in our day. We can read and examine them and learn from them as the Lord teaches us from them.

Now the bad thing. The people who had started to criticize and leave the Church, turned on it with a vengeance. They not only said horrible things, but they also did horrible things. They could leave the Church, but they could not leave it alone.

In early 1832, Joseph and Emma had moved to Hiram, Ohio, about thirty miles away. Several months before the move, Emma had her baby, or I should say babies. Just as she had suspected, they were twins, a boy and a girl. I'm sorry to say that they died shortly after being born, but the strange thing was that a family who lived nearby, the Murdocks, had also had twins, a boy and a girl, at about the same time. And sadly, their mother passed away not long after their birth. Well, Brother Murdock already had several children, and he had no idea how he would care for newborn twins. So, he asked Joseph and Emma if they would adopt his twins. Emma was so happy to finally have babies in her arms that she readily took them. They named them Joseph and Julia

The Smiths had moved in with the Johnsons in Hiram, and Sidney Rigdon had moved out there as well. A conference was to be held there, and of course, Father needed to be present for that. He took Mother with him to Hiram and left us children in the care of our great neighbor, Sister Huff. We were getting old enough to mostly take care of ourselves, but Sister Huff kept track of us, fixed our meals, made sure we washed up and ate our food, and were in bed early. And she watched after Swain, which was a full-time job all by itself. Luckily, Brother Huff, the kind and loving soul that he was, took a particular liking to Swain, and of course, Swain reflected that love right back to Brother Huff. Secure in the knowledge that we were all taken care of, Mother and Father stayed on in Hiram for several weeks.

Father told me that one afternoon in February of 1832, some of the Church leaders were gathered in the Johnson home continuing work on the new translation of the Bible that had occupied them for some time. On this particular day, the Prophet had been pondering the idea that many important points about the salvation of man had been taken from the Bible or lost from it somehow. If everyone was to be rewarded for what they had done while on earth, surely there must be more than one heaven because one person's level of spirituality and dedication to doing good differed so widely from others. He was working on retranslating the Gospel of John when quite suddenly a vision was opened to him, but the peculiar thing was that the same vision opened to Sidney Rigdon. The two of them started describing what they were seeing, and Father and John Whitmer started writing it all down.[10] The rest of the men sat in chairs around the room. When Joseph described things that he was seeing, Sidney would say, "I see it, too." Then Sidney would describe things and Joseph would say, "I see it, too." This went on for some time, and when the vision was over, Sidney was pale and limp as a rag. The Prophet explained, "Brother Sidney is not used to this as I am."

Apparently, having a vision drains a person of a lot of energy.

CHAPTER ELEVEN

Ogden, Utah 1904

Keeping Covenants

"Papa!" Fred exclaimed. "I have read and reread that section of the D&C so many times without knowing that my grandfather was there writing it down as it was given. Now it is even more special to me."

"Yes, Son, and it is a pivotal revelation in the history of the Church." Ezra seemed to be a little drained himself.

"What does it say that makes it so special, Grandpa?" asked Joseph.

"I will tell you a little bit of it, but then you must study it for yourself to really understand it. Will you do that, Joseph?"

"I think I would like to do that." The boy sat up straighter in his chair. He had always been taught the gospel from the time he was very little but didn't pay attention to the details until recently, since getting to know his grandfather. Now it seemed to be more of a priority to him

Ezra went on. "Father and Brother Whitmer read back to the people in the room the things they had written down as not everyone could hear the Prophet or Sidney clearly. It was amazing. They described three heavens, or degrees of glory, one of which each of us will be assigned to when we die. The lowest degree will be the home for those who have no faith and have not lived according to the teachings of the Gospel of Jesus Christ on the earth. The middle heaven will house those who are good people, and may even have faith in Christ, but have not been valiant in their testimonies or received a fulness of the gospel. And the third will be comprised of those who have tried valiantly to live according to the teachings of the Gospel of Jesus Christ, those who have kept the commandments, sacrificed when necessary, and stayed true and faithful to their covenants. They will be living in the presence of God and His Son, Jesus Christ."

Ezra looked directly at his son and grandson and went on. "Isn't that what we all want? I know that is what I want, every day and every hour."

"To be in their presence, and to have my family with me is worth anything I have to go through on this earth," said Fred.

Ezra nodded. "Yes, Son. That is the prize, the pearl of great price, you might say."

"Grandpa, you mentioned something about keeping the covenants. I don't know what that means," said Joseph

"At the time, I didn't know what it meant either, but I learned that it means to stay true to the promises we make to God at baptism and in the temple. We promise to stand as witnesses of God in all things and in all times and in all places, and to do whatever He might ask us to do. Sometimes, that includes moving to a new place that is unfamiliar and leaving everything you know behind, and maybe even learning a new language, or any number of other things."

"Like moving to Mexico and leaving all your friends and family behind to go somewhere that you know nothing about and having to learn Spanish," said Fred.

"Dad, did you do that because of a covenant you made with God?" asked Joseph.

"That's right, Joe."

"But why do we have to make them? Can't we just live a good life?"

"Making and keeping covenants sets us on a path back to God, to be able to live with him forever. Baptism is the first step of many," Fred explained. "Covenants are his way of teaching us how to become like him. The best gift he has to give us is eternal life with him, and with our family. That is why covenants are so important, and why we should want to keep them."

Ezra continued. "This revelation was one of the most glorious documents ever to be given on the earth. I can't begin to tell you all that was revealed in it, so you must read it for yourselves. It is recorded in what we now know as the 76th Section of the Doctrine and Covenants. You should read it often. We all should. So many magnificent things were revealed at that time, but to me, the most glorious part of this revelation was this statement by the Prophet and Sydney."

Ezra quoted from memory:

And now, after the many testimonies which have been giv-
en of him, this is the testimony, last of all, which we give
of him: That he lives! For we saw him, even on the right
hand of God; and we heard the voice bearing record that
he is the Only Begotten of the Father—that by him and
through him, and of him, the worlds are and were created
and the inhabitants thereof are begotten sons and daughters unto God.[11]

"They had seen Jesus Christ Himself! And what a testimony they had born of Him. I'm sure the people in that room were in total awe of the significance of the whole thing."

When Henrietta came into the room, she took one look at Ezra and hesitated, then softly said, "Maybe that is enough for today, Doctor. Dinner is ready. Let's go eat, and then I'm putting you to bed."

Joseph and his father lifted Ezra into the wheelchair and took him into the dining room. Joseph thought that Ezra was lighter than the first time he had helped him into the chair a month before. *Maybe I'm just getting stronger.* He didn't want to think there was any other reason.

◆

When morning came the next day, Fred said to his son, "Maybe Grandpa won't want to talk to us today, Joe. I was a little worried about him last night."

"Maybe we should ask Grandma what she thinks," answered Joe.

The father and son found Henrietta busy in the kitchen fixing breakfast. "How did Papa fair the night, Mother?" asked Fred. "I hope we didn't tire him out too much yesterday."

"I was a bit worried myself, Fred, but he slept well, and the first thing he said to me this morning was, 'I need to get on with that story.' Need I say that he feels an urgency? I'm sure you can tell."

"I know," answered Fred. "I just … I just want to be careful and considerate of his condition."

She put her arms around her son's neck and kissed his cheek. "Joseph and I will be leaving for Smithfield in a day or two, and you and your father can have a nice long restful time while we're gone."

After a hearty breakfast of flapjacks with maple syrup, fried potatoes, eggs, and bacon, they once again made Ezra as comfortable as possible, and he resumed the story.

"Now where was I?" he asked, as he usually did.

"You were talking about the revelation on the three heavens," answered Fred as he opened the journal to write everything down.

"Oh yes, I knew that." He looked at Joseph and winked.

CHAPTER TWELVE

HIRAM, OHIO 1832

Good, Evil, and Loss ...
Through Ezra's Eyes

Father told me that Joseph Smith seemed to feel safer in Hiram, away from many of the people who were so critical of him and the Church in Kirtland. But he also said that the truth was quite different, which became apparent as he told me what happened next.

He reminded me that Joseph was warned at the time of the First Vision in the grove where he first saw God and Jesus Christ, that *your name will be had for good and evil.* He couldn't escape the evil that seemed to follow him everywhere he went, not even in Hiram, Ohio.

On a cold March night, just a month after that glorious vision of heaven, an angry mob broke into the Johnson house where the Prophet and Emma were staying. Joseph had been up late taking care of one of the twins who had measles. The men dragged Joseph outside, swearing terrible oaths, calling him all kinds of evil and vicious names, and threatening to kill him. They grabbed him by the throat and choked him until he temporarily lost consciousness, tore off his clothes, and tried to push hot tar and a bottle of acid into his mouth. Joseph clenched his teeth so hard that the bottle broke one of his teeth, chipping it badly. Some of the mob held him tightly while others beat him and scratched him deeply all over his body, then covered him with the hot tar. To add insult to all this, they tore open a pillow and covered him with feathers which stuck to the tar. Sidney Rigdon was also dragged from where he was living across the road from the Johnson home and was also tarred and feathered. When Joseph saw Sidney lying nearby, he thought for sure that his dear friend was dead.[12]

Some of the neighbors who had heard the noise made by the mob came out of their houses and witnessed a part of it happening. Some went to the aid of Sidney, whose head was severely injured as the mob dragged him by his feet, head bobbing up and down over the frozen ground and the stones in the walkway and the road. Many thought Sydney would surely die from the inhumane treatment.

Others ran to help the Prophet. The Johnsons, at whose house they were staying, also rushed to help. "Go get Dr. Williams," screamed Emma who had fainted when she first saw Joseph covered in what she thought was blood but had quickly revived. "He is staying next door with the Harrisons."

My parents came immediately and spent most of the night trying to remove the tar from Joseph's skin. They even had to remove it from inside his mouth. It was a delicate job, and very painful for Joseph.

As a doctor, I've often had to remove bandages that have stuck to tender skin, and I know how painful that can be. But I can't even imagine the pain that the Prophet endured, caused by having tar removed from all over his body, especially where it had been applied to open wounds caused by the scratching, biting, and beating of the mobsters. In many places, the skin tore off with the tar.

"I'm so sorry," said Father as Joseph winced. He looked at Father with pain-filled eyes and tried to say "thank you."

Sister Johnson had made a fire in the stove, and Mother helped Emma put a big pot of water on to boil. When it was ready, they added it to the water they had already put in the bathtub until it was the perfect temperature, not quite hot enough to burn. Father put Epsom salts and soothing oils into the water and stirred it around. Finally, he and Brother Johnson eased Joseph into the warm water and let him soak there until the water cooled down. When they got him out and dried him off, Father dressed the worst of his wounds. At last, they were able to put him to bed. Joseph, struggling to talk, was finally able to say, "Will you pray for me, Frederick?"

"Of course, my dear, dear friend." Father took Joseph's hand and bowed his head.

"Our beloved Father in Heaven," he began. "We ..." He paused, trying to get hold of his emotions. "We need Thy help, Father. Thy servant, Thy faithful servant Joseph needs Thy help. Please, Father, heal his wounds this night, both those seen and unseen. Let him rest, send Thy ministering angels to buoy him up, succor him and reassure him of Thy love for him."

Father again stifled a sob before going on. "Bless his dear wife Emma and the children, especially little Joseph. Pour Thy blessings down upon this family that has already in their young lives seen so much pain and sorrow, but also so much of Thy majesty and mercy. And please be with the Johnsons who have so generously accommodated the Smith family while here in Hiram.

"We ask for these same blessings for Thy faithful servant Sidney, dear Father, and for those who are caring for him. Bless us all to know what best to do to help these men heal and resume their hallowed lives of serving Thee. And Father, we ask a special blessing on those men who were so filled with anger this night that perhaps this incident will help them see more clearly the need for the restoration of Thy gospel and the role Joseph is playing in it. Bless them to be able to turn themselves to Thee."

He stopped to swallow, and to clear his throat, then went on. "And Father, help us forgive them for what they have done. Help us to love them and to bring them back to Thee. We humbly ask these blessings in the name of Him Who suffered so much that we might have eternal life, even Jesus Christ, Amen."

Father sat by the Prophet's bedside the rest of the night, knowing he would most likely experience a fitful sleep. Joseph woke up about every hour, crying out in despair and pain, as if he were in the middle of a nightmare. Father reassured him that he was safe, and that Emma and the babies were safe as well. Then he redressed Joseph's wounds as needed and administered pain-relieving herbs and ointments.

Sister Johnson watched over baby Julia, and Mother took little Joseph Murdock from Emma. The baby boy was struggling to breathe, coughing and sneezing from lying exposed to the cold on the bed where the mobsters had thrown him when they first broke in. The front door had been left open when Joseph was dragged outside, and the baby, who was already very ill with measles, most likely took a chill. Mother held him on her lap in the rocking chair, holding his head up so he could breathe more easily, and encouraged Emma to get some rest. Sister Johnson put Emma to bed in a different room so Joseph would not disturb her during the night and sat by her side until morning. I think she probably prayed for Emma as Father had prayed for the Prophet.

The next day was Sunday. Joseph got up and dressed, then preached to the members of the Church as usual, recognizing that some of the men in the congregation had been in the mob that had tarred and feathered him the night before. Joseph spoke with a whistle from the broken tooth for the rest of his life.

A few days later, little Joseph Murdock Smith passed away, breaking the hearts of the grieving Emma and Joseph once again.

About a week later, Joseph organized the presidency of the Church into a more formal structure. He remained the president, of course, with Oliver Cowdery as assistant president, Sidney Rigdon as first counselor, and Jesse Gause as second counselor. Eventually, it became standard protocol to have a president and two counselors as we have today in the Church, but in the beginning, there were no set rules for running the earthly aspects of the organization.

When Mother and Father came home from Hiram, they brought Emma with them. She was having some problems in Kirtland with people who thought she should be different from what she was, or in other words, they thought she should be perfect, and of course, she was not. Because of the tar and feathering incident in Hiram, Joseph no longer felt it was a safe place for her there, and sensing his concern, Mother offered to keep her at our house until things settled down. Since we had not yet moved back into Kirtland, it could be the perfect solution. Emma seemed happy to come home with the Williamses, partly because she and Mother had become fast friends, just as they had both hoped when they first met, but also because she thought perhaps my sisters would help her with baby Julia.

Did they help her? Oh, my yes! They never left that baby alone and would argue over who got to take care of her. They even fought over who got to change her diapers. It's a miracle she ever learned to walk, because when Lovina and Lucy were around, her feet never touched the ground. She was just starting to say cute things, mostly *ma-ma* and *da-da,* but in such a charming way that she lit up the house with happiness, something that Emma desperately needed.

One day when Father came back from seeing his patients and working with Brother Joseph, he brought mail. We didn't get regular mail delivery in those days, and often we would get quite a bit all at once. This day there was a letter for my mother. She took it from Father slowly and carefully, as if it might burn her, and held it gingerly in her hands for some minutes.

Emma must have noticed her reluctance because she asked, "Why don't you open your letter, Rebecca? Who is it from?"

"I don't dare open it, Emma. It is from my father. I wrote him some time ago explaining all about the restoration of the gospel, and he wrote me an angry letter, telling me to repent and leave this foolishness behind. His strict English upbringing can make him too proud to accept much change. I wrote back a long letter, and this time I poured out my heart. I told him all about our conversion to the only true Church on earth, Frederick's mission and meeting the Prophet, and so much more. I told him how happy and blessed I am to be part of this newly restored Church of Christ. I bore my testimony as to the truthfulness of it all, but I am afraid he still won't accept any of it."

"And what about your mother, Rebecca? Sometimes women are a little easier to convince."

"My mother died when I was not quite fifteen years old. Something tells me she would have been more receptive than my father, but right now, he is all I have. So, I hold this letter unopened, hoping that whatever it says does not destroy me."

"You are stronger than you think, Rebecca. But I have to be honest. My parents have reacted much the same way. I was fortunate to have my mother with me when I delivered and then lost our first baby in Pennsylvania, but how I longed for her to be with me when the twins were born. My father would not allow her to come."

"I'm sure you could've used your mother's love and understanding when you lost your twins. There is just no substitute for a mother's love when you are hurting. I worry for you, dear Sister Emma, because you have so many burdens and so much on your mind. It would help so much if you were able to have your mother with you. That is the way I felt when I was having my babies. Oh, I am so blessed to have had Frederick deliver my children, and he is so good and kind and gentle. But if I could have had my mother with me … Well, you know exactly what I mean."

"Yes, of course I do, Rebecca. I sometimes wonder if I will ever be able to have a baby that will live more than a few hours. I love my little Julia, don't get me wrong, but I am so desperate to have Joseph's child, and …"

Mother put her arm around Emma's shoulders and gave her the clean hanky she kept in her apron pocket to wipe the tears. She temporarily forgot the letter she held in her other hand, and said, "When I was pregnant with Lucy, I was a nervous wreck the whole time, worrying that she might have problems like Joseph Swain has. He is such a sweet child, Emma, and he fills our lives with love, but he will never have a normal life, not without a great miracle. I guess it is a normal part of motherhood to worry about our children."

"You're right. I could worry myself sick. If it happens, my being able to have Joseph's child, then it happens, and I will feel blessed beyond measure. And if it doesn't, well, I still have my beautiful little Julia."

She stopped to caress the child who had made her way to her mother, then continued, "We need to remember the promises found in the Scriptures. The one I repeat over and over is Proverbs 3 verse 5: 'Trust in the Lord with all thine heart and lean not to thine own understanding.' It has gotten me through some rough times, and it will get me through this."

"That is a great Scripture. I will remember it always."

"So now, dear friend, you must trust in the Lord, and open that letter. No matter what it says, it will be all right. Everything will work out in the end."

Mother held the letter in front of her, then closed her eyes as if in prayer, took a deep breath, and opened it. She read,

Rebecca, Your stubbornness over this so called religion leaves me no choice. As of this day, you will not be an heir to any of my estate, and I forbid you to write to me or anyone else in this family again. Do not try to contact us in any way until you come to your senses. I am sorry, Rebecca, that it has come to this. I have given you a chance, and you have not repented. You have rejected me and your brothers and sisters in preference to some crazy idea that we want no part of.

Isaac Swain.

"Oh no, Emma." Mother looked up from the letter as she dissolved into tears of pain and sadness. "He didn't even sign his name as *Father*. Now I have no mother *or* father. I can't bear this."

She crumpled into inconsolable sobbing.

CHAPTER THIRTEEN

OGDEN, UTAH 1904

A Good Lunch and a Great Horse Ride

Ezra sat up straight and stared at nothing in particular for several moments as he thought about the pain his mother must have gone through when her father disowned his baby girl. When he finally came to himself, he looked around to see Joseph's bottom lip quivering, and Fred wiping his eyes.

Just then, Henrietta came into the room, and when she saw the somber faces, she laid her hand on Fred's shoulder. He turned toward her and put his arms around her waist and hugged her close. The silence in the room spoke loudly of the love they all shared with each other, as well as the empathy they had for the trials of their brave ancestors. Eventually, Henrietta was the one who broke the silence. "I have made creamed cauliflower soup with cheese and rolls for lunch. We can put it off for a while if you boys would like to."

"Give us a few moments, my love, and we will come in to lunch." After she picked up the Doctor's hand and kissed it, Henrietta left the room.

"I just can't believe what some people have had to go through for the gospel," said Joseph somberly. "I guess I've had it pretty easy."

"I hope it stays that way for you, Joseph," Ezra said softly. "I never dreamed when I was a young child in Kirtland, Ohio, the kinds of things I would have to face in my lifetime."

Joseph sighed. "How did the Prophet stand it? Why didn't he just give up?"

Ezra, straightening his back, looked right at him, and answered, "Joseph, my boy, I have wondered that same thing many times, but now I know the answer and I will give it you. The Church of Jesus Christ of Latter-day Saints, the one the Prophet Joseph was called to restore to the earth, is the only true and living church. I know it, your grandmother and your father know it, and you can know it, too, if you don't already. We know it by the power of the Holy Ghost bearing witness to our spirits, just as if we had seen it all take place or had felt the hands of the apostles on our own heads. But the Prophet Joseph *knew it* because he was there. He did not have faith that all these things were true because he had the *knowledge* that they were. He knew those gold plates intimately. He knew the Angel Moroni as well. He knew he had translated that book by spiritual means. He did feel the hands of ancient apostles on his head. He saw God the Father and His Son, Jesus Christ. How could he possibly deny any of this without incurring God's wrath. And that is why he never quit or waivered for one moment, not because he was afraid of God, but because he knew Him."

"Do you think he ever wanted to quit, Grandfather?"

"Of course he did. Do you think it was fun for him to endure the kinds of things he had to put up with? Do you think he enjoyed being tarred and feathered? Of being ridiculed and mocked by people who were once his friends? Of worrying about his family for fear the mobs would turn their vengeance on them? No, Joseph, he did not like being treated that way. Anyone else would have quit long before if not for one reason, and it isn't money. No amount of money would have been worth everything he endured. The real reason he did what he did could only be because he was called of God to re-establish the Church of Jesus Christ on the earth, and all that he claimed to have happened, did happen. That's it. I know for a fact he had no money. He worried about his own monetary destitution all the time, not to mention the Church's financial situation."

Exhausted, Ezra dropped back against the pillow Fred had put behind him. "There was no earthly gain in this for Joseph. Many people who knew of him outside the Church could not speak a civil word about him, judging him mostly or solely on hearsay. His name truly has been known for good and evil even today, just as God told him it would."

"So, I guess that is why your mother didn't give in to the will of Isaac Swain, right, Grandfather?"

"That's it, Joseph. She had a strong testimony of the gospel from the very first time she heard it preached. Not even losing the love and trust of her father could dissuade her."

"I know it must have been hard for Isaac Swain to see his daughter leave everything behind that he had taught her and go off with a lot of unknown people with new ideas," said Fred. "But I could never turn my back on you or any of your siblings, no matter what, Son. You know that don't you?"

"I do, Dad. Thank you."

They sighed a collective sigh, and then Ezra said, "Well, we can't do anything about old Isaac now, and I'm hungry, so let's have some of that cauliflower soup."

"Wait, Grandfather. Will you answer one question before we go to dinner?"

Ezra agreed. "All right, Joseph, but only one. I'm hungry."

"Who is Jesse Gause? I thought your father became the second counselor to the Prophet."

"Well, I'll tell you, Grandson. I don't know who he is. Or was."

Joseph gave his grandfather a confused look.

"He seemed to appear out of nowhere, and then disappear just as suddenly. I have no idea where he came from or where he went. In his absence, Father served in Brother Gause's position as second counselor for nearly a year before being called officially in March of 1833.[13] I think Brother Gause is a sad little footnote in the history of the Church."

Fred nodded. "Yes, it seems very sad for him, Papa. Look at all he missed out on."

"So true, Son, but it gave your grandfather a chance to continue serving with Brother Joseph and the other Church leaders, and that was a real blessing for him and us."

Fred and Joseph put Ezra into his wheelchair to move him to the dining room. Turning his attention to the food-laden table, Fred asked, "Did you raise this cauliflower yourself, Mother?"

"I certainly did." She took her place at the table.

"Well, that will make it all the better, Grandmother. And I am hungry!"

———————◆———————

The next morning, Henrietta called Joseph to her, and said, "I have heard from my friends in Brigham City and in Smithfield. They are all willing to have us stay with them on our trip. That means we can start getting things ready and be on our way next week. Joseph, are you sure you still want to do this?"

She could not hide the excitement in her eyes.

"You know I am, Grandma. I can't wait either!" Then he asked, "Is Grandpa all right today?"

She stepped to the bedroom door and peeked inside. "He is still asleep, Joseph. Let's let him sleep for a while so he can build his strength up a little bit before he starts telling stories again." She sighed deeply. "I must be honest, Joseph. Bringing up all these memories about his life as a child in Kirtland is hard on him, but he is determined to tell you and your father everything."

"How much more does he have to tell, Grandma?"

"Mercy, child, he has barely got a good start. Some of the things he has to tell you are marvelous indeed, but some of them are going to be very hard for you to hear. Your father has heard some of it before, but it is all new to you."

Joseph was trying to understand what she was telling him when the thought crossed his mind that maybe Ezra would not be around to finish the story. Then he took a deep breath and asked, "Grandma, would it be all right if I took Dodger out for a ride? I miss riding my horse so much, and I have some things I need to think about. I do my best thinking on horseback."

"Sure, Grandson, I think that is a good idea. Just make sure it is all right with your father."

After checking with his father, Joseph put his hat on and went out to saddle up the riding horse that Ezra had named Dodger after his father's horse of long ago. He rode the horse for a few miles up Ogden Canyon, thinking all the time about the things Grandpa Ezra had been telling him, and wondering what he might possibly still hear. He couldn't help but ponder about what trials might lay ahead for him. Would he marry? Would he be able to support a family? Would he ever have children of his own? Would he be able to teach them the important things of life and of the Gospel of Jesus Christ? What if he ended up losing baby boys as his father and grandfather had? Or baby girls? Would he really lose this grandfather that he had just barely come to know, and who he already loved so dearly?

When he got to a big open clearing, he dug his heals into Dodger and let him run full steam. It felt so good to have the wind in his face, and to be alone for a few minutes on horseback. His concerns seemed to blow away with the wind, at least for a little while. After letting the horse rest and graze, he rode back down the canyon. It was steep in places, and he had to hold Dodger back to keep from losing control. He loved being able to be the master of such a powerful horse and make him go where he wanted him to.

When he got home, he found that Henrietta and his father had helped Ezra out of bed, got him all cleaned up, and had fed him a late breakfast.

"Where have you been, youngster?" asked Ezra, back to his old spunky self.

"I just went for a little ride on Dodger, Grandpa. I miss my horse a lot, and it felt good to be in the saddle again."

"Well, I can't blame you for that. I wish I could have gone with you." Ezra settled into the rocking chair.

"Are you sure you are ready for another installment, Papa?" asked Fred. "We don't have to do this every single day, you know, if you need to rest."

"I don't want to rest." Ezra almost snapped at Fred.

"All right, we are ready for you to go on," Fred said in a calming tone. "I just don't want you to think we are pushing you. Sometimes, it is hard to stir up old memories."

"I'll be all right, Son, just remind me where I left off."

Fred was reticent to remind his father of the emotional ending of the night before. "Umm, you were telling us about living in Kirtland as a young child."

"Oh. Now, I remember." He turned to Joseph. "Do you remember your baptism, Joe?" It was the first time he had called his grandson by the more informal name, and Joseph smiled.

"Of course I remember, Grandpa. I was eight years old. It was in November of 1896. My friend Ira Hurst and I went down in the fields to the big irrigation ditch where Brother Joseph Wright was making molasses. Brother Wright baptized us right there in that big ditch. The next day was Fast Sunday, and my dad confirmed me a member of the Church." Then to Fred, "Did I get that right, Dad? That is how I remember it."

"Yes," said Fred, seeming to smile at the memory. "That about sums it up."

"Now I will tell you about my baptism," resumed Ezra.

CHAPTER FOURTEEN

KIRTLAND, OHIO 1832

A Baptism and a Bully ...
Through Ezra's Eyes

By April of 1832, we had moved into our house back in Kirtland, and I was very happy to be closer to my friends. William Kimball and I had been spending a lot of time together, in fact, we were together just about every day. One warm spring day he was over at our house when we thought it might be fun to take Swain for a walk down by the river. I had asked Mother if it would be all right, and she said, "Ezra, that would help me so much. I've been very busy trying to get things planted in the garden, and your father ..."

I knew what she wanted to say but didn't. Father was gone so much of the time now, and he wasn't a lot of help around home.

"Don't lose track of him or let him get hurt."

"Mama, are you forgetting that I am eight-and-a-half now? I can take care of him, and anyway, William will help me, right, Will?"

"Yes, Sister Williams. We will take good care of him."

We ran to get the wheelbarrow. Father had made a little contraption that we could push Swain in so that he didn't have to work so hard to keep up with us. It only had one wheel and reminded us of a wheelbarrow only much smaller, so that is what we called it. We were having a good time taking turns pushing him. We would run for a few steps then suddenly stop. That pitched him forward a little and made him giggle. Then we would push him in a snaky pattern and tease him about dumping him out. He laughed and squealed with delight, which made us laugh, too.

Just then we saw a man coming toward us down the river path. As he got closer, we could see that it was the Prophet Joseph. We got Swain out of the wheelbarrow and waited for the Prophet to walk up to us.

"Catching any fish today, boys?"

We laughed, and I said, "We aren't fishing today, Brother Joseph."

"We're just taking Swain for a walk," added William.

Joseph bent over to talk directly to Swain. "Hello, Master Swain. Are you having fun today?"

"Ezwa and Wioyum make me waff. They aw my fwends."

"It looks to me like they are good friends, too."

Swain came back with, "I yuv dem."

"I think you love everyone, Master Swain. You could teach a lesson to a lot of people around here."

The Prophet turned to look at us, studied us for a few minutes, then asked, "Have you boys been baptized? It just occurred to me that I haven't seen your names in the membership records."

William and I looked at each other a little bewildered, then we both stammered out, "n-n-no, not yet," or something like that.

"Well, it seems to me that it is time to take care of that. Both of you run home and get your parents, and we will take care of it right this minute. I'll stay here with Swain until you get back."

A few minutes later we were back. Mother and my sisters came with me, and William's mother and sister Judith came back with him. We found the Prophet teaching Swain to count on his fingers, and Swain was doing his best to say "one two fwee foa fie," and point to some of his fingers at the same time.

"Wook, Ezwa. I can count. One, two, fwee." He grinned that goofy grin as he showed us with pride what he had learned.

"There are the men of the hour," said Joseph to William and me. He turned to our mothers, and asked, "Sister Rebecca and Sister Vilate, do I have your permission to baptize these two fine young men?"

"Yes," said Mother, "only I wish Frederick were here, too." William's mother said the same thing about Brother Kimball.

"I won't ask where they are, since I am the one who has sent them both on errands. All right now, who is going to be first?"

William spoke right up and said, "Ezra will be first because he is older than I am."

I gave William a scowl, but then the Prophet took me by the hand and led me down into the river. It was running quite high with the spring runoff, which also made it cold, but some of the men had dug out a little pool near the riverbank that was used as a baptismal font where the water would run slower than the main current.

I shivered as Brother Joseph took hold of my hands with one of his while I clenched my nose shut. Then he raised his other arm to the square and said the same words the missionaries had said to my parents and sisters, "Having been commissioned of Jesus Christ, I baptize you …" Then he put me down all the way into the water, but just for a second. When I came up, I was not only shivering with the cold, but also with that same tingling feeling I had when I witnessed my parents and the girls being baptized. Mother quickly wrapped me in the blanket she had brought with her, and I suddenly felt very warm.

My sisters both came and hugged me. Lucy whispered in my ear, "Do you feel the tingle, Ezra?" I just looked at her and smiled.

The Prophet repeated this same routine with William, and when he came out of the water, his mother wrapped him up in a blanket, too. We looked at each other and laughed, but then we hugged each other, somehow knowing that we had just experienced something precious beyond words.

Although the water was cold, the air was warm, and since the grown-ups seemed to be talking about something serious, Will and I threw the blankets down, put our arms around each other's shoulders, and started to walk away from the river.

All of a sudden, Mother screamed. We turned around to see Swain running toward the river saying, "I wanna be batized yike Ezwa. I wanna be yike Ezwa."

We both ran toward him as fast as we could, and luckily, Swain couldn't run very fast, so we were able to catch him, but it scared me.

"I wanna be yike you, Ezwa," he said with sadness and longing in his voice.

"Tell you what. Let's see what Papa says when he gets home. If he says it's all right, we will get you baptized then."

"All wight, Ezwa." He put his arms around my neck. "I yuv you."

"I love you, too, Swainy. Come get back in the wheelbarrow, and Will and I will push you home."

As we were getting Swain in the wheelbarrow, the Prophet stopped to shake our hands. "Congratulations to both of you for taking such an important step in your lives. I know the Lord loves you for it."

We both shook his hand with enthusiasm and thanked him for baptizing us, then he left. Mother hugged and said goodbye to Sister Kimball as she left for home with Judith.

As Mother walked past us, she said, "Hurry on home now, Ezra. I'll be putting dinner on the table before Brother Hyrum comes to confirm you." Then she turned to the girls and yelled, "Come home quickly, girls."

"We will," they both yelled, and then turned back to whatever was so interesting to them, whispering and giggling.

A young man was walking toward them from the direction of the Whitney store. As he walked past my sisters, he tipped his hat.

Will and I pushed Swain over behind the girls, feigning interest in skipping rocks across the river, even though they all immediately sank to the bottom. I was very curious about the identity of the stranger.

"Who is that man?" Lovina, who was now fifteen and a half, asked Lucy when the man was out of earshot. Will and I had inched up closer behind them, just close enough to hear what they were saying.

"I don't know," Lucy answered, "but I think I know how I can find out. He is staying at Caroline Grace's house."

"Lucy, you find out for me, will you? I'm going to marry that man."

"Oh, Lovey, what are you thinking? You know nothing about him."

"I know he is handsome. And sophisticated," said Lovina, as the two of them stared after him.

Lucy shook her head. "Sometimes I worry about you. Come on, let's go home. Mother is waiting dinner on us."

We turned to go home as well and had only gone about a block when a group of children came toward us. They were older than we were, and I knew right away they meant trouble because their ring-leader was ol' Henry Jones, the town bully.

"What's the matter with your brother, Ezra? Why do you have to push him in that old thing?" sneered Henry.

"Yeh, what's the matter with him? Why doesn't he have friends of his own?" said another of their gang.

"He's too dumb to have friends," someone said. They all pointed and laughed at my brother.

Someone else said, "He's so dumb, he has to hang around with the little kids." The laughter started again.

"Can't you talk, Swain?" said Henry. "Why don't you say something to us?"

"Maybe his tongue got bit off by a rattlesnake," said a fourth boy. "Maybe a cat got his tongue." They laughed even louder.

"Open your mouth, Swain. Let's see if you have a tongue." At Henry's comment, they roared with laughter. Swain looked bewildered. He didn't know what to do with this kind of negative attention, and just looked at me as if I had the answer.

"Hey, Swain, what's two plus two?" someone else yelled. "Hahaha, you don't even know what two plus two is, do you, Sawaain." He exaggerated Swain's name in mockery. "How stupid are you?"

Well, I had had enough, and I ran toward those bullies and yelled as loud as I could, "You leave him alone!"

"Oooo, the big tough guy, huh?" said Henry, and some of them started throwing rocks and sticks at us.

"Why can't he talk, Ezra? Say something, Swain, so we can hear you talk," they yelled, still pelting us with rocks.

"He can too talk," I yelled. "He just doesn't want to talk to people like you!"

Someone yelled, "I think Joseph Swain's a freak."

At this, they all started chanting, "Joseph Swain's a fre-eak, Joseph Swain's a fre-eak," and ran off down the road.

I could still hear them laughing and chanting even after we had started again for home.

Swain had a sadly perplexed look on his face and tears ran down his cheeks. "Why don't dey yike me, Ezwa? I yuv dem." He paused, looking over his shoulder at their retreating figures as if trying to understand it all. Then he added with evident pain in his voice, "Jesus yuvs dem."

I stopped pushing the barrow and went around to the front of it where I could see his face, and said with authority, "Listen, Swain."

He looked up at me, and I wiped his face with the corner of my still-damp shirt. I crouched down, held his face in my hands, and looked into his face. "You are my brother, and I count myself lucky to have you. Do you understand?"

Swain nodded his head slowly.

"I feel sorry for those bullies because they just don't know who you really are. But I do. I know that inside that head of yours is a very incredible person. You just sometimes have a hard time letting all that wonderfulness come out, that's all."

His tears started up again. "I won't ever let them hurt you as long as I am alive, do you hear me?"

I put my arms around his heaving chest. "It doesn't matter what other people say, you are the best brother anyone could ever have."

I was trying so hard to be brave and not cry, but when I looked at Will, tears were already running down his cheeks.

I took a deep breath. "Let's go home, men. I think my mom has chicken and dumplings ready for dinner, and you know how you love chicken and dumplings, right, Swainy?"

"Yes," he said as he brightened up a bit. "I yuv dem. Wio," he said to my buddy. "Do you yuv chicken an dumpwings?"

We were all able to laugh again and continued on home.

Father was still gone when we sat down to dinner. Mother started us off reading the Book of Mormon, and it somehow meant more to me that night after all that had happened that day. We read about how Alma the Younger and his friends went around doing bad things, just as Henry Jones and his gang had been doing to us earlier that day, only maybe even worse. But Alma the Younger was able to completely change. Maybe there was hope for Henry Jones.

When the dishes were cleared from the table, I finally got up the courage to ask Mother what she had been talking to Brother Joseph about after my baptism.

"He told me that Brother Hyrum wants to come around this evening and confirm you and William members of the Church," she answered. "Then I asked the Prophet if Swain should be baptized. I worry so about him." She paused for what seemed like a very long time.

"And what did he say?" I had started to wonder if she was going to answer me.

She took a deep breath and continued, "He told me that people like Joseph Swain are in no need of baptism. They are pure and innocent before the Lord. Swain is here, not to prove himself, but to prove those around him. I guess that is supposed to be comforting to me, and it is, but at the same time …" she hesitated again.

I stepped closer to her and, in my childlike way, tried to reassure her. I put my arms around her waist and leaned into her, and she ran her hand through my hair. "It reconfirms to me that he is not going to get any better. He is twelve years old, Ezra. We have hoped and prayed for a miracle for so long, but if a cure were coming, it would have likely come by now. I can see now that it probably won't happen, at least not in this life."

We were both silent, letting the finality of Swain's situation sink in.

"Mama, I need to tell you something. After you grown-ups left, a gang of children came toward us and started making fun of Swain."

She just sighed and asked, "Was Henry Jones one of those kids?"

"Yes. He was so mean to Swain. They all said such mean things! They even threw rocks and sticks at us, and it really hurt." I rubbed the top of my arm where I had been hit. I continued to tell her the whole story, and when I had finished, she told me she was proud of me for standing up for Swain.

"Isn't that what brothers do?"

"Yes, Ezra, it is what they are supposed to do. Maybe they don't always do it, but you did."

Perhaps she was thinking about her brothers and wondering if they stood up for her to their father when she chose to join the church.

In any case, I knew that she knew I had done the right thing. Then she asked, "How did Swain take it?"

"He cried, Mama, and asked why those boys didn't love him because he loved them."

She swallowed hard. "That is the heart of a hero, Ezra. That's the kind of love we should all have. Swain is the best example of that, far better at it than I am." She hugged me tight, and then said, "Now, go get cleaned up because Brother Hyrum will be here any minute to confirm you."

CHAPTER FIFTEEN

OGDEN, UTAH 1804

Trip to Smithfield, Part One ...
Henrietta Tells Her Story

"And that is how I came to be baptized by the Prophet Joseph Smith, and confirmed by his brother, Hyrum."

"Papa, that is an amazing story," said Fred.

It was easy to see that Ezra was getting tired. He had been very emotional telling about the circumstances of his baptism, and about the children who were mean to Swain.

The next few days were occupied with getting ready to go to Smithfield. Joseph stuck by his grandmother and did whatever she asked him to do. He had pulled the buggy out of the barn and was wiping the dust from it when Henrietta came out to inspect it.

"I think we can leave in the morning, Joseph. Everything is ready to go. I will get the flowers the last thing before we leave."

"Flowers?" asked Joseph. "Do you think we will have room for them?"

When he saw the disappointment in her eyes, he knew they would make room for the flowers no matter what else they may have to sacrifice. "All right, Grandma, we will take the flowers."

She hugged him and kissed his cheek, then went to get a shovel to dig up the flowers. Joseph helped her dig them up and transfer them into the pots that she had collected. He had to admit they looked beautiful standing there in a row in all their array of colors.

Henrietta had planted a wide selection of flowers in the hopes that she would be able to take them up north. Roses, lilies, mums, petunias, snapdragons, and many others, but she knew some of them would not transport well, so she only dug up the ones that would last through the two-day journey over bumpy roads. She had decided to put them in pots, roots and all, so that they would stay fresh during their travels.

At the end of that long day of preparation, she said, "Joseph, you better get to bed early tonight so you won't be tired in the morning."

He obediently and willingly did just that.

✦

At last, the morning of the great adventure dawned. It was a beautiful first day of September, the cloudless sky a deep ocean blue, and the trees on the mountainside just starting to show signs of putting on their fall colors.

Question after question swirled around in Joseph's head at the prospect of having his grandmother all to himself. She had not had the opportunity to tell her story, and he couldn't wait to hear it. She got up early and fixed a nice breakfast for Fred and Joseph, deciding again to let Ezra sleep as long as he could. She was too excited to eat much breakfast herself, but Joseph, as usual, wolfed down as much as possible without seeming too rude.

Fred helped them load everything into the buggy and then he hooked it up to Woodrow, the carriage horse. Henrietta grabbed a shawl and put on her bonnet. Then Joseph climbed into the driver's seat and helped his grandmother up beside him.

"Kiss your father for me when he wakes up, Fred. Tell him I will miss him," she said.

"Don't worry about a thing, Mother. I will tell him, and we will be just fine," Fred reassured her. "You two have a great trip."

As they pulled out of the yard, Henrietta turned and blew her son a kiss, and Joseph lifted his hat to his father. Fred waved back with both arms high overhead.

"Well, Grandma, we are on our way." Joseph kept Woodrow at a steady trot as they headed up the dirt road. He did well at avoiding the occasional pothole and keeping the ride as smooth as possible for his grandmother.

The road was two lanes wide, one going north and the other going south. Both had grooves from wagon and carriage wheels. Still, it was smoother than any road Joseph had seen in Mexico.

Ezra had told him that a crew regularly pulled a road grater behind a team of horses to keep the road evened out. Recently, he said, they were using a truck to pull the grater. Apparently, that was a vast improvement.

Joseph knew he should take every opportunity to stop to water and feed Woodrow, and let his grandmother have a break as well. Each time they stopped, Henrietta took great care to make sure the flowers were watered and standing upright.

She had packed enough food for the two-day journey, and after they had eaten some of it for lunch, Joseph asked his first question. "Grandmother," he said, and then waited for a reaction from her.

After a minute or two she answered, "Yes, Joseph?"

"Grandmother, I've been wanting to ask you some questions."

"Oh really, Joseph? You?" she asked, a little sarcastically. "How did you get this far down the road without asking them?"

"Well, is it all right if I ask you about some things now?"

"I would be disappointed if you didn't."

"All right, then, here goes. Where did you come from?"

She looked around as if trying to find the answer outside herself. "I came from the moon, Joseph. Did no one ever tell you?"

He looked at her in shock, but when she laughed at her own joke, Joseph relaxed and laughed as well. He started to feel as if he could ask her anything but wondered if he would ever get a straight answer. How he had come to love this feisty little woman.

"No, not really, Joseph, although I'm sure some people think I did. I was actually born and raised in Boston, Massachusetts. Have you heard of that place?" She exaggerated her accent by saying "Bah-stn" for Boston and "bahn" for born. She always spoke with a slight accent, but when she wanted to, she could really make it noticeable.

"Yes, I have heard of it, Grandma. My dad told me that is why you speak with a different accent than most people."

"Oh, do I have an accent?" She put her hand to her mouth as if she had done something wrong.

Joseph laughed. "Yes, you do, and it is one of the things I love about you."

"And all these yeahs I thought it was everyone else who had accents."

They both laughed again, then she went on. "I will tell you about my life in Bahstn. My parents were very rich. Mother was an only child and stood to inherit a huge fortune from her mother, Elizabeth Pope Phillips, whom they called Betsy. Her father, Ebenezer Phillips, had passed away in 1818, leaving Mother with a second fortune.

"My mother, Elizabeth Phillips, named for her mother, of course, became interested right away in a young man by the name of John Crombie who had recently moved to the town. He also came from a wealthy family, so it was no surprise that the two of them ran in the same circles, and inevitable that they would meet.

"They combined their fortunes when they married in 1826. A year and a half after they were married, I was born, and my two brothers followed soon after, William in 1829 and John Henry in 1832."

"Did they live, Grandmother? I mean, were they able to grow up?" He knew baby boys sometimes died in this family.

"Yes, they did, although William was only thirty-seven when he passed away. I had a baby sister, too, but she died when she was two years old. I was eleven when little Mary left us, and I thought my world had come to an end. How I loved that little girl."

"That is so sad, especially to lose a girl, and your only sister. Were your brothers nice? I mean, did they stick up for you?"

"Yes, they were very nice," Henrietta smiled, "and they did stand by me. But we lived such a privileged life that we never faced bullies or any kind of negativity to speak of. We were all well-educated. I went to St. Ursula's Finishing School, and ..."

"Finishing school? What kind of school is that?"

Henrietta gave a little laugh as she realized Joseph would have no idea about finishing schools. "It's a school for 'upper class' girls."

"Upper class girls?" questioned Joseph.

"More succinctly put, rich girls. That was me," she went on. "We learned the so-called social graces, cultural refinement. We learned how to embroider and how to properly set a table, how to arrange the food on a dish to make it beautiful and appetizing. We learned etiquette, which includes how to eat properly, how to sit and stand and even walk properly, and all kinds of manners."

"I've never heard of such things, Grandma. Does it really matter how you set the table, or sit on a chair?"

"It does to some people, the 'upper class' specifically. I would have known how to act in the presence of the Queen of England if I had ever had the chance to meet her." Her eyes seemed to glow at the thought.

"You said you learned how to arrange the food, Grandma, but did you learn how to cook it?"

"Oh, heavens no, Joseph. We would never have cooked for ourselves. We had servants to do that for us."

Joseph shrugged. "Are those refinement things all you learned? It seems like a waste of time to me."

"Oh mercy, no!" she exclaimed. "We learned grammar, penmanship, literature and philosophy, history, mathematics, and creative writing. We learned to swim and ride horses, two things I loved to do. We also learned to dance and play the piano, my favorite subjects of all. In short, we learned many of the same things you learn in school, only with a different focus."

"What was that, Grandma?"

"Everything we learned in school was designed to teach us how to act properly around young men so as to catch a wealthy husband. We were educated in many areas but were also taught not to display too much intelligence around the young men for fear of scaring them off."

"What? You were taught so many incredible things and then warned not to let anyone know that you knew them?"

"That's about it." She laughed. "Sometimes it is very hard to be female."

"That is terrible, Grandma."

"I have to agree, Joseph, but it's the way it was. The rich girls were expected to marry sons of wealthy men so the money would stay in the family. Everyone was concerned with protecting the family fortune. And if a young man felt threatened by a young woman in the sense that she might be smarter or better educated, he would look elsewhere."

"Oh, poor Grandma," he teased, finding her hand and patting it softly. "The hardships of being wealthy must be so difficult to bear."

She smiled, giving him a playful nudge on his arm. "It was tough," she sighed, "but we endured it the best we could."

They both laughed at the irony of the situation.

"But here is the really good thing about having a lot of money. With wealth comes freedom, Joseph. We were able to do anything we wanted to do and go anywhere we wanted to go. I had beautiful clothes, and servants to take care of everything that I didn't want to do. I never had to wash the dishes or empty the chamber pots."

"You never did the dishes, Grandma? Or make your bed or sweep the floor?"

"No, Joseph, not one time, not until we left Boston."

Joseph was overcome by his grandmother's life of ease as he contrasted it with his own.

"I'm sure I would have spent a year or more in Europe if it hadn't been for two things that happened, one very sad and one very happy."

"Oh no, Grandmother. What happened?"

"I'll tell you about the sad thing first, Joseph." A look of thoughtful reflection came over the usually cheerful face. "In 1841 when I was thirteen years old, my father passed away. He was only forty years old, not nearly old enough to die. Although Mother had married for money, as they say, she deeply loved my father. I adored him, and he was my brothers' best friend and teacher. But he was gone, and there was nothing any of us could do about it."

"What happened to him, Grandma?"

"I don't know," she said, lifting her hands palms up and shrugging her shoulders. "He just dropped dead. Your grandfather says it was likely a heart attack, but I guess no one will ever know for sure. It was so sudden that we were all in shock for quite a while afterward, and we all missed him so much. My brothers who were only eleven and nine missed him the most, I suspect. It was especially hard for them to grow up without a father.

"My mother now had the huge responsibility of raising us to be proper adults all by herself. She had a hard enough time helping me through the trauma, but for her to be mother and father to those two young boys," Henrietta shook her head at the sad memory. "She didn't really know how or what to do. So, she put them in boarding school, a very high-quality military-like school that could teach them about becoming men. I think it was a good decision on my mother's part, but I missed my brothers terribly. It was lonely at home with just my mother and me."

Joseph let his head hang down in sympathy with his grandmother when she suddenly raised her head and looked around. "I think we are getting very close to Brigham City, Joseph. We will both be ready for a good night's rest, don't you think?"

Joseph had secretly been hoping that they were getting close because the sun was making its way toward the western horizon. "It will be a welcomed sight to be there, Grandma. We've been sitting in this buggy all day."

They entered Brigham City, a small town near the northern border of Utah and Idaho, nestled up close to the mountains. Henrietta was able to direct him right to the Harrises' home just off the main road through town, where they were welcomed with a nice meal and comfortable beds.

Henrietta and her friend Abigail Harris stayed up well past suppertime, talking and laughing long after they had cleared the table and had done the dishes. How great it seemed for her to be reunited with this dear friend.

Joseph loved seeing his grandmother so happy, but he couldn't miss the comparison of Henrietta's life now with what it could have been if she had stayed in Boston. Being very tired, he went to bed, dreaming of the life of ease that he someday might have.

At breakfast, Joseph and Brother Harris talked about the easy time he and Henrietta had had getting as far as Brigham City. The dirt road had been almost a straight shot north since leaving Ogden and had been well maintained for the most part. The little buggy had followed right along behind Woodrow, and they stayed right on course. The horse paid little attention to the automobiles that whooshed past them from time to time at speeds that must have exceeded fifteen miles per hour.

Because of what his grandfather had told him about Sardine Canyon, he was a little apprehensive about the next leg of their journey. He asked, "Where do we go from here, Brother Harris?"

The older man looked at this young man, not yet sixteen years old, and said, "Joseph, I know you must be an expert driver, or your father and grandfather would never have let you make this trip so I will just tell you this. The road up the canyon is quite steep and has some pretty tight twists and turns. It will not be the straight shot you experienced getting this far. However, as long as it doesn't rain and there aren't too many cars on the road, I expect you will do just fine."

Joseph wasn't sure if that made him feel more or less apprehensive. "Where does the road up the canyon start?"

"Come outside with me and I will show you."

The two of them walked out the front door and into the road. "Go to the corner here, then turn left onto the main road, the same one you came in on. Then just stay on that road, pay attention to what is going on around you, and you will be fine."

"Do you think it will rain, Brother Harris?" asked Joseph, expecting a negative answer since the skies were currently cloudless.

"It's hard to say, Joseph. It doesn't look like rain right now, but this late in the summer, anything could happen."

Joseph took a deep breath and walked to the corner. Looking to the left at the mountain ahead of him, he was suddenly grateful he had taken that ride up Ogden Canyon a week before on Dodger. It had taught him some things about horses on steep roads to which he had quickly adapted. But pulling a buggy up a steep incline might be a different story, he thought. He had handled some pretty amazing situations while driving a wagon for his father in Mexico, and so surely he could handle this canyon. But then again, none of those roads had been as steep as this one purported to be. His thoughts went back and forth from apprehension to confidence until his grandmother called him back into the house.

"Joseph, the Harrises have asked us to kneel in prayer with them before we leave," she said. He dropped to his knees by Henrietta, and Brother Harris offered the prayer. He asked a special blessing on the two travelers and their horse, and then petitioned the Lord to remember young Joseph, asking that he be blessed with understanding of how to handle any situation that may arise on the road. Joseph appreciated that very much. That prayer gave him the push he needed to remember that he should place his trust in God as his mother had taught him, and everything would be all right.

Everyone hugged everyone else, and Joseph helped his grandmother into the buggy. Abigail took hold of her friend's hand one last time. "We will be looking forward to seeing you on the way back."

"Perhaps we shall have a great adventure to tell you then, Abigail." Henrietta looked at Joseph. "I just hope it isn't too great of an adventure."

———◆———

As they started up the side of the mountain, Joseph had the feeling that everything would be fine. He would just keep Woodrow at a steady gait, watch for automobiles, and pray that it wouldn't rain. That had to be a formula for success.

It was a beautiful clear morning, and the height of the mountain to the east kept the road in shadow until about 9:00 a.m. When the sun finally reached them, its warmth felt good on their faces and arms. The leaves on the mountain trees were already showing off their autumn reds, golds, and oranges, a couple of weeks ahead of the trees on the mountains around Ogden.

Woodrow was having no problem pulling the buggy up the incline of the road. Everything was going along well enough for Joseph to think he could safely remind his grandmother of what they had been talking about before they reached the Harrises. "So, Grandma, you told me of the bad thing that happened to you as a young girl in Boston, but you never told me the good thing."

"Mercy, Grandson!" she exclaimed. "I forgot all about that." She chuckled her little grandma chuckle and went on. "Around the early spring of 1845, there was a lot of excitement in our little corner of the world. Some men came into our neighborhood asking people to attend a meeting at the public school. They would be telling us about the restored gospel of Jesus Christ, a new religion that taught what Christ taught, with a living prophet and real apostles, and with the authority given them of God to do so, just the way Jesus had set his church up many centuries before. Mother was not interested at all and forbade me from attending any meetings. I think that might have been in part because her mother, Betsy, who effectively owned Charleston, a city next to Boston, wanted nothing to do with it. When Apostle Parley P. Pratt approached my grandmother's house, she chased him off the property with a broom, yelling, 'I shall sit on the top of the topless throne while the devil pitches you into the bottomless pit!'"

Joseph laughed at Henrietta's dramatic outburst.

"That would put the fear of God into just about anyone, including my mother, and so she chose not to listen to the missionaries at that time. But I was very interested and wanted to hear all that they were teaching. I would tell Mother I was going for a walk, but instead I went to the meetings. We were religious people, members of the Mount Vernon Congregational Church, but the more I listened to these missionaries preach this new religion, the more the truth of it was borne into my heart. I soon told Mother what I was doing and finally convinced her to attend meetings with me. These missionaries later came to our house to teach us more and more about this religion, which led to our baptism on May 1, 1845, in the famous Boston Harbor. Do you remember hearing about Boston Harbor in your history lessons?"

"Let's see, Grandma, I think I do. Wasn't there something called *The Boston Tea Party*, where the villagers dressed as Indians, boarded a ship that had been sent from England with a load of tea, and dumped it into the harbor?"

"What a smart young man you are! That is exactly what happened."

"Well, maybe not so smart, Grandma, because I don't remember why they did it," he admitted.

"England was ruling the colonies with an iron fist, still claiming that the King was their rightful sovereign. The colonists said, no, we came here to be free. England was extorting a huge tax on the tea before it could be unloaded, and the colonists refused to pay it. You must understand how much those people loved their tea, so it was a huge sacrifice for them to dump it all into the harbor, but they weren't about to pay that tax. By dumping it overboard, the colonists deprived the King of making any money from all that tea, and in fact, he lost money on the proposition. But more importantly, the colonists were asserting their right to be free from the oppression of the King."

"Wow, Grandma. Did you know any of the people who dumped the tea?"

"Mercy, Joe, I hope not. It happened in 1773, over fifty years before I was born. But my grandfather Ebenezer was twenty-three and living in Boston at the time. He likely knew many of them. I guess he could have even been one of the Indians who did the dumping."

"I hope he was, Grandma. What a famous ancestor I would have, and how brave they all must have been to board that ship. I wish I had been there!"

Joseph's enthusiasm was contagious, so Henrietta decided to milk it for all she could get out of it. "People claimed for many years that the water of Boston Harbor still tasted of tea, but I couldn't detect any tea in it at all."

"You tasted the harbor water?"

"Oh yes, I did! When I was baptized there in 1845, I accidently got a big gulp of it, and it just tasted like nasty water to me."

"Oh, Grandma! You swallowed it?" Joseph giggled. "You're not making this up, are you?"

"Would I do that? The fact is, I was baptized by Elder Ezra T. Benson, one of the missionaries who had been working with us. He took me into the harbor but neglected to remind me to hold my breath and didn't give me a warning about when he was going to put me under. Just as I was about to go down, I panicked a little and took a big breath. Unfortunately, I got more water than air, and I came up sputtering and spewing the water everywhere, even in Elder Benson's face. I coughed and coughed, and my arms and legs were flailing."

Joseph laughed out loud at the picture she had painted. It seemed to get funnier and funnier until they were both out of control and roaring with laughter.

"Elder Benson had to put me down in the water all over again," she was finally able to say, "and this time he told me when to hold my breath." This started another paroxysm of gaiety between the two of them. After a good long and hearty laugh, she tried to gain some self-dignity, but when she looked at Joseph and saw that he was still struggling to keep a straight face, they both laughed again. Finally, she said with that little twinkle in her eye, "Mother's baptism went much smoother than mine."

It took them a few minutes to regain complete composure, but they both needed the release this episode provided them, Joseph because of the apprehension he had about taking her up the canyon, and Henrietta because of the emotions that had been dredged up talking about her years in Boston. Finally, she said, "Joseph, now I must repent. I did not mean to make light of such a sacred ordinance, especially because I am so grateful to have been baptized."

He grinned. "I know, Grandma, but sometimes sacred things happen in a funny way. I was baptized in an irrigation ditch, for crying out loud."

Henrietta giggled a little cute grandma-giggle and put her head on Joseph's shoulder. He put his arm around her shoulders and gave her a big hug.

"It just goes to show what we would do for our testimonies of the truthfulness of the Gospel of Jesus Christ," she said as she patted his knee.

"Yes, it does." Joseph couldn't help but wonder again what trials lay ahead for him.

Henrietta, who would be seventy-seven years old in a couple of weeks, knew her trials and had met them head on, but Joseph was just getting a good start on his life. Anything could happen.

And anything did.

Just then, Joseph felt a drop of rain fall on his hat. He hadn't noticed the clouds gathering while his mind had been wandering all over Boston and laughing with his grandmother. A few more drops fell, but it was still nothing but a very light sprinkle.

He pulled the horse over while he got Henrietta her umbrella and a lap robe out of the back of the buggy, and just as a precaution, he pulled the rain cover that the buggy was equipped with up over their heads.

Thank goodness for that, he thought.

After studying the sky for several minutes, he could see there were no threatening thunderheads or heavy clouds but knew he must be even more vigilant as he continued to take the horse and buggy up the mountain.

As they neared the relatively large town of Logan, the road became considerably more twisted, and more automobiles were passing them, both going up the canyon and down. Still, Woodrow paid them little attention, and he negotiated the twists and turns of the road with apparent ease. Joseph's confidence grew a bit. The rain stopped a few minutes later, but the clouds didn't go away. He decided to get his grandmother's mind focused on her story again while he inwardly prayed that everything would go well.

"So, Grandma, what happened next?"

The little sprinkle had cooled the air down, and Joseph enjoyed it, but Henrietta wrapped her shawl around her tightly and tucked the edges of the lap robe under her legs. "All right, Joseph, I am ready to go on with my story," she said. "Let's see, we were discussing … What were we discussing, Joseph?"

"Your baptism, Grandma." They both snickered again, and Henrietta took a deep breath.

"How could I forget that?" she said more to herself than to Joseph. Then she went on. "The meetings with the missionaries continued, and Mother and I were very committed to the gospel until they talked about the Lord wanting those who joined the Church to band together in one body. They had told us all about the Saints being driven from Ohio, then from Missouri, and now from Nauvoo, Illinois, and that they were preparing to move far away to the west. The Prophet and his brother Hyrum had been martyred in Carthage, Illinois, and things were no longer safe in Nauvoo. The saints were working hard to finish the temple so that Church members could all receive special temple blessings, but they knew they had to leave as soon as possible. Despite all of this, the Lord had asked the new converts to gather with the Saints in Nauvoo to receive the blessings of the temple, and then to move west with them to a place where they could live in peace. We had never seriously thought about leaving Boston before this time.

"Mother and I talked a lot about what that would mean for us if we accepted this challenge to move west. We would have to get the boys home from school and convince them that what we had been taught was the truth. We would have to sell our house and all our belongings. Our belongings! We had so much, Joseph. We really didn't know what we would do with it all. Mother, as you might recall, was to inherit three huge family fortunes. Now with this new call to move far away, she would have to turn her back on it and move to an unknown place in a wild, uninhabited country with no luxuries at all. She and I studied every day, and the more we did, and the more the truth of it was burned into our hearts, the more we knew we were going to have to do exactly as the Lord directed, despite how difficult it would be to let go of our favored position in the community and our very comfortable lifestyle."

"Wow, Grandma, I knew it was hard for people who had little to move to an unknown place, but I never stopped to think how hard it would be for people who had everything to leave it all behind and go to having nothing."

"Yes, Joseph, and that is just what we did. As soon as we received our own assurance that we should go west with the Saints, and relying on our testimonies of the Gospel of Jesus Christ, we started selling things off. I was nineteen years old the year we left for Zion. Since my grandmother was still alive, Mother asked her to take care of all the money matters. Although she in no way condoned what we were doing, Grandmother gave us enough money to get us on our journey in as good a style as possible, and to outfit us for the trip west. Two years to the day after our baptism, May 1, 1847, Mother and I and my two brothers, now seventeen and fifteen, left Boston and turned our faces to the west. We left at noon that day with the Alvin Farnham Company for the land of Zion. We were able to make the journey to St. Louis mostly by boat, but it was a very hard journey."

"I thought you were heading to Nauvoo, Grandma. Why did you go to St. Louis?" He remembered his grandfather telling him that he had "gone down to St. Louis," it being downriver from Nauvoo.

"The idea was to go to St. Louis first because we could procure wagons and teams there for the trip across the plains. Many Saints were gathering in St. Louis for that very reason, then going up the two hundred miles on the Mississippi River to the temple in Nauvoo to receive their blessings before heading west. Those who had already received their blessings could just get on the Missouri River right there in St. Louis and travel all the way to Winter Quarters."

"Oh, that makes sense."

"The day we left our beautiful big home in Boston, taking with us only things we really needed or could sell easily along the way, was a day of joy and sadness. It was hard to leave everything we knew behind, all our friends and loved ones in Boston, all our earthly possessions, and especially Grandmother Pope. Our whole way of life. But we were going to Zion, and that is all that really mattered to us anymore."

"Where did you go from Boston, Grandma?"

"We went around Cape Cod, then down to New Jersey, and from there we took a steamer to New York. We rode on boats that were so crowded we had to sit on the deck on a box, if we were lucky enough to find one. Otherwise, we sat right on the boards of the deck. Soon, I was escorted to the side of the boat to cast up my accounts to the fishes."

"Oh no, you were seasick, weren't you!"

"So seasick. I get a little queasy in the stomach just thinking about it. One morning, we were able to get on the ferry boat for Philadelphia. We finally arrived at the hall where we were to stay that night, but we had to sleep on very uncomfortable benches.

"The next day we secured the services of a canal boat from a Dutchman to take us further on, and what a time we had! We had to wait for the Dutchman to unload the boat which took a long time, and then reload it with his wares, and all the belongings of those of us going with him. People piled in and found whatever place they could to sit or lay down on the boxes that were strewn everywhere. I sat astride the upper corner of a dry goods box and felt lucky to have it. And that is how we spent the night."

"That must have been some change from your nice soft bed in Boston. No pillow even, Grandma?"

"We hardly had room for that kind of luxury, Joseph. I just rolled up whatever article of clothing was handy and used it, and then used my shawl for a blanket at nights. And to cook on a canal boat in that thinly settled land. Mercy, Joseph, with nowhere to buy or sell, we had to get along with whatever was at hand, which was not very much."

"I would have died of starvation, especially if I had grown used to eating the kind of food you fix for me."

She smiled before she said, "You would have made it, Grandson, certainly not comfortably, but you would have made it."

She went on. "One day when we were on the Susquehanna River, I was disembarking when the man at the keel, out of mischief, started the boat moving before I made it to shore. Mr. Eldredge had my right hand as he sat in the stern of the boat, and Mr. Howell took my left hand as he walked the path on shore. The man at the keel laughed all the while as he gave me a ride through the raging canal. I had a good swim and wetting to their merriment."

Joseph could not help but laugh at this scene until Henrietta poked him in the ribs. "Ouch, Grandma," he said, pretending pain.

"Serves you right for laughing at my misfortune," she said, with a merry smile on her lips. "Looking back on it, I guess it was funny to some people, but it was one of the best things that ever happened to me."

"What?" His smile turned to confusion. "How could that have been a good thing?"

"Well, as a result of getting wet, I became quite ill, and by the time we made it to St. Louis, Mother sought out the aid of a physician to heal me."

"Ohhhh," said Joseph, dramatically drawing out the word as the dawning of the situation came suddenly. "She took you to Dr. Williams, didn't she."

"Well, we happened onto him, I'll say. After some similar experiences with other boats, it was a relief to finally be on the steamer which took us the rest of the way to St. Louis. Even then the trip was not easy. Sometimes all the passengers had to get off and walk while the steamer negotiated rough or shallow water that sometimes appeared in the Ohio River. But we were going to Zion to receive all the blessings promised to us before we left Boston, and that was worth whatever we had to go through to get there.

"When we made it to the Mississippi River, the going was much easier, although I was sick and weak when we arrived in St. Louis on May 12, 1847. What a place it was compared to the eastern cities I had known all my life, and what a change from our home in Boston. It seemed wild, even savage, and unsophisticated and rough. We had to walk from the levee to the home of Brother Hubbard who helped new emigrants get on their feet, and we stayed a few days there. Mother got employment at the planter's house as a dressmaker. I can't tell you what a shock it was to see my mother working as a laborer for the first time in her life. My brother William worked as a waiter, and brother John as a pantry boy. What a change of lifestyle for us. We met Dr. Ezra G. Williams while we were there at Brother Hubbard's when he was treating one of their family members. Mother engaged him to care for me. He was tall and handsome, and smart and funny, and I fell for him the moment I saw him. He ..." She stopped abruptly.

Joseph emitted a comical snort when he realized her mistake admitting it was love at first sight.

"Well, he was very nice, and ..." she tried to cover up the faux pas. "I mean, I ... well, I liked him right away and ..."

Joseph, by now doubling over in laughter, told her, "It's all right, Grandma. Your secret is safe with me." They both laughed a good hearty laugh.

When she could finally talk again, she said, "Dr. Williams said I had the *dumb ague,* something that we had never heard of before. We did not know what to think. Was he really fooling us because we were new arrivals? But he prescribed for me and in a few months, I was myself again. Even after I was well, he continued to pay attention to me. I had begun working at the planter's house with Mother, the first time in my life to work for other people as well. But we were going to Zion, and that made the burden lighter.

"The doctor was soon treating Mother and my brother John for complaints of their health, and both were soon well. It was his success at curing us that gave us implicit faith and confidence in him, and it turned to marriage for me. On a beautiful Sunday in August, the ceremony was performed by Apostle Orson Hyde. It was quite a wedding at Rebecca's home. She had gone out of her way to make it as nice as possible, and I believed I was the happiest person on earth at the time."[23]

Just then, Joseph felt another raindrop on his hat, then a few more and a few more. Within a matter of a few minutes, the weather had turned from a light sprinkle to an all-out storm. They were both getting soaked, and Woodrow was finding it hard to keep his footing as the steep road became muddier and muddier, so Joseph pulled the buggy over near a stand of trees.

He got Henrietta down from the buggy, retrieved one of the blankets that she had made sure to bring, and wrapped her up in it. He found a place under a tree that sheltered her from the rain quite well and left her there while he attended to Woodrow.

He saw it coming out of the corner of his eye. A truck was fishtailing down the steep grade of the canyon in their direction. He felt the panic rise in his throat as he struggled to keep a clear head and react appropriately. Should he pull the horse forward, or move him backward, or should he stay where he was. He prayed out loud, "Dear Lord, give us the protection you promised us," and he stayed where he was. The truck continued to career out of control and came sliding sideways right for them, completely splattering Joseph, the horse, and the buggy with mud. At what seemed like the last possible moment, the truck miraculously fishtailed into the opposite direction, leaving Joseph safe.

But it was so unexpected to Woodrow that he bolted down the side of the road and into the brush, spilling the contents of the buggy all over the ground. Joseph ran as fast as he could to stop Woodrow, while the horse, half blinded by the mud and finding it hard to run in the long, wet grass, slowed down enough for Joseph to grab the bridle and regain control. He turned the buggy around and saw his grandmother standing there with horror written all over her face. He ran to her and scooped her up into his arms. They both cried, and thanked God that they were all right.

The rain stopped as suddenly as it had begun, amounting to nothing but a summer cloud burst, and the sun began to peek through. They surveyed the devastation of their belongings strewn down the side of the road.

"My flowers!" Henrietta cried. "Oh, Joseph, my flowers! What will I put on the graves?"

Every one of the flowerpots had broken to pieces, and the flowers were torn apart and scattered everywhere.

"And this looks like what remains of our dinner," bemoaned Joseph, picking through any little thing that was edible and eating it up. He offered his grandmother a piece of soggy bread. She looked at it with disgust, then started retrieving the rest of their things.

"Hello, folks. Looks like you haf hat a bit of trouble. Can I gif you a hand?" A large man with a friendly smile and driving a wagon had pulled up behind them.

Joseph thought he detected some kind of accent in the way the man spoke, but he couldn't say from where. He said, among other oddly pronounced words, "gif" instead of "give," and he seemed to growl his r's. Joseph extended his hand to the man, who in turn offered Joseph a big, meaty hand that looked like it could pound nails without a hammer. He gripped Joseph's hand so hard that the boy had the inclination to cry out.

"I'm Joseph Williams, sir, and yes," he said, trying to disguise the pain in his voice. "As we were coming up the canyon, a truck started to slip on the muddy road and nearly ran over us. It spooked my horse, and he took off, spilling everything out of the buggy when he hit the barrow pit."

"Are you hurt?" asked the man.

"No, I had just pulled over because of the rain, and had wrapped her in a blanket," he said, motioning to Henrietta. "So, we were not in the buggy when the horse bolted."

"Dat vas lucky," said the man. He was an older man, maybe around sixty-five or so, but apparently still as strong as a bull. He had a short, tidy beard, but no moustache.

"I tend to think it was something more than luck, sir," replied Joseph.

"I haf no doubt about dat. My name is Hans Peterson, I lif here in Hyrum, just a couple of miles avay, and vould be wery happy to take you to my house and let you get cleaned up."

He started helping Joseph gather up their things when he noticed Henrietta standing nearby, still wrapped in the soaking blanket with a forlorn look on her face. He walked over to her and asked, "Are you all right, ma'am?"

"My flowers," she said, motioning to the broken pottery and the ruined plants.

"Oh dear," he commiserated. "Dey vere special to you, no doubt."

"I—I—I—" she stuttered, unable to form a coherent word.

"She brought them with us from Ogden to put on her children's graves in Smithfield." Joseph had come up behind them, wanting to rescue his grandmother from the whole situation, and explaining to the man what they were doing in Sardine Canyon with potted plants.

"Ohhh," he said. "Vell, dat can be remedied, you know." He put a big, muscular arm around her and escorted her to his wagon. "Come sit in here vhile your son and I finish cleaning tings up."

Henrietta looked up at the man and said with pride, "He is my grandson."

"Really? Forgif my mistake, ma'am," said Hans Petersen. "You look so young dat I couldn't imagine you haffing a grandson dis old."

"Oh, you're just teasing me," she said, finally able to smile. She was quickly feeling at ease around this big man.

After Joseph and Mr. Petersen got everything back in the buggy, the man went over it to make sure it was still in working order. "Looks like you haf a couple of cracks in two of de spokes, son."

"Oh no. What am I going to do about that?"

"Vell, lucky for you, I am a vheelwright, and I can fix it."

"You're a wheelwright?" asked Joseph, hardly believing his good luck.

"I guess I do a little of everyting," the man said, obviously not wanting to brag about himself. "Let's yust say I like to fix tings."

"You're a handy man to have around," said Joseph, raising his hand to pat the man on the back. Then, thinking better of it, he just dropped his arm to his side.

"Tell you vhat," said the man. "I'll take your grandmodah vith me in the vagon, and you follow us in de buggy. Vhen vee get to my house, vee can clean everyting up and get you somezing to eat. Are you hungry, Yoseph?"

Joseph's stomach started growling at the mere mention of food. "Grandmother had packed enough food to get us to Smithfield, but it was all ruined when it flew out of the buggy and onto the ground. I guess that is my nice way of saying, yes, I am starving."

The man laughed a deep and hearty laugh. "You are a man afteh mine own haht," he said and pounded Joseph on the back. It was all he could do to keep from coughing at the impact.

Joseph followed Hans Petersen's wagon, all the while listening to the creaking of the broken spokes of the buggy. He was grateful when the man turned right off the main road and onto a side road. They hadn't gone very far when the man pulled the wagon to a stop in front of a modest but well cared for house. A sturdy, handsome woman came out of the house and greeted them. Hans jumped out of the wagon and introduced his wife. "Dis is min kone, my vife, Yulia."

He told Julia briefly what had happened and why he had brought Joseph and Henrietta with him.

"Velcome to owah home," she said to them, motioning Henrietta to come in.

Henrietta, noticing the accent as well, said, "Where are you from, Julia?"

"Hans and I came from Danmark many years ago," she said. "You vould tink afteh all dese years, de accent vould go avay." Then she said to Henrietta, "I taught perhaps you haf a little accent yourself."

Henrietta smiled. "I come from Boston, Massachusetts, born and raised there." She exaggerated "Bahstn" for Julia's sake, and said "bahn" for born and "theh" for there.

Joseph had stayed outside, helping Hans Petersen bring the horse and buggy into the barn. He saw to Woodrow, rubbing him down with a dry towel and making sure he had water and hay. "Thank you, Mr. Petersen, for your help, for letting me put Woodrow in your barn and have some hay. I'm not sure what we would've done if you hadn't come along."

"No problem, son, I am wery glad to help."

The big man had started to remove the broken wheel from the buggy. It seemed to Joseph that when the man spoke, he was mixing his letters up and putting them in the wrong places.

Joseph asked, "What can I do to help you, sir."

"You can go in de house and get somezing to eat. Den vhen you are full, I vould like your halp."

Joseph did not need to be asked twice. He took his wet boots off outside the door, then went inside, removing his wet hat as he entered. He could see the two women sitting by the fire, talking and laughing together as if they had known each other all their lives.

"Oh, Yoseph," said Julia as he walked in the door. "Come here and sit by your grandmodah and I vill get you both some dinnah." She had already made mutton stew with biscuits and fresh corn on the cob before they had arrived.

Joseph sat down to eat and was not ashamed of the amount of food he tucked away, although maybe he should have been.

Julia remarked, "I haven't seen anyone eat so much since my boys vere at home. It does my haht good."

"How many sons do you have, Julia," asked Henrietta.

"I haf tree big, handsome Danish sons, Robert, Henry, and Teodore," she said with evident pride. "Aldough none of dem haf been to Danmark," she added. "And one beautiful dattah, Valdorg Elvira. Dat name probably sounds funny to you, but it is a good Danish name. Ve call her Elvira, dough."

"What a nice family, Julia. I'm sure they bring you much joy."

"Of course, dey do, yust as I am sure your family does."

"My son Fred is visiting us from Mexico, and he brought his son Joseph with him. That is why I am so lucky to have my grandson with me today."

Joseph stood up, thanking Julia for the great meal, and left the house for the barn. He found Hans turning two new spokes for the wagon wheel on a little lathe.

"Here, Yoseph," he said, "you verk de foot pedal for a minute, please." Joseph did as he was asked, and Hans stood next to him, fashioning a tongue on each end of the two spokes he had made. He had previously taken the iron tire off and had taken the wheel apart. He explained that he had removed the two broken spokes in order to duplicate them exactly. Now, he inserted the new ones into the wheel and secured the iron tire back around it. Joseph was fascinated by the whole process and was amazed at Hans Petersen's skill.

"Dere you ah, son, as good as new," said the big man. The two of them put the wheel back onto the buggy and rolled it a few feet in each direction. Obviously satisfied at the results, Hans said, "I tink dis vill get you to vhere you ah going in safety."

"Thank you, sir. I really don't know how I can repay you."

"I don't want you to pay me, Yoseph. Yust take care of dat grand-modah of yours," he said.

Joseph was growing to like that Danish accent.

"I will do that. And now we had better get on our way to Smithfield."

"I recommend dat you stay de night vith us, and ve vill get you moving early in de morning," Hans offered. "I tink your grandmodah vill be better off dat vay."

"That's all right with me, but I know she is eager to visit those graves. I'll ask her, though."

When they went inside, Henrietta took Joseph by the arm and said, "Julia has offered to let us stay here tonight, Joseph. I think it would be a good thing to do."

"Really, Grandmother?" He motioned to the big man. "Brother Petersen had just made me the same offer."

They stayed the night with the Petersens in warm, clean beds while their belongings dried out near the fireplace. Early the next morning, they repacked the buggy, harnessed Woodrow up, and were ready to go.

Henrietta put her arm around her newfound friend, and said with sincerity to both Julia and Hans, "I don't know how we can ever thank you enough for your hospitality." Then looking at Hans, she continued, "and for repairing that wheel. What a stroke of good fortune and blessing from God it was for you to find us."

"Det var så lidt," said the big Dane. "It vas notting."

Joseph hesitated when Hans offered his hand, but finally decided he could take it like a man.

"We will never forget you." He stifled a grimace as his hand was engulfed in Hans's vice grip.

"Nor vill vee forget you. God bless you on your yourney."

"He already has, friends. He brought us to you," said Henrietta.

Joseph helped her into the buggy, and they were once again on their way north toward Smithfield.

CHAPTER SIXTEEN

SMITHFIELD, UTAH 1904

Trip to Smithfield, Part Two...
A Solemn Visit to the Cemetery

When the two travelers finally made it to the Hansen home in Smithfield later that morning, Joseph heaved a sigh of relief. Hans Petersen's repairs made to the broken wheel proved to be sturdy and strong, and Joseph had no further problems with the buggy, with Woodrow, or with oncoming vehicular traffic.

As they pulled into the yard of these good friends of his grandmother's, what a surprise it was when Brother Hansen came up to the buggy and said, "Velcome to owah home." He sounded just like Hans Petersen. He was big and strong, but clean shaven with curly blond hair

"Are these people from Denmark?" Joseph quickly and quietly asked Henrietta.

"Yes," she replied under her breath, and gave him a sly smile as if to say, *Surprise!* Joseph couldn't help but stifle a laugh.

"Oh owah little Henrietta is heah at last," the man said as he helped her down from the buggy and gave her a hug. Then turning to Joseph, he said, "I hope you had a safe yourney up heah from Ogden."

He extended a hand. "I am Peter Hansen." Although very strong and vital, Peter Hansen's handshake was a bit less painful than Hans Petersen's vice-like grip.

"It is very nice to be here in Smithfield, sir. We have had quite the time getting here."

"Vell, come into de house. Yosephine has lunch ready for you," replied the Dane. "A good meal is a cure for many ills." He gave Joseph a sturdy clap on the back.

Where did these Danishmen get their great strength and good hospitality?

Once again, he tried to keep from coughing at the impact. "I vill take care of your horse, Yoseph. You get inside and get some lunch." Joseph didn't have to be asked twice. He started for the house.

"Vhat is his name?" Peter yelled after him.

"Woodrow," Joseph called over his shoulder as he hurried toward the house.

"Voodrow," echoed Peter Hansen loudly. "Vhat a good name for a horse."

When Joseph went into the house, he found his grandmother weeping into her hanky. He ran to her side. "Grandmother, what's the matter?"

"Look, Joseph." She motioned to a nearby table. There stood four pots of beautiful flowers. "My dear friend prepared these for us to take to the cemetery." The tears flowed freely from her eyes once again, then wiping her face and remembering her manners, she said, "Josephine, this is my grandson, Joseph Williams."

Joseph looked from Henrietta to the flowers, and then to Josephine, dropped his chin in disbelief and said, "How did you know?"

"I knew dere vere four Villiams graves up in de cemetery, and I knew Henrietta vould vant to put flowers on dem. I had no idea dat she vould try to bring flowers from Ogden, so I had Peter halp me dig dese up. It vas yust a happy coincidence."

Joseph was speechless as he tried to prevent the tears that had welled up in his eyes from falling down his cheeks. Josephine Hansen came up behind him, took him by the shoulders, and directed him to a place at the table. "Let's get you two somezing to eat so you can get up to de cemetery as soon as possible."

She had made a Danish concoction that she called *smørrebrød*, open faced sandwiches with fish, cooked eggs, pickles, and an assortment of other things. Joseph wasn't so sure he would like it.

"In Danmark, ve put de eggs on top raw, but I haf found most

Americans don't like it dat vay," she said.

Joseph's stomach did a little flip-flop at the thought of eating all this with a raw egg thrown on for topping. She also served Danish red cabbage which had a pungently sweet taste to it. Joseph tried each thing carefully, not wanting to offend, but also not wanting to eat something with gusto that he didn't like. He tried the red cabbage first and decided it was quite good. Then he tried the smørrebrød and surprisingly, found it much to his liking. He ate most of it up, but slower than he usually ate. Just as he was finishing it, he found Sister Hansen bringing him a plate of *æbleskiver*, round balls that tasted somewhat like pancakes with bits of apple cooked into the middle and covered with powdered sugar and jam. Now those he knew he would like. He ate several with the gusto he had held back before.

At last, Henrietta said, "Joseph, are you ready to go to the cemetery?"

"You know I am, Grandma. Let's go." He grabbed his hat and went out to the barn.

After getting Woodrow hitched up and carefully placing the flowers in the back of the buggy, Joseph helped his grandmother up onto her seat, and off they went to finally reach their destination. He was glad to see that the weather was cooperating—not a cloud in the sky anywhere. But he was a bit nervous about his grandmother. He could see her twisting the lace hanky in her hands. After seeing her so emotional while visiting the grave of John Albert at the Ogden cemetery, he thought he knew what to expect when she would be reunited with the burial places of these three precious babies.

"Here, Joseph, turn up this little lane. The cemetery sits up on the brow of that hill. Do you see it?"

"Yes, I see it." Woodrow trotted along, pulling them up the little hill and into the cemetery. Joseph pulled the buggy around to the right and onto the brow.

"Stop here, Joseph. This is where they are buried," she said. Already, her emotions were choking her words.

Joseph hopped out of the buggy and went around to help his grandmother down. She put her arms around him and for just a moment, laid her head on his chest, trying to catch her breath.

He held her close to him, and then said, "I know we have come a long way, Grandma, but you don't have to do this if it's too much for you. We can turn around and go home."

"No, Grandson," she said quietly. "No, I have to do this. It hurts, but frankly, it always hurts. I think of them every day, just as I do John Albert and Francis. A mother never forgets her children, not for a moment."

They only had to take a few steps from the buggy, and there they were, three little headstones, and one a bit larger. He lay the still-folded blanket he had brought over from the buggy on the ground in front of the headstones for Henrietta to sit on. He helped her sit down, and then took a good look at each headstone.

He first saw a small one that read, *Heber C. K. Williams, May 18, 1862- September 18, 1863.*

Sixteen months old.

Just about the same age as his little sister, Naoma. How cute she was, walking all over and jibber-jabbering like babies do … and how hard it would be to lose her now.

Then he stepped to the next grave, which read, *Brigham Y. Williams, May 18, 1862-January 22, 1863.*

This was Heber's twin brother.

Both of them were named for great leaders of the Church, but Brigham only lived to be eight months old.

How devastating to lose these two precious boys so soon.

Next, he came to a nice bronze-cast marker that read, *Pioneer of 1849, Rebecca Swain Williams, Aug. 3, 1798- Sept. 25, 1861. Wife of Dr. Frederick G. Williams.* He had a million questions about this great lady, but they would have to wait.

He moved to the last of the four markers and read, *Joseph S. Williams, March 10, 1858-October 24, 1860.* Two-and-a-half years old! Very close to the age of his little brother Rolla who had turned three just before he and his father had left Mexico to come to Utah.

He looked at Henrietta who had begun carefully cleaning off each stone, pulling the overgrown grass from around them, and brushing away any dirt or debris that had blown onto them. He thought, *If I am feeling such pain, how must Grandma be feeling?*

He sat down by her and put an arm around her shoulders. He thought of the funeral processions that must have brought the bodies to this very spot. He thought of the people who had stood right here where he was, watching the bodies of their loved ones being lowered into the ground. And he thought of how his grandparents' hearts must have ached to leave their sons here in this cold earth to go home with empty arms. Although his heart swelled with pain for these lost children, somehow it felt as if his great-grandmother was there with him. He thought he heard her say, *Don't worry, Joseph, I'm taking good care of them. You will get to meet them someday, and we will all rejoice together.*

"The pain never goes away, Joe," Henrietta said in a low, slow voice. "My mother-arms long for them every day."

He was going to say, *I know,* but he didn't know. How could he? All he could do was comfort her to the best of his ability.

He said softly, "As I was reading each headstone just now, a voice whispered to me, Grandma. I think it was Great-grandmother Rebecca's voice. She told me not to worry about these precious babies because she was taking care of them, and we will one day all be together in a joyful reunion."

Henrietta touched Rebecca's headstone with tenderness. "I know that is true, Joe, I know it to my very core. If I didn't know that, if I didn't have any hope of being with my children again, I would lay down right here by them and die myself." She turned to her grandson. "Joseph, go get the flowers, will you please?"

He brought each potted plant over, and Henrietta ceremoniously placed one on each grave. "This is Joseph Swain, named for your grandfather's only brother, you know. John Albert was six months old when this very active two-and-a-half-year-old suddenly fell ill with whooping cough and quickly died. I have always been grateful that I had John Albert to rock and kiss and take care of when my arms ached so badly for his brother, but I couldn't help but worry that he, too, might get the dreaded disease. I don't know how many tears I dropped onto John's head while I fed and rocked him and mourned for Joseph Swain."

She placed the next plant on Brigham's grave. "How blessed I felt to be delivered of two beautiful healthy baby boys when these twins were born. It eased the pain of losing Joseph, and I certainly kept busy with two newborns and a two-year-old."

She smiled but then went on, her brow furrowing. "Whooping cough was still running rampant in northern Utah at the time, and the Doctor was very busy, running from one family to the next, trying to help their children recover, and then he would come home to his own sick babies. Hyrum Royal, Electa Jane's little boy, also had the whooping cough at the time, so there we were with a house full of sick children and no good solution to the sickness. As I have told you, Hyrum lived, grew up, and had a big family, but my little boys, my Brigham and my Heber, both passed away.

"Oh, Joseph," she sobbed, "if you could have heard them cough and cough that deep, horrible cough and not be able to stop. The Doctor tried every kind of medicine, herb, and idea to heal them, and of course, gave them priesthood blessings. I nursed them to the best of my ability as well, keeping poultices on their chests and boiling water on the stove in hopes that the steam would open their lungs. Brigham was the first to give in to the horrible illness. Heber responded to the treatments at first, and we had hopes of keeping him, but Heavenly Father had other plans for him, and a few months later, the disease hit again, and this time, his weakened body could not fight it off."

Joseph could not help it. He wept openly with his grandmother as she placed the next flowerpot on Heber's grave. She continued through sobs of pain. "Once again my arms were empty, and as I looked at those two little empty beds, I wondered if I would ever feel happiness again."

"How did you do it, Grandma? How did you ever learn to smile again?" He wiped his eyes with the backs of his hands and tried to appear brave for her.

She swallowed hard a few times. "It was a process, Joe. First, time will dim the hurt. I told you it never goes away, not completely, but it does get to a point that you can function in spite of it. You learn to cope with it, I guess. And sharing the pain with your grandfather helped tremendously. He hurt as badly as I did, you know. We could talk about that pain and the loss of the boys, but most of the time, we didn't even have to say anything. We would just hold each other and weep until we could go on.

"Second, God blessed us with a beautiful baby girl not too long after Heber's death. How she lit up our lives. I would hold her tight and kiss her and rock her and pray to God that he would not take my precious girl, and he didn't. He let her stay for twenty-five years, until she had given birth to five beautiful children of her own, as I told you once before."

She sighed deeply. "But the third way is what really gave me the courage to get back to my own self, and that was the grace of a kind Heavenly Father. Although I had to bear that grief that no one could take from me, he carried it with me, and he promised me that I would have my babies back someday. That is how I made it, Joe."

The two of them sat pondering on what had been said, and what could be said until finally, Joseph asked, "And what about Great-grandmother Williams. Was her death hard on you?"

Henrietta placed the last pot of flowers on her grave and then said, "Rebecca was about the best mother-in-law anyone could ask for. She was patient and kind and loved me the best that she could. Your grandfather and I were all she had left by the time we came to Utah. She helped me so much with John when little Joseph was so sick and finally passed away, but it wasn't too long after that when she herself was buried here next to him."

"How did she die, Grandma?"

"I want to say she died from old age, but she wasn't all that old, only sixty-three. Mercy, I passed that landmark long ago, and I don't feel old yet. I think she died of sorrow, sadness from not having her husband with her, sadness from losing her son Joseph Swain, and her two daughters, Lovina and Lucy, sorrow from not knowing whatever happened to Lovina's little girls. She loved us and she loved our children, and she had a good life here, but her heart was somewhere else. A person can only live so long like that."

"If she had only lived a few more years, then maybe I would have known her, Grandma," he said wistfully.

"Let's see, what year were you born?" she asked as she calculated how old Rebecca would have had to be to live to see Joseph born.

"1888."

Henrietta laughed her little chuckle and said, "She would have had to be 90 years old just to see you born. She never could have lasted that long."

After a few quiet moments, he asked, "How long do you think you will live, Grandma?" He hoped she might say at least one hundred.

"Who knows, Joe. I hope I make it to ninety, but it appears I won't have my man with me, and that will make it hard, very hard, I am sure." She hung her head and sighed deeply.

"When I am old enough to travel by myself, I intend to come up here and see you once a year, Grandma. I want you to know my children and my wife, if I ever get them."

"Nothing would bring me greater joy than seeing you often, Joseph."

She then turned her attention back to the graves. She seemed to be thinking or meditating for quite a while, and he knew he shouldn't disturb her. She moved from one grave to another, caressing each stone that would have to substitute for the person it represented until some future time.

At last, she said, "Help me up, Grandson. We have done what we came here to do, and it is time to go home."

He pulled her to her feet, and they stepped back to get a full view of the final resting places of these beloved people and admire how beautiful the flowers were that adorned them.

The next day, after a breakfast of Danish *Æggekage*, egg omelets made with flour, milk, sliced bacon, tomatoes, and chives, and a serving or two of Danish pastry, Joseph took his grandmother all over Smithfield where she visited old friends and showed off her handsome grandson.

That evening the Hansens treated them to a dinner of *Frikadeller*, Danish meatballs made with minced beef and pork, egg, chopped onions, breadcrumbs, and milk, fried in beef fat and served with boiled potatoes and cheese. The smell of that luscious food cooking on Josephine's wood-burning stove made Joseph's stomach growl in anticipation of eating it. Both he and his grandmother commented on this delightful food, and it tasted as good as the aroma had promised.

But by the following day, Henrietta was ready to start for home.

"Are you sure, Grandma? I am in no hurry to go home, you know."

"I know, Joseph, but I miss the Doctor. I'm sure your father has taken great care of him, and I hope the two of them have had some good conversations, but it is time for me to return."

"All r-r-r-right, min *bedstemor*," he said, miming the Danish accent by growling the "r" at the beginning of "right" and using the phrase for "my grandmother" that he had often heard the Hansens say these past few days. "Your vish *er min* command," and he bowed deeply to her.

He had picked that phrase up from a Hans Christian Andersen fairy tale that Josephine had insisted on reading to them the night before. She was delightful to listen to, mixing in a little Danish with her broken English. Joseph was really starting to love Josephine's Danish food and that captivating Danish accent, and most of all, just being around these incredibly happy and hospitable Danes that he hardly knew existed before this trip. He thought he would miss them a lot.

The rest of the day was spent preparing for their return trip. Joseph decided to ask Peter and Josephine some of the questions that had been building up inside him for four days and were finally demanding to be asked. "Brother Hansen," he said, addressing himself to Peter, "how is it that Danish people are so big and strong and yet so happy and friendly?"

"Vell, Yoseph, I vill tell you. Many yeahs ago, our ancestors vere Wikings. Have you heard of the Wikings, Yoseph?"

"Huh? Wiking—Oh, Vikings? Yes, of course I've heard of them. I used to wish I was a Viking when I was little, and my brothers and I would play at being Vikings all the time. My brothers are all younger than I am, so I always came out on top in our Viking battles."

"The Wikings—Vikings," Peter corrected himself, "vere big and strong, and ruled de nordern seas. I haf to admit dey vere quite ruteless, claiming lands for demselves dat did not rightfully belong to dem, and trampling ower people who got in dere vay. I vould not have called dem 'friendly' at dat time, Yoseph."

"I guess not," he shrugged.

"But somezing changed all dat," interjected Josephine. "I tink it vas de Christian missionaries who came and taught dem about Yesus Kristus."

"Yes," Peter agreed. "After dat, a large group of Danes decided dat de Viking vay of life did not lead to happiness, and so dey decided to change. 'Vhat vould bring us happiness?' dey asked each udder. De answer vas, live like Christ had lived, as de missionaries had taught dem. And dat is vhat dey decided to do. Aldough dey did not have de fulness of Christ's teachings as ve have now, dey had enough to know how to treat each udder, and it vorked."

"That is amazing. That explains so much. Thank you, and thank you for letting Grandmother and me stay here this week."

He turned to Josephine. "I have fallen in love with your Danish cooking, Sister Hansen. Maybe I can even figure out how to make some Danish food for my mother when I get home to Mexico. Imagine eating Danish food in Mexico."

The thought seemed to make them all laugh.

Joseph went on. "Do you know Hans Petersen who lives in Hyrum?" He and Henrietta had told the Hansens all about how helpful the Petersens had been when the accident happened.

"Yes," said Peter. "Ve sang in a choir dat he had put togeder from Scandinavian peoples some years ago. It vas a lot of fun."

Joseph somehow had a hard time visualizing that mountain of a man with his huge hands directing a choir.

"It seems funny to me that he is Hans Petersen, and you are Peter Hansen. Are you related somehow?" Joseph wanted to know.

"Probably not, Yoseph. You see, in Danmark, ve had a vey of passing names down trough de generations dat is different dan here," he replied. "My great-grandfader vas Carl Yensen, his son, my grandfader, was Lars Carlsen. His son, my fader, vas Hans Larsen, and I became Peter Hansen. It is called patronymics. You make a new last name out of de fader's first name and stick on 'sen.'" He spelled out s-e-n, then explained, "Dat is de Danish vord for *son*. Since I am de son of Hans, my new last name became Hans son, or Hansen."

"Ohhh," said Joseph. "If we had been Danish, I would be Joseph Fredericksen, right?"

They all laughed at the idea. Then Joseph said, "And my father would be Frederick Ezrasen, and speak Danish."

That really struck him as funny since he had known his father only in Mexico, as completely at ease speaking Spanish as he did English. Then he said, "So your sons are all Peters sons, right?"

"Dey vould be if dey still did it dat vay," said Josephine, "but in dis modern volrd, it vas getting too confusing, so everyone stayed vith de last name dey had at de moment vhen dey decided to change de system."

"I see," said Joseph. "What about your daughters? Did they keep the Hansen name?"

"Vell Yoseph, ve didn't have any girls, yust tree boys. But if we had, dey would have kept de Hansen name now," replied Peter. "My grandmodah, dough, vas Kiersten Pedersdatter. D-a-t-t-e-r," he spelled out the word, "is the Danish vord for daughter." He pronounced it more like *dettah*. "But when she married my grandfadah, she took his last name of Carlsen. She vas den Kiersten Pedersdatter Carlsen. Nowadays, de girls usually use de family name, radder dan being called somezing like *Pedersdatter*. Again, it is for clarity and making de system more modern and easier to use."

"Whew," sighed Joseph, "it was a confusing way of keeping track of people."

"It vorked for a wery long time, doh, Yoseph," said Josephine. "In some vays, I am sorry to see it go. I liked being identified as a 'datter.' Now ve females are lumped in vith de males."

"I guess it all depends on what you get used to," said Joseph.

Peter took Josephine's hand in his. "I could never tink of you as a lump, my deah."

Everyone laughed, and Josephine put her head down on Peter's shoulder. He put his big arms around her, gave her a squeeze, and kissed the top of her head.

Henrietta, who had been busy packing their belongings into baskets and bags, came into the room and announced, "I think we are all packed and ready to go, Joe. Let's get up early and get down the canyon before there is very much traffic."

"That sounds like a good idea, Grandmother. I think."

Henrietta knew from what he had said earlier that he was a bit reluctant to leave this place.

"It is a good idea," said Peter, "but now ve have dis evening, so let's not vaste it."

They each took a turn telling a little of their life's stories. Peter and Josephine started by recounting their early lives in Denmark, how the Mormon missionaries had come to their town, how they had listened and believed, and then had to make the decision to leave everything behind and come to America with their three small boys. Josephine said that her sister Christine had come across the ocean at about the same, and that she and her husband, Thomas Nicol, had brought their widowed mother with them. Josephine told how grateful she was to have a sister not too far away, and her mother close enough that she could see her regularly. She mentioned how very difficult it had been for her to learn English, and how she still felt ill at ease with the language.

"If it had not been for you," Josephine said to Henrietta, "dis American misfit may haf turned around and gone back to Danmark."

"You were never a misfit, my dear girl, just basically friendless in a new and different land. The Lord blessed us both when we became friends." And with that, Henrietta launched into telling her story of joining the Church in "Bahstn," having to make the same hard decision to come west with her widowed mother and learn a new language. "Well, it wasn't exactly a new language, just a very new way of using it. There were so many things to get used to. Work, for example."

They all had a good laugh over that. She went on to tell about life with her doctor husband on the frontier, having to move to Smithfield when President Brigham Young called them to do so, and of finding a great friend in Josephine Hansen. "How you have enriched my life by being here," she told her friend.

Then Joseph took a turn, telling of moving away from his grandparents at age two, and only recently realizing what he had missed out on. He said he also had to learn a new language in Mexico, but that he had been so young when he learned Spanish that he now did not remember ever not knowing. He said he loved being bi-lingual.

Everyone he knew in Colonia Dublan, Mexico, spoke both Spanish and English with ease. He told of watching his parents go through many hardships and how he had learned to love them all the more for that. Although living in Mexico seemed entirely normal for him, he knew it wasn't that way for his parents.

They continued talking well into the night until finally Henrietta said, "Well, Grandson, it is time for us to get to bed so that we can be on our way in the morning. Your eyelids have been getting steadily heavier for the last hour."

"I know, Grandma. I just hate for this night to end."

"Here, Yoseph," said Josephine. She had gone into the kitchen a few minutes before. "Here is a *lidt sen aftensnack*, a little late-night snack for you," and she handed him a plate of cheese, jam, and the rye bread, or *rugbrød,* that Joseph had grown to love.

"Oh, thank you so much, Sister Hansen. You know I will miss you, right?"

"I hope so, Yoseph." She gave him a quick kiss on the cheek.

"It makes me happy that our names are so much alike, you know. Joseph and Josephine. It feels like being part of your family."

"You vill alvays be part of our family, Yoseph."

The next morning, they were up and ready to leave almost before the sun came up. Josephine had fixed a grand breakfast of soft-boiled eggs, ham and fried potatoes, flakey cheese Danish, and an assortment of Danish buns, fruits, cheeses, and jams. After they had finished eating, Josephine packed all the leftover food up and sent it with them on their way.

Joseph had asked Peter to teach him a few words in Danish that he could say to Josephine as they left. "*Tak fordi du gjorde os så hyggelige og for den gode mad.*" Thank you for making us so cozy and for the good food. The Danes are big on *hygge,* or being cozy, and Peter had told him that saying that to Josephine would be a big compliment.

"*Det var så lidt,*" Josephine replied as the buggy drove out of the yard. "It was so little" is the Danish way of saying you're welcome. "*Vi elsker jer begge.*"

Henrietta turned her face back toward her good friends, and

yelled, "*Vi elsker også jer.*" We love you, too. She had picked up on a Danish word or two herself.

As they started on their way down the canyon, Joseph suddenly noticed something. "Grandma! What is that white stuff on the tops of the mountains?"

"Joseph, don't you know? It is vanilla icing. The mountains have been turned into giant cakes."

"Grandma, you're teasing me again. It's snow, isn't it?"

She laughed. "Yes, Joe, it's snow."

"But it's only the second week of September!"

"The rain often turns to snow up high in the mountains like that. It is probably only an inch deep and will melt quickly as the sun warms it up. It won't snow down in Ogden for another month to six weeks, maybe even two months. But here in Smithfield and Logan, we are higher up in the mountains, and they often see snow even in the valley by the first of October. When we lived up here, I was amazed every year at how cold and snowy it gets in the winters. Truth be told, I'm not crazy about the cold weather."

"Maybe you should come live with us in Mexico, then. It never gets really cold down there."

"That might be nice, Grandson. I just might do it one of these days."

They were pretty quiet the rest of the trip down the canyon, and after spending another nice night with the Harrises in Brigham City and telling them all about the excitement they had experienced in the last several days, they were finally on the straightaway to home.

After going a few quiet miles, Henrietta suddenly asked, "Are you all right, Joseph?"

"What do you mean, Grandma? Of course, I'm all right."

"Well, after asking about the snow on the mountains, you didn't ask me a single question all the way down the canyon, and you have hardly said a word so far today. I'm starting to think you aren't well."

Joseph laughed. "I guess I've been thinking about all I've seen and heard the last week, being with you up here, and about all the great people we have met. And I wanted to be sure we didn't have another incident in the canyon to tell about."

"Yes, I've been thinking about it all myself. What a good time we've had, right, Joe?"

"Oh yes, we have, Grandma." He was quiet again for a few minutes and then said, "I do have a question, though. What happened to your mother? You have told me about Rebecca, but you never told me what happened to Elizabeth."

"All right," she said, "I will tell you that story." She put her parasol up to shade her from the sun.

"After my marriage in St. Louis, Mother and the boys lived with an older couple who needed the help that my brothers could give them. The boys and Mother continued to hold down their jobs but helped with household chores whenever they could. Neither Mother nor I knew anything about household chores, or even how to make a bed. Some people could have helped us by teaching us how to do things because we were willing to learn, but instead, we were often the brunt of demeaning jokes."

"Nooo, Grandma," Joseph moaned. "Tell me they didn't make fun of you."

"They did, Joe, but it's all right. We soon learned for ourselves how to be Westerners and take care of ourselves. It was just so different from what we were used to."

"Westerners? You called St. Louis 'the west?' What do you call Ogden, then? The way, way, way west?" he laughed.

Henrietta laughed right along with Joseph, and then said, "Yes, but St. Louis seemed very far west for those of us who lived on the East Coast. We had no idea at the time just how far west we were going to end up. We all saved every penny we possibly could to pay for our journey to the 'far west.' Then something sad happened again. In November, dear Rebecca received a letter, informing her of the ill health of her oldest daughter, Lovina Riggs. She left for Quincy at once to nurse Lovina back to health, or so she hoped. But her health did not return, and she died at the end of November. It was almost more than Rebecca could stand, Joe. You will recall that Joseph Swain had died in 1838 and ..."

"Wait, Grandma, I didn't know that."

"Yes, he had died. I'm sure Ezra will tell you all about that. And Lucy had died as well, so Rebecca was bereft of comfort. She tried to bring Lovina's two little girls back to St. Louis with her, but it didn't work out. Their father, Lovina's husband Burr, refused to let them leave Quincy, and even though he had become so addicted to alcohol that he was in no shape to take care of them, he was their legal guardian. So, Rebecca arranged for Lucy's mother-in-law to take the girls. Betsy Pinkham, who was a member of the Church but no relation to Lovina, raised those two little ones. What a good woman she was. Her son, Lucy's widower, Nathan Pinkham, helped his mother raise his sister-in-law's little girls. He was a wealthy entrepreneur and lived in a big, beautiful house there in Quincy."

"What's an ontra-pen-"

"Entrepreneur. It is someone who organizes businesses and isn't afraid to take a few risks in the hopes of making some money. He had a lot of business knowledge and did very well for himself."

"Did Rebecca ever see those little girls again, Grandma?"

"No, I'm pretty sure she did not. I was with her throughout the rest of her life, and I don't know of her ever being able to see them again. I believe it is one of the things that broke her down. She did bring Lovina's adopted son back with her, though. His name was James Goddard, and he crossed the plains with us. I think he was about ten at the time, and he turned out to be a great help to us."

"At least she had him. But I can see that her heart must have been broken," said Joseph. "Did you leave for the west when she got back?"

"Not immediately. We were all quite content to stay in St. Louis for a few years. We all had jobs, Rebecca was taking in boarders, and Ezra had many patients. The emigrants who were flooding into St. Louis often brought disease with them, and many others had injuries from different accidents along the way, so he was called upon daily to care for them. Then one day he received a letter from Heber C. Kimball. It was about February of 1848, as I recall, and it came from Winter Quarters, where the Saints who were migrating west could stay throughout the winter and be put into companies that would travel together the rest of the way to the Salt Lake Valley in the spring.

"The Williamses and the Kimballs have always had a close

relationship. Heber's son, William, who was baptized the same day as your grandfather, has stayed in close touch with Ezra through all these years.

"When plural marriage was first introduced to the Church, it became the practice of Church leaders to marry the widows of those leaders who had died. They did it, not to live with the widow, but out of respect for her husband, to take care of her and give her the name of a Church leader as a kind of protection while coming across the plains. The point of all that is that Heber C. Kimball had married Rebecca in 1846, just as the first company of Saints was getting ready to move west, and four years after Frederick's death. Heber was always concerned for her and made sure she always had whatever she needed. So, at this time, he felt the need to encourage her and Ezra to leave for the west right away. That is essentially what the letter said. He told Ezra that he would have more doctoring to do there in Kanesville, the nearby city in Iowa, than he had in St. Louis. He asked him to bring all the medicine he could, and also would he please make a little kit of medicines up for him and his family to take with them as they were about to start their journey to the Salt Lake Valley.

"So, our plans abruptly changed, and we got ready to head west. We left St. Louis the first of April on a steamboat called the *Mandan,* and up the Missouri River we went. We were in a company of Saints led by Ezra T. Benson who had baptized Mother and me. There were the four of us who went together, Mother Williams, James Goddard, Ezra, and me. But, Joseph, there was one more who went with us that I haven't mentioned yet. I was expecting our first child and was already four months gone."

"That must have been so hard, Grandma."

"It was and it wasn't, Joe. I was thrilled beyond words at the prospect of becoming a mother, that was the good part. But my condition made it very uncomfortable to have to sleep in the poor accommodations on the crowded boat. I think those were the days that I missed my soft, clean Boston bed more than at any other time. But the Doctor was so good to me, rubbing my back, and giving me any extra bedding he could spare just to make my bed a little softer. He put his arm under my head for a pillow which I am sure made his arm numb by morning. But he never moved it all night for fear of waking me."

"What a grand husband he was, Grandma. I want to be like him when I am married."

"I have no doubt you will be an extraordinary husband, my boy. Some young lady is going to be very lucky to be your wife."

"I hope you are right. So, I guess you made it to Winter Quarters eventually, though."

"Yes, we did. It was on the west side of the Missouri River, but we crossed back to the eastern side to Kanesville and stayed there for a year. Kanesville is what the Saints called the town, but it is known as Council Bluffs today. The Doctor built us a log hut with a dirt floor and a mud roof. We did have a glass window in the back, which was nice."

"As nice as your Boston house?" Joseph teased.

She playfully poked him in the ribs and said, "Oh, yes, it was a palace. A mud palace in the middle of nowhere. In September, we moved into a log house with a shingled roof, two windows, a brick chimney, and doors made from lumber. We had a cook stove and locks on the doors. When I was a child in Boston, I could never have foreseen the day that I would have thought those things were luxuries."

"Not quite a palace, then?"

"Not quite, Joseph. But Ezra worked so hard to make it especially nice for us, as nice as was possible on the plains with little or no money or other resources, and I worked right along with him. One evening before the house was finished, I had done a big batch of ironing and eaten nearly a whole watermelon. Rebecca teased me about getting sick from eating so much, and I did get sick, oh so very sick. But it wasn't what you think. I had gone into labor. Ezra, ever the attentive doctor and husband, sprang to my side and coached me through the whole ordeal. As I am sure you know, sometimes women can be in labor for many hours, but my sweet Lucy made her appearance into this world in just six hours. She was born at 3:00 a.m., early on a Saturday morning, September 30, 1848, leaving Mother Williams and your grandfather enough time to get some sleep and get up the next morning to begin their fast for Sunday fast meeting. In those days, we fasted all day on the Saturday before Fast Sunday."

"And where was your mother during all this?" Joseph was still curious about his original query.

"I guess I got a little sidetracked, Joe. Please forgive me. Remembering all of these things gets me a little shook up."

"It's all right, Grandma. I have just been thinking that Elizabeth Crombie is as big a part of me as any of the others, and that is why I want to know."

"You're right, Grandson. Mother and the boys came with us to Winter Quarters and stayed nearby when we lived in Kanesville. Mother was not strong, and I began to worry about her. She was so very happy to have a granddaughter, though, and at that time, I thought she would just get stronger and stronger and would make it across the plains just to be with Lucy. But when it came time for us to leave and go west, Mother said she needed a little more time to prepare physically for the trip, so we left her in the care of my brothers and started west without her. I never saw her again."

"Oh no, Grandma." Joseph was thinking about his own mother, still in Colonia Dublan, and whom he had not seen for over a month. How his heart would break if he never saw her again.

"I kissed her goodbye on the morning of July 4, 1849, and she held me tight as if she knew she would never see her only daughter again."

"Oh, that is so sad."

"It was, Joseph, but we had to continue on. Remember, we were going to Zion, and as hard as it was to leave my mother and brothers, that is really all that mattered. There were the five of us now, going together, and we did not have it as rough as a lot of people did. We had two ox-drawn wagons, eight cows, two steers, provisions for a year, and a splendid stock of medicines. We had borrowed money from a company of Welch saints, $135.00, which Heber Kimball had convinced them to loan us so that they could have a doctor on the trail with them. Ezra was the only doctor for three companies, so you can see his services were badly needed. Grateful to God, we were able to repay the debt within a year."

"It sounds fun to me, Grandma. Did you ever get to drive the wagon?"

"Oh, Joseph, you wonderful boy. I guess you could say we had occasional fun, but it was mostly hard work. No, I never had to drive the wagon, thankfully. Grandma Rebecca drove her own wagon, and James Goddard, who was a blessing indeed, drove mine. He was only ten, but he could handle a wagon very well. I had a nine-month-old baby to care for, and she was a full-time job. Sometimes, she would sleep in the wagon while I walked alongside on the trail, and sometimes, I got to ride in the wagon with her. And sometimes, I just carried her on my hip. She seemed as light as a feather to me, Joe."

"That was a blessing. But why didn't Grandfather drive one of the wagons?"

"Your grandfather rode his horse most of the way so that he could get around to the different companies and care for the sick."

"Oh, that makes sense."

"The next morning, as early as we could, we ventured into the unknown territories of the great western wilderness. About a year later, after we were settled in the Great Salt Lake Valley, we received a copy of the newspaper that was occasionally published and distributed along the pioneer trail and in the valley called the *Frontier Guardian*. In it, I read about my mother's death. It said, *died*, On Monday July 20th at 1 o'clock, P. M., *Mrs. Elizabeth P. Crombie*, formerly of Boston, Mass, aged thirty-eight years."

"How do you remember all that it said, Grandma? You must have a great memory."

"I read it and reread it until it was burned into my brain, Grandson. This was about my mother who I would never see again in this life. It was all I had left of her. I kept that piece of newspaper with me for many years, until it literally disintegrated into nothing. I learned later from my brother John that he had been alone with her when she died. She had contracted cholera, and people don't want to be around other people with cholera for fear of getting it themselves. But my brave brother stuck with her to the end and did not get sick. He came to Utah a year later, and what a nice reunion we had."

The travelers continued on in silence for quite a while, eventually stopping to rest the horse, stretch their own legs, and eat the lunch that Abigail Harris had packed for them that morning. It was already quite late in the day, and they were both hungry. Sister Harris had made sandwiches on thick homemade bread with slices of cheese, roast beef, onions, and freshly churned butter. She had included a big pickle that she had cut into sandwich-sized pieces, an apple and a peach for each of them from their orchard, and two slices of carrot cake. Joseph couldn't help thinking of the lunch that had been strewn along the side of the road the week before on their way up the canyon and found himself being very thankful that this food was going into his stomach. Woodrow seemed grateful as well to be able to graze on the lush greenery to the point that Joseph had to stop him from eating any more so he wouldn't get sick.

"Well, Joseph, we are about to start our last stretch before arriving home. Do you think we will make it?" Henrietta teased as she finished the last of her lunch.

He laughed at this adorable woman that he had come to treasure so highly. "I think we will just barely make it, Grandma. I hope they have dinner ready for us."

She laughed right back at him. "How can you think of food after the big lunch we just had?"

"I'll be able to eat again soon, I promise."

"That is a promise I think you can keep, right?"

"I wouldn't have said it if it weren't true." And they both laughed again, as they packed things away and prepared to make the final leg of their journey home.

CHAPTER SEVENTEEN

Ogden, Utah 1904

All's Well at Home, and a Sticky Story

It was with a sigh of relief that Henrietta found everything well at home. Fred had been true to his word, having taken excellent care of his father.

"We both had a feeling that you would be home today," said Fred as he picked his mother up in a big bear hug. "We have been watching for you all day, haven't we, Papa?"

Ezra was sitting up in his wheelchair, all cleaned up, beard and hair trimmed, teeth brushed, and dressed in a fresh nightshirt. Fred had even given him a little cologne to splash on his face, so he smelled sweet.

When Ezra saw Henrietta, his bottom lip started trembling, and he couldn't speak. It seemed to be getting harder for him to control his deep emotions the older he got. She came to him and put her arms around him. He pulled her down onto his lap.

"Don't you hurt yourself now, Ezra," she warned.

"How could the best medicine I could ever have hurt me?" He embraced her with all the strength he had left. She hugged him back, and pulling his head close to her, she kissed the top of it.

After tending to Woodrow, Joseph came into the house and found himself embraced in hugs from both his father and his grandfather. "Well done, Son, you made it home safely. I assume you had an incredible time," said his father.

"Yes, Grandson, well done," added Ezra.

"You were perfect, Joe, and I will always be grateful for this trip that you executed so expertly," his grandmother boasted.

"Three cheers for Joseph Williams," they yelled, "Hoorah, hoorah, hoorah," clapping their hands at the successful completion of the journey.

The next day, after spending the morning putting things away from their trip and cleaning up the buggy, Joseph and Henrietta told their story to Ezra and Fred, who in turn told of their time alone together that whole week.

"There isn't a lot to tell," said Fred. "Father behaved himself very well and we mostly just talked."

"I can see you did more than just talk, Son," said Henrietta. "Everything is neat and tidy; your father is happy and well fed, and the garden has been harvested and plowed under. How did you get Dodger to pull a plow? He does not like to pull things."

Fred winked at her. "Magic. I promised him that I would take him for a ride up the canyon if he would behave himself and do as I directed, and he did it. For some reason he loves to run in that canyon, so I let him run."

"That is magic."

Later that afternoon, Ezra motioned to his grandson to come sit by him in the parlor. He said, "I have something to tell you." He had a bit of a gleam in his eye. "When I was young, I had a friend named Sammy. He always seemed to have a runny nose, so it wasn't long until we started calling him Sammy Snotface."

"Oh, Grandpa, that is terrible," he giggled.

"He didn't like the nickname, Joe, but it stuck," said Ezra as he let out a big roll of laughter.

"It stuck? Oh, it stuck!" Joseph laughed. "Just like glue, right, Grandpa?"

"It clung to him tenaciously," said the old man. Then leaning in closer to Joe, he whispered, "Just like Henrietta's oatmeal mush sticks to the roof of your mouth." They both dissolved into peals of laughter.

Henrietta could hear the commotion from the parlor. It did her heart good to hear the Doctor's laugh mingled with Joseph's. But when it didn't stop, she thought she had better go see what they were up to.

"Shhhh," said Ezra when he saw her coming, putting his finger to his lips in warning to Joseph not to say anything that would incriminate him.

"And what do the two of you find so funny?" asked Henrietta.

"Funny?" asked Ezra. "I don't know of anything funny, do you, Joe?"

"No, Grandpa, nothing funny here," he answered, trying not to betray Ezra's trust by bursting again into laughter. But when the two of them looked at each other as Henrietta was leaving the room, the inevitable happened, and out it came in deep, hearty peals once more. Henrietta turned back around and looked at them with a puzzled but accusatory expression. "I was just asking Grandpa if he is ready to go on with his story," Joseph said, shrugging his shoulders while feigning innocence.

"Right," she said, looking from one to the other, she seemed to be trying to discern who the hilarity had been directed at. "And what was the answer?"

"Oh, um, he said of course he was ready." Joseph nodded his head in affirmation.

"Yes, Madame," added Ezra in a very stilted and rather pompous voice, "I am extremely disposed to providing the opportunity to press on with the advancement at this point in time of the history of my juvenile adventures."

That made Joseph snort, but he turned it into a cough as if his mischief was caused by something in his throat.

"You two!" she said accusingly but with a shake of her head as she left them alone again.

They looked at each other and had another good laugh, trying to let it go but not being able to.

"Grandpa, that was a sticky situation," said Joe.

"It was nothing to sneeze at, but we slid right through it, Joe."

"We were on a slippery slope, Grandpa."

"Yes, Joe, it could have been the gelatinous end to the both of us."

"We could have been in an ooey, gooey mess," said the boy.

"It could have gummed up our future," laughed his grandfather.

They burst into another paroxysm of laughter, until they just couldn't laugh any more.

Joseph said with a huge sigh, "Oh, Grandpa, you are the best."

"I know," said Ezra, rolling his eyes in self-mockery. "Now, go find your father so he can scribe for us before I lose my last bit of strength today."

—•—

When Fred came into the room with the book and pen several minutes later, he said, "Papa, are you sure you are up to this tonight? We can wait until tomorrow."

"My son, I know you want to protect your old dad, but I have to do things when and how I can, and right now, I am ready to talk. So, let's get at it."

"All right, Papa," he replied, wondering if he was too much like his mother in his desire to protect his father. "I am ready to write when you are ready to begin."

"Read me that last paragraph, Fred, so I know where I left off," said Ezra. "It's been nearly two weeks, you know."

"Now, let me see … Oh, here we are," he said while turning to the last written entry. Clearing his throat, he read, "That is the heart of a hero, Ezra. That's the kind of love we should all have. Swain is the best example of that, far better at it than I am. She hugged me tight, and then said, Now go get cleaned up because Brother Hyrum will be here any minute to confirm you."

"Oh yes," said Ezra, "the day of my baptism."

CHAPTER EIGHTEEN

KIRTLAND, OHIO 1832

An Answer to Prayer and a Reprimand from God...
Through Ezra's Eyes

True to the Prophet's word, Hyrum Smith came that evening to confirm me a member of the Church of Jesus Christ of Latter-day Saints. I wish I could remember everything he said in that blessing, but I do remember the feeling. I felt that I wanted to do what God wanted me to do to the best of my ability. Sorry to say, I have not always done it, but I keep trying. I keep trying.

Throughout that summer of '32, more and more people, most of them new converts to the Church, were moving into Kirtland, many more were building houses on what used to be Father's property, and even though we were living in our old house, Father felt as if he was a boarder there. He had deeded everything that he had over to Joseph. The crop production came under the supervision of Father Smith, and Joseph and Emma lived with him from time to time. I suppose it was a relief to Father not to have to worry about farming, and Father Smith shared the produce liberally with us, but I missed working the earth by Father's side.

As the Church grew, so did the opposition, which mostly came from people who had formerly been members of the Church. It seems like when people leave for whatever reason, and often the reason is not much compared to the blessings they are turning their backs on, they want to attack, hurt, and disable things they previously treasured. I always think that if people want to leave, it is their right to do so.

But why come back on people they formerly loved to hurt and injure them? Makes no sense to me. I just wished they would leave us alone.

One day, Father came home from being with the brethren all day and made an announcement. "Well, I guess I have another job."

"What job would that be? Will it mean an increase in pay?" My mother was never the kind who wished for riches, but like any of us, she was concerned for her family's well-being, and especially now that Father was not bringing in as much from his medical practice or the farm.

"No," Father laughed. "It actually will not be much of a change at all. Joseph has asked me to be his official scribe. I guess it could mean I will be gone a bit more, but probably not too much."

"Wait, Papa," said Lucy. "I thought you were already his scribe. What is different now?"

"That's true, Lucy. I have been scribing for him quite a bit. But now it is an official calling. I will scribe for him every day, sometimes all day, writing whatever the Prophet needs me to write."

Father was already an experienced clerk, having served as the first clerk of the newly created Township of Warrensville, Ohio, an elected office he held for four years back in the 1820s.

"I feel honored to have this calling," he said. "It is a privilege to scribe for the Prophet of God."

I guess you might say none of us was excited about hearing this news, and we reacted without much energy. We thought it would mean he would be away from home more than ever, and none of us wanted that.

Finally, Mother went to him and gave him a hug. "It truly is an honor, dear, and one that we all share. It is just … well, it is just that … we are all so happy for you, aren't we, children?"

She turned to us, indicating that we should congratulate our father on his new calling.

"Congratulations, Papa, I know you will do the best job of anyone," I said to him, whereupon Swain jumped right up and said, "Conlat …" He turned to me and whispered, "what is da wood, Ezwa?"

I whispered back to him, "Good work, Papa."

"Dood woke, Bapa," he said as loudly as he could, beaming with pride at doing it.

From that day on, Father was with the Prophet many hours every day. After his calling to the first Presidency, Father acted as Joseph's personal scribe, writing his sermons, helping him keep his diary, writing his letters, and writing down many revelations. He kept track of everything.

I remember the time Father came home and told me about an experience he had that day. "Ezra," he said. "I want you to hear this from my own mouth." So, I sat at his feet and listened to what he had to tell me.

"One of the things I do is to keep Joseph's letter book, where I copy letters that the Prophet sends and receives into a book.[14] But the first thing we did in the first letter book was to write Joseph's own history. I recorded everything as Joseph spoke of his first glorious vision in the grove of trees on his father's farm in 1820, the very time when God the Father and his Son Jesus Christ appeared to him. He told me that after he received that first vision, only his family believed him. Everyone else who knew about it either made fun of him or tried to hurt him in some way. I continued to write as Joseph dictated an account of the visitation of the Angel Moroni three times in one night and once again the next day, of finding the plates where the angel had directed him, of his marriage to Emma Hale, his association with Martin Harris and how Martin had been responsible for losing the first one-hundred-sixteen translated pages of the Book of Mormon, pages that had been revealed to the Prophet and laboriously scribed by Emma and by Martin himself. I wrote these words as they came from Joseph's mouth, his remembrances of all those who had helped him in the translation of the plates, and of how the Lord sent Oliver Cowdery to scribe for him in 1829. We ended the session with a sad note about how Emma's father was about to turn him out with nowhere to go, until the Lord provided him a place."

He stopped and looked at me right in my eyes, and said, "Son, as Joseph told me these things, it was as if I were seeing it all as it happened. I felt the Lord's Spirit so strong that I could hardly breathe. I want you to know that I know he was telling the truth about every bit of it, and I know it by the power of the Holy Ghost, just as we are promised at the very end of the Book of Mormon."

I was young and had only experienced feeling the Holy Ghost a few times, but that day as my father bore his testimony to me, I felt it so strong, and I knew this experience would shape the rest of my life. I would follow Christ to the best of my ability, and I loved my father for setting the example for me.

Joseph began a retranslation of the Bible in 1832 for which Father was employed as one of the scribes, first redoing the New Testament, and then moving on to the Old Testament which is nearly all scribed by my father. So many things were included in these writings that clarify misconceptions allowed to persist in the Bible before this work was completed.[15]

Of the many revelations Joseph received in Ohio, Father was the scribe for a good part of them. Some people don't realize that the Prophet also received many revelations that were not canonized or included in the Doctrine and Covenants simply because they didn't pertain to the Church as a whole or were of temporary importance. Father was the scribe for many of those as well.

By 1833, Father was so busy that we hardly saw him. He was trying hard to do everything that was asked of him, plus maintaining his large and demanding medical practice and taking care of us at home. His calling as the Prophet's counselor in March of that year kept him busy during every minute he wasn't scribing or doctoring. He was involved with something called the United Firm, which oversaw the physical needs of the growing Church membership. With the high influx of newly baptized members of the Church, those physical demands could be overwhelming, to say the least. But he was determined to serve the Lord and be of service to His Prophet, and he did everything in his power to fulfill the responsibilities. The only problem was that it left us without him much of the time. We ceased to read from the scriptures every day, and Father didn't have time to teach us many of the great things he had learned like he was doing before.

I missed him.

Mother shouldered so many of the duties at home that Father would normally have taken care of, and, knowing how capable and conscientious she was, allowed Father to worry less about us and focus more on the things he had to do in connection with his Church calling. But, although she never complained, I could see that it was hard on my mother, and she was starting to wear down. One thing that worried her a lot was that her children were growing up, and she wasn't entirely sure how to handle the associated problems.

My sister Lovina had become a lovely sixteen-year-old and her suitors were lining up. It seemed like all the young men wanted to court her, both for her innate loveliness, and for the prestige of courting and marrying the daughter of a leader in the highest offices of the Church. Some of those suitors were unsavory, to say the least, and she was showing the slightest signs of teenage rebellion.

One such suitor was Doctor Philastus Hurlbut. He was not a doctor, but rather his first given name was Doctor, somewhat presumptuous of his parents, I should think. He was made an elder in March of 1833, but was soon excommunicated for his conduct toward a woman while on a mission in the East. When he came home in June, his membership was restored, but two days later he was again excommunicated because he had deceived the Church leaders in his repentance. In other words, he hadn't really repented but continued in the same unchristian-like ways that had gotten him in trouble in the first place. He became a bitter enemy to Joseph Smith and threatened to kill him, and he spent a lot of time with people who ended up writing vicious anti-Mormon literature.

Hurlbut was handsome, pompous, energetic, but poorly educated. He had sought a high position in the Church and strove to marry a daughter of any of the leaders to get it, Lovina being his number one target. I think he was a fraud and a counterfeit who wanted things but didn't want to have to work for them, so he tried to get them by deceit. He was not the kind of man any parents would pick for their daughter to marry. When he gave her the old line about receiving a revelation that he was to marry her, she responded with "when I receive the same revelation, I will marry you."

She never received that revelation.

I suppose, I guess I should really say I know, that whenever things of God are revealed and a group of people come together to live in righteousness, the evil one raises his deceitful and jealous head, trying to make counterfeits of the truth. You can count on that happening, and it is to me a testimony of the truth. We have been taught that there is opposition in all things, and we must learn to expect that whenever we choose the right, good choices will be challenged by the spirit of deception. We must be prepared for it to happen, but Father in Heaven must allow it because we could not have the precious gift of freedom of choice if there was nothing to choose between. Therefore, the Lord allows the evil one to tempt and deceive the hearts of man, and let me tell you, I never saw it stronger in action than when I was a child in Kirtland, Ohio.

There was a group of people living on a farm outside of Kirtland who had been baptized but had not yet been instructed in their duties. Many false spirits were introduced, many strange visions were seen, and wild enthusiastic notions were entertained. Men would run out of doors under the influence of these spirits, some getting up on tree stumps and shouting weird sayings, a few that were understandable but obviously false, and others that were unintelligible to the human ear. Their bodies would be twisted into strange and unnatural configurations and contortions, driving the Spirit of God from them. One man said he saw something flying in the air that he chased until he came to a precipice. This man, called Black Pete, had been self-designated as a "revelator." He claimed that he saw angels who offered him and other men letters from heaven. It was when he thought he saw one such letter caught up in the wind that he ran after it, resulting in his stepping off the twenty-five-foot-high river embankment, saved only by a tree that broke his fall. He then fell from the tree into the Chagrin River.

Much like Doctor Hurlbut, Black Pete wanted to marry Lovina Williams, but again she was smart enough and close enough to the Spirit to recognize the evil intent of this man, despite him also telling her he had received a revelation that she was to marry him.

But the man whose behavior was the worst of all, according to some Kirtland residents, was another of Lovina's "revelation-suitors," a man named Burr Riggs. Levi Hancock, a friend of my father's in Kirtland, recorded some of Burr's odd behaviors. As I recall, Brother

Hancock said Burr claimed to receive revelations, and to see angels fall down, frothing at the mouth. Brother Hancock said he witnessed Burr swinging on the joists of an unfinished house, and then falling as if he were dead, lying there for an hour or two. Then he would wake up and prophesy and tell what he had seen, things that were dark and sinister. But at other times, he appeared to be so honest and nice that Brother Hancock was temporarily led to believe all that Burr said.

Another early Kirtland resident, James Rollins, told Father some things that happened after Father and the other missionaries had left for the west. Elder Cowdery and Elder Pratt had to put some inexperienced men in charge of the Church because there was no one there who had any experience. These men were timid and afraid to denounce the actions of men who were operated upon by different kinds of spirits, such as receiving revelations written on parchment as Black Pete said he had and professing to receive them from heaven. Others were lying like they were dead in meetings, and on coming to, they rushed to the river and jumped in amongst the flowing ice, thinking they were going through a form of baptism, until someone had to jump in and save them.[16]

This is what was going on with Burr Riggs. He was the young man Lovina and Lucy had seen walking by the river right after my baptism.

I don't know if Lovina knew these things about Burr or not, because she had already made up her mind to marry him. He was handsome and sophisticated and did not push her as many of the other suitors did. He was different, in her eyes, and therefore could not be lumped in with the other apostates. He had been called in and counseled by Church leaders, maybe even Frederick G. himself, and shown how to repent and change his ways. He promised to do so, but apparently, he did not keep his promise, because he was excommunicated in February 1833 for, basically, failure to repent. Looking back on the situation from the perspective of time, I suppose I thought that she was smart enough and strong enough, as she had been with many others, to avoid falling for the old line, but now I see that Satan finds our weaknesses and plays off them. Her weakness seemed to be falling for his charisma, his playing hard to get, so to speak, and not pushing himself on her as the others had done. And he played it to the hilt. I can imagine him telling her over and over that he had made changes, would continue to make changes, and that he desperately wanted to be back in the Church if she would just give him time to make the changes and prove to everyone that he was sincere. I'm sure he told her that he would do anything for her because he loved her so much, and blah blah blah. I think she fell for his line because she wanted to believe it. That is the way we mortals operate sometimes. And she continued to see him.

Meanwhile, Father was struggling. By May of 1833, he was so burdened by his many responsibilities that it seemed he never smiled. He was trying his hardest to do everything that was asked of him, but he kept feeling farther and farther away from God's comforting spirit. One night he came in very late and found my mother waiting up for him.

"What are you doing up at this hour, Rebecca? I thought you would have been asleep long ago."

"I couldn't sleep so I thought I might as well get up and wait for you. I'm worried about you, Frederick, I feel like you are pulling away from me, and it is scaring me."

"Oh, my dear sweet wife, nothing could be further from the truth. I do everything I do because I love you and want to be with you forever."

"Then why are you gone so much? The children hardly know you anymore, and I am shouldering both of our loads. Is that really the Lord's will? I can't believe that it is."

Father sat down next to her and dropped his head into his hands. He started to sob, and when he finally lifted his head, his face was streaked with tears.

"I don't know what to do, Love. My responsibility is so great. I have three full-time jobs, or so it seems. Which one do I let go? They all seem to be of equal importance, and I can't really let any of them go."

Mother took the hem of her apron and wiped his face. He lay his head down on her chest, and she comforted him as she would have one of us children. He put his arms around her waist and hugged her hard.

Finally, he said, "If I didn't know with all my being that this gospel is true, it would be so easy to walk away from it. I could just cast away my responsibilities and lead a normal life."

"Is that what you want, Frederick?" she asked in a low, soft voice.

He raised his head, sat up, and looked her in the eyes. "Rebecca …" he hesitated before going on. He took both of her hands in his, kissed her fingertips, and said again, "Rebecca, I did not join this Church until I was sure in my own soul that it was right, and that the Gospel of Jesus Christ embodies truth and light, all the truth and light that exists on this earth. No matter how broken I feel right now, I cannot and will not ever abandon that conviction."

"Then what are we to do, Frederick? What would the Savior have you do if He were standing right here?"

He thought for a minute, and then she saw a dawning of light come over him. "I know what to do, Sweetheart. I will ask him in faith, just as the Book of Mormon says to. I ran across a passage the other day that hit me very hard, and at the time, I wondered why. The Spirit whispered to me to memorize it because I would need it. Now, I need it."

"Did you memorize it, my love?"

"Partially, but I will complete the memorization tonight." He dug around for his Book of Mormon, then turned to the book called Mormon, near the end of it. He thumbed through a number of pages, seeming to know what he was looking for because he stopped when he found a page that he had marked heavily with his pencil. He scanned down the page until he found the part he wanted, and then he read it to her, "Here it is, Rebecca: *Behold, I say unto you that whoso believeth in Christ, doubting nothing, whatsoever he shall ask the Father in the name of Christ, it shall be granted him; and this promise is unto all, even unto the ends of the earth.*[17] All I have to do is ask, and He will tell me what to do." He looked up from the book. "Why didn't I realize this sooner?"

"Because you were too busy trying to do what was right. I think sometimes we get so caught up in checking things off a list, things that must be accomplished within a certain amount of time, that we don't stop and listen to God's voice."

"I think you are right. Kneel down with me, Love, and we will solve this problem together."

He took her by the hand, and the two of them prayed, each taking turns asking God for guidance in just how to fix what was so troubling to Frederick.

Father slept better that night than he had for weeks. The next morning, we were all surprised to see him sitting at the breakfast table.

"What are you doing home, Papa?" asked Lovina. "I thought you would be long gone to work."

Swain, who was sitting next to him, took hold of Father's arm, laid his head against it, and said, "I yike you to be heow, Bapa."

"I like being here." He tousled Swain's hair, gobbled down the end of his hot cakes and eggs, picked up his coat, and ran for the door. As he was leaving, he turned and called, "I'm going to try to be home for dinner tonight. I love you all!"

Lucy looked at Mama. "What was that all about?"

"I think he knows he needs to be home with us a little more."

"Oh goody," I said.

"Oh doody," echoed Swain. "We yike Bapa to be heow wif us, don't we Ezwa?"

"Yes, we do, my brother, even if it is for only a minute like it was this morning. It is better than nothing."

"Yay for Papa!" shouted Lucy. "I can't wait for supper when he will be here!"

"Yay for Papa!" we all yelled, more or less together.

As Mother watched us celebrate, she didn't seem entirely happy about it.

"What's the matter, Mama? Aren't you happy to have Papa home for supper?" asked Lovina.

"Of course I am, children. I just hope he can follow through on the promise. I don't want you children to be disappointed."

"He'll be here," I said. "I just know it."

That morning when Father finally arrived at the Whitney store after making his medical visits, the Prophet was waiting for him in the upstairs room that was used for official Church business.

"Get your paper and pen, Frederick. The Lord is about to send us a message."

Father got the ledger he had been writing in the day before, a quill pen and an ink bottle, and sat down in his accustomed place. Sidney Rigdon and Brother Newel Whitney were already there as well.

"I'm ready whenever you are, Brother." He knew that these things could take time.

After a prayer imploring the Lord to reveal the truths they needed to know that day, Joseph the Prophet began by saying, *Verily, thus saith the Lord: It shall come to pass that every soul who forsaketh his sins and cometh unto me* … [18] and he continued on, speaking about the Savior, hearing Christ bear record of who he is, and what he intends to do in the last days. The revelation continued, speaking now of John who received such a strong personal testimony of Christ as he wrote his own testimony of the Savior's glory. Then Joseph dictated, *if you keep my commandments you shall receive of his fulness and be glorified in me as I am in the Father…* [19]

Those words hit my father full force, but he didn't know why. He was trying to do everything he should be doing, and yet he had shared with Mother the night before that he knew something was wrong.

He continued to write many more amazing things, about the agency of man and of temples, light and truth, and how the wicked one takes away light and truth. Then he was stopped in mid-sentence as he heard the Prophet speak the next words as he wrote, *I have commanded you to bring up your children in light and truth. But verily I say unto you, **my servant Frederick G. Williams,** you have continued under this condemnation; **you have not taught your children light and truth**, according to the commandments; and that wicked one hath power, as yet, over you, and this is the cause of your affliction.*[20]

Father continued to write, but he was doing so automatically, and couldn't remember what he was writing, because his mind was stuck on those lines addressed to him. "I have not taught my children light and truth! I have not taught my children light and truth!" Those words ran through his mind at least a hundred times.

Joseph seemed to notice Father having a hard time concentrating. He stopped and asked him what was going on.

"I have not taught my children truth and light," he repeated out loud. "That is the answer!"

"Explain, my friend. As those words came to me, my first thought was that you would be very upset to hear them. What are you seeking an answer to?" asked Joseph.

With tears stinging his eyes, Father swallowed hard. "I have been troubled for some time about what I lack. I knew something was amiss, but I also thought I was doing everything I knew to do, trying to fit everything in that I have been asked to do. Still, I would go home late at night after my children were in bed and sit pondering on what I need to do better and leave again early in the morning before they were awake.

"But this …" He pointed to the things he had been writing, then looked at the Prophet and started to laugh.

"Hold on, Brother," said Joseph. "I have never seen a man so happy to be called to repentance."

"Last night I asked for an answer. I begged the Lord to tell me what more I should be doing. I sensed it had something to do with my family, so I got up early to have breakfast with them. And now, this moment, my Savior shows his great love for me and my family by telling me plainly what I need to do to fix things."

"Frederick, look at what you wrote after that line. Read it out loud."

Father read, "*Verily I say unto my servant Sidney Rigdon, that in some things he hath not kept the commandments concerning his children …*"[21]

Brother Sidney sat up straight, and with concern in his voice, said, "I knew it. I knew something was wrong as well, Brother Frederick, and this is the answer."

"There is more," said the Prophet. "Write this down, Frederick."

Father commenced writing down the rest of the revelation as it fell from Joseph's lips. "*And now, verily I say unto Joseph Smith,*

Jun.—you have not kept the commandments and must needs stand rebuked before the Lord …"[22] then, *"My servant Newel K. Whitney… hath need to be chastened and set in order his family …"*[23]

The Prophet stopped for a moment. He looked at Brother Whitney, waiting for his confirmation.

"Yes," he said softly. "I have had similar feelings."

"What are we to learn from this, brethren?" Joseph asked the three men in a slow, soft voice.

"I am learning that I need to put my family first, that they must be taught light and truth, even if I have to let some other things go," Father answered.

"Yes, yes, yes! We have not put enough emphasis on the importance of our families," said Joseph, raising his voice to a higher, more forceful pitch, "but I am telling you, brethren, that this is what God wants and expects of us. The power of eternity is based on the family. Your question has opened this up to all of us, Frederick. You know that questions to God are powerful, and He often waits for us to ask before he pours out knowledge to us. I had a question once, when I was fourteen. Do you remember my telling you this?"

"Of course, Brother Joseph. Your question was 'which Church is the one I should join?'" said Sidney.

"And what happened? My question was answered in the most powerful and unexpected way imaginable. Now, your question is the seed for how important families are in the Lord's plan, Brother Frederick. I want to bring to your minds the very last verse of the Old Testament. Do you know which one I am talking about?" the Prophet asked.

Sidney spoke up without hesitation, *"And he shall turn the heart of the fathers to the children, and the heart of the children to their fathers, lest I come and smite the earth with a curse.* That's Malachi 4:6."

"Exactly, Brother. And what did the Lord mean by that?" asked the Prophet. Then answering his own question he said, "He means that unless we save our families, the earth will have had no reason to exist. All of us will be lost." He put his arm around Father and hugged him close. "So, thank you, Brother Frederick, for asking your question. It is crucial to our eternal salvation. We must teach our children light and truth. And now we must finish this revelation, so prepare to write more."

Father took up his pen and ink and continued writing as the Prophet spoke. The Lord called Sidney, Joseph, and Frederick on missions. In addition, they were to *hasten to translate my scriptures, and to obtain a knowledge of history, and of countries, and of kingdoms, of laws of God and man, and all this for the salvation of Zion.*[24]

"Wait," said Frederick, "I thought we already had too much to do, and now we are going on missions?"

"That seems to be the Lord's way. He gives us so much to do, and then we must figure out how to balance it," answered the Prophet.

"We will do it," they all agreed.

"One way or another," added Father.

Father did make it home for dinner that night and told us all about the revelation that Joseph had received earlier in the day.

"Oh, Freddy," exclaimed my mother, "that is a direct answer to our prayer. God is good, dear husband. What did he say you could stop doing so that you can spend more time with us?"

"He didn't. In fact, he told us to do more, and we are to leave on missions as soon as we can."

"What? For how long this time, Frederick?" Father had left for about three weeks after he was ordained to the First Presidency back in March. He and Joseph were mission companions during that time. And now he was leaving again? It was a little hard for my mother to grasp. "And are you going?"

He looked at her with some pain in his eyes at leaving them just when he had learned how important it was to be with them. "I will go and do the thing that the Lord commands, Rebecca, and trust that it will all work out. It has to."

Mother sighed deeply and hung her head. "I know, my righteous man. It's just that I was so excited about you being able to spend more time with us and …"

"I know. I was very surprised myself. But when I get home, things will change around here, that I can promise you."

"Who will be your companion this time?" asked Lucy.

"The Lord has asked me to be companions with the Prophet

again. We work extremely well together." Looking at the disappoint-ment on all our faces, he continued, "I don't think we will be gone long because the Lord also told us to hurry and finish the translation of the Bible, to learn of history, and of countries, and of kingdoms, of laws of God and man. I'm pretty sure that is what I wrote down as Joseph spoke. All of this, ALL of this," he emphasized, "is for the salvation of the Lord's children. That includes us, you know."

"Can I go with you, Papa," I asked, not able to keep the pleading out of my voice or off my face.

"How I would love it if you could, Son, but not this time."

The First Presidency *cum missionaries* left, not knowing how long they would be gone. Father always said the Lord called him to be there, wherever *there* may be, and he would remain until the Lord called him home.

As Father suspected would be the case, the mission was very short; they were called home after only three weeks. True to his promise, Father made some changes. He was home for dinner every night after that, generally speaking, and was always there for breakfast. Sometimes, he would leave again after dinner to see a sick patient or take care of some important Church business that couldn't wait until morning, but it was so nice to have him home more of the time. We started reading scriptures together again and praying together as a family. We thought up new games to play together, we even took walks around town a few times. Most importantly, we had fun and laughed together. And through it all, he continued to teach us things we needed to know. He also invited me on his medical rounds much more often. I was nine years old, going on ten by then, and eager to learn more about what he did. All our lives improved because he was there, our father, our hero.[25]

CHAPTER NINETEEN

Ogden, Utah 1904

Loving and Losing Babies

"What a blessing that must have been." Henrietta was standing in the doorway. She must have been there unobserved for a while, not wanting to interrupt the Doctor. She had brought in the unwelcome medicine bottle, intending to give some of its contents to Ezra, who, as always, protested.

"I don't want to take it," he insisted.

"I know, but it really does seem to help you feel better. Just do it for me."

He looked up at her with resignation, sighed, and let his shoulders droop, then obediently opened his mouth for her to put the dreaded spoonful in. Grimacing and contorting his face, he said, "It somehow hasn't gotten any better tasting."

She handed him a big glass of water, and he drank it all down, swishing it around in his mouth to get rid of the last vestiges of the nasty taste.

Fred and Joseph lifted Ezra into the wheelchair and Joseph pushed him into the bedroom. He and his father lifted him out of the chair and set him on the edge of the bed. Fred helped his mother get him into his night clothes.

"Lie down, now, Doctor, and I will massage your legs so you can sleep easier."

Ezra seemed more than happy to comply with that offer, and under Henrietta's skillful and loving hands, was soon asleep.

As Fred and Joseph retired to their bed, Joseph asked, "Dad, what was it like for you?"

"What do you mean, Son?"

"Losing all those babies. Did it hurt worse or get easier with each one? Grandma seems to still be filled with pain for every child she has lost, even after all these years."

Fred didn't answer for a long time, and Joseph began to wonder if he had gone to sleep. Finally, he said, "No, it did not get any easier. If anything, it got harder. Every time we had a new baby, we were hopeful of keeping him. It got so that we hoped for girls because they seemed to survive easier than the boys."

"I know where my younger brothers are buried, but where are the older three?"

"We were living out in the Uinta Basin, far away from family and friends, when Frederick Ezra was born, because I couldn't find work here. It was just your mother, little Lizzy, um, Elizabeth, and me. We have all called her Lizzy so long it just doesn't seem right to call her anything else. Lizzy was only two years old, but already showed signs of being the motherly type. She had a little baby doll that I had made her, and Mother had made a little dress for it. She carried that poor thing around until it finally fell to pieces."

He smiled at the memory. "And when we told her that a new baby was coming to live with us, she was so excited. Frederick Ezra was born in January of 1879, and just as we anticipated, Lizzy thought that baby was hers. Of course, she wasn't old enough to really care for him, but we helped her hold him on her lap, and she snuggled him and kissed him every moment she could. As he started to grow and develop, we all laughed at his precious antics, his funny smile, and easy giggle."

"How old was he when he died, Papa?"

"He made it until November of that same year, ten months we had him. Winter came early out in Ashley Fork, and he soon succumbed to what started out to be a bad cold. I suspect it was probably whooping cough because he coughed his poor little self to exhaustion. We tried everything we knew to help him recover, but finally resigned ourselves to bowing to the Lord's will. Lizzy, who was almost three by then, sat by that baby's side as long as we would let her sit there. When he finally passed away, she was inconsolable. Mother and I were broken-hearted, but at least we could understand that we would have that precious baby in the eternities, but Lizzy only knew that *her baby* was taken away, and we were back to just the three of us."

"Poor sister. No wonder she wanted to become a nurse. I can see how all of your hearts were broken, Papa."

"Then you can understand how happy we all were a year later when Josie was born, a beautiful little girl who became Lizzy's playmate, and the delight of her parents. Things weren't easy for her either, though, and we almost lost her. But she pulled through, as you know, God be praised."

"Was she born in Ashley Fork, too?"

"No, we had moved back here to Ogden, or very close to here. This is also where your brother Frederick Enoch was born, named for your Grandpa Burns, but he didn't survive. He passed away at six months. When we had Alonzo in 1884, and he made it to a year old and then two years old, we were sure we were going to get to raise him. But we left for Mexico in '86 to avoid prosecution for polygamy, and the trip was hard on a two-year-old. In fact, the two-year-old son of one of our traveling companions passed away as we were making our way up Spanish Fork Canyon, and we had to wait there for them to take his little body back to Springville to bury. While they were gone, Alonzo passed as well. Now, it was our turn to go to Springville to bury our son."

"Oh, Father. How I could cry for you right now."

"Not just for me, but for your mother and sisters as well. Those girls sobbed and sobbed when they lost their third brother. Lizzy was seven years old by then, old enough to take care of the baby in some ways, and such a help to her mother. Josie was almost three. They clung to each other and to us, and we tried our best to comfort each other.

"We traveled on to Fairview and stayed there for a couple of years. That is where you and Flora May were born, you know. My second wife, Kathena Hegsted, passed away there, and since I was no longer in a plural marriage, we went home to Ogden. Her death and the loss of Alonzo were too devastating and too hard on our spirits to make us want to keep going. We were terrified that we would lose you, too, but you can tell that we didn't."

"Yes, I seem to still be here," Joseph said, pinching himself all over as they both laughed out loud at the absurdity.

"Now we had three girls and a boy and thought we couldn't be any happier. But the next year, 1889, I was called to take a third wife, which is when I married Nancy. Our Bishop, Winslow Farr, had just been released from the Utah Territorial Prison for plural marriage and was determined never to go through that again. He said he was leaving for Mexico, and anyone who wanted to go with him could do so. Even though your mother was already expecting Hazel, we decided we had better take advantage of the opportunity, and again left for Mexico."

"I think I remember Aunt Nancy losing a baby, too, Father. Is that right?"

"Yes, she did, Son. I was worried that Nancy might also lose her baby boys, but she surprised us by losing a one-year-old baby girl, Louie Bell, her first child. Then a few years later, she lost another girl, sweet little Delta, also only a year old."

"That wasn't a very good surprise, Dad."

"I know," replied Fred. "It wasn't meant to be funny."

"But Leonard was born before that, right?" He looked at his father for confirmation of the date.

"Yes, Leonard, then Orlando and Vernal, too, and you finally had brothers who lived."

"Yes, I was so happy to finally have little brothers, even if they were quite a bit younger than I am. Were you secretly afraid they would die?"

"I don't think it was a big secret. We just hoped and prayed that they would live to be your playmates. And it seems like all of a sudden, I had four sons. What a blessing each of you were. But then ..."

Joseph picked up the narrative. "But then we lost Ivan and Clyde. They were just little babies, weren't they," Joseph said, not so much as a question but as a statement of fact. "Papa, did you love them as much as the babies who lived longer? It seems like you hardly knew them."

"Son, one day you will understand that as soon as you see your child born, as soon as that baby is no more than one minute old, you would gladly lay down your life for him or her. If those babies had died in one day, or even one hour, we would have grieved all the same. Or even if they had never taken a breath."

"I think I am starting to understand, Papa. Grandma told me that a mother never forgets her children. I guess a father doesn't either."

"No, Son. A father doesn't either. They are our children, and I look forward to spending eternity with them, just as I look forward to having you forever."

"I think I will be happy to get to know my five brothers, Papa. I just wish I had them now. And I won't forget my sisters, either."

Fred didn't answer for a few minutes, then he sleepily said, "Be grateful for who we have," and drifted off to sleep.

Joseph silently said a prayer of thanks to God for the rest of the babies who had lived; Henrietta, Orin, Rolla, and Naoma. And once again he wondered what life had in store for him.

It was about a week before Ezra expressed the desire to go on with his story.

"Fred," he called one evening after supper. "Get your pen and paper. I have more to tell you."

Fred hurried to his father's side, making him as comfortable as he could. It was only a few minutes before Joseph appeared in the room as well.

"Where was I, Fred?" Ezra asked as usual.

Fred turned to the last page he had written and read, "Most importantly, we had fun and laughed together. And through it all, he continued to teach us things we needed to know. He also invited me on his medical rounds much more often. I was nine years old, going on ten by then, and eager to learn about what he did. All our lives improved because he was there, our father, our hero."

"Oh yes," said Ezra, "the good ol' days."

CHAPTER TWENTY

KIRTLAND, OHIO 1833–1834

More Missions and Zion's Camp...
Through Ezra's Eyes

Even though Father was home a lot more, he still had a lot of responsibilities. Oh, the number of meetings he had to attend! I swear they had meetings to plan meetings. There were especially a lot of council meetings and conferences, held in the room above the Whitney store or the schoolroom, the printing office, our barn, or private homes, including our home. Father was involved in organizing and administering the establishment of the high council, the calling of the Twelve Apostles, ongoing ordinations and mission calls, Church publications, instructing and training leaders, and much more. They also tried to handle all the complaints of one member against another, everything from dereliction of duty, breaking the Word of Wisdom and dancing (some people thought it wasn't appropriate), to questionable financial dealings and the teaching of false doctrine.

The meetings were not very comfortable, I assure you. Few of the venues they used were very big, and the number of people wanting to attend was so great that they had to crowd in or be turned away, and once inside, they usually had only hard benches to sit on. It was hot in the summer and cold in the winter. Not everyone could hear what was going on, forcing the speakers to shout. It didn't help that mothers often attended with crying, hungry babies and children, and if someone needed to use the commode, they had to go outside to a cold, dark, and smelly outhouse, which was even worse in the summer for the stench it emitted. If the meetings continued into the night, something that often happened, they had to light lamps to see by, which never made the rooms bright enough. Oftentimes, people came fasting in hopes of witnessing spiritual manifestations, which resulted in people passing out as a result of the unfavorable conditions made worse by an empty stomach. Father was the scribe for most of the meetings held in 1833 while he was employed by Joseph, and so he was always in attendance.

Joseph Smith, as President of the Church, spoke more often than anyone else, of course, but Sidney Rigdon, Oliver Cowdery, and Father also spoke frequently. President Rigdon gave the longest talks, usually for an hour or longer, and Father gave the shortest ones. Father was just more comfortable writing everything down than he was standing up in front of people. The Prophet once said of him, *Brother Frederick G. Williams is one of those men in whom I place the greatest confidence and trust, for I have ever found him full of love and brotherly kindness. He is not a man of many words but is ever winning because of his constant mind.*[26]

That sums my father up very well.

He was called on another short mission in May of 1833, and again was paired with the Prophet. A fourth call came to him in July of 1833, this time to be the companion of Sidney Rigdon. This call came as they completed the retranslation of the Bible, or as Sidney recounted in a letter, "I am going off immediately with Brother Frederick to proclaim the gospel … Having finished the translation of the Bible a few hours since and needing some recreation, we do not know of one way we can spend our time more to divine acceptance than in endeavoring to build up his Zion in these last days, as we are not willing to idle any time away which can be spent to useful purposes."

It was sometime during that summer while they were all home from missions that the Prophet announced that a temple was to be built in Kirtland. I think Papa could see it coming, but now it was to become real. The leadership knew that they should be building a temple in Independence, but the Church was financially unable to do that, and the anti-Mormon rhetoric in Missouri was getting worse and worse to the point that it was unsafe to build a temple there at that time. So instead, they were given the charge to build one immediately in Kirtland. In June of 1833, they discussed dimensions of the building, what it was to look like inside, and where it was to be built. It was a foregone conclusion to us that it would be built somewhere on what had been Father's land since it included the whole heart of the city. Plans were drawn up, the site was chosen, and everyone had faith that it would all work out.

Father was home with us throughout the winter, but at the first sign of spring, February 24, 1834, he was called again to go and preach, this time with Hyrum Smith. Can you even imagine how close-knit this band of Church leaders had become? They each had their own strengths and weaknesses, but when they came together, they were extremely strong and supportive of one another and completely focused on the work of building Zion that the Lord had given them to do.

Then came Zion's Camp.[27]

"Brethren," said Joseph at the beginning of a meeting in the spring of 1834, "our people in Missouri are in a lot of trouble, as you have heard, and it behooves us to go to their aid. Brothers Parley P. Pratt, Lyman Wight, and W. W. Phelps have come from Missouri to tell us what is going on. Brother Parley, please tell the council just what is happening in Jackson County."

Parley P. Pratt came forward to address the council. "Thank you, President. Our brethren and sisters in Jackson County have been robbed and plundered of nearly all their belongings and forced off their lands. These are lands that are rightfully theirs, having been bought and purchased with monies they have earned through honest labor.

"As you know, the Lord has revealed to the Prophet that Independence is to become the earthly headquarters of the Church, which is why Joseph and others traveled there in 1831 to dedicate the land. Many of those people that the five missionaries baptized in 1830-31 have banded together to establish the Church there, and many more have been sent from Kirtland to join them. Well, it scares the citizens of Independence. They have concerns that the Saints might eventually outnumber the Missourians who are already there. They feel threatened by the belief of Church members that Jackson County is to be the gathering place of Zion, and they object to the large numbers of Saints moving in. That is a problem because the Church is decidedly against slavery, but Missouri wants to remain a slave state. If enough Saints move there, they could swing the vote in favor of abolition, and there is just too much at stake with keeping Missouri a slave state for them to allow that to happen. So, the persecutions have started up. People have been driven off their land and their property stolen. They have been threatened with their lives if they don't leave."

Next, W. W. Phelps stood to speak. "I have written editorials in the newspaper we have been printing, *The Evening and the Morning Star*, trying to explain our position to the people of Jackson County, trying to relieve the tension between us and them, but nothing I nor anyone else has said seems to help. The mob gave us fifteen minutes to agree to move all the Saints away. We could not make that promise. God had called us there; he had called me personally to be there and to be able to print anything that was needed. But the mob broke down the door of my house, threw out the printing press, and destroyed my home. I had to take my wife and children away, and the only place we could find to stay that night was an abandoned stable. And we are not the only ones who have been treated so badly. We really had no choice but to capitulate and agree to their demands to evacuate. Most of the Saints have moved north to Clay County. None of us have any idea how we will get our land back in Jackson County."

When the two were through speaking, the Prophet Joseph stood. "Thank you, brethren. I intend to go to assist the Saints there in redeeming Zion. I ask every one of you who can, to avail yourselves of the opportunity to do likewise. Who is ready to go with me to Jackson County now?"

Several of the men raised their hands and shouted their willingness to follow Joseph Smith wherever he tells them the Lord needs them. Joseph thanked them for their faithfulness. "Now, I will tell you of a new revelation that I just received. In it, God tells us that the Saints in Missouri are not perfect. We already knew that, I'm sure. But He is calling them to repentance and telling them that if they will do everything he asks them to do now, they will start to prevail against their enemies.

"Brother Parley, Brother William, and Brother Lyman, the Lord has instructed that you do not go back to Missouri until you have as many men as we can gather to go with you. As soon as we have gathered at least a hundred men, we shall go to redeem Zion."

After the meeting was over, the Prophet approached my father. "Brother Frederick, the Lord has need of you going on this march with us to Missouri."

"You know I will go if you need me, Brother Joseph, but I am getting old and may not be able to keep up with the younger men. Besides, I may be needed here to keep things in line." He was most likely thinking of what happened in 1831 when he and the four other missionaries first went to Missouri.

"I understand your reticence, Brother, but the Lord has asked for you to go. He needs your medical expertise and also needs your organizational skills. He has asked that you be paymaster for the company, and you may be given other responsibilities as well. As for keeping things in line here, both Brother Sidney and Brother Oliver will be staying, also some people who will begin work on the temple, as well as the older brethren. The people will be well cared for while we are gone."

"I will make arrangements to go then, Brother, it's just that ..."

"I know, I know, Frederick. Your responsibilities are great, and your family needs you badly. But I promise if you go with me, your family will be highly blessed."

Father heaved a big sigh, and replied, "All right, Joseph. I am with you completely. When do we leave?"

"As soon as we can get things prepared and packed. The sooner the better."

"I'll go tell Rebecca, then, so that she can make arrangements for my absence."

When we sat down to dinner that night, Father told us all that was going on. Mother said that she had already heard rumors that "an army" was going to Independence.

"An army? Really, Papa? Are you going to war?" I thought that was the best adventure possible. "Can I go? Please, please, please? I'm almost eleven and look how tall I'm getting." I stood as tall as I could and put my hand flat on the top of my head.

"I'm taow too, Bapa," mimed Swain, standing up beside me and cupping his hand on his head.

"Yes, I've noticed how tall you are both getting to be, and that's why I feel safe leaving Mother and the girls here in your care. To be honest, I don't really want to go, but I have been called, and you all know how I feel about that."

"Yes, Papa, we know. 'I will go and do what the Lord asks me to do,'" Lucy recited. "It is just something you have to do."

Mother asked, "Will it be dangerous, Frederick? I mean, is there a possibility of people getting hurt?"

"Oh no," said Father. "I don't think any of us will be in harm's way."

I noticed that he did not look up at Mama when he said this. She looked down at her hands, and at the time, I didn't know why.

He continued, "We are just going to talk some sense into the leaders of the state so that they will lend their aid to the Saints in getting their land back. That's all. We will be back before you know it."

"Why do so many people have to go then?" asked Lucy. "I don't think I want you to go."

"I know, but it isn't up to you or me, sweet girl, only to God, and He wants me to go."

"But why, Father?" she went on, nearly in tears. "You are a lot older than the other men. It seems to me they could choose someone younger than you are."

Father closed his eyes for a moment, as if he were asking God for the strength to continue. He took a deep breath and went on. "Let's all sit down and counsel together for a few moments. Let me finish my side of the story, and then anyone who wants to tell theirs is welcome to do it. Agreed?"

We all nodded.

"All right then. Here are the reasons I don't want to go. One, I will miss you all terribly."

We said back to him all at once our own versions of how we would miss him.

Swain went over and hugged him and then, trying to be brave, said, "I wio miss you, Bapa." He found his way onto Father's lap, snuggled his head into Father's chest, and with tears streaming down his cheeks, he said, "I don't want you to go."

"I know, Son, but I won't be gone long," he promised. "How old are you now?"

Swain held up all of his fingers.

"Well, I'll be home before you are all of those fingers plus one."

"But I don't have any moe feeners, Bapa."

"Then let's count this big toe right here." He took hold of Swains big toe, wiggled it back and forth, then tickled his foot.

Swain giggled, and we all laughed at them both, breaking the tension in the room for the moment.

"Now where was I? Oh yes, reason two. If I go, you will all have to take more responsibility while I'm gone. But you have done it before, and I know you can do it again with the Lord's help. Third reason, who will treat my patients? And fourth, I'm getting too old for this kind of thing. Listen to my bones creaking as I walk." He stood and walked across the room, making a covert creaking sound as he did.

Lovina walked into the room. "Those are all good reasons, Father. So why are you going?"

"Here are the reasons I must go. One, the Lord has called me to go. Two, I promised Him when I joined this Church that I would do his will. Those are reasons enough, but I have a third: the company needs a doctor."

"But, Papa," said Lucy. "What about your patients here?"

"That is a good question, Lucy. But there are other doctors around, you know. I will have to entrust my patients to them."

I scowled. "But you're the best doctor anywhere."

"That may or may not be true, but the Lord will provide for them while I am gone. Which brings me to reason four. My faith needs to be tested. And I suppose that means your faith needs it as well, all of you. Now, whoever has a reason for or against me going, bring it up at this time."

No one said a word. I believe we all had good reasons to keep Father at home in addition to the ones mentioned, but none of us said a word. We knew he was going, and we knew it was God's will.

My mother told me later that Father held her in his arms the whole night before he left. "My love, I cannot lie to you or keep the truth from you. This could be a dangerous mission, and it is possible that I won't come back."

She put her head on his shoulder and cried.

The company left within days of the Prophet asking them to go, walking much of the eight hundred miles. In addition to being the camp doctor for the two hundred people in the company, Father was also appointed paymaster and historian. As a big part of that job, he wrote to Oliver Cowdery every week, explaining where they were, what places they had passed through, and the experiences they had had. I tried to find those letters so I could read them firsthand, but it appears they were lost, or possibly Oliver discarded them after the Camp returned. Father, along with other men, had to fill in the historical parts of the mission from memory.

Joseph's goal was to meet with Missouri Governor Daniel Dunklin to get him to call out the state militia to escort the Saints back to their lands in Jackson County. He felt that if he could convince the governor to do that, then once they were back on their own lands, the Camp would be able to protect the Saints so they would not be driven out again. And so, for the next six weeks, the Camp marched through Ohio, Indiana, and Illinois with that goal in mind. They covered as many as forty miles a day, which was a brisk speed to be moving all those men and all their equipment. To make matters worse, the food was poor, and it was hard to get clean water. Sometimes the ground was very muddy, the deep mud oozing over the tops of their boots. They also had a suspicion that spies from Missouri were following them.

Although the pay wasn't great, the men in the camp who had left families in Kirtland sent them money as often as they could. On June 4, Joseph wrote to his wife Emma, sending her a large bill of money, for how much I do not know, but she was told that Joseph and Frederick did not have any change for the large bill, and that Emma and Rebecca were to share it to get the things that they needed. And then a very unexpected thing happened. Father wrote a personal note to Mother at the bottom of the Prophet's letter. My mother made a copy of the part of the letter that was addressed to her. It read:

> *I embrace this opportunity to fill up this sheet to you, my beloved companion, not that I have anything important to communicate, but remembering your request to write to you while on the road, but as I write every week to brother Oliver, you will know all the particulars of our journey.*
>
> *Tell the children to remember that passage of scripture which says, "children obey your parents in all things," for this is right, and God will bless them. For want of room I must stop writing, but in due time after I arrive to my place of destination will take an opportunity to write more fully. Be assured that I always remember you to my Heavenly Father and hope you will do the same for your   F. G. Williams*[28]

About the middle of June, the Camp neared their destination; they camped one night between two forks of a river called Fishing River. When my father told me about this, I asked, "Couldn't any river be called Fishing River?" It seemed funny to me that any river would be singled out to be a fishing river.

As they prepared their places to camp for the night, a large group of men came toward them, swearing and threatening to kill them. The brethren had heard rumors that many Missourians who lived around Jackson County were angry that the Camp even dared to cross into Missouri and swore to kill whoever did. The Missourians felt such hatred toward the Saints that they were ready to shed blood.

Father thought perhaps there were a thousand men in this group, and truth be told, the Camp members were scared.

Then a miracle occurred. A small black cloud appeared in the west, and soon it grew until the entire sky was black with thunderclouds. It rained in sheets, the winds blew, and the lightning flashed. The thunder sounded louder than any of them had ever heard it, and hale began to fall, breaking trees down, and the river began to swell so fast and high that they could not leave that place. But the miracle was that their enemies could not reach them. They were all reminded that the Lord had promised to fight their battles for them, and it seemed that he was doing just that on this night.

A couple of days later, Joseph learned that Governor Dunklin was not willing to call out the militia on behalf of the beleaguered Saints, so the Camp could not protect them nor escort them back to their lands. At this point, Joseph did not know what to do, so he did what he always did—he turned to God. As a result, Joseph received a revelation that instructed the members of Zion's Camp to disengage. In other words, they were told that they no longer needed to fight for the Saints in Missouri, and that the Lord would fight their battles for them. You can read all of this in what is now called Section 105 of the Doctrine and Covenants. The revelation goes on to say that they needed to be endowed with power before Zion could be redeemed. That power could only come by having a temple built, a House of God, where he could bless his children with that promised power. I suspect Joseph knew what God meant by that, but most of the men had no idea. Some of them were very upset that they weren't going to get to fight. Others were very relieved, especially when they heard the part of the revelation where the Lord said, "I have heard their prayers and will accept their offering." What they had already done was enough. Their faith had been tested, and although there was nothing they could do at that time to help the Missouri Saints, the Lord had accepted their acts of faith. He could see that these men, knowing that they were putting their lives on the line, were determined to do what they had been asked to do. Because they knowingly put their own lives in peril, Father in Heaven knew he could ask anything of them.

Now that Zion's Camp was disbanded, many men turned their faces east to go home to Kirtland. Father was so excited to get back to us, but little did he know his most difficult work had only begun.

On June 21, 1834, the Camp was hit with an outbreak of cholera, the most feared disease that my father ever treated. Three days later, the full force of cholera broke out among its members. The Prophet Joseph wrote in his journal:

> *June 24 This night the cholera burst forth among us, and about midnight it was manifested in its most virulent form. Our ears were saluted with cries, moaning, and lamentations on every hand, even those on guard fell to the earth with their guns in their hands, so sudden and powerful was the attack of this terrible disease. At the commencement, I attempted to lay on hands for their recovery, but I quickly learned by painful experience, that when the great Jehovah decrees destruction upon any people, and makes known His determination, man must not attempt to stay His hand. The moment I attempted to rebuke the disease, I was attacked, and had I not desisted in my attempt to save the life of a brother, I would have sacrificed my own. The disease seized upon me like the talons of a hawk, and I said to the brethren, "If my work were done, you would have to put me in the ground without a coffin."[29]*

Father had his hands full with treating the sick and dying of the dreaded cholera as it began to decimate many Saints and members of Zion's Camp. About sixty-eight Saints suffered from this disease, of which thirteen Camp members died, and two members of the Church living in Missouri also died. Among those who perished were

Algernon Sidney Gilbert, who had a store in Missouri, and Joseph's young cousin Jessie Smith. The disease raged for about four days when Father and others hit upon a cure. They put the afflicted person into cold water, or poured it over them, then gave them whiskey thickened with flour. I'm not sure how that helped, but it somehow did. It must have been through the power of the priesthood because I see no medical basis for it. Father also made sure his patients had doses of herbal tea several times a day, which helped to rehydrate their emaciated bodies. Perhaps that was the best thing he did. We now know that cholera occurs when food and water have become contaminated, and sanitation is poor. It is best to avoid contact with it, if possible, but I have treated a few cases.

As the Camp broke up, men began to divide themselves into smaller groups to make the trek back to Kirtland. There were nineteen men in the group that Father came back with, including the Prophet, Hyrum Smith, William E. McLellin, Martin Harris, Orson Hyde, and others. They left Missouri with few provisions, and it wasn't long before they were hungry and thirsty. They stopped at various farm homes along the way, but no one seemed to have even a drink of water for the men. Finally, one lady said she had some buttermilk. Although it wasn't fresh, many of the men drank as if it were the sweetest thing ever to cross their tongues. One of these was my father who reportedly drank a whole gallon by himself. I think it saved their lives.

Apparently, the cholera epidemic was going on in many areas of the country, which is why the Camp, with the poor living conditions and less than nutritious food, was hit so hard. But we were hearing of outbreaks in Detroit, Cleveland, Fairport, and as far away as Buffalo, New York. As soon as the health of the Camp was on the mend, Father was told to go to Cleveland and administer to the sick there. Before he left, Father, Joseph, and Oliver united in prayer, asking for the Lord to grant the blessings of healing for the people there, and for the glory of the Lord.

He finally made it home to Kirtland toward the end of August.

CHAPTER TWENTY-ONE

OGDEN, UTAH 1904

Making a List, Checking It Twice

"These excerpts from the Prophet's diary as well as a few letters written between my parents are among the papers I want you to have, Frederick. I have been saving them here for you to take home with you."

"Thank you, Father, I shall cherish them, and then pass them on to my children. How lucky for us that you saved them all these years."

"I'm sure the papers are important," Joseph piped up, "but they aren't very interesting without the stories to go along with them, Grandfather."

"I agree with you, Joe," Ezra replied. "That's the main reason I wanted you and your father to come up here. These stories need to be told and retold."

"I've learned so much from them already," said Joseph. "And I'm really glad my dad is writing them all down."

Ezra turned to face Joseph straight on. "Well, we are nearing the end of things, but the biggest lessons are yet to come."

Ezra was visibly tired, so Fred put down the writing book and excused himself. He found his mother in the kitchen and said, "I think Papa has had enough for tonight. We are all getting a little tired by now anyway."

"All right, I will come and get him ready for bed. Why don't you go ahead and crawl into bed as well?"

"Joseph and I will get him into the bed, Mother, then you can come work your magic and tuck him in." He hesitated for just a moment before leaving, took Henrietta's hand in his, and said, "Thank you for taking such good care of him, Mama."

Henrietta smiled and squeezed his hand.

She was soon at Ezra's side, ready to administer to the doctor who had done likewise for so many other people. She took healing oils into her hands and started to massage Ezra's feet and legs as Joseph, who was not quite ready to leave his grandparents yet, looked on.

Ezra said, "Mother, I am sure there are things in this life that are more soothing than what you are doing right now, but I don't know what they are. You have an angel's touch."

"Grandma," said Joseph, "I think I would like to try rubbing down Grandpa's arms. Would that be all right?"

"Hold out your hand." She poured some of the aromatic oil into it. Joseph rubbed his hands together, and then started massaging the oil into Ezra's arms. Ezra's body relaxed, giving in to the treatment, and the Doctor was soon asleep.

Henrietta pulled the covers up over Ezra's body, and then with her arm around her grandson, turned out the lamp and left the room.

The next morning, Ezra seemed uncharacteristically chipper and full of life. After they had made him comfortable in the parlor rocking chair, and as soon as they had finished helping Henrietta with clearing up the breakfast dishes, washing them and putting them away, Ezra summoned them to his side.

"Boys," he yelled as loud as his strength allowed, "I have thought of some things that you need to hear."

"All right, Papa," said Fred. "We're coming."

When they got to him, he said, "Early this morning I remembered some things that I have not thought about for years. Here, Fred. I made a list of some things on this paper to remember to tell you. Read it, please."

Fred took the paper from his father, and could tell right away that Ezra's handwriting, which had previously been meticulous and beautiful, had deteriorated.

He read, "*Child reservation, Kirtland Sally Soccer, School of the Probelties, Signs of Zombies*," Fred looked up quizzically from the paper. "Papa, I must not be reading this correctly. You don't have a child on a reservation, do you? And who on earth is Sally Soccer. Tell me you didn't learn about *probelties* in school, and worst of all, you saw *signs of zombies?*"

"Oh, Fred, for Pete's sake, did no one ever teach you to read English? Give me that paper and hand me my glasses."

Fred handed the list back to his father, and Joseph jumped up and got his grandfather's glasses. Ezra put them on and read, "Chile revelation ..."

"Wait, Papa, I'll make a new note here as you read it to me."

Ezra looked at his son in surprise, then the fact of what was happening dawned on him, and he said with a touch of sarcasm, "What a good idea, Son. Print in large letters so you can read it properly."

Fred was serious. "I'm sorry, Papa. I would read your list if I could."

"Then read it. I don't know why you can't read it."

Suddenly Fred said loudly, "Oh, I know what the problem is. You're a doctor. Everyone knows doctors can't write legibly."

"Where did you ever get that idea? I'll have you know I ..."

Henrietta walked in, interrupting the banter. "What is all this noise about? Boys, please stop."

Joseph, who had started to laugh, said, "They are arguing about who was in the wrong, the person who couldn't write the list, or the person who couldn't read it." He started to laugh again as the two did not let up on each other, and the more they argued, the louder Joseph laughed.

Henrietta stomped her foot. "I said stop!"

Everyone immediately stopped and looked at her.

"Let me see that list. *Child reservation*. Ezra, explain please."

"It clearly says *Chile revelation*, Henny. Surely you can see that."

"Well, Chile revelation isn't much better than Child reservation."

Joseph couldn't stop the chuckling under his breath.

Ezra's eyebrows furrowed and his lips pressed into a thin line. "Write that down, Fred. Chile revelation."

"All right," Fred obeyed.

Henrietta looked closely at the paper. "Then what is this second thing, Kirtland Silly Socrates?"

"Henny, whose side are you on here? It says, 'Kirtland Safety Society.'" Ezra spoke slowly, pronouncing each word in a very exact and exaggerated way.

"I see that now, dear. At least I got 'Kirtland' right the first time. Now, what is the next thing on the list," she said, tilting the paper a little to the left and then to the right. "Ummm, School of the Properties?"

"Ai yi yi," said Ezra, hitting his forehead with the heal of his hand. "School of the Prophets. Prophets!"

"Mercy, Ezra, stay calm. This is not an easy task."

"Oh, Mother, it couldn't be that hard," he whined.

"Here is the last line. Let's see …" She looked at it for quite a while, and finally inhaled sharply as she exclaimed, "Signs of Zombies?"

"My love, you make me want to cry," he said in a soft, steady voice. "It says, *Songs of Zion.* I don't know about the rest of you, but I am exhausted. I never dreamed it would be so hard to get my thoughts across to those I love. Fred, please take me to my room for a while. I think I need a little nap."

"This early in the morning?" asked Henrietta as Fred and Joseph got him into the wheelchair and took him into his bedroom.

"I'm afraid so, my love. Surely, I'll feel better after lunch." She followed as they lifted him onto the bed, then left her alone with her husband. She picked up the knitted Afghan and tucked it in around him. She turned to leave, but Ezra stopped her. "Oh, Henny, there is something I left off the list. Would you add it please?"

"Of course I will, Doctor."

"The dedication of the temple."

"I'll write it down right now." She looked at him a little sheepishly and said, "I'm sorry, Ezra, I didn't mean to make such a mess of things."

He reached for her hand and said, "You didn't make a mess, my love. It's just that I am so focused on getting the most important parts of the story across to Fred while I still can."

"The temple dedication?"

"No, even more profound than that." He closed his eyes and turned his head away from her, as if to say, *I can't talk about it right now.* "You will know soon enough."

------◆------

Henrietta knew that Ezra had not been sleeping well. He had insisted on sleeping in the downstairs bedroom a few years before so as not to wake her in the night. It was also easier for him, as his legs became less cooperative, not to have to climb the stairs every day. He was often awake for a couple of hours around 3:00 a.m., and really the only thing he could do was get up and pace the floor a bit, read a bit, or write a bit. Now, he could not get out of bed by himself, but he still slept in this smaller main floor room. *She needs her rest too badly for me to wake her up,* he reasoned, and she continued to sleep upstairs in one of the bigger bedrooms. Despite their nightly separation, Henrietta still knew when her husband was having a bad night because she crept down the stairs two or three times a night to check on him. He seemed to be awake more and more in the nighttime now so she was happy to let him rest during the day whenever he could.

He was awake for lunch, though, and as soon as they had finished eating a great meal of roast beef, pickles, cheese, and lettuce on thick slices of buttered homemade bread, with home-canned grape juice to drink, he seemed ready to attack the list of items he had made that morning.

"Do you have any pie and whipped cream?" he asked her.

"Sorry, Ezra, not today. I'll make some soon," she replied.

"Then we might as well get on with the story."

"Let's start with the Chile revelation," he said to Fred and Joseph when they had settled him into the rocking chair and assumed their positions that had come to signal Ezra's story telling.

"Yes, please, Papa, I am so curious about what that even is."

"Well, the first thing I want to tell you about it is that nobody really knows where it actually came from," said Ezra.

"All right," said Fred, "but what exactly is *it*?"

"Among some of the writings Father made was a purported

revelation about just where the Nephites landed when they came across the Pacific Ocean," he explained. "It says something to the effect that Lehi traveled from Jerusalem to the place where the ship was being built in a southeast direction. Then they traveled southeast across the sea until they came to the South American continent and the country that is now called Chile. Since it is written in Father's hand, many people assumed that it was a revelation given to the Prophet Joseph and scribed by F. G. Williams, telling him where the boat had landed. Some even thought it could have been a revelation given to Father, because there is no attribution on the page as to who the author was. But Parley and Orson Pratt were both telling people about it before Father had even joined the Church. Some of the earliest Church members assumed that Lehi and family had landed on the coast of Chile, most likely because of this document. It seems that Father had just made a copy of the paragraph, to what purpose we will forever remain in the dark. No one ever claimed authorship of it."[30]

"And what is your opinion, Papa?" asked Fred.

"I will tell you a personal experience, since you asked. I turned to the Lord one day and asked him if this was a revelation from him to Joseph or to my father, and he said to me, 'I am not ready yet to reveal just where it was that Lehi landed, and it will remain hidden until I am ready to reveal it,' or words similar to that effect. The overall feeling I got was that God doesn't want that specific place known yet, for whatever reason he might have. I respect that. Still, the most logical solution is that it came from the Lord to Joseph and my father later copied it. There were some strange characters written with it as well, and no one knows where they came from or what they really mean. On the other hand, just because it is written in Father's hand does not mean it came from Joseph. It's true that Father scribed many things for Joseph while he was his scribe, but he also wrote things for other people. That paragraph could have come from an illiterate person who believed he had received a revelation and came to Father to have him write it down. Because many people in those days were uneducated, it was not unusual for them to hire someone to write things down for them. It is not common knowledge that this document even exists, which reinforces my personal testimony that since the Prophet died, no one really knows where Lehi landed, and, as I said, I think that is because the Lord has his reasons for not making that known."

"What do you think those reasons could be?" asked Joseph.

"Let's say we know exactly where Lehi landed. Many people would flock to that place looking for artifacts to prove that it is the place, and thereby reinforcing the truth of the Book of Mormon."

"What would be so wrong with that, Grandpa?

"Well, the strange thing is, someone could also use the same evidence to disprove it. I think I've mentioned this before, but I want to say it again. Every time something good happens in a person's life, or we could say, in the life of the restored Church in this case, the Adversary has the ability to create a counter point to disprove it."

"Who is the Aver—"

"Adversary," said Fred.

"The Adversary? I've never heard of him," said Joseph.

"Yes, you have, you just know him by his more common title of Satan," said his father.

"Oh." Joseph was surprised. "I never knew that."

"God has to allow Satan to try to convince people that the truth is error, and that right is wrong," continued Ezra.

"Wait," said Joseph. "He *has* to let Satan tempt us?"

Fred picked up the conversation here. "He does, Son. If God did not let us choose for ourselves, He would cease to be God. And if there were no opposition, there would be no choice to make."

"So, are you saying that the Adversary," Joseph went on, "could somehow make things that would prove where Lehi landed look like they were disproving it?"

"Something like that," said his father. "This is a good lesson for you to learn. Expect opposition whenever you make a great choice. Just gear up for it, and pray about it, and God will tell you which version you should believe. Do you remember the verse at the end of the Book of Mormon that says, *By the power of the Holy Ghost, you may know the truth of all things?* Learn to call on that power, Son. The Holy Ghost cannot lead you astray."

"But the Adversary can, right?"

"He can and he will if there is any way at all that he can tempt you away from the truth," said Fred.

"Some things are better left alone, such as where Lehi landed. That way, Satan cannot turn such a place to his benefit, right?" Joseph was working hard to get this straightened out in his mind.

"Yes, now you are starting to understand," said Ezra.

"I'm not sure I totally understand that whole idea, but I'll work on it."

"That's good enough for now, Joe."

"So, can we check child reservation—uh, Chile Revelation— off the list, Papa? What would you like to talk about next, *School of the Probelties?*"

Ezra glared at his son.

"Oh, oops, I meant to say *School of the Prophets,* Father. I don't know what I was thinking."

"Humph," the old man growled. "Yes, I will tell you about the School of the Prophets." He said it slowly, emphasizing *prophets*. Ezra seemed to settle back into his accustomed position and attitude toward the story he had to tell.

"The School was a group of men, all ordained high priests, who met together regularly in a room above the Whitney store, and later in a room dedicated for it on the top floor of the temple. I think it is important for you to know that when Father and Sidney Rigdon were ordained to the Presidency in 1833, they were accounted as equal with Joseph Smith in holding the keys of the Kingdom of God on earth, which included the keys of the School of the Prophets. No other first presidency since then has been given those keys."[31]

"Tell us more about the temple, Grandpa."

"Don't worry, Grandson, I have a lot to say about it. But for now, I will say that the work had started to progress because in order to tell you all that I can about the temple, I have to tell you about the School of the Prophets. That is why I put it on my list. The School was instituted as a result of revelation about the time Father was ordained second counselor to the Prophet, and as I said, they met in an upper room of the Whitney store. It was crowded and stuffy, but the things they learned in that room made up for the discomfort. The Prophet received many great revelations there, most of them scribed by F. G. Williams.

"Joseph told his counselors that the two main objectives for the School were first, to learn how to preside over the Lord's kingdom in preparation for his return, and second, to teach the worthy men who were there what they needed to know to be the leaders that the Lord would need to accomplish the first objective. The School became the foundation for learning Church doctrine and how to administer it."[32]

CHAPTER TWENTY-TWO

KIRTLAND, OHIO 1834

So Much to Learn...Through Ezra's Eyes

I talked to my father a lot about the School of the Prophets because I wanted to know what he was doing there. He went to school every day with the other Church leaders in the upstairs room of the Whitney store, and I went to school along with the rest of the Kirtland children in a small, nearby building that was built for that purpose. I somehow had the feeling that Papa was not learning the same things I was. When I came home from school one day, Papa was there at home, something that was not an everyday occurrence.

"How was your school day, Ezra?" he asked.

"Just a normal day."

"Well, what did you learn?" he persisted.

I gave a big sigh and said, "We are learning the twelve times tables, Papa. They are not so easy. What did you learn at school today?"

He smiled and said, "I am learning how to be a better Church leader."

"Well, that doesn't sound so hard."

He laughed a little laugh. "There is more to it than you think, Son. Each day we start with fervent prayer, praying for direction from God, because we know we cannot do this job on our own."

"Does he answer you?"

"Oh yes," he said without hesitation. "He always answers us, and sometimes in very miraculous ways."

"I would like to see a miracle, Papa. Can you tell me about one?"

I always hoped that he would tell me about seeing angels or some other heavenly manifestations, the way Joseph had seen them before he came to Kirtland.

"I can tell you some things that you might not see as miracles right now, Ezra, and I could also tell you some things that truly are miraculous," he assured me. "But I want to tell you about what happened not too long ago. As you know, so many of the brethren liked to smoke pipes and chew tobacco, both rather nasty habits that I have never seen the need to indulge in. But many of them continued to puff away so much that a cloud of blue smoke hung over our heads all through our sacred meetings. Worse than that, those who chewed the disgusting stuff would spit their tobacco juice all over the floor. Of course, no one cleaned up after himself, leaving Sister Emma and Sister Whitney to take care of the mess, and they weren't very happy about it, either."

"I know Mother would not like to clean it up."

"Well, one day, we were about to administer the sacrament when we suddenly realized that there was no wine. Some of us were about to leave to go get some when Joseph told us to stay put. He said the Lord was about to reveal something to us. More often, Joseph received revelations at more private times, but this time, the Lord spoke to him right there, giving him what we now call the Word of Wisdom.[33] The Lord told Joseph not to use wine in the administration of the sacrament, but just to use water."

"Why did God not want you to use wine, Papa?"

"I guess He knew that some men would abuse it and become drunkards, for one thing. Also, it was very expensive, and the Church didn't have very much money, and since we could just as effectively use water, Heavenly Father told us to make the change. Both water and wine have great symbolic meaning to the Savior, so I guess he didn't mind which one we used. Also, water is readily available, whereas wine is not. Then he went on to forbid us from using any strong drink, meaning all alcoholic beverages. When it is abused, alcohol can be deadly, not only to the body, but to the spirit as well. I have seen men under the spell of strong drink who would give up anything, including their own families, or do anything, even breaking the law, to get it."

That all made sense to me.

"We were also told not to use tobacco because it is bad for our bodies. It can cause diseases that most people don't even know about, in addition to making a mess. And as you know, He gave us other health guidelines that we immediately adopted, and I have found them to be very helpful in keeping myself, our family, and even my patients healthy and well. Father in Heaven wants to give us the best chance at good health. He wants us to take care of our bodies because to Him, they are sacred, and they should be to us as well."

"Are you the one who wrote that revelation down?" My interest in what Father was doing with the other Church leaders stemmed from being proud to be his son, and I knew the Prophet trusted him and gave him important responsibilities.

"Yes, I was, Ezra. I am the clerk for the School, and as such, I have the responsibility of writing down everything that happens there. It is a job I enjoy very much, and I often have the privilege of writing down amazing things."

"Were the men mad that they had to give up smoking and chewing?"

"No, Ezra. They all immediately took their pipes out of their mouths and the tobacco they may have had in their pockets and threw it all into the fire. To my knowledge, none of those men ever used tobacco again unless it was for healing sick animals as instructed in the revelation."

"That was a kind of miracle itself, wasn't it, Papa?"

"I would say it was, Son. I had never seen some of those brethren without a pipe or a chaw. And once they stopped using tobacco, they all wondered how they could ever have used it."

"I think it smells funny."

"I do, too, which is one reason I was never disposed to using it. That, and my father never did either."

"What else are you supposed to learn at your school?"

"Everything."

"Everything?"

"Yes. The Lord told us to study the scriptures together and teach each other. Then He told us to learn everything we could about literally everything. I know that is a big order, but we are trying to learn everything we can about as many subjects as possible. As near as I can recall, the Lord said to learn things of both heaven and earth, and things under the earth, things which are to come, at home and abroad. He said to learn about wars and nations and judgments and countries and kingdoms. He said we need to be prepared in all things, so we are able to fulfill our missions and callings.[34] Doesn't that sound just about like everything to you, Son?"

"It's a lot more than the twelve times tables, Papa. It must be a lot of fun to learn so many things."

"Yes, it is. There are so many things to learn, things I never dreamed of. There is no way we can learn everything in one lifetime, but it is fun to try. And of course, the School is where Joseph told us about building the temple. We came up with a sketch of what it should look like. I will show you sometime when we are over at the Whitney store."

"I would like that a lot, Papa." Then I added, "I think you learn better things in your school than I do in mine."

"We all have to start somewhere, Son, so put first things first, learn your twelve times tables, and in due time, you will learn about everything I am learning."

"Promise, Papa?"

"I promise, Ezra."

CHAPTER TWENTY-THREE

OGDEN, UTAH 1904

Spanish Lessons and a Beautiful Song

"And so did you learn everything, Grandpa?"

"What do you think, Joseph?"

"You sure know a lot about many things, but I will guess that you don't quite know everything yet."

Ezra laughed out loud. "You are right, Joe, I don't quite know everything yet. In fact, I don't know half of everything, or a fourth of everything. I guess I don't know one-hundredth of everything. The universe is so vast that to learn everything is going to take us all a long, long time.

"One of the things the Lord told the Church leaders to learn should interest you, Joe. He told us to learn languages. Do you know how many different languages there are on the earth, Grandson?"

"Umm, twenty?"

"Let's see if we can name them. German, Spanish…"

"I already know that one, Grandpa."

"Oh yes, you do. But I don't, so you might have to teach me."

"What about Japanese and Chinese, and Portuguese, French, Dutch, Danish, Swedish, Norwegian, Finnish, Italian, Romanian, Turkish, Greek, and Russian?" Fred said. "How many are we up to, Joe?"

Joseph had been keeping track on his fingers. "Counting English and Spanish that is seventeen."

"Are we done?" asked Ezra.

"I don't think so, Grandpa. We haven't mentioned African or Canadian or Greenlandian, or Hawaiian. That makes twenty-one."

"Wait a minute. How many African languages do you think there are? Many more than just one. Probably more than twenty all by itself."

"Really, Grandfather? That is amazing."

"Yes, really. But in Canada they speak either English or French so we can't count Canadian. And I'm not sure about Greenlandian."

"Well, they have to speak some language, don't they?"

"Yes, that is true. I guess calling it Greenlandian is as good as anything."

"And what about the languages of the Pacific Islands? There is Samoan and Tongan, and Fijian and Phillipinian and …"

"Wait, Joe," said his father. "When did you learn about all those island countries?"

"In school, Dad. We have to learn something, you know."

"Good point, Son. And what about all the countries of the East like Saudi Arabia and Persia, and India?"

"And the Indians that live here in the United States," added Ezra. "Every tribe has its own language, and there might be a hundred of them."

"How will we ever learn them all? Did your father learn them all?"

"Oh no," said Ezra. "The School decided to concentrate on one language at a time, and that first one was Hebrew, one we have not mentioned yet."

"Hebrew? What is that?"

"It is the language spoken by the ancient peoples who wrote most of the Old Testament. The Church leaders thought they would learn a lot about Scripture by learning Hebrew."

"And did they?" asked Fred.

"They tried, Son. They actually hired a Hebrew teacher to come and teach them. My Father had his own Hebrew Bible at one time. They all did, and I think they learned a lot about the early Scriptures from studying that language."

"What other languages did they learn?" asked Fred.

"I don't think they ever got around to any other language, other than how to read a little Egyptian hieroglyphics. It is very hard to learn everything, as they were finding out."

"*Supongo que tengo mucha suerte de saber dos idiomas, Abuelito,*" said Joseph. "I guess I am pretty lucky that I know two languages, Grandpa."

"Yes, I would say that you are. I wish I knew another language," said Ezra.

"I can teach you Spanish."

"Oh, wouldn't I love that!" said his grandfather. "What should I say first?"

"Say, *Hola mi amor,*" Joseph coached.

"*Oluh me armour,*" Ezra said slowly. He was trying his best to copy the way Joseph said it, but it wasn't easy for him.

"Pretty good for a first try, Grandpa. Try it again. *Hola mi amor.* Now you say it."

"*O-la me amor,*" he tried again.

"Yes, that was much better. Now say it again and again after me." The two of them went back and forth like that for some time.

Finally, Ezra said, "By the way, what am I saying?"

Joseph laughed. "You are saying, *hello my love.* You have to say it to Grandma."

And right on cue, Henrietta came in to tell them it was time for dinner.

"*Ola me amor,*" Ezra said to her.

She looked at him quizzically and said, "What is that supposed to mean?"

"I'm teaching Grandpa how to speak Spanish," said Joseph. "He said, *Hello my love.* Those are his first Spanish words."

Henrietta looked at Ezra, then Joseph, then back to Ezra, and she said, "Oh, that is so nice. I love you, too, my dear." Then she leaned over to Joseph and whispered in his ear, "How do I say, 'Now get ready for dinner?'"

Joseph whispered back, "*Ahora prepárate para la cena.*"

She looked at him cross-eyed, but she gave it a try. "*A-ora,*" she looked at Joseph. He started coaching each word, telling her to roll the Rs.

"Like this, Grandma," he said, then he rolled a long span of Rs with ease.

"*Duh-der-duh-der,*" she sputtered.

"Say this, Grandma: *uhduh, uhduh.* Just keep saying that and pretty soon you will be rolling them." She tried but wasn't having great success. "I know," he suggested, "for now, just replace your Rs with Ds. Now say *ahora* again."

"*A-oda,*" she said.

Joe: *prepárate*

Henrietta: *prepawtay*

Joe: *para*

Henrietta: *pada*

Joe: *la cena*

Henrietta: *lazanya*

Then she turned on her heels and left the room. "Well," said Ezra, "I guess she didn't want to be outdone."

Joseph looked over at his dad who said, "*Bueno, creo que es bueno que ella no tiene que hablar español, hijo!*" and they both chuckled as quietly as they could.

Ezra looked at Joseph and said, "What did he say? I couldn't understand a word of it."

"He said, 'I think it's a good thing she doesn't have to speak Spanish.'"

◆

October came and went in Ogden, Utah, and November rolled in, cold and stormy. The morning after a particularly cold, rainy day, Joseph could see what he thought was snow on the tops of the mountains. He ran to find his father.

"Dad," he yelled, as he looked all over the property for him, "Dad," he yelled again.

Fred poked his head out of the barn with a look of concern and said, "What is it, Joe? Is there an emergency?"

He pointed to the highest mountain he could see. "Look," he said breathlessly. "Is it snow?"

Fred looked at the ten-thousand-foot-high peak overlooking

the Weber Valley and said, "It sure is, Son. That mountain is Ben Lomond Peak."

"I knew it," he said, jumping up and down. "How long before we have snow down here in the valley, Dad?"

"Once it starts dusting the mountain peaks, it won't be long until we see it down here."

"Oh, I can't wait," said the boy. "I can't wait for a snow fight and to build a snowman, and maybe an igloo. It will be so fun. Is it going to get a lot colder than this?"

"We will go downtown tomorrow and get you a warm coat and hat, some good boots and mittens. You are going to need them."

"I guess that means yes. I think it will be worth it to get to play in the snow, though, won't it, Dad?"

"If you like that sort of thing, Joe."

"What is that supposed to mean?" Joe was starting to get a little worried that snow wasn't going to be all that great.

"I'm just teasing you, Son. You will love it."

Henrietta came out of the house. "Fred," she called. "Fred, can you come here a minute?"

He looked at his son, shrugged his shoulders, and raised his hands in defense. "I guess I am the popular one around here today."

"Lucky," said Joseph sarcastically.

Fred walked toward his mother. "How is Father," he asked before Henrietta could say anything.

"He is asking for you and Joseph. He says he hasn't told you any more of the story for some time, and it is starting to worry him."

"All right, Mother, we will go to him right away. Should I be concerned?"

"I don't think so. He's just anxious." She went on. "Fred, I have an idea and want to see what you think. It is your father's birthday in a couple of weeks. Wouldn't it be fun to invite some family members over and have a party for him? Joseph has been wanting to meet some cousins, and this just might be the opportunity for that."

"I think that is a great idea, Mother. I would love to see my brothers and sisters, too."

"I think that this might be his last birthday, Son. It would be fun to make it special." Tears welled up in her eyes and she brushed them away. "I will write some letters to family members and see what they think. Meanwhile, go to him at your earliest convenience."

◆

Fred and Joseph found Ezra sitting up in bed and flipping through the pages of the scrapbook Henrietta had put together with some of the old papers.

"Hello, boys," he said. "It's time to get on with the story so that we can get to the end of it before it's too late. You know, I'll soon be eighty-one, don't you?"

"Yes, we know you are getting up there, Papa."

"You're not gone yet, though, Grandpa. You have too much to tell us."

"Yes, you are right about that, so let's get to it. Where were we last time, Fred? Can you find where we were?"

"Sure can. We were going through the list you made. Do you remember that?"

"Of course I do, Fred. That's what I meant. Where are we on that list?"

"I think we are on *signs of zombies,* Papa."

Joseph stifled a laugh as his father and grandfather went at it again. "Hey, I don't even know what a zombie is. Can one of you tell me?"

"I'll tell you, Joe," said his dad. "Zombies are made-up creatures that can't seem to die. I mean, they are dead, but they are not dead. They walk around in dead bodies and scare people. When living people try to kill them, they can't because they are already dead, except that they are still alive a little bit, but not really. And that is what a zombie is." Fred nodded his head quickly.

"Hmm," said Joseph. "So, what are signs of zombies?"

"Well, I guess if you found a disembodied and rotting hand lying around the house, that would be a sign that a zombie had been there."

"And exactly where did you learn all this?" asked his father.

"Uh, well, I read a book about it a long time ago."

"Hmm," said Ezra. "Have you ever seen signs of zombies, Son?"

"No, I can't say that I have. But then again, somebody made them up."

"Hmm," Ezra and Joseph said at the same time.

"Soooo," said Ezra, drawing out the word. "Let me tell you about the Songs of Zion."

"What?" asked Fred.

"You know, the thing I put on the list in the first place. The Songs of Zion."

"Oh yes, I nearly forgot. Joseph, did you remember that?"

Joseph was trying so hard not to laugh, and finally said, "Uh, I think I do."

"All right, Papa, I am ready to write this story down. Let's hear it."

Ezra became very somber. "I've been looking through this box of papers, wanting to find some things Father wrote that are very spiritual in nature."

"Did you find them, Papa?"

"Yes, I did, Son, and they will be part of what I turn over to you, but you might consider giving them over to the Church."

"I'll consider that, Papa."

Ezra continued. "Right from the start, the Prophet Joseph Smith was in touch with many things needing to be restored. One of these things was the prophecies of Enoch. Do you remember who Enoch was, Son?"

"Yes, of course I do, Father. He was the great-grandfather of Noah. Do you remember learning about him, Joe?"

"The name sounds familiar, but I don't remember much else about him."

"You can read a lot about him and about his revelations in the Pearl of Great Price," Ezra told him.[35] "He was an extremely righteous prophet who taught his people so thoroughly about the will of God that they all tried to live the gospel as perfectly as they could. As a result, God took Enoch and his whole city up into heaven."

"So, what does that have to do with the Songs of Zion?" asked Fred.

"They are a commentary on Enoch. You will have to study them to find out more about that, but right now, I am going to share one of the five he wrote down."

"Wait a minute, Papa. Who is *he*?"

"My father, of course. Who do you think we have been talking about all this time? He wrote five beautiful hymns that he called 'Songs of Zion.' They are based on the teachings of Enoch. One of them was sung at the dedication of the Kirtland Temple, you know. The song was entitled 'Ere Long the Veil Will Rend in Twain' and was sung by the choir just before President Rigdon gave the opening prayer. Here, Fred," he handed him three or four pages from the scrapbook. "You are our resident poet. Please read the last song."

Fred was eager to read these words of his grandfather's. Ever since he found out that President Williams was somewhat of a poet like he was, he felt a closeness to him that he had not experienced before.

He took the pages from his father and looked them over. "There are nine verses, Father. Did the choir sing all of them?"

"I don't know, Son, but they are short verses. Go ahead and read them to us."

Fred began to read:

> "1. *Ere long the veil will rend in twain*
> *The king descend with all his train;*"

"Wait," said Joseph, "he's coming on a train?"

"No," explained Ezra. "That just means everyone and everything that comes with him. Father could have chosen a different word, such as entourage, or company, but it wouldn't have rhymed."

"Ohhh, I see. That makes sense then."

Fred continued:

> "*The earth shall shake with awful fright,*
> *And all creation feel his might.*
>
> "2. *The trump of God, it long shall sound*
> *And raise the nations underground*
> *Throughout the vast domains of heav'n*
> *The voice echoes, the sound is given.*
>
> "3. *Lift up your heads ye saints in peace*
> *The Savior comes for your release*
> *The day of the redeem'd has come*
> *The saints shall all be welcom'd home.*

> *"4. Behold the church, it soars on high*
> *To meet the saints amid the sky*
> *To hail the King in clouds of fire*
> *And strike and tune th'immortal lyre."*

Joseph spoke up again, "Wouldn't an immortal liar be a bad thing? One of the commandments says, 'Thou shalt not lie.'"

"In this case," answered his father, "it is spelled, l-y-r-e, and is a kind of musical instrument, sort of like a harp."

"I see. That's why it says to tune it, kind of like a guitar."

"Yes, that's right." Fred continued:

> *"5. Hosanna now the trump shall sound*
> *Proclaim the joys of heav'n around*
> *When all the saints together join*
> *In songs of love, and all divine.*

> *"6. With Enoch here we all shall meet*
> *And worship at Messiah's feet*
> *Unite our hands and hearts in love*
> *And reign on thrones with Christ above.*

> *"7. The city that was seen of old*
> *Whose walls were jasper, and streets gold*
> *We'll now inherit thron'd in might,*
> *The Father and the Son's delight."*

"Wait, Son." It was Ezra who interrupted this time. "Do you see the connection here to Enoch? 'The city seen of old' is Enoch's city, the one that was taken into heaven, and is supposed to come back to earth at the Savior's second coming."

"Oh yes, I see that now, Father. That's really great how Grandfather did that." He continued reading:

> *"8. Celestial crowns we shall receive*
> *And glories great our God shall give*
> *While loud hosannas we'll proclaim*
> *And sound aloud our Savior's name.*

> *"9. Our hearts and tongues all join'd in one*
> *A loud hosanna to proclaim*
> *While all the heav'ns shall shout again*
> *And all creation say, Amen."*[36]

"I like the way it ends," said Joseph, "but some of the lines don't rhyme exactly."

Fred looked up at his son. "I want you to try writing a poem, Joe. Especially in a long one like this, you will find that getting all the words to rhyme exactly and still getting the idea across is not as easy as you might think. And please notice that each line of Grandfather's poem has the correct number of syllables. Sometimes he has to leave out a letter in a word to make sure it is read in one syllable rather than two, such as heavens, normally a two-syllable word. He wrote *heav'ns* to make it sound like one. Still, it is quite a feat to be able to write such a beautiful poem with those restrictions."

"I never thought of all that, Dad. Maybe I will try writing one someday."

Ezra shifted in the bed a bit to try to get more comfortable. "A lot of the things that happened over the next year or so are a matter of Church History, and you can read it all there. But I will tell you a little about the things that I saw. What time is it, Son?"

Fred pulled his watch out of his pocket. "It's only 11:00 a.m., Papa. Are you hungry?"

Ezra began to cough, and had quite a spell of it before he could get hold of himself again. After a deep sigh, he looked at Fred and asked, "Now, what did you want to know, Son?"

"I just asked if you were hungry."

"Hungry? You know it is a funny thing, but I haven't thought much about food lately. It seems like my head is full of spun sugar sometimes. Are you hungry?"

"No," laughed Fred. "Just worrying about you."

"I wanted to see if I have time to tell you a few more things before your mother comes in here wanting to feed us. Women are like that, you know. They always want to feed everyone."

"Thank goodness they do, or we men just might starve to death, Papa. What is on your mind right now?"

"My sister, Lovina. I want to tell you about her wedding."

CHAPTER TWENTY-FOUR

KIRTLAND, OHIO 1834

A Wedding and Gifts from Father...
Through Ezra's Eyes

During the latter part of 1834, Father received another mission call. The six men, all in the top leadership of the Church, were to leave on October 16.

"Papa, I don't want you to go!" It was the standard reaction from us children every time he told us he had to leave. He had returned from the grueling journey of Zion's Camp only a few months before, and none of us was prepared to have him gone again so soon.

"How long will you be gone this time?" asked my sister Lucy.

"Lucy love, you know the answer to that question by now, don't you?"

She looked down at her feet and said, "Yes, Papa, until the Lord calls you home again."

"Can I go with you this time, Papa, please, please, please?" I begged.

Swain jumped up beside me and mimicked, "Can I go, Bapa, peas, peas, peas?"

"Now boys, you know I need you here to take care of your mother and sisters. You are my solders for Jesus, remember?"

"I'm almost eleven, Papa. I think I am ready to go with you to preach the gospel."

"I want to go wif you, Bapa. I am ..." he turned to me and asked in a loud whisper, "How many am I, Ezwa?"

"Fifteen," I whispered back.

"Fitteam," he proudly said. "An I'm weely big," he added, standing as tall as he could.

Father gathered both of us to him. "I'll tell you what. If you will be strong and help your mother every day, I will bring you all something from Michigan."

At the mention of the word, my mother looked at him and exclaimed, "Michigan? You're going to Michigan, Freddy? Please tell me you will look for Sarah and find out how she's doing!"

Sarah was Mother's sister, the one she was on her way to visit when she met Father who was piloting the big transport boat down Lake Erie. She had not heard from Sarah for a while and was worried about her.

"That was my first thought when I found out where we were going, my love. Of course, I will look for her."

Mother stood and threw her arms around his neck. "Will you take something to her from me, and a letter, and, and ..."

"I will take whatever you want me to. We are going for the purpose of strengthening the Saints in the area, so I will most likely have time to find her."

Lovina came into the room. "What is all the excitement about?" she asked.

Lucy turned to her sister. "Papa is leaving on a mission to Michigan, and Mother is excited to think that he might see Aunt Sarah."

"Oh," Lovina's eyes widened. "I see. When will you be home?"

"You know, Lovey, he comes home when the Lord calls him home," said Lucy.

"Well, I just hope he calls you back in time for my wedding." Her eyes never left Father.

"Your wedding? I have not heard about this. Did you know about this, Rebecca?"

"I have known that it was likely to happen fairly soon but had not heard a date."

"It will be November 19, Papa, so I hope you are here by then," she sounded a bit deflated.

He went to his firstborn, and put his arms around her, holding her close to his heart. "My beautiful daughter, I will do whatever I can to be here. I promise."

She looked at him and then said with pleading in her voice, "I was hoping you could marry us, Papa."

Father had been a justice of the peace, in addition to everything else he was doing, for some time.

"Lovey, I intend to be here, as long as the Lord approves, which I think he will, but I can't promise you I will be here for the preparations. Let me ask J.C. if he will perform the ceremony. Is that all right?"

His friend J.C. Dowen was a justice of the peace, also.

"And besides, then I can be free to give you away." He held her at arm's length and looked in her eyes. "Are you sure about marrying Burr?"

"Yes, Papa, I am sure. I love him. And he is trying so hard to stay faithful to the Church and the Prophet right now."

"I'm wondering why he has not come to me to ask for your hand."

"He wants to, Papa, but he is afraid you won't approve of him."

He sighed a deep sigh, and said, "If it is truly what you want, I won't stand in the way. I just hope he is sincere and strong enough to overcome all the trials that are bound to be in your future. I just want what's best for you, Lovey."

"I know, Papa. I have faith in Burr. I know he loves me and wants to do what is right."

"Then have him come see me." He gave her another hug. "I can't believe I will have a married daughter in a matter of a few weeks," he said to no one in particular.

Father left on the mission with the other five men: the Prophet Joseph, his brother Hyrum Smith, David Whitmer, Oliver Cowdery, and Roger Orton. While in Michigan, the brethren called and set apart leaders for different callings in the different branches and strengthened them as much as they could. Joseph was able to give the local leaders and members a lot of good instructions, and all the brethren bore testimony of the truthfulness of the restored gospel of Jesus Christ.

It was already getting very cold in Michigan. Father had no warm gloves, so he went looking for a good pair to buy. He found a shop that sold all kinds of knit goods: sweaters, hats, scarves, and beautifully knitted mittens in all sizes, from baby to adult. Suddenly, his four offspring came to mind, and his promise to take them a surprise. He went inside.

"Who knit these superb mittens?" Father asked the shopkeeper.

"My wife spends a great deal of time knitting them for me to sell," he answered. "She is from Norway, which is where she learned to make these patterns from her mother." Each mitten came to a point at the top, like the roof of a little house, and the rest of the mitten was knitted in a beautiful Norwegian pattern.

Father tried a pair on. He was impressed by the intricacy and beauty of the patterns that formed such an amazing fabric.

"How did you meet a young lady from Norway? That seems like a long way away."

"Yes, it is," answered the shopkeeper. "Her family came in contact with missionaries from a new church called the Church of Jesus Christ of Latter-day Saints. They believed what they were taught, joined the Church, and emigrated here to America to be near others of that faith. Have you heard of that church by any chance?"

"Heard of it? I am on a mission myself to the people here in Michigan from that very church. One of my mission companions is none other than the Prophet Joseph Smith himself."

"What? Right here in Michigan? What is your name, brother?"

"I'm Dr. Frederick G. Williams, second counselor to the Prophet. He is not very far from here. I'll bring him to meet you."

"Oh my. Oh my," the shopkeeper kept repeating. "I must go get Solvejg. She will not want to miss this."

Father went to get Joseph and the others to bring them back to the little shop, while the shopkeeper went to get Solvejg, his wife.

◆

When he first saw this couple, Joseph thrust out his hand to the shopkeeper, and shaking it hard, said, "I am Joseph the Prophet. Who do I have the pleasure of meeting?"

"Uh, uh, uh," he stammered.

"He ist Yames Phillips, yoa honah," said Solvejg, answering for her husband in a strong Norwegian accent.

"Oh, please don't call me *your honor*, Sister Phillips. I am just a plain, ordinary man."

"Who just happens to have been chosen to restore the Gospel of Jesus Christ to the earth in its original form," said Hyrum Smith.

Joseph laughed. "I was chosen because of my plainness and lack of education, and I have plenty of that."

"Well," said Father, "Sister Phillips is neither plain nor ordinary. Just look at these magnificent clothing articles she knits." He showed everyone the mittens, sweaters, slippers, and other things that Sister Phillips had made, all in the intricate Norwegian patterns she had learned as a child from her mother in Norway.

A few of the brethren made purchases, and then addressing her directly, Father said, "I need a pair of these mittens for each of my four children, and larger pairs for my wife and myself."

She helped him pick out the right size for each child. He then picked out the best pair for Rebecca. Solvejg wrapped them all up for him, he paid her for the goods, put the ones he had bought for himself on his hands, and put the others in his bag.

"Tank you foa brringing da Prrophet to meet us, Prresident Villiams," she called to my father as he and the other men left.

"My pleasure," he called back as he exited the shop.

The next day, Father set about to find my Aunt Sarah, which turned out not to be too hard of a task. And what a nice surprise she had for him! Sarah joyfully told her brother-in-law that she and her husband, John Clark, had joined the Church of Jesus Christ of Latter-day Saints. When Father gave her the letter Mother had written to her along with the blanket Mother had knitted, she received them with delight. In return, Sarah wrote a happy, cheerful letter back to Mother, full of hope and love that one day they could meet again.

Father returned from his mission on Tuesday, November 18, the day before Lovina's wedding and incidentally, the day after my birthday. I was now officially eleven years old.

"Papa! You made it back in time!" Lovina cried when she saw him come through our front door. She ran and threw her arms around him, and he hugged her back.

"My beautiful little girl is about to be a bride. What is left to do before the big day? Is there something I can help with?"

"Yes, Papa. Walk with me over to the temple site, and let's decide how we should walk up to the front door."

"You're going to be married in the half-finished temple? That doesn't seem like the best choice to me," he said quizzically.

"Not in it, Papa, just on the front steps. I know it isn't finished, but that's where I want to take my vows."

"It's cold out there, Lovey. And what if it rains, or snows, or the wind blows? Any of those things could happen around here tomorrow."

"I know, Papa, but we have prayed about it, and have decided that even if it is cold, we will be all right. And I asked the Lord to hold off with the wind and snow for one more day, and I just know he will."

The two of them walked over to the temple site, and practiced how they would walk up to the steps of the unfinished temple, where Burr Riggs would be waiting to make her his wife.

◆

The day dawned cold, but clear and beautiful. All those who attended wore coats and most of the women and children wrapped themselves in blankets as well. There were two porches on the front of the temple, the one on the right being the chosen side where my sister, Lovina Susan Williams, would become Mrs. Burr Riggs. Father was dressed in his nicest suite of clothing and had a little white mum pinned to his lapel as did Burr, and Lovina carried a small bouquet of white mums. She wore a long white, lacey wedding dress, and was wrapped in a heavy white shawl that Mother had made some time before. She looked for all the world like a snow angel come down from heaven with her dark hair trailing down her back in ringlets. I think Burr thought the same thing, because as he watched her walk up the new concrete path to the temple steps, it was plain to see the love in his eyes. Father looked so proud to have this beautiful daughter on his arm. Then with tears in his eyes, he gave her away. Under the direction of Justice Dowen, she and Burr exchanged their vows, and were pronounced husband and wife. What would life hold for this young couple so full of hope for a happy future?

After the wedding, as Father was changing out of his best suit, he reached into the inside pocket and brought out a letter. "Mother, in all the excitement of the wedding, I forgot to give you this."

"What is it?" She took it out of his hand and after only a moment, recognition came over her, and she tore open the letter her sister Sarah had written and given to Frederick to take home with him.

As her eyes scanned down the page, suddenly her hand flew to her mouth as she cried, "She's joined the Church. She and John have joined the Church! Oh Frederick, what happy news you bring me! Thank you so much."

She jumped around unable to hide her joy at hearing that her sister had accepted the Gospel of Jesus Christ. "What about the children, Frederick? Have they been baptized?"

He took her hand to calm her. "Yes, they have each been baptized."

"And what about Father? Has my father accepted her or rejected her as he did me? If he has accepted her, maybe there is hope for me."

"I'm sorry to say he has rejected Sarah as he did you, my love, but she is strong and stands with you in defending the truth."

Mother dropped her head but then clutched the letter to her heart and said, "At least I'm not alone anymore. I have my sister on my side."

She looked up at my father with tear-filled eyes. "Thank you, Freddy. I need to go write her back this very minute." She hurried away leaving us all to watch her go.

"Oh! There is one more thing I nearly forgot." Father looked at us with a sly glance. "How did you children behave while I was gone?"

Swain was quick to answer, "We were shodows foe Jesus, Bapa."

We laughed at this innocent boy as he did his very best to report to Father that he had done what he had been asked to do. I had reminded him the night before, after Father had come home, that we had been trying our best to be soldiers for Jesus. Swain looked at me and motioned to me to stand beside him, as he so often did. "We were shodows foe Jesus, huh Ezwa," he said, wanting the reassurance that he had done the right thing.

"Yes, Father, we did our best."

"That is all I can ask, boys. I'm very proud of you." Then looking at my sister, he asked, "And Lucy, how did you do?"

"I tried to do my best, too, Papa. But we miss you so much when you are gone."

"Well then, you might remember that I promised you something from Michigan if you did your best. Everyone, close your eyes."

Mother joined us. "What are you all up to?"

"Mama, close your eyes. Papa has a surprise for us," I said.

There we all stood with our eyes closed and our hands extended in front of us as Father put something in each hand. Finally, he said, "You can open your eyes now."

Mother and Lucy gasped. "How beautiful."

They tried on the Norwegian mittens Father had brought.

I have to admit I was a little disappointed. I was hoping for a toy, or maybe chocolate, or some other rare treat, but as the weather turned colder, I came to appreciate those mittens more than chocolate or a toy. I put mine on and helped Swain put his on, and we all marched around the room, showing off to one another. Lucy was trying to make us believe that hers were the nicest, and despite my mild disappointment, I reassured her that mine were the best.

Swain said, "I wuv dem all. Mama, do you wuv dem all?"

Mother hugged him. "Yes, Son, I agree with you. Every pair is the best."

We held hands with our mittens still on, knelt in family prayer, and Father thanked the Lord for one of the most beautiful days our family had ever had.

CHAPTER TWENTY-FIVE

OGDEN UTAH 1904

Whipped Cream for Lunch

"Doctor Williams!" Henrietta called to Ezra from the next room. "Would you like me to bring your lunch to you or do you want to come to the table?"

"We finished just in the nick of time," said Ezra to Fred and Joseph.

"I will try to come to the table," he yelled back.

His voice had lost its yelling strength, so Joseph ran to tell his grandmother that Ezra was going to come to the table. Ezra had opted to stay in bed a lot lately, and only rarely came to the table or sat in the parlor. When Joseph came back, he and Fred lifted the old doctor into the wheelchair.

Grandfather is getting lighter still.

They had an exceptional meal of Chicken Pie, Henrietta's signature fluffy buttermilk rolls with butter and apricot jam, squash stirred up in a frying pan with onions, mushrooms, and covered in tomato juice. She had made cinnamon scones for dessert, and even topped them with Ezra's favorite, whipped cream.

"Oh, Grandma, that was a delicious meal, but the whipped cream was the best," Joseph told her.

"What did I tell you, Joe? There is nothing quite like whipped cream," said Ezra.

After the meal, they got Ezra settled back down in the bed with the pillows behind his back, and each took his accustomed places near him as they prepared to hear more of his story.

"You know," he said in a low, secretive voice, "Henrietta could not always cook like that. I hate to say it, but if my mother had not been around when we first made it to Salt Lake City, I might have starved to death."

They all laughed a conspiratorial laugh, then Ezra went on. "Mother taught this young girl who had lived a pampered life in Boston how to cook, and many other things. Sometimes I catch my girl's wistful look, as if she wished the old Boston days were back, where everything was done for her. But alas, they are not, nor will they ever be in this life. She had to learn to work, and she has done a great job of it."

"Papa," said Fred, "Are you sure …"

"Now Fred, I know what you are going to say. Yes, I am sure I want to go on with the story. You see this box of papers here?"

That box had been by Ezra's bed for a couple of weeks. In addition to the scrapbook, it contained other books and many loose papers as well. "It holds important things for you to know. To tell you the truth, so much of it makes me sad to read, but I must let you know what they are all about while they are still on my mind."

"Couldn't I just read them later and save you the pain, Papa?"

"I don't think you could make sense out of most of them. That's why I'm eager to put the facts with the stories."

"That's the way I like it, Grandpa. You make it sound so fun."

Ezra heaved a deep and heavy sigh before continuing. "There are some fun parts left to the story, Joe, but much of it …" He swallowed hard and cleared his throat several times before he could continue. "Let's just say, the hardest part is yet to come. That's why I must finish it while I still can."

CHAPTER TWENTY-SIX

KIRTLAND, OHIO 1835–1836

A Temple for Kirtland…
Through Ezra's Eyes

By the end of the year, the interior of the temple was nearly completed. One afternoon the brethren were through with their work at the School of the Prophets earlier than usual. It had been a few weeks since Father had visited it, so he decided to walk up the hill to the temple site to see for himself how the work was progressing. Samuel Rolfe, one of the main carpenters, was just putting all his tools away when Father walked in.

Obviously proud of his work, Carpenter Rolfe wanted to know what Father thought. Luckily, a young man, twenty-five-year-old Truman O. Angell, was out of sight on the second floor. He overheard what happened next and wrote it all down, or I suppose the conversation would have been lost. This is what he recorded:

The work on the Lower Hall was to the point of finishing the stands and pews, and the plastering and painting was complete. About this time, Dr. Frederick G. Williams, one of President Joseph Smith's counselors, came into the Temple. Carpenter Rolfe said, "Doctor, what do you think of the House?"

He answered, "It looks to me like the pattern precisely." He then related the following. "Joseph received the word of the Lord for him to take his two counselors, Williams and Rigdon, and come before the Lord, and He would show them the plan or model of the house to be built. We went upon our knees, called on the Lord, and the building appeared within viewing distance, I being the first to discover it. Then all of us viewed it together. After we had taken a good look at the exterior, the building seemed to come right over us, and the makeup of this hall seems to coincide with what I there saw to a minutia."

Joseph was accordingly enabled to dictate to the mechanics, and his counselors stood as witnesses, and this was strictly necessary in order to satisfy the spirit of unbelief in consequence of the weakness or childishness of the Brethren of those days.[37]

This vision came in fulfillment of a prophecy given to Joseph Smith in which the Lord declared that the manner of construction would be shown to three persons and would not be after the manner of men.

◆

On top of everything else he had to do, Father had been asked to draft the plans for the temple, and so, of course, it meant that much more to him to see it realized. Father was also asked to draft plans for the temples in Far West and Independence, which of course were never built, and for city plots in several locations. Like everything else he did, he proved to be very good at it. But I think the Kirtland Temple gave him the most joy because he was able to watch it take shape.[38]

Meanwhile, the Church had its ups and downs in Missouri. Father had expressed a desire to move there more than once and even went so far as to ask Joseph if that was something he should do.

"Frederick," said the Prophet, "here is what the Lord has to say to you." Father scribed down these words from the Lord through Joseph:

Blessed be Brother Frederick, for he shall never want a friend, and his generation after him shall flourish. The Lord hath appointed him an inheritance upon the land of Zion: yea, and his head shall blossom, and he shall be as an olive branch that is bowed down with fruit.[39]

"So, it looks like you will at some point be living in Missouri, my brother," said the Prophet. "And apparently, you will have a large posterity. What a blessing for you, Frederick."

"Thank you, my dear friend, but now that I know it will come to pass, I'm not sure I want it to. How could I ever leave Kirtland? I have lived most of my life here."

The Prophet answered in a somber voice, "The time will come when we will all move to Missouri, but I don't see it as the happiest of times." Joseph looked down at his shoes for several minutes. Then he looked up at Father. "Perhaps I am wrong."

"I can't imagine you being wrong, Joseph. Maybe none of us should go there then, especially in light of the trouble the Church has already had in Jackson County."

"It is, or will be, the gathering place of Zion, Frederick, we know that from revelation. It just doesn't seem too promising at the moment." After another thoughtful pause, Joseph went on. "Do you think things will change for the better?"

The Prophet was not in the habit of asking opinions from very many people, but he did respect Father's point of view, possibly because Father was older than him, and well educated.

"I think we still have a lot of hardships to go through, as you have reminded us frequently," Father answered. "I wish there was some way we could still build the temple there."

"Perhaps you are right, Frederick. I have this nagging feeling that we should try harder to build the temple in Independence. I can't help feeling that the truth and light we would find in the temple would counteract the darkness and evil that has come over that country."

"That is probably right, but it is economically impossible until we pay off the debt we have encumbered here. We are bankrupt, or nearly so. But perhaps the Lord will send us a way to raise some revenue yet."

"Let's make it a point of business with the Counsel of the Twelve, or at least with those who are in town, at our very next meeting. In the meantime, we have a temple here in Kirtland to dedicate."

Finally, the day came for the dedication of the temple, March 27, 1836. Father was at the temple the entire day. It seemed to me that he had been there all day every day for weeks. It was a beautiful building, with its walls shimmering in the sun from the broken bits of blue glass that had been mixed in with the stucco, and the big, elegant windows. We were all very proud of that building because we knew it was the House of God, and all the Saints in Kirtland had sacrificed so much to build it.

My friends and I did not go to the dedication. Our parents said we could have our choice to go or not because it would be a long ordeal, and the space we would take up was needed for the grown-ups. So, several of us chose to stay home, and subsequently, the Rigdon children said we could all go sit up on the porch roof of their house, something some of us had done a few times when their parents weren't home.

The Rigdons had built a sleeping attic across the top of their house. Many houses in the area had one. It was a low-roofed room the full width of the house, with small windows across the front to let fresh air in. It wasn't a comfortable place for sitting, and we couldn't see much out of the windows, but from it, we could crawl out onto the porch roof. It gave us a perfect view of the Temple, and because the river was close by, it often caught the evening breeze.

The meeting had already been going on for quite a while by the time we got up on the porch roof. We could see everything that was happening at the temple because the Rigdons' house was right across the street from the temple, a little to the southeast as I recall, but we had a straight line of vision to the building.

There was quite the group of us this time. In addition to Swain, Lucy, and I, there were three of the Rigdon children. Eliza Rigdon was fifteen, and a good friend of Lucy's. Her brothers Sidney A. and John Rigdon were fourteen and twelve, the same ages as Lucy and I. Andrew and Daniel Cahoon were also fourteen and twelve. Horace Whitney was twelve like John, Daniel, and I, and as I recall, Sara Ann Whitney was a year younger, only eleven. My little sidekick, William Kimball, going on ten, was the youngest, but he seemed much older for his age, and we all included him whenever we could. Swain was the oldest of all of us, being sixteen at the time, but he was also the smallest. Anyone would think he was only eight or nine.

The whole bunch of us crawled through the windows and onto the porch roof. When Horace Whitney spotted William, he asked, "William, where is your sister Helen? Why didn't she come?"

"She went to the dedication with my mom. I told her she could come here with us, but she said she wanted to stay with Mother," answered William.

"Oh," replied Horace, a little disappointed. "Well, tell her I said hello."[40]

As we were each claiming a place on the roof, John said to his brother, "Sidney A, are you sure Father won't be mad if he finds us up here?"

Sidney A. wiped his hands on his trousers from the grit on the roof. "What's the matter, John? Are you afraid?"

We all laughed as we found places to sit. John was a little put off by our reaction. I guess he was used to his brother's teasing, but John was the thoughtful sort, and it was often hard to tell what he was thinking.

"No, John," said Sidney A. "I don't think Father will mind us sitting up here. I think he knows we've been up here before. Anyway, he has been too busy with getting things ready for the Temple Dedication to worry much about us."

Their sister Eliza said, "Papa said we might see things we've never seen before if we are patient, didn't he, Sidney A.?"

"I don't know about that, but I do know he told the three of us to stay where we could see the temple, and to stay out of trouble."

"Seems like we're in a pretty good place for both of those things," added William, "if we don't fall off the roof."

"Well, I hope it's worth the climb up here," said Daniel Cahoon. He paused, then asked, "Eliza, what kinds of things did your father think we might see?"

"I don't know, Daniel. He just said to be patient and keep our eyes on the temple, and we might see miracles. We've learned to listen to Father when he says things like that. He knows stuff."

"Yeh, our papa is like that, too," I said.

The Cahoons, Whitneys, and William Kimball agreed that their fathers were also saying weird things like that from time to time.

Everyone was quiet as we seemed to be thinking about miracles, and all that had happened to our families since the gospel had been restored.

Finally, Andrew said, "Boy, there sure are a lot of people over there."

Daniel's eyes grew wider and wider. "I hope the temple can hold everyone. It looks like it may burst at the corners. Look at all the people hanging out of the windows."

Lucy put her arm around Swain to keep him safe. "What do you think is going on in there?"

"I don't know, Lucy," answered Eliza. "I guess they're talking about heaven."

"Do you really think so? What would they be saying about heaven?"

"I wonder," I piped in. After another few moments, I continued, "What do you think it's like?"

"What?" William asked.

"Heaven," I returned.

Eliza said dreamily, "I think it must be the most beautiful place on earth."

"Well, if it is *heaven*, it can't be the most beautiful place on *earth*," chided Sydney A.

Sara Ann said, "If I were in charge of heaven, everything would be pink and purple." A faraway look came over her face as she appeared to be lost in her imagination.

"Pink and purple?" said Horace. "Blehch! Why would you choose pink and purple?"

"What's wrong with pink and purple? I like pink and purple," Sara Ann retorted.

Horace said, "Well, I'm not living there if that is what it's like."

"That might be a plus." Sidney A. laughed.

John Rigdon playfully hit his brother on the arm. "Maybe you won't be there either, Sidney A."

Everyone laughed at Sidney A.'s expense. He didn't think it was so funny.

We were silent once again, until Lucy said, "I hope we are all there together someday." She pulled Swain a little closer to her and then continued. "And I wouldn't even mind if it is pink and purple."

"Maybe there isn't really such a place at all. I don't see how we can know such things," said John, and the mood became serious.

"Well, if there is no heaven, where would we go when we die?" said William.

"Maybe we don't go anywhere. Maybe we just *phfft!* disappear." John snapped his fingers.

We stopped talking once again; it seemed we were all thinking about what had just been said.

"It's such a beautiful building," said Lucy, breaking the silence. "It's hard to believe it's finished. Seems like they've been working on it forever."

"Look how it shimmers in the sunlight," added Eliza.

"I wanna see," said Swain, speaking for the first time all evening. He didn't know where to look to see the temple, so Lucy took hold of his face and directed it at the building.

"All you have to do is look right over there, Swainy." She pointed in the direction of the temple. "See? See the temple right there?"

"Ohhhhh," he exclaimed, clapping his hands in delight.

"Oh, Swainy, you make me laugh!" Lucy said as they giggled together.

"I yuv you Woocy," he said, and laid his head against her.

"I love you, too, Swain. Now watch because we might see an angel."

"An angel? Where did you get that idea?" laughed John.

"From Papa," Eliza answered for Lucy. "Don't you remember? I told you that he told us to be patient and keep our eyes on the temple, and we just might see things we've never seen before."

"I didn't know that included angels."

"Well, he told Lucy and me that we might just see angels."

John suddenly sat up straight with a start. "Hey, I didn't know they hired soldiers to guard the temple, did you, Sidney?"

"Where?"

John pointed toward the temple. "Look, up there in the turret!

Can you see the men standing there with … what do they have in their hands? It looks like …"

"Rifles!" Andrew finished his sentence. "It looks like rifles, or some kind of guns!"

"I see them!" gasped Lucy. "I've never seen those men before around here, and …"

"And there is something different about them," I added, "something …"

"Something … heavenly," finished Eliza.

Swain, not wanting to miss out on the excitement, said again, "I wanna see dem."

This time I took hold of his head and pointed it toward the temple. "Look, Swain. They are right there. They have straps across their chests. Horace, is that what it looks like to you?"

Horace seemed unable to believe it, because his eyes were as big as melons, and he couldn't take them off that turret. He said very slowly, "Are … they … real?"

Eliza, also in a daze, said, "Of course they are real. I think."

I asked her, "Do you think they are angels? I mean, when your father said we might see angels, I didn't think he was serious. And I've never seen an angel carrying a gun."

"You've never seen an angel at all, Ezra," Lucy quipped.

From the temple came loud shouts of *Hosanna, hosanna, hosanna, to God and the Lamb.*

Suddenly, I noticed something else strange. "Who are those other people? There, up on the roof of the temple."

Andrew noticed them about the same time I did. "What are they doing up there?" He went toward one of the windows.

"Where do you think you're going?" asked Daniel.

"I'm going to go tell Papa that there are people on the roof. Do you think they are trying to get in the temple? Maybe they want to cause trouble."

"Andrew, don't go!"

He stopped moving toward the window when he heard Lucy's command.

She was staring wide-eyed and talking slowly. "Those aren't people.

This time … they really are angels. Look at them! Look at their feet!"

Andrew gasped when he turned around and saw them again. "Their feet aren't touching the roof! It's like they're …"

"It's like they're floating," Eliza cut in.

Sarah Ann could no longer keep silent. "Look how brightly the lights are shining from the windows. They must've lit a thousand candles in there."

"I hope it doesn't catch on fire," said Horace. "It looks like the roof is on fire right now!"

"It *is* on fire, Horace. Only it is a different kind of fire."

"What do you mean, Eliza?"

"Can't you feel it, Horace? She means it is the Spirit of the Lord," said Lucy.

"I see Jesus," Swain said with a bit of urgency while pointing at the temple.

"I can feel it," I said, ignoring Swain's comment. "William, can you feel it? It makes me want to … well, it makes me want to cry … and I'm not even ashamed."

Sarah Ann said, "I can feel it!" She wiped the tears that were falling onto her cheeks. "Horace, can you feel it?"

Horace, almost unable to talk, put his arm around Sarah Ann and pulled her close. "I feel it, Sister."

Andrew and Daniel were also hugging one another, and the big tough guys could not prevent the tears from running down their cheeks, either.

When I could finally speak again, I asked, "What's that sound?" We all heard the whooshing sound.

"I don't know," answered my sister. "It sounds like the wind, but I don't feel any wind here."

Swain, again pointing at the temple, said, "I see Jesus." We were so caught up in our own amazement that we still did not react to what he said.

The townspeople who were not attending the dedication began to gather outside the temple and were looking up at it in amazement. We could hear their voices murmuring but were too far away to understand what they were saying. They seemed to be seeing what we were seeing and were apparently as moved by it and astonished at it as we were.

Suddenly, we heard the congregation inside the building sing the song, "The Spirit of God Like a Fire is Burning."[41] We all joined in, singing as loud as we could, right along with them. *We'll sing and we'll shout with the armies of heaven. Hosanna, hosanna to God and the Lamb.* Soon the townspeople outside were singing, too. *Let glory to them in the highest be given henceforth and forever, Amen and Amen.* I can't say for sure, but I felt as though my whole being was lifted into the air. It was the most glorious moment of my life.

At the end of the song, all the sounds stopped, and I guessed they were closing the meeting with a prayer, and then people began to exit the building. We all crawled back through the windows and went down the stairs. Lucy and I each held one of Swain's hands and half-carried him so we could go faster. As soon as we were outside, I picked up Swain piggyback style, and with Lucy, we ran to meet our parents at the park bench on the south side of the building where we had been told to meet up with the rest of our family. Mama, Lovina, and Burr were already there waiting for us. Lucy and I started talking at once, trying to tell them all about what we had seen.

"Stop, children, I can only hear you one at a time," Mama said. "Take a deep breath, then Lucy, since you are the oldest, you talk first."

Lucy began pouring out her heart, telling them all of what we had talked about and what we had seen. The three of them were amazed at what we saw and heard. Then they started telling us about what they saw. Lovina told of the wind rushing in and out of the windows with a great whooshing sound. We told her that we had heard that sound, too, and wondered just what it was. Mama said it was the power of the Holy Ghost manifesting itself to us. Burr said he knew Joseph, Oliver, Father Smith, Papa, and others were seeing some kind of vision, but he didn't know what it was.

Finally, Mama said, "All right, Ezra, your turn."

I told them of the Spirit I had felt, and how I wasn't sure if I was still attached to the earth. Mama said she had had that same feeling. It was as if fire had engulfed the building, she said, but it didn't burn up. It was a very good kind of fire, warm and full of love.

Just then, we saw Papa coming toward us. He was kind of staggering and holding his heart. We made room for him on the bench, and as he sat down, he quietly began to tell us his experience. "I—I saw so many things, I—I don't know—I don't know where to—start."

Tears welled up in his eyes, and he began to tremble. "I saw angels," he said. He could no longer hold the tears back, and they spilled out of his eyes. He found it difficult to talk, but he managed to say, "One came and sat right next to me! He was a glorious being of light and love. I—I couldn't talk, I—didn't know what to do but stare—and feel. I felt the most incredible love imaginable."

Swain had made his way onto Papa's lap. He put his hands on each side of my father's face and said, "I saw Jesus."

Papa hugged his broken boy to his chest and rocked him in his arms, he whispered, "I know you did, Swain. I saw him, too!"[42]

They sat there like that for quite a while, as one by one we put our arms around them. We all just hugged and loved and hugged and loved.

We didn't want it to end.

CHAPTER TWENTY-SEVEN

Ogden, Utah 1904

A Birthday Party and Another Poem

"Well, I suppose that is enough for tonight, boys," said Ezra as he wiped the tears from his cheeks.

"Grandpa, that was a beautiful story," said Joseph, shamelessly letting the tears fall. "I just want to hug you right now."

"Come and do it, then, Joe," answered Ezra.

With Joseph hugging him on one side, and Fred hugging him on the other, the scene from Kirtland, Ohio, in March of 1836 was in part replicated.

Joseph did not go right to bed that night. Instead, he asked his grandmother for some paper and a pencil after she had settled Ezra down for the night. He told her he wanted to write to his mother, which was the truth, and he wrote her a long letter about how much he missed her, and everything he had seen and heard in Utah. But he had something else in mind that night as well. He sat at the dining room table until after his father and grandmother had gone to bed, composing something for Ezra's birthday. He wrote:

Today my grandpa's eighty-one.

"What rhymes with one," he thought. "Ton, run, sun, bun, fun. That's it. Fun."

Maybe we'll have a lot of fun.

"That's not that good," he thought, and crossed the lines out.

Today my grandpa's eighty-one.
Maybe we'll have a lot of fun.

He sat and drummed his fingers for a while, then tried again:

Happy Birthday, Grandpa dear,
Cousins are coming from far and near.

"Hmmm, a little better but still not great," he thought as he crossed it out.

Happy Birthday, Grandpa dear,
Cousins are coming from far and near.

Next, he tried,

Can't wait to meet my aunts and uncles.
I hope that no one skins their knuckles.

"Completely stupid!" he thought. "That is painful." And he crossed it out.

Can't wait to meet my aunts and uncles.
I hope that no one skins their knuckles.

Then:

When I came to Utah I didn't know
How much I would come to love you so.

"That's more like it," he thought. He tried for quite a while, but when nothing more would come to him, he went to bed.

"Where have you been, Son?" Joseph jumped when his father's voice came unexpectedly out of the darkened room.

"Dad, I thought you were asleep. You scared me." He changed his clothes in the dark and crawled into the double bed with his father.

"I was just trying to write a poem, like you told me to, Dad. You're right, you know."

"Really? About what?"

"It's not so easy. I have written exactly two whole lines, and I'm not so sure they are very good."

"Perhaps it will be easier tomorrow after a good night's rest. Now go to sleep."

Henrietta had been busy planning Ezra's birthday party for some time. She wrote to all of her children, telling them about the party, and how Joseph was hoping to meet some of his cousins. She asked them to make a special effort to bring their children who were around Joseph's age. All of them lived fairly close by except Hyrum. It would be a houseful, but Joseph could hardly wait to meet so many relatives, all of his living aunts and uncles except Uncle Hyrum who couldn't make it down from Idaho.

And then a miracle happened. On the morning of Ezra's eighty-first birthday, Joseph awoke to a foot of snow. It was the most glorious thing he had ever seen. He ran outside and picked some up. It was cold in his hands, but he didn't care. He threw handfuls of it into the air and watched it fall to the earth in fluffy white snowflakes. He even tried eating it, but the frozen water burned his tongue.

Fred came out of the house. "Don't eat the yellow snow, Son."

"What?" Joseph yelled back.

"I said…" thwunk. Suddenly, Fred had a face full of snow.

"What are you…? Why you little…" Fred chased Joseph all around the yard, pelting him with snow.

Joseph threw snowballs back at him as fast as he could.

Finally, Fred caught Joseph and threw him to the ground. He pinned him down, took a big armful of snow, and stuffed it down Joseph's shirt.

Giggling harder than he ever remembered before, Joseph wiggled out from under his father's grasp, grabbed more snow with his bare hands, and stuffed it down Fred's back.

"No, no, have you no respect for your elders?" Fred tried to catch his breath from the exertion and laughter.

Henrietta came to the door and yelled, "Boys, breakfast is on the table. Hot cakes and sausage. Come before it goes cold."

"We better do as we're told, Son, if we don't want to catch it from my mother. She can get pretty mean," Fred teased.

They both untucked their shirts to let the loose snow fall to the ground.

Fred put his arm around his son's shoulders, and Joseph did likewise to Fred, and the two of them marched in the back door.

Right when they reached the top step, a huge bunch of snow slid off the roof and onto their heads. They looked at each other's impersonations of snowmen, both covered from top to toe in the white stuff, and dissolved into laughter again. Before they dared enter the house, they shook off the snow from their clothing, then hung their coats on hooks in the back entryway and kicked off their shoes.

"Snow is so cold, Dad. I knew it would be cold, but it is freezing!"

"Yes, Joe. Snow is frozen water."

Henrietta came to inspect the two of them before they came into the kitchen.

"Oh, Grandma," said Joseph. "Snow is the greatest invention ever!"

"You think so, do you? Well, wash your face and hands before you come to the table, Joe. And dry your hair."

He did as he was told, surprised to feel the burn of the warm water on his freezing hands and his red, glowing face that sported a runny nose. Then he towel-dried his hair. "Don't forget to blow your nose, Grandson," she called.

He came into the kitchen massaging his cheeks. "They feel stiff, like there isn't much feeling in them."

"Welcome to winter in Utah," said his father. "Next time you go out in it, be sure you have your warm winter clothing on. That's why we bought it for you."

"Can I just play out there all day?"

His grandmother looked at him and put her finger to her lips to quiet him. Then she said, *sotto voce*, "I will need your help all day to get ready for the party tonight, Joe."

"Ohhhh, yessss," he said, drawing the words out in a soft hiss. "I nearly forgot. What do you want me to do?"

"I want you to keep the Doctor occupied whenever he is awake, and Fred, you can please help me set up the tables and chairs and get the turkey in the oven."

Fred looked at Joe. "Looks like you get the easy job, Son."

"I think it will be tough, Dad, but somebody has to do it. What time do you expect them, Grandma?"

"The ones who live close to us should be here about 4:00, and the rest will be here hopefully by 5:00 or 5:30. Here, Joe." Henrietta handed him a plateful of hotcakes, sausages, jam, and butter. "Take this to the Doctor and be sure he eats all of it."

"Yes ma'am," he replied, and marched off to Ezra's room with the food-laden plate.

He found his grandfather just rousing from sleep, but when Ezra saw the plate Joseph had in hand, he was eager to sit up.

"Happy Birthday, Grandfather," said the boy with formality. "Sorry, there is no candle on the hotcakes, but you can blow on them anyway."

He put the tray on the bed, set the food on it, and put several pillows behind his grandfather's back. His father had made this thing for Ezra. It just fit across the Doctor's lap and had legs on it that raised the food up high enough for him to eat comfortably while sitting up in bed. Fred had put a trim around the edge of the tray so that the dishes or glasses would not slide off it.

"I don't want to blow them away, Son. I will, instead, suck them right into my mouth and down the gullet."

"What's a gullet, Grandpa?"

"I guess you might say it is slang for stomach. It basically means I want to eat them."

This is a good sign.

Many days, lately, his grandfather had not wanted to eat much of anything.

Joseph buttered the hotcakes and spread them with the strawberry jam. Then he cut them up into bite sized pieces and cut the sausage up as well. Ezra took a few shaky bites. "It sure tastes good this morning, Grandson."

"It's your birthday. It is supposed to be a perfect day."

He laughed. "I'm too old for perfect days, Joe."

"No, you're not, Grandpa. It will be a perfect eighty-first birthday."

"All right, Joe. We will make it a perfect eighty-first birthday."

"Did you know it snowed last night, Grandpa? When I went out in it, I found that it was clear up to my knees. I had such a great time. My dad came out, and we had a snow fight. It was great. Did you ever have a snow fight with your dad?"

"Yes, many times. As I've told you before, it gets very cold and snowy in Ohio. You know we lived just a mile or two from the great Lake Erie, don't you? The so-called 'lake effect' sometimes gave us peculiar weather. Lakes like that often affect the weather in ways that inlanders don't understand. It makes the snow fall deeper than it might in other places, for example."

"Are we inlanders here, Grandfather?"

"I guess you could say we are. Ogden is a little too far north to get much lake effect from the Great Salt Lake, although we sometimes experience a bad odor when the wind whips up all the rotten stuff from the bottom of the lake. And that lake is only a puddle compared to Lake Erie. Look on a map sometime, and you'll see what I mean."

"Did you like living in Ohio, Grandpa?"

"I did until I was old enough to know what was going on."

"What do you mean by that?"

"Joe, it is a pretty well-known fact that when the Church was first organized, it struggled to stay viable."

"What's viable, Grandpa?"

"There was no money to run the Church."

"I didn't know it took money to run a church, Grandpa."

"It takes money to run any organization, Son. When Joseph Smith finished translating the Book of Mormon, how do you think they got it published? There was no money to do it. The Prophet had been a poor farmer with only a third-grade education. He had no worldly knowledge whatsoever. Do you remember the Book of Mormon story about Nephi and his brothers having to return to Jerusalem to get the brass plates?"

Joseph nodded.

"When the Prophet translated that part right near the first of the book, Emma was acting as scribe. When the story mentioned that the brothers had to wait outside the walls of the city, Joseph turned to Emma and asked, 'Did the city of Jerusalem have walls around it?' From her reading of the Bible, Emma knew that it had, but Joseph had no idea that some cities had walls. I tell you that only to illustrate how little Joseph knew of worldly matters, and to show you how completely Joseph had to rely on God's power to translate that book. At the time, he and Emma were living with her parents because they had no way of paying for a place of their own. How, then, would he ever get the book published?"

"What did he do, Grandpa?"

"First and foremost, he relied on God. He trusted that God would provide a way for the book to be published, since he was the one who wanted it done."

"Oh, I know," said Joseph. "I will go and do the things which the Lord commands, for I know that the Lord gives no commandment unless he prepares a way for the commandment to be fulfilled."

"Yes, Joe. That is about what Nephi said. And that is what Joseph said as well. The Lord sent him Martin Harris, who happened to be willing to sell some of his property to pay for the publication, but even that did not pay for the total cost of printing. So, he borrowed money using the rest of his land as collateral."

"What's collateral, Grandpa?"

"It's something of value that the person who wants to borrow money is willing to put up against the loan, so in case he doesn't or can't pay it back, the lender will take the collateral as payment for the loan."

"You mean they would have taken Martin's farm if they hadn't paid the loan back?" he asked.

"That's exactly what I mean," answered his grandfather. "Martin staked everything he owned on it, Joe, and the book was published. Gratefully, they were able to pay the loan off, so Martin didn't lose his farm, but it wasn't easy. Nothing in those early days was easy."

"When did it start getting easier, Grandpa? It seems easier now."

Joseph was surprised to see tears well up in his grandfather's eyes.

"Perhaps it is somewhat easier now, Joe, but nothing in any of our lives was easy for many long years, with the exception of having the Temple. After it was dedicated, we used the building for everything, which seemed very nice. It was used for Church services, of course, but it also housed the offices of the First Presidency. That is what the Prophet and his two counselors were called, and still are called today, although in those days, Joseph had an assistant president. That was Oliver Cowdery. There are five big rooms on the upper floor of the temple, or at least there were when we lived there, and that is where my friends and I went to school once it was dedicated. The School of the Elders moved there as well. That is what the School of the Prophets came to be called, and anyone could attend, even women. And members continued to learn as much as they could about everything. But the main purpose for the building was so that the Lord had a place where he could come to reveal his will, to commune with his prophet, the counselors, and the Quorum of the Twelve Apostles to give them the instructions they needed to continue the restoration of the Church of Christ on the earth. That's the way Jesus had organized his Church when he was upon the earth, and that's the way he wants it organized now."

Ezra stopped and looked at his grandson for a long moment. "Joseph," he finally said, "I have some hard things to tell you, but before I do, I want to tell you something happy. In June of 1836, Emma Smith gave birth to a healthy baby boy, who she and Joseph named Frederick Granger Williams Smith. What do you think of that?"

"Wow, Grandpa, that is amazing! The Prophet must have really loved your father to give a child his whole big, long name. Did he name a son Oliver Cowdery Smith, or Sidney Rigdon Smith?"

"No, Joe. Father was the only one of their eleven children that the Smiths named after a non-family member."

"It seems funny that my great-granddad would be the only one Joseph would name a son after. Why do you think that was?"

"I can't say for sure, Son, but I believe it was because the Prophet and Frederick had such love, trust, and confidence in each other that they became as close as any brothers could be. Joseph knew that he could ask Frederick to do anything, and Frederick would do it, no matter the cost in time or money, if Father happened to have any money, of course. Do you remember what Christ did at the end of the last supper?"

Joseph thought for a moment, then answered, "Yes, Grandpa, I think I do. Jesus took a basin of water and a towel and washed all the apostles' feet. Is that right?"

"Yes, Joe, that is exactly right. Do you remember why he did it?"

"Uh, not for sure. Didn't he say something like, 'If I wash your feet…' I can't remember the rest."

"Can you see my Bible down there under the bed, Son? Get it please and open it to the book of John."

Joseph found the ancient book, and opened it as instructed. "What chapter, Grandpa?"

"Let's see, I think it is chapter thirteen," said the wizened scriptorian. "Read it, Joe. I think you should start at about verse 4."

Joseph read,

4 He riseth from supper and laid aside his garments; and took a towel and girded himself.

5 After that he poureth water into a basin, and began to wash the disciples' feet, and to wipe them with the towel wherewith he was girded.

"Stop there, Joe. I want you to understand something you may not have known before. Only servants would wash someone else's feet. If someone washed another person's feet, he would be saying, basically, 'Now I'm your servant.'"

"You mean Jesus was saying he was their servant?"

"Skip down to verse, uhhh, the one that starts with 'So after he washed their feet.' Do you see it?"

Joseph ran his finger down the column of Scripture, and when he found the right verse, said, "Yes, Grandpa, verse 12."

"That's the one. Read about four verses there please," he instructed.

12 So after he had washed their feet, and had taken his garments, and was set down again, he said unto them, Know ye what I have done to you?

13 Ye call me Master and Lord: and ye say well; for so I am.

14 If I then, your Lord and Master, have washed your feet; ye also ought to wash one another's feet.

15 For I have given you an example, that ye should do as I have done to you.

Joseph looked up at his grandfather. "So, why did Jesus do that, Grandpa?"

"Why do you think? He was saying, 'I am the Lord of all, and yet I am here to serve you. Now you need to do likewise.'"

"Is that what the Prophet was doing? Serving others?"

"Yes, that is exactly what he was doing. But the thing that is so precious to me is that my father jumped up as soon as Joseph was through, and in turn, washed the feet of the Prophet. Father told me later that he had been moved upon by the Holy Ghost to do it as a token of his fixed determination to be with Joseph in suffering or in rejoicing, in life or in death, and to continually be on his right hand."

Joseph looked directly at his grandfather and said, "That is a great story, Grandpa. Thank you."

When Ezra did not start right up talking again, Joseph said, "Now, what is the hard thing you want to tell me?"

Just then, Fred stuck his head into the room and called for Joseph. "Son, could you come here please?"

The two spoke in low tones outside Ezra's room for a few minutes, then Fred went back into the room with his father. "Mother needs Joe's help with some errands so I told her I would sit with you for a while."

"I'm getting kind of tired anyway, Son, so maybe I'll just take a little nap," he said as he lay back on the bed.

"Then I'll sit by you until you are asleep, Papa." He rearranged the pillows so Ezra could lay down, then took his father's hand and watched him almost immediately fall asleep.

***

For the next few hours, Henrietta directed Fred and Joseph in what she needed them to do. She had a couple of folding tables she asked them to bring up from the cellar, and then they gathered extra chairs from all over the house, as well as a few that were borrowed from the neighbors.

When everything was about ready, Joseph said, "May I be excused for a little while, Grandma? I have something I need to do."

"All right, Joseph, as long as you will come if I call you."

"Of course, Grandma." He quickly retreated to the room that he and his father had made theirs for the last few months.

As 4:00 approached, Henrietta started a routine of going to the front door, opening it, and looking up and down the street. Soon, she saw a buggy coming and ran to tell Fred, "I think the first one is here, Son. Oh, I'm so excited to see them."

But the buggy drove on by.

Henrietta's face fell.

Fred put his hand on her shoulder. "Don't worry, Mother, they will be here soon."

"I know, but it's been so long since I've seen them. I wish they would hurry."

A few minutes later, she opened the front door and again looked in both directions. She saw two more buggies pass by, as well as four or five automobiles. Finally, a buggy pulled into the yard. It was Thomas Budge, the widower of Francis Williams Budge, Henrietta's youngest child who had died at twenty-five years of age. He was accompanied by his two sons, Thomas, sixteen, and Louis, almost fifteen. The boys jumped out of the buggy and ran into the house. They found their grandmother, threw their arms around her, and lifted her right off the ground.

"Boys, put me down this minute," she yelled at them as they laughed with merriment. As she touched down onto the floor, she put her arms around them and gave them both hugs and kisses. "I have someone I want you to meet." She raised her voice, "Joseph! Joseph, come here please!"

"Coming, Grandma." Joseph ran into the room.

"Joseph, I would like you to meet your cousins, Thomas and Louis Budge."

They all shook hands, and Joseph asked them about what kinds of things they liked to do, and they asked him back the same questions. The boys were very close in age to Joseph, and it soon seemed as if they had known each other their entire lives. The three of them went outside to build a snow fort which deteriorated into snowball fights.

Soon, another buggy pulled into the yard. It was Mary and Joseph Gardner and their son Andrew, fifteen. After hugs and kisses,

Henrietta assigned them tasks to do to get things ready for the party. Andrew joined the boys outside in the snow, and suddenly, Joseph knew three cousins.

Fred had not seen his sister Mary for at least fifteen years, so the two of them had much to talk about. After a few minutes, he said, "Mary, come with me to get Papa ready for his party."

When the two of them walked into Ezra's room, he said, "Where have you been, Fred. I am just about starved to death."

"Well, I have brought you something better than supper, Papa. Look who is here." Mary, who had been hiding in back of her brother, suddenly stuck her head out from behind him.

"Is that Mary?" said Ezra. "What are you doing here?"

"I came for your birthday party, Papa," she said as she ran to him and threw her arms around his neck.

"The whole family is coming for your birthday, so Fred and I are going to get you cleaned up."

They proceeded to get their father washed up, shaved, and dressed in the nice clothes that Henrietta had laid out for him.

Mary called to her husband to come help Fred lift Ezra into his wheelchair. They wheeled the man of the hour into the dining room where all the activity was about to take place.

It wasn't long before another buggy pulled in. This time it was Ezra Henry Granger Williams, whom they called Henry so as not to mix him up with his father. He brought his wife Sarah and their three youngest daughters, Annie, nineteen, Sarah, seventeen, and Elizabeth, fifteen. Fred was very glad to see his brother, and soon the three siblings along with Henry's wife, Sarah, and their brothers-in-laws, Thomas Budge and Joseph Gardner, were talking and laughing, and just being happy to be together.

Before long, an automobile pulled into the yard. Who could that be, everyone wondered.

"It has to be the Godfreys," said Mary. And sure enough, Lucy and William Godfrey, with their youngest daughter Minnie, fifteen, got out of the automobile and came into the house.

"When did you get that fancy car?" Henry asked his oldest sibling.

"Oh, we've been saving for it for quite a while," Lucy answered. "Want to go for a ride?"

Henrietta said, "Not before the party. We will be ready to start before long."

For the next several minutes while the women put the finishing touches on the dinner, the men chatted away, telling stories, and catching up on everyone's lives.

Joe Gardner said to his brother-in-law, "Henry, are you still following the baseball games?"

"I am, Joe, I like to follow the Chicago Cubs. What team are you following?"

"I like the Cubs, but the New York Giants are number one in my book," answered Henry. "They won a hundred and six games this year, Joe, and the National League Pennant."

"Well, the Cubs came in a close second with ninety-three wins," defended Joe. "I don't know. There is just something I like about that team."

Ezra, overhearing their conversation, volunteered, "I used to have some friends who loved to play baseball, you know."

"Is that right," said Henry. "Tell us more, Papa."

"Oh yes," he said. "My two friends Sam and George loved to play baseball, and George got to be a pretty good pitcher. Sam got really sick, and when he was dying, George went to see him. George said, 'you know, Sam, we have loved baseball for years, and I just have to know if there is baseball in heaven. When you get there to heaven, will you please come back and let me know?'

"Sam said he would, and then he closed his eyes right then and there and died.

"Two nights later, George woke up in the middle of the night to see Sam standing there in the room. 'Is that really you?' he asked the ghost. 'Yes, George, it is really me. The Good Lord let me come back to give you the news.' 'Oh, that is great, Sam. Let's hear it.' 'Well,' replied Sam, 'there is good news and bad news.' 'All right,' said George. 'Let me hear the good news first. Tell me, is there baseball in heaven?' 'All right,' answered the ghost. 'There is definitely baseball in heaven.' 'Oh yes,' said George. 'That is wonderful news.' 'Now the bad news,' said Sam. 'You're pitching tomorrow night.'"

At that, everyone had a great rolling laugh. When it had died down a little, Ezra went on.

"Did you know I used to be a baker?"

"No, Father," said Fred. "When on earth did you do that?"

"Well, I gave it up because I couldn't make enough dough."

"Ahhhhh," they all groaned.

Then Henry said, "You couldn't rise to the occasion, Papa?"

More groans.

"Maybe you should have quit loafing around," said William Godfrey.

"I tried to roll with it, but I got toasted," answered Ezra.

"Let's face, it, Papa," said Fred, "you're just too crusty."

Lucy, who had recently come into the room, wanted to join in the game, but couldn't think of a good comeback, so she just said, "Let's put some butter on it."

Everyone stopped talking and just looked at her. Then suddenly, everyone burst out laughing at the least funny line of the night.

Sarah, Henry's wife who had been helping Henrietta in the kitchen, walked in just as Lucy delivered her line and said, "Lucy, that makes no sense."

"Oh, is it supposed to make sense?" she asked innocently, at which, everyone laughed again.

Henrietta, who had followed Sarah into the dining room, said, "Speaking of butter and rolls, it's time to get up to the table. Dinner is about to be served."

Soon, the four boys were called into the house. They got out of their wet snow clothes and washed up. The ten grown-ups crowded around the dining room table. The four boys sat at one small table, and the four girls sat around the other one, but the teenagers soon pushed their two tables together so they could get to know one another better.

The Utah cousins had all heard about Joseph, but he knew nothing about them until this day. They were amazed at Joseph's ability to speak Spanish, and made him say everything twice, once in

English and once in Spanish.

And there was so much food! Everyone brought a favorite dish to go with the roasted turkey that Henrietta had prepared. For dessert, there were several different kinds of pies with homemade ice cream that the Godfreys had made in a hand-crank ice cream maker, and which was now packed in ice.

Joseph thought he might actually burst open with food, but it would be a good kind of burst. As he watched all of his relatives interact with one another, he started to miss his mother terribly. When he looked at Thomas and Louis, though, he realized that they were never going to get to see their mother again, not in this life. They never really got to know her before she had passed away, as Louis was not even a month old, and Thomas wasn't much more than a year and a half.

After dinner, the dishes were cleared away, the leaves were taken out of the dining room table, the extra tables were removed, and the room was made to feel as big as possible. The chairs were placed around the room in a sort of lopsided circle.

Fred stood up to get their attention. "Well, Father," he started. "We are all here to honor you on your eighty-first birthday. This is quite a sight to see so many of your progeny in one place."

"Are all these people mine?" asked Ezra, at which everyone laughed. "How many are here? I don't know if I can count that high."

"All of your living children are here except Hyrum, Father," said Fred.

"And eight of your sixty-seven grandchildren," added Lucy.

"Are you sure there are that many? That doesn't seem possible. Mother, are there really that many children?" he asked Henrietta.

"Yes sir, Doctor, there are that many."

"What a blessing!"

"And Father, we are all here because we love you," said Henry.

"I thought it would be a good idea for us to go around the circle and let everyone tell you something that they especially love about you," said Fred.

Everyone spoke at once with words like, "Yes, that is a great idea," and "I have something great to tell," and "this will be easy," etc.

Fred said, "Since I am already standing up here, I will start. Papa, thank you for teaching me how to be a man and how to take care of a family."

Everyone agreed with that, nodding their heads and confirming with one another.

Then Fred said, "Lucy, since you are the oldest, you will be next."

Lucy gave a deep sigh, then stood up and said, "One of the things I like best about you, Father, is that you have always made me feel like I was your favorite."

"No, you can't be his favorite, I am," said more than one person.

William Godfrey said, "I love that you helped create the most perfect wife a man could have," and he put his arm around Lucy and hugged her.

Their daughter Minnie said, "Grandpa, I love you because you brought Grandma and Mother across the plains in safety."

Henry said, "Thank you, Papa, for teaching me how to fix broken things and broken people." Henry wasn't really a doctor, but like his brother Fred, had a gift for healing.

Sarah said, "Thank you, Father, for being such a wonderful grandfather to our children."

Mary said, "Papa, you know how much I love you, and you also know that I am the real favorite in the family. Right?"

At this, Lucy feigned indignance.

Joe Gardner said, "Thank you for the love and trust you have given me to take care of my darlin' Mary." And he put his arm around her shoulders.

Then Thomas Budge, the Scotsman, said, "Aye, Papa, Ye knew that I needed an extree halpin' of yer lovin' when I lost ma Francis, and ye gave it t'me. For that, I will always be lovin' ye."

And so, it went around the whole family. The rest of the grandchildren told of their love for him and thanked him, each in their own way until it was Joseph's turn. He stood up in front of his grandfather, pulled a folded piece of paper out of his pocket, and began to read.

My father is a poet, and he tells me that it's hard
To make the words come out just right and put them on a card.
Today's your birthday, Grandfather, and so I thought I'd say
The words that I am thinking in a very special way.

When I first came to Utah I didn't even know
The many things you'd teach me, and just how I would grow
To love you and respect you for all that you have done,
And just how very proud I am to be Ezra's grandson.

So, thank you for the stories that you've told me day and night,
For laughing and for crying and for teaching me what's right.
I know I'm not so good at poems, but this one thing is true:
I thank my Heavenly Father every day that I have you.

The room fell silent for a few minutes while Joseph walked over to his grandfather and hugged his neck. Ezra patted his shoulder as he hugged back.

Then Aunt Lucy started to clap and say, "That was so nice, Joseph."

Others soon joined in, saying things like, "That is exactly the way I feel, too." And there was more than one tear-filled eye.

When the time came for everyone to leave, each one of the aunts and uncles and cousins said a special goodbye to Ezra, and then to Joseph. He felt as if he were losing his best friends as he said goodbye to Thomas, Louis, Andrew, and all the girls. They had spent the hours getting to know one another, and just when he felt comfortable with them, they were gone.

As soon as everyone had said their good-byes, Fred could see that his father was tired, and asked, "Are you ready for bed, Papa?"

"I am exhausted, Son, but this night was worth every second that we spent together, tired or not. Whose idea was this, anyway?"

"It was Mother's idea. She wanted to make this day especially great for you, Papa. And I agree. How blessed we have all been."

Ezra slept in late the next day. It was already 11:00 when he awoke. Henrietta took his breakfast into him and sat by his side while he ate, helping him butter the toast and cut up the fried eggs and ham.

Fred and Joseph busied themselves by sweeping the floors and the carpet and putting party things away that they didn't get to the night before. As soon as Ezra finished eating, Henrietta came into the kitchen to tell Fred that his father was ready to talk.

"Really, Mother? I thought he would be too tired today," said Fred.

"He said he has some things to teach you and wants to do it now."

So, Fred got the journal and pen out, and called Joseph, who took his seat near Ezra's head.

The old man seemed more serious than usual. "Joe, if I remember correctly, yesterday I told you I had some hard things to tell you. Do you remember? Before the party?"

"Yes, I do, Grandpa. We never quite got to it, did we?" said Joseph.

"Well now it is time to tell you. Have you got the paper and pen, Fred?"

"Yes, Papa, I'm ready to go. What is it you have to tell us?"

"I need to tell you about the Kirtland Safety Society."

"Oh," said Fred. "Is that a scary topic?"

"I don't think *scary* is the right word, not now anyway, but it is important that you know about it. The thing is, I don't think I totally understand it myself. I was just a boy of thirteen when it all went down in 1836 and '37. But I certainly understand some things that happened because of it."

CHAPTER TWENTY-EIGHT

KIRTLAND, OHIO 1836–1837

Broken Bank, Broken Trust, Broken City...
Through Ezra's Eyes

After the temple was dedicated, the Church was insolvent. The temple cost about forty thousand dollars in 1836 dollars, and although a good deal of that was donated by Church members, enough of it fell on the Church leadership to make them wonder what to do.

New converts continued to pour into Kirtland, people who had very little themselves and who were expecting the Church to take care of them. Church leaders had their backs against the wall just trying to find adequate housing and provisions for the newcomers. Many of the new converts went on to Missouri but faced the same problems there. And most of the resident members had already given all they could spare to the building of the temple and had no way to help provide for the influx of converts. My father was one of the few with any wealth at all, and he had already given everything he had, all of his property and many of his belongings, to the Church.

What could be expected to come of this other than what did?

I think it is a hard thing to have the kind of faith that moves mountains. Here was the Church, the restored Church of Jesus Christ, that should have had amongst its members men and women who had unending faith and strength, or so one would think. They were asked to build an expensive building, go on missions that meant leaving their homes and their families without income, care for members who had nothing, take care of the immigrants who daily poured into the city, and do it all without viable means. They were trying hard to do everything the Lord asked of them, but in the end, they were mostly uneducated people of little means with not enough faith to move this mountain before them. On top of all this, the enemies of the Church were growing in power and number. Day by day, they grew angrier and more determined to destroy the Church. It was a messy situation.

Despite these problems, there was a spirit of optimism after the Temple Dedication. The Lord had promised so many great things if we would have the faith to build the temple. Now that it was built and dedicated, surely the Lord was about to pour down these blessings in abundance, we thought.

But things didn't get better immediately. When searching for answers to this difficult problem, the idea came to Joseph and the other leaders to open a bank. If they could get enough people to deposit their money in the bank on one side, they reasoned, they would have enough money to make loans to other people in need on the other side, even including the Church itself. So, Orson Hyde went to the State Legislature in Columbus, the capital of Ohio, requesting approval for a charter for a bank in Kirtland. The State turned down his request and tried to explain to Brother Hyde what a risk he would be taking by opening a bank. The possibility of failure was real. Banks were on the verge of failure all over the State.

However, the Church leaders would not be dissuaded and decided to open their own "bank" that they called the "Kirtland Safety Society Antibanking Company" to make it sound like it wasn't a bank for legal reasons, and Joseph encouraged Church members and others to invest in the Society. Now, when the Prophet counsels you to invest in something, your first reaction would be that it is a safe investment and likely to make you some money. That is what people thought, and so that is what they did. The spirit of optimism grew as many people invested money in the bank, and many others received loans. So many new homes and buildings were being built that it was easy to be hopeful that the days of poverty and adversity were over.

As I understand it, this is how a bank works. It has to rely on enough people wanting to deposit their money in savings accounts and investments long enough to earn interest on it and not draw it out for a while. Then the bank can loan out that money in the savings accounts to others that need to borrow it and who would be paying it back with interest. The bank would make a profit on the difference between the higher interest rate the bank received from those who made payments on the money they borrowed, and the lower interest rate paid to those who invested. It is a delicate balance but usually works just fine. The people who come to the bank wanting to withdraw some or even all of their money would receive it with no problem, as long as not too many people came all at once. And for a while in Kirtland, things worked just like that.

It seems all the members of the Church were borrowing money from the bank, amounts large enough to buy land, or little enough to buy a pair of pants. Everyone, it seemed, was going into debt to the Society, creating a false sense of prosperity. People became greedy, seeing it as a way to improve their standard of living, or to get rich by borrowing money for some scheme or another. Soon, as Brother Warren Cowdery put it in a newspaper article, many members were "guilty of wild speculation and visionary dreams of wealth and worldly grandeur, as if gold and silver were their gods, and houses, farms, and merchandize their only bliss or their passport to it." Kirtland seemed to have become a place of great prosperity, and everyone expected to become rich.

The Church leadership started borrowing money to open stores in hopes of generating a little more income. But then they had to borrow money to purchase goods to stock the stores. That doubled or tripled their debt. These stores and their inventory plus the land that the Church had to buy to build them on, created great debt to the Church.

Now, I'm no banker, and I don't know exactly how it happened, but I did see the fallout from it. People who had borrowed money thinking they would use it to make a lot more in some business or other, were defaulting on their loans. Many people got scared and tried to pull their savings out all at once, and there was not enough money to pay everyone for the money they had put in. Those are the things that caused the trouble. Banks all over the country were experiencing the same kinds of things, but as the State Legislature had feared, it was particularly bad in Ohio. And the worst place in Ohio was Kirtland. Most people, having no cash, had put up their farms as collateral, so when time came to repay the loans and they couldn't make the payments, they lost their land.

And, of course, the enemies of the Church never seemed to sleep. Some people began going all over the area buying up all of the Safety Society banknotes they could find, then later, they went to the Society and demanded the face value of the notes in coin all at once. This one thing was one of the biggest reasons the Society went bankrupt.

One night during this time, Father came home visibly downcast. My mother often waited up for him when he was late, and I sometimes stayed up with her, as I had that particular night.

"What is it, Frederick?" Mother asked.

He heaved a huge sigh, then sat down heavily on the couch in the parlor. "I don't see how all of this will work out," he told her. "The spirit of speculation is rampant in the Church, and faultfinding and dissension are on the rise."

"What can be done about it?"

"That's just it, love. I don't know if anything can be done. People have been borrowing so much money, sometimes for good reasons, but sometimes for investing in some scheme or other. I'm afraid they are all going to start losing a bunch of money, and the Church leadership will have to take the fall."

"Sit down, Freddy, and I'll bring you a nice cup of warm milk. That might help to soothe your nerves."

"Papa," I said as I slid in next to him. "What happened?"

"Everything and nothing, Son. I guess the worst thing is that a lot of our enemies have bought up most of the banknotes we have written. That means they can come to the Society at any time and demand the face value of the notes. We don't have half enough money to cover them all."

"Why did you keep selling them, then?"

"It is the way banks work, Son, and it usually is not a problem. But there are so many people around here who hate us now that they would do anything to destroy us. And maybe they will."

I had never seen my father so down and depressed before and it scared me.

"What did we do to make them hate us? I don't think we are so bad," I reasoned.

"We didn't have to do anything, Son. Throughout history, the forces of good and the forces of evil have always fought. The dark hates the light because it is light, and it does everything it can to put out the light."

"But that makes no sense, Papa. How can the dark hate the light because it is light?" I asked.

"I know, Ezra. It makes no sense to me either. But haven't you noticed that some of the very people who were once so strong in their testimonies of the Gospel of Jesus Christ are now the ones who have turned on it? They can leave the Church, but they can't leave it alone. When the light of the restored gospel of Jesus Christ burst upon the scene when Joseph walked into that grove of trees, everything changed. Do you remember what Moroni told Joseph when he came to tell him about the Book of Mormon?"

"I don't know, Papa. Remind me, please."

"He said, Joseph, God has a work for you to do, and your name will be had for good and evil among all nations, kindreds, and tongues, or that both good and evil shall be spoken of it among all people."

He looked directly at me. "Think of it, Ezra, *all* nations, *all* kindreds, and in *all* languages, people would speak of Joseph Smith, either to believe him or to despise him. So here we are in little ol' Kirtland, Ohio, and guess what. People either love him or hate him. The Saints who have gone on to Missouri have found the same thing there. Because they belong to the Church founded by Joseph Smith, they are either hated or loved by the people in Missouri, and I dare say, there are more that hate them than love them. I suppose we have to expect opposition if we are associated with Joseph the Prophet."

"Do you mean because he is like the light, Papa?"

"Because he has restored the true Gospel of Jesus Christ, which is light and truth, Son. The forces of evil will do anything and everything to prevent the truth from coming to light."

As time went on, everything that Papa was worried about came to pass. The Society lost more and more money every day. People demanded their money back from the Prophet, but he had warned them that if the spirit of speculation and greed overtook them, they would not prosper. And that is exactly what happened. Joseph and the other leaders started to feel that everything they had worked for in restoring the Gospel of Jesus Christ was about to fall apart. The powers of evil were at work trying to overthrow the Church. Enemies without and within the Church worked against it together and then blamed Joseph for everything that happened. Even some of the members of the Quorum of the Twelve had begun to side with the enemy.

It wasn't long until many people left the Church.

As Church leaders sought ways to get the Church out of debt, Joseph felt that his back was against the wall. He had been hearing of people buying land and then selling it for more than they paid for it, and decided this just might be the answer he was looking for. He had to have some money to buy the land, and so even though he was the biggest debtor in the Safety Society, he was willing to borrow more money.

With all this pressure on the Prophet, what I saw happen next was no big surprise to Father, although it shook me to the core. The Prophet himself went to the Safety Society to borrow money to invest in this new idea. He came to Father who was then an officer of the bank, to request another loan, but Father refused him. I happened to be with Father that very day, and I saw Joseph come into the bank and make his demands.

"Frederick, I should like to borrow some money from the bank to invest in some land that we can then sell at a profit. It looks like we could make a lot of money doing this," said the Prophet.

"Joseph, you know I can't authorize money for that kind of speculation," Father replied.

Joseph, quite red in the face, became indignant with Father for not believing in this new financial scheme. "Frederick, I demand that you give me that money."

"Now, Joseph, knowing what I do about banking, it would go

against all the rules and conventions of good practices to loan you the money for that kind of thing, especially when we are so close to bankruptcy."

As Father insinuated that he knew more about the banking business than Joseph did, the Prophet became all the more insistent.

"Frederick," he said, starting to lose his self-control, "you give me that money right now or I will break you of your office as justice of the peace!"

"Then go ahead and do it, sir, but I still cannot give you the money," said Father, raising his voice and showing his anger, something I rarely saw him do.

Other ugly words of condemnation were shouted back and forth at one another until Joseph turned and stomped out of the building. My face must have shown the great shock I was feeling, because Father gently said, "Don't be too surprised to see Joseph upset, Ezra."[43]

"But Papa, he is the Prophet of God, isn't he?" I asked, not able to hide my disappointment and confusion.

"Son," he said, putting his arm around my shoulders, and taking a deep breath to settle himself down. "Let me explain something. First of all, prophets are not perfect, you know that. Let's both stay calm and think about this for a few moments. Adam, the first of all prophets, had a son who murdered his brother. Noah got drunk. Moses could hardly put a sentence together that could be understood. Even the great prophets Abraham, Isaac, and Jacob had serious problems. Abraham's family life was a mess. Isaac tricked his father-in-law into giving him the best of the herds and flocks. Jacob conspired with his mother to trick his father into giving him the choicest blessings and steal the birthright of the priesthood away from his brother.

"Jacob had twelve sons, as you know. Do you remember that those boys tried to murder their younger brother Joseph and would have, if one of them hadn't said, 'Hey, we can make some money off him by selling him as a slave? Then we can lie to Father about what happened.'"

"I know, Papa," I protested, "but this is Joseph Smith. I truly thought he was nearly perfect. But he was so angry with you, and you were angry, too!"

"Yes, we were, Son, we were showing our humanness, weren't we? Something all of us Church leaders have had to learn is that, like many other men, Joseph is quick to anger."

"Are you serious, Papa?"

"Yes, I am, Son,"

"Then how can he be a prophet?"

"For me, this is easy to understand because I have worked so closely with him for the last several years. Joseph is an imperfect man, but when the Spirit of the Lord works through him, he becomes different. It is like he rises above being a mortal as he speaks with authority from God. His demeanor changes, even the tone of his voice changes, and his skin even changes as the light of God shines through him."

"I think I have seen him shine like that, Papa. I never said anything because I thought you might think I was making it up."

"No, Son, you did not make that up. If you pay attention to him, you will find it is very easy to tell when he is speaking as a prophet and when he is acting as a regular everyday man. He doesn't have to warn us when he is speaking for God, nor does he need to tell us when he is not. Today, you saw a man who has the weight of the world on his shoulders. For a few minutes, you saw him lose his temper and become angry with me. That does not change the fact that he is God's chosen Prophet of the Restoration, but it does show that God acts through imperfect men who are trying their hardest to become perfect, just like the rest of us."

"So which Joseph do you see more often, Joseph the Prophet, or Joseph the imperfect man?" I wanted to know.

"The first year or so that I knew him, I would say he spent more time being the imperfect man than the prophet. But now, I would say it is the other way 'round. Every year, I see him progressing toward being more like Christ, as we are all trying to do, but his progress seems faster than most of the rest of us. Joseph was quick to anger today, Son, but he is also quick to forgive and to ask forgiveness. You know, there was only ever one perfect Man, and neither I nor Joseph is that Man. No one who has ever walked this earth has been perfect except our Savior, Jesus Christ. He is our only perfect exemplar, Son, and if you put your total faith in anyone else, whether it's me or Joseph Smith, you will be disappointed because he will one day let you down."

"But you are my hero, Papa. You would never let me down. I want to be just like you," I said as the tears started to sting my eyes.

"I love to hear you say that, Son, but the truth is, I am far from perfect. I wish I were more… Well, I wish I were better, that's all. I wish I were different in many ways."

"In what ways, Papa? I can't imagine you any other way."

Father put his hands in his pockets and looked down at his feet. When he finally spoke, he took a deep breath and said, "What if I could translate and prophesy like Joseph Smith? What if I could give a sermon like Sydney Rigdon? What if I could be a strong leader like Brigham Young? What if I could—"

"I don't want you to be different, Papa," I said, interrupting him. "I love you the way you are."

He hugged me for a long moment, and said in my ear, "Don't you worry for a minute about Joseph Smith."

Then moving me back away from him so he could look into my eyes, he said, "I know that Joseph is a prophet of God. The Lord has taken a man from a poor family and with little education, and no knowledge of how to run a church or a bank or anything else and worked a miracle through him. That is exactly the kind of person God wanted to restore His Church. Then everyone with any knowledge of Joseph would have to say that all he did to restore the gospel had to have been through the power of God because he couldn't have done it any other way. Do you see that?"

I looked at the floor and shrugged. "I guess so."

"Every time I read the Book of Mormon, I see more and more things that would have been impossible for Joseph to know in 1829, or even now. And I have no doubt that more incredible things will surface as time goes by to make us all shake our heads and say, 'How could he have known to include *that*?' There is no way that young man could have written this incredible book," he said, as he motioned to his own copy on the desk. "He is exactly who God needed to bring forth this *marvelous work and a wonder*—unlearned, but incredibly smart and willing to learn and do God's will, no matter what."

I sighed a deep sigh as I tried to take this all in. "Joseph will be back, Son, you wait and see."

We sat down together as Father went on. "You cannot imagine the kind of pressure the Prophet is under. This Society is going to fail, I can feel it coming, and he knows it, too. Everyone will lose all their money, and they will blame him. People who have been so strong in their testimonies are starting to apostatize, some of our closest friends. Some even call Joseph a fallen prophet. He is supposed to be the leader of this people, but it is hard to lead those who are so focused on the things of the world that they forget the things of a better. I would take some of that burden from him right now if I could."

Just then, as Father had predicted, the Prophet Joseph Smith walked into the room, crying like a child as he came to Father and fell to his knees. "Frederick, can you please forgive me?" he begged. "I know I was wrong. I should never have asked for more money, not for the reasons I told you, or any other reason for that matter. You were right."

Father slid to his knees beside him and said, "I will forgive you if you forgive me. I was not very charitable just now in how I talked to you, my dear brother. I let my emotions rule me."

"Will you continue by my side, Frederick? Can we remain friends as we once were?" he pleaded.

"Didn't I promise to be by your side no matter what? I meant it then and I mean it now."

The Prophet threw his arms around Father, and the two of them hugged in reconciliation, renewing their pledges of friendship and their service to God.

Right after that, Joseph Smith withdrew from the bank, told people to stop investing in the Society, and not to accept the Society's banknotes. In his absence, F. G. Williams accepted the appointment of president of the bank in June 1837.

In his own quiet way, Father was able to shoulder some of the load for Joseph. For his work there, Father was paid a total of $36.

But he paid a much heavier price than he ever received. In taking this burden from Joseph, he also took the blame for the failure of the Kirtland Safety Society which went under within a month. People came to him demanding their money, to which, all Father could tell them was "there is no money."

This caused a lot of anger and bitterness among the members themselves, even among some of the Apostles, and a lot of criticism and secret glee from those outside the Church who wanted to see it fail. Some people believed that Father made sure he didn't lose any money personally, but the truth is that he lost everything just like everyone else.

It wasn't too long after the bank failed, at a conference held September 3, 1837, in Kirtland, that three members of the Counsel of the Twelve Apostles, Luke S. Johnson, Lyman E. Johnson, and John F. Boynton, were rejected and disfellowshipped.

These were incredibly hurtful things to all of the remaining leaders, but especially to Joseph Smith. Of the original twelve who Father had helped choose to be Apostles of the Lord Jesus Christ, more than half of them left the church at this time. A couple eventually came back, but most of them never did.

By the end of that year, most members of the Church had left Ohio and moved nearly a thousand miles away to Missouri, including my sister Lovina and her husband, Burr Riggs, who were expecting their first baby, and who had left for Far West at the end of 1836.

"But I don't want to leave Kirtland, Papa," I cried to my father. "I've lived here my whole life, and all my friends are here. Can't we stay?"

"All of your friends are leaving for Missouri, Ezra. There will be nothing left here for us except our enemies. Is that where you want to stay, Son? You will be very lonely if you do."

"Do you want to leave Kirtland, Papa?"

"I don't think any of us wants to leave this town, but we can't go on living like this where no one is safe. It is not good to live in fear and danger all the time."

I heaved a sigh of resignation as he went on. "I know it is not easy to leave a place where we have so many great attachments. The things that have happened here have been miraculous, indeed. And to think of leaving our beautiful temple…"

He put his arm around my shoulders, then continued. "Do you remember in September of 1831, just after I got home from that first mission, that Joseph received a revelation telling me not to sell our land here because *I, the Lord, will retain a stronghold in Kirtland for the space of five years?*"[44]

I turned to look into his face in disbelief. "He told you that, Papa? Heavenly Father talked right to you?"

Father gave a little hint of a laugh, then said, "He sent that message to me through the Prophet, but Father in Heaven confirmed to me the very same message. And he has talked to me many times since. I've found it is always wise to listen and do what he tells me to do. So, I kept that land until I knew Joseph and the Church needed it more than we did. Well, that five years has come and gone, and now it seems that it is time for us to leave."

I pondered all that information for several minutes, then asked, "Do you think Heavenly Father would talk to me sometime, Papa?" I really wanted to know the answer to that question.

"There is no doubt that he will, but you have to learn how to listen. Our Heavenly Father wants to talk to us so much. We are his children, and he has wonderful things to teach us, but too often we don't stop to listen for his voice."

"Can you teach me how, Papa?"

"You know I will."

CHAPTER TWENTY-NINE

OGDEN, UTAH 1904

How to Hear the Lord's Voice

"And so did he teach you, Grandpa?" asked Joseph.

"Of course he did, Joe."

"Well… can you teach me?"

"I would, but maybe you ought to ask your father. I already taught him."

Joseph turned to his father who quickly said, "We'll talk about it tonight when we go to bed."

Later that evening, as they were getting ready to retire, Joseph knew he couldn't put off asking his father about how to hear the voice of the Lord.

"So, how do I do it, Dad?"

"Do what? Oh, you mean how do you hear the Lord's voice, right?"

"Yes, I need to know."

"Of course you do, Son, and I will teach you. I'll start by asking you this. What is a recent book you have read, Joe?"

"Well, last year in school we were told about a great new book called *Call of the Wild*. It's about people up in Alaska where the weather is always cold, and where they had to rely on sled dogs to travel on the frozen snow," Joe told him. "It sounded like something I would like to read, and since we had to read a novel for our English class, I decided I would read that one. I had to put my name on the waiting list at the school library before I could get my hands on it, but when I did, I couldn't stop reading it."

"Tell me about it. Who is the main character?"

"The main character is a dog named Buck."

"Really? And what about the humans in the book?"

"Well, some are good, and some are bad. Some of Buck's owners loved him and took good care of him, and some beat him and sometimes even starved him."

"And does Buck speak? Or is it realistic literature."

"Really, Dad?" He rolled his eyes and laughed. "No, he doesn't talk."

"Then how do you know he is the main character?'

"By what he does."

"And you feel that you really came to know this dog, despite him not speaking one word out loud?"

"Of course, Dad, I knew him very well by the time I was finished with the book. I knew what he liked and how he did things, and what he was likely to do, even where he liked to sleep and what he liked to eat. I just loved that dog." Joseph stopped to study his father's face for a moment or two, then said, "What does this book have to do with hearing God's voice, Dad?"

"Since you learned so much about the dog and the other characters in the book by reading it, where might you turn to learn what God and Jesus are like, how they do things and what they will likely do?"

"Ohhh," said Joseph as understanding dawned on him. "The scriptures!"

"Yes, that is a good place to start if you want to learn to hear the voice of God. You must learn to know him, learn what he is like. Have you been reading the scriptures?"

"Probably not every day like I should, Dad. Sometimes I don't understand them very well."

"Then you are like just about everyone else who has ever tried to read them, right, Son?"

"I suppose so."

"I'll give you some ideas to make it easier. First of all, start with the Book of Mormon. It is the easiest scripture to understand. Second, read the New Testament. It is specifically about the life of Christ and is mostly easy to understand."

"All right, Dad, I think I can handle that. But will I hear his voice in the scriptures?"

"Like the dog in the story you read, you will come to know God by all those same things. Every new thing you learn about God and his Son Jesus Christ makes it easier for us to hear and recognize their voices," he explained. "But there is more for you to do. You and I have prayed together just about every night since we have been here in Ogden, right?"

"Yes."

"How many times have you stopped to listen for an answer? We tend to thank God for our blessings and ask his further blessings on those we love and who desperately need the blessings, and those are good prayers, Son. But why do we ask things when we do not wait for the answer?"

"I guess I never thought of that."

"Give it a try for a week, Joe, and then let's talk about whether you have heard God's voice. At the end of your prayer, wait and listen, and see if he answers you. Are you willing to do that?"

"I will, Dad. But ..."

"But what?"

"But what if he says something to me that scares me? Or something I don't want to hear?"

"I think I can safely promise that he won't scare you. That isn't God's style, if you know what I mean. Some people might be afraid of him, and maybe for good reason, but I don't think he will speak in answer to your prayers by scaring you. You may never try it again if he does, and that is definitely not what he wants."

"Oh. I guess that makes sense."

"As far as him saying something you don't want to hear, well, you just have to learn to have faith that what he tells you is best for you, even if you don't want to do it. Do you think Jesus wanted to be crucified and to suffer for what we do?"

"I'm pretty sure he didn't, Dad. Who would want to do that?"

"Exactly. He even prayed that Father in Heaven would not make him do it, while he was in the Garden of Gethsemane. Do you remember that?"

"Sort of."

"These are the kinds of things you need to read and know about if you really want to know God and Jesus Christ because I don't think they are going to want to talk to you too much if you don't put forth the effort to know them. After Jesus asked his father to take this horrible task away from him, he said, 'but I will do your will, Father, not mine, no matter how hard it is.' That is what we need to do as well."

"I guess it depends on how badly I want to hear their voices, right, Dad?"

"I would say so. Now, let's go to sleep, and we can talk about this again in a few days."

As they snuggled down in the comforter that covered their bed, Joseph said, "Thanks, Dad."

"You're welcome, Son. I love you."

"I love you, too." Joseph was silent for a few moments, then said. "Dad."

"Yes, Son?"

"Thank you for bringing me with you to Utah."

"I'm glad you came."

❖

Despite the sadness the rehashing of these memories of Ezra's young life seemed to create in him, the very next day he looked as if he were eager to finish the story.

"It's time to tell you about Far West," he said to Fred and Joseph as they took their accustomed places beside him.

"We're ready, Granddad. Let's do it."

CHAPTER THIRTY

FAR WEST MISSOURI 1837

A Hard Journey West and Broken Hearts...
Through Ezra's Eyes

Far West was in a rather isolated place in northern Missouri where no one seemed to care if the Saints lived, even though the members of the Church had been run off their lands in nearby Jackson County. When the first company of Saints got there in 1836, it was nothing but a vast, empty piece of real estate. But soon, as more Saints came west, it became a bustling city with houses and cabins going up everywhere, crops being planted, stores being opened, and a temple being planned.

Our family left for Far West in the fall of 1837 after packing what belongings we could and sending everything else on ahead in a teamster's wagon. We headed for the Ohio River, some ninety miles away from Kirtland. It was hard to leave that place, the only place I could remember living, our home, many of our possessions, our friends, and of course, our beautiful temple.

Father did not leave with us because he had to be in court over lawsuits filed against him and others regarding the Kirtland Safety Society. So many people were very angry over that whole affair, and inevitably, Father took the blame. So, we left without him. He made sure we would be well taken care of, though, purchasing our fares beforehand as much as possible, and making sure Mother knew exactly where to go and what to do at every step of the way.

"Ezra," Father said to me as we were about to leave. "You are the head of this family during this journey. Many men have had to take on the responsibility of caring for their families when they were your age, and now you must take care of your mother, sister, and brother. Then give me an accounting of what you did when we are all in Far West together. You can do it, I know."

"I will do it, Father." I wanted to cry, but I was able to control my emotions now that I was fourteen, or nearly so. I was determined to make him proud of me.

As we traveled along in our little buggy, I thought about the day Lovina and Burr had left nearly a year before, and how all of our friends were invited over to see them off. Father gave them each a blessing before they left, and Joseph Smith, who was there with us, told the Riggses that he could see them in his mind's eye having a little accident before making it to Far West in which the wagon would tip over, but not to worry. Everything would be all right, but to please be careful. I wondered if Lovey had had a hard time giving birth, and whether the baby was a boy or a girl. That baby might be six months old by now. We had not heard from her for several months, although Mother had written to her at least once a week. She did not understand why Lovina didn't write back.

I thought about Father and wondered how he would feel when he was able to leave Kirtland for the last time. He must have felt sad about how things had turned out. I'm sure he was embarrassed and hurt that people blamed him for things he did not do. One lesson he had learned in a hard way was that people do not like their money tampered with, and when they end up losing even a part of it, let alone all of it, they look for someone to blame. He just happened to be in the wrong place at the wrong time, I guess. But these were his neighbors and friends, the people that he had served and loved so deeply, who no longer had confidence in him to whom integrity was so important. And now he had to be in court, trying to justify what everyone else had done. I prayed that everything would work out for the best, but I had an uneasy feeling in my stomach.

I think he must have also been brokenhearted about losing so many of his close friends to apostasy. He worked with those men every day in the leadership of the Church, and with the Spirit of the

Lord in attendance. They were all truly as close as brothers, so to lose them was almost like a death in the family.

I looked over at Swain who seemed very uncomfortable. He looked a little pale to me. "How are you doing, Swain?" I asked my brother.

"My beowie is gwaowing, Ezwa. I'm hungwee. I want to go home."

"I know, buddy, but we are going to a new home now." I was trying to be as happy about the move as I could be.

"Wio Bapa be dere?"

Mama cradled him to her. "He'll be coming soon, sweet boy."

Father had hired a driver for our buggy, and the four of us were squashed into a seat that was built for three. Mama held Swain on her lap and supported him as he leaned against her. She rubbed his head and back and tried to make an uncomfortable situation tolerable for him. Swain did not take well to new situations, and I could see he was not the least bit happy about this trip. Most of the time, he stretched his legs out over Lucy's lap and onto mine. Lucy, uncomfortable herself, rubbed the weariness out of them as much as she could. She was like a little second mother to Swain. We had all learned to make accommodations for him and to put his needs first. But like Swain, I thought that road would never end. The ride was bumpy and hot during the day, and bumpy and cold in the mornings and evenings.

"We will get something to eat very soon," Mama promised Swain. He closed his eyes and silently cried himself to sleep.

Once we got to the Ohio River, we traveled most of the rest of the way by water which was great when our accommodations included a room of our own. But a few times we had to go some distance on a packet which meant we had no private room, or anything else for that matter, no bed except the bare planks of the deck, no bathroom facilities, and no food, except what we could bring for ourselves. Swain did not like his schedule disrupted, and he really did not like it when the boat hit a big wave and threw us all over the place.

He got very seasick and had to "cast his accounts to the fishes," as Henrietta is fond of saying.

When we finally arrived in Far West, Burr Riggs met us at the river and then drove us to their place where we would stay until we could figure out something else.

"How is the baby," Mother asked before anyone else could say anything.

"We lost the baby, Mother Williams," he said with great sadness in his voice. "We named him Frederick Burr and buried him in the cemetery here. I dug his grave myself, and we had nothing to put for a marker except a slab of wood."

"Oh no." Mother's hands flew to her face and tears leaked through her fingers. Her heart had to be breaking to have lost her first grandson without ever having seen him.

She composed herself, and after a lengthy silence, she asked, "How is Lovina?"

"You will know in about two minutes," said Burr. We pulled up to a rather crudely made house.

"Here is our little cabin." Mother jumped out of the buggy, leaving Swain with Lucy, and she ran to see her other daughter.

The door flew open, and Lovina ran out onto the porch. "Mama!" cried Lovey. "I've missed you so much."

The two of them hugged for what seemed like forever.

"I lost the baby, Mama."

Mama nodded and pulled her daughter closer. She and Mama wept together for several minutes until Mama was finally able to speak.

"Burr told us, dear girl. I am so very, very sorry."

"He didn't weather the journey very well, Mama, and he came early," she said through her tears. "We had a little accident, just as the Prophet said we would, and although both Burr and I came through it, and the horses were not hurt, it is what brought little Frederick too early. He was so tiny. And… I'm sorry, Mama, that I didn't write back right away. I knew you would be as brokenhearted as we were, and I just couldn't bring myself to burden you with that pain on top of everything else."

She stifled a little sob. "It will be all right, though. More babies will come."

She was actually able to smile a little when she said that to Mother, and we soon learned why. She was expecting again.

The next day we found the land that Father had purchased. We were surprised to find that Burr had arranged for some men to start digging out a place for a foundation for a little house. It was rather far away from everything, but that was all right. Some of our Kirtland friends were fairly close by.

Meanwhile, Father was in court in Ohio once again over the Kirtland Safety Society. He had had to go to court several times over the last few months as he and a few others were being sued for thousands of dollars by a man named Samuel D. Rounds, who was not a member of the Church. Of course, Father didn't have that kind of money, nor did the others, and he believed that Mr. Rounds was not only trying to create a windfall for himself from the misfortune of others, but he was also trying to punish Father simply for being associated with the Society. Right before we were to leave for Missouri, he and others were summoned to court again, but the judge could soon see that Mr. Rounds did not have a case against them, and they were all free to go.

But just as Father was ready to leave Ohio to join us in Far West, he was arrested in Willoughby, a nearby community to Kirtland, on what he called "a frivolous and vexations process." He sent for help to a friend of his, Sylvester Stoddard, who Father knew was still in Kirtland. Brother Stoddard came as soon as he got the message, and told what happened next:

I found Dr. Williams in the custody of an officer named Cranston. He was about to have his trial before Esquire Bates that evening at candlelight. I wisely took the doctor's horse and buggy away from the jail and into the neighboring county so it could not be taken possession of by the court. Then I went back to the jail and told Dr. Williams that I would let him borrow one of my horses which was much faster than a horse and buggy would be, and that I would hold it for him across the street. I had noticed that the key to the courtroom was inserted into the lock on the outside of the door, so I sat down next to that door. As Cranston and Dr. Williams were walking towards the door of the courtroom, I could hear Cranston bragging to the judge about how he had never lost a prisoner. The lamplighters were just starting to light the candles, so it was still quite dark inside. I opened the door and let Dr. Williams slip out, unseen by Cranston. I quickly shut and locked the door and threw the key several feet away. Those who were inside started yelling, "open this door, open this door."

I directed Dr. Williams to my waiting horse, which he mounted and rode away as fast as he could, while I casually and quietly walked down the street toward Kirtland. Cranston finally succeeded in getting out of the courtroom by going through a hatch into a shop below. He caught up with me and slapped me on the shoulder, asking where Dr. Williams had gone. I replied, "I am not his keeper;" whereupon he gave me a second and third slap on the shoulder and demanded of me to inform him. I had been shooting squirrels that day, and had my powder flask in my pocket, which I took out and told him I would let him know where the doctor was, and snapping the spring of my flask at him several times, he ran off. Looking back over his shoulder to see if I was following, he tripped and fell but kept running several rods upon his hands and feet. When he got back to court, he reported that he had narrowly escaped with his life.[45]

Father finally came to Far West about a month later, exhausted from the long trip and worn out from having to be in court for so long. Mother told him about Lovina's baby, but had more to tell him as soon as she got up the courage.

"My love," she said later that night after she had fed us supper and put Swain to bed, "I have more bad news."

"Well, that won't be anything different, then, will it? It seems like there is bad news every way we turn. Let's have it; what is it?"

"There was a conference held here about a month ago. Everyone was asked to sustain the First Presidency and the Quorum of the Twelve, and ..." she had to stop and take a deep breath. "They dropped you from the presidency." She burst into tears and hung her head, sobbing.

Father sat in stunned silence for several minutes, then taking a deep breath, said, "Well, I can't say I am surprised. I know how everyone has been feeling about me since the Safety Society mess."

"But, Frederick, they had just sustained you in Kirtland in

September. What could change in two months?"

"I don't know, Rebecca, but I will try to find out. Do you know where Joseph is staying?"

"Yes, he is staying with the Kimballs until he can leave for Kirtland to get Emma and the children."

"Do you know where that is, Ezra?" he asked me, and of course I did because William Kimball and I were very good friends.

He picked up his hat and motioned for me to go with him.

For a long time, he didn't say anything, and neither did I. He could have easily found the Kimballs' house by following my simple directions, but I think he wanted me with him because he felt that he had just lost all of his friends, and knew that if I were there, he would at least have someone on his side.

"Oh, Frederick, it is so nice to see you. When did you get into town?" asked Sister Kimball as she invited us in. The Prophet gave a start as he walked into the room and saw Father standing there, hat in hand.

"Hello, friend," he said, holding out his hand to Father.

"Am I?" asked Father. "Can you explain to me what happened?"

Joseph heaved a huge sigh. "Sit down, Frederick, and I will try to." He pulled out a chair for Father to sit on, and one for me as well. "When I nominated you at conference to continue as my counsellor, Elder Wight opposed it. He said you had written a letter that said some things that he found objectionable."

"Seriously?" said Father. "What was that? Did you read the letter?"

Joseph hung his head and said, "No, brother. I did not. I just took everyone else's word for it."

"I thought you knew me better than that, Joseph. Who else opposed it?" Father wanted to know.

Again, the Prophet sighed, then said, "Elder Marsh, Elder Emmet, and Elder Grover."

"They hardly know me!" he said.

"A lot of people don't know you, Frederick. You don't stand up for yourself. You are quiet and have a way of staying out of the limelight. Anyone who knew you would have known that letter meant nothing."

"And yet … Did anyone vote in my favor?"

"Yes, Bishop Partridge seconded your nomination and said he had read the letter and saw nothing criminal in it. And David Whitmer also spoke up for you. But Thomas Marsh said some things that seemed to turn everyone's head away, so Sidney got up and nominated my brother Hyrum to take your place."

Father looked down at his hands. "I guess that passed with ease," he said, not looking up. "So let me make sure I have this right. You nominated me, and I was seconded by Bishop Partridge, but no vote was taken." He finally looked up at Joseph. "Sidney nominated Hyrum, and only then was a vote taken. Was Sidney the conference moderator? I thought that would have been the President of the Quorum, who is Thomas Marsh."

"You are right, Frederick. It should have been Thomas," said Joseph. "I have to admit my mind has been miles away, wondering what we are going to do next if we are run out of this town. I fear for my family's safety, and the safety of all of us. Our future is not secure, Frederick." Joseph stopped speaking. He looked down at his hands before continuing, "And then I was put in a bad position." He looked up into Father's face. "Once he was nominated, how could I not vote for my own brother?"

"I see," said Father. "It seems like the odds were pretty much against me."

No one said anything for what seemed like an hour, which made me very uncomfortable. Finally, Father said, "I understand. No one trusts me anymore since the Kirtland Safety Society failure. I have to say I was not surprised when Rebecca told me about this."

I don't think Joseph knew what to say because there was another lengthy pause before he asked, "What will you do, Frederick?"

"What will I do?" Father seemed surprised at the question. "I will do what I have always done, Joseph. I will do my best to help you in any way I can."

"I'm so sorry, Frederick." Father stood, put his hat on, and we left.

I could tell he was hurting, so I put my arms around him from where I sat behind him on the horse and lay my head against his back. I tried to let my love seep into him all the way home.

CHAPTER THIRTY-ONE

Ogden, Utah 1904

Hard Lessons and a Strange Recipe

"What finally happened, Papa?" asked Fred.

"There were a lot of things working against him at the time. First, Father was not in Far West to defend himself when all this happened, so he had no say in the matter at all, nor could he defend himself against the accusations.

"Then, there was a procedural misstep by Sydney Rigdon jumping up and nominating Hyrum that the rest of the leadership did not correct. It was not Sidney's place to do that because he was not the President of the Quorum, but once Hyrum's name came up, it was obvious that everyone would vote for him, right or wrong.

"And then there was the matter of the letter that Father had written. Someone mentioned that it possibly contained negative things against the Church, even though almost no one had read it."

"How is that fair if no one had read the letter or even really knew what it said?" asked Joseph.

"Do you remember the story about the man who had spread some lies about someone, and afterward regretted it?" asked his grandfather. "He went to the leader of the village and said, 'What can I do to receive forgiveness?' The leader said, 'Go and get a feather pillow, rip it open, and spread the feathers all over town.' The man thought, *this is too easy. I will have this done in no time.*

"He completed the task quickly and went back to the village leader to tell him he had done what he had been asked to do. The leader then said, 'Now go gather all the feathers up and you shall be forgiven.' Of course that was an impossible task. Once people hear a lie, gossip, or rumors, it is impossible for them to 'unhear' it. To take it back, or erase it from people's minds, whether it is true or not, is out of the question. And since many people already had a bad taste in their mouths over losing money in the Safety Society, it was easy for them to believe Father had written something bad because they had lost faith in him. I have found that when people lose money, they become preoccupied with the loss, thinking about what they might have done with that money if they still had it. Then they get angry that they no longer have it. Then the person who they blame becomes a bigger and bigger target until they just can't let it go, and the blame turns to something like hatred."

"Yes, I can understand how that could happen," said Fred. "No one likes to be the loser in speculation gone bad, even if it is their own fault. It makes them feel stupid and taken advantage of. They simply can't admit that they themselves are really the ones to blame. I've seen it happen."

"That's right, Son. That is why Joseph was so adamant about people being careful not to get trapped in some money-sucking speculation, even though he dipped his toe into it himself. He knew the Lord would not approve of it, and a lot of people could get hurt, which they did. Just the thought of making a lot of money in an easy way is something many people dream of, especially when they have been working so hard to get ahead but still live in poverty. When it seems that there really is a way to do it, they easily fall for the scheme. I guess it's human nature."

"Maybe it would be better to stay poor," said Joseph.

"Perhaps so, Grandson. Poor and honest is better than rich and dishonest," said Ezra. "A kind of weird thing happened about this time that I find interesting.

The leadership in Kirtland who supported Father wrote to those in Far West, telling them that they would like to have Frederick's position reconsidered, but yet, nothing was ever done about it."

"That doesn't seem fair, either, Grandpa," said Joseph.

"No, it doesn't, but when we look at the whole picture, it might have been a blessing in disguise. There was trouble on every side in Missouri. Perhaps Father was spared a lot of that by being on the outside during this time. For one thing, he was able to work on getting the Church's money out of the Gilbert estate, and for another, he was able to continue with his medical practice, helping to heal many people who needed his help. It would have been hard for him to do those things if he had been in Liberty Jail."

"Yes, Papa," said Fred, "you were going to tell us more about what was going on in Missouri."

Henrietta came through the doorway. "Let's eat lunch before going any further, please."

It was easy to see that Ezra was a little used up, so they were happy to take a break. Fred and Joseph put Ezra into the wheelchair so he could sit up to the table. He seemed to need to be around his family this day.

They had a tasty lunch of boiled beets with melted butter, baked potatoes, buttered biscuits, and beef steaks that some friends had given Henrietta, saying that they had too much meat stored for the winter and would not be able to eat it all before it went bad. Henrietta was glad to get it, and the boys were glad to eat it. She browned it in butter with sautéed mushrooms and onions and seasoned it with garlic and other herbs. Then she fried it until it was perfect.

"Grandma," said Joseph, "what is this red sauce?" Everyone else was spooning it onto the potatoes and meat.

"Here, try it, Joe," his father said and spooned some onto his plate. It was sweet, tangy, and spicy all at once.

"It is delicious!" he exclaimed. "Is it ketchup?" He had heard about ketchup but had never seen nor tasted it.

"No, Joseph," his grandmother said conspiratorially. Then in a low voice near his ear, she said, "It's a secret."

"Oh dear," he said softly. He figured that she was up to something.

"It's chili sauce," she whispered.

"Chili sauce?" he questioned. "No, it's not, Grandma. You are tricking me again, aren't you." It was a statement, not a question. "Who would make sauce out of chilis? Especially when it tastes this good."

"I'm not playing with you this time, Joe. Would you like the recipe to take home to your mother?"

"Yes, I would love that," he said, still wary of what she might have in store.

She pulled what looked to be a recipe card from a cupboard, then after looking both ways as if someone might hear her, she started to read it in a mysterious voice as she crept around him:

> "Fillet of a fenny snake,
> In the caldron boil and bake;
> Eye of newt and toe of frog,
> Wool of bat and tongue of dog,
> Adder's fork and blind-worm's sting,
> Lizard's leg and howlet's wing,
> Cool it with a baboon's blood,
> Then the charm is firm and good."[46]

She gave a little witch-like cackle, and Joseph just looked at her with his mouth open.

Fred rolled his eyes and shook his head. "Oh, Mother," he said, "if you're going to give the boy a recipe, give him the right one. You know we never liked that one when we children were little."

"Oh, all right." She turned the card over and handed it to Joseph. "I copied the recipe for you on the back."

Chili Sauce

½ bushel tomatoes (28 pounds)
2 onions minced
5 ½ cups sugar
1/2 cup salt
2 Tablespoons Ground Cinnamon
1 Tablespoon Ground Cloves
2 teaspoons Allspice
1 teaspoon Nutmeg
½ teaspoon Cayenne Pepper
5 cups cider vinegar
3 tablespoons Paprika

Peel and quarter tomatoes. Cook tomatoes and onions slowly 15 minutes or until soft. Bring to boil. Cook slowly until mixture is reduced – ¾ previous quantity. Stir frequently. Combine sugar, salt and spices – except paprika – stir into tomato puree. Add vinegar. Continue cooking, stirring frequently until of desired thickness. Add paprika during last 5 minutes of cooking. Pour the boiling hot sauce into jars and seal. Makes about 12 pints – 3 chopped sweet red peppers can be added to tomatoes and onions before cooking.[47]

Joseph read through the recipe, then looked up at Henrietta. "Grandma, there are no chilis in this recipe. Is that a mistake?"

"I don't know, Joe. I just know that is the way Mother Williams made it, and we all loved it so much that she gave me the recipe, just like that. It took me a while to learn how to make it without burning it."

Ezra rolled his eyes and then winked at Joseph.

◆

After the dishes were cleared, washed, and put away, Fred took Ezra to his room where he lay down on the bed and fell asleep.

It seemed to Joseph that lately, he never knew when Ezra would want to resume his story. Sometimes he was ready to get back at it after lunch, but sometimes it was days before his grandfather called him and his father to their places at his bedside.

This particular time it was about three weeks before he called for the boys to come to him. It was January by then, and Christmas had come and gone. On Christmas Day, Joseph had been able to see his cousins again, and everyone made merry with food and gifts and love all around. Ezra seemed to enjoy everyone being there, but he didn't say much.

On this cold January day, Fred and Joseph were happy when Ezra, without much preamble, jumped right back into the story. He didn't even ask Fred where they were.

"Today is one of those days when I have to tell you hard things. Life was not easy in Far West, despite our great hopes of a better life there."

CHAPTER THIRTY-TWO

Far West, Missouri 1837–1838

Life in Far West, Sadness and Loss...
Through Ezra's Eyes

After his release from the First Presidency, Father continued with life, putting much more energy into his medical practice, making us think that his dismissal had little or no bearing on his happiness, but somewhere inside me, I knew that was not right. It was December, and very cold, but in spite of that, he went to work finishing our little house, and asked if I would help him.

Of course, I said I would. I was fourteen years old by then and learning how to build a house seemed like fun to me.

We had to work hard and fast to get our little place finished before snowfall, but we did it. It wasn't very big, but after having to crowd in with the Riggses for several weeks, it seemed like a mansion. We made it as cozy as we could, and when we were able to retrieve the things that we had sent on ahead with the teamsters, it started to feel like home.

Meanwhile, the leadership met together daily to plan our future in Far West. There were already signs that the Missourians might not leave us alone, but we did our best to ignore them, and we carried on as if we were going to live there forever. The leadership had announced that we would be building a temple there in the immediate future. For some families who remembered the hardship of the Kirtland Temple, this was not entirely good news, but for others who remembered the disappointment of not being able to build a temple in Jackson County, it was good news, indeed.

The planning went forward, and despite his no longer being in a leadership position, Father seemed to be involved in all the decisions made by those members of the First Presidency and Quorum of the Twelve who were currently in Far West. And he was always happy, or seemed to be, to do Joseph's bidding.

When spring rolled around, we were all very relieved to get outside and move without the constraints of walls around too-small rooms. We had finally come to call Far West, Missouri, our home, and felt far enough away from the Ohio mobs to feel safe. The Missourians were always at the back of our minds, though, as they began giving us veiled threats about running us out of the state. We frequently heard of mischief they had inflicted on other communities, but we tried to pay no attention to them as best we could. At least for now, Far West was being left alone.

But then more trouble started up within the Church. Joseph had not yet returned from his trip to Kirtland to get Emma and the children, and in his absence, the leaders who were there did their best to run things the way they thought Joseph would do it. But in February, Stake President David Whitmer's two counselors, John Whitmer and W. W. Phelps, were tried by the high council for misusing Church funds. They were subsequently removed from their positions and were excommunicated from the Church. And then President David Whitmer, himself, was accused of willfully breaking the Word of Wisdom, among other things, and was released from his position. Thomas B. Marsh and David W. Patten were sustained as acting presidents until Joseph Smith arrived.

He and Emma, who was again expecting, arrived in Missouri in March. Many of the Saints met them as they got off the boat and accompanied them to Far West. Just knowing that the Saints were so happy to see him again lifted Joseph's spirits after all the problems of Kirtland. I doubt he had any idea of what lay ahead for him, or he might have stayed in Ohio.

A lot was picked out for the new temple, and a group of men went to look for four large flat stones that would become the cornerstones. It took about ten men and the strategic placement of ropes to move one of those huge stones, but eventually, each one was unloaded and ready to lay. Despite all our misgivings and fears about being in Missouri and all that implied, the town was alive with excitement at the thought of another temple. Even those who had not initially been in favor of trying to build another temple at this time and in this place, knew that it would mean the Lord would shower down his blessings, and how we needed his blessings. But for some, the blessings would have to wait. Lovina gave birth to a little girl, Emma Rebecca Riggs, who only lived a few days. Burr buried her next to her brother.

Things were still not going well for Papa, either. Algernon Sidney Gilbert, a storekeeper in Independence, had died during the cholera epidemic of Zion's Camp March. The Church had a great deal of money tied up in Gilbert's store, and it fell to my father at the request of the Prophet to figure out how to get that money back. As was his style, Papa worked hard to get it back, but he didn't make a big deal of it. In addition to that, he had to go to Kirtland because of more vexatious charges leveled against him and other members still living there. They were accused of stealing from the very people who were persecuting them. Would these people never leave him alone? Father was nearly a thousand miles away in Missouri and could do them no harm, but they would not let it rest.

"No, Papa, you didn't steal, did you?" I cried to my father before he left once more for Kirtland.

Frederick heaved a big sigh and explained, "Ezra, the hatred and misunderstanding in both Kirtland and Missouri get worse every day. I am sometimes tempted to think we have seen the worst of it, then something happens to prove me wrong. People from Kirtland came to Missouri to get away from persecutions in Ohio while some of the Saints here in Missouri think it might be best if they go back to Kirtland. I have a feeling that false evidence is being planted to incriminate the members of the Church in Kirtland so that those scoundrels can take what property the Saints still retain there, away from them."

Many of the persecutors in Ohio were delighted to see Father return because they knew Church members still there would likely side with them against Father because of the money they had lost in the Safety Society. Honestly, I can't figure the whole thing out myself.

Can I just say it was a big mess? But Father was again arrested and put in jail on frivolous charges, although he was quickly released because of a lack of evidence.

Once he was released from jail, he continued working on the Sidney Gilbert estate. Part of the reason it was taking so long was that Brother Gilbert's estate was mixed together with Newel K. Whitney's properties because the two of them had owned the store together, and since Brother Gilbert was not there to claim what part was his, it fell to Father to figure it out. He had to go to court in Richmond, Missouri, then in Independence, and back to Kirtland. I'm not sure why he had to go back to Kirtland, but he did. Like me, most people had no idea what he was doing. They just knew he was not around, which was especially noticeable when they needed his medical skills.

At a conference held in April, the Prophet called Thomas B. Marsh, David W. Patten, and Brigham Young as the new stake presidency in Missouri. In reviewing the status of the Quorum of the Twelve Apostles, they found that there were only six of the brethren that they could commend as being men of God.[48] These men who were released were men with whom Father had worked closely, and whom he admired and looked up to. It was all very difficult for him to watch. But the worst was yet to come.

About this same time, Oliver Cowdery was charged by the high council for persecuting Church leaders with vexatious lawsuits, and a whole list of other complaints. Both Father and the Prophet were called upon to testify against Oliver, which must have been incredibly hard because those three men were about as close to one another as anyone could be, as I've mentioned before. But they both knew that Oliver was involved in activities that were not in line with Church doctrine, and of course, they had to tell the truth about the situation. I'm sure it was especially hard on the Prophet to have to implicate his closest friend and confidant, the man who had been with him from the very beginning, who had scribed most of the Book of Mormon, who was one of three special witnesses privileged to see the Angel Moroni and touch the very gold plates from which the book was taken, who had experienced many of the same manifestations and miracles as Joseph himself.

I understood that Oliver was always concerned about making money, so when the bank failed, he didn't know how he would ever support a family or make anything of himself, and the temptation to put money and property first is what finally drove him out of the Church. Oliver wrote a letter to the Church leadership saying that the Church did not have the right to dictate how he should conduct his life, and asked that he be excommunicated, to which request the council complied.[49]

Oliver Cowdery's exit from the Church impacted Father perhaps more than it did even the Prophet. You see, Oliver had urged Father to write a statement of facts regarding our Kirtland farm, so he did. It simply said that he had given Joseph a lot of money and other things, including the use of his Kirtland farm, for which Father never took or received any money. He also let the Prophet have oxen, chains, a sled, a wagon, and other things amounting to several hundred dollars. But then in a revelation, the Lord told Church leaders to "give up all notes and demands against each other," which meant that Father never got anything at all for the farm. I don't think Father knew or could even guess that Oliver wanted to use the statement against Joseph Smith, and Father seemed to have forgotten all about it. He gave the farm and other things over to Joseph of his own free will. But others in the community did not forget about it, and Father's name began to be grouped with the dissenters.

More disappointing news came when the high council had to excommunicate David Whitmer, who, like Oliver, was one of the Three Witnesses to the Book of Mormon, on charges of usurping too much authority, breaking the Word of Wisdom, and other things. Martin Harris, the third of the three witnesses who saw the Angel Moroni and the gold plates from which the Book of Mormon was translated, was also excommunicated at this time.[50] The list kept getting longer of seemingly stalwart men who lost their testimonies over worldly things. These excommunications of men of tremendous spiritual strength were hard for everyone, but Joseph felt it most. Father said Joseph knew the Church needed to be cleansed of so many bad practices going on, but it was still painful to watch. It seemed to me that excommunications were becoming as common as baptisms.

Emotions in Far West were creating a roller coaster ride for everyone. Bad things were happening all over town, but great things were happening as well. The brethren had picked a date for the laying of the cornerstones for the new temple, and there was to be a big ceremony when they were laid. We all looked forward to the celebration, something that our little town needed to lift our spirits and pull us together.

The day before the ceremony, Papa had left home early to help the brethren check and double check that everything was prepared for the laying of the cornerstones. A little later that morning, Mama asked me to go get Swain up. He usually didn't sleep in, but there had been a lot of excitement the night before over stories of Missourians mistreating the Saints, disappointment over the departure of Oliver Cowdery, and of course, the upcoming laying of the temple cornerstones. Mother had lost track of the time, mixing up Swain's routine so that he was exhausted before he went to bed later than his usual bedtime.

When I tried to wake him, I couldn't seem to rouse him. "Swain," I said, jostling him, but with no response. "Swainy," I said again. "Wake up or you will miss the big celebration today." I gently shook him, and still no response. He looked gray and was cold to the touch.

"Mama," I screamed, "come here quickly." She knew the moment she saw him that her boy had died. We cried and cried, Mama and I. We held Swain and we held each other. Mama kept saying, "My poor baby, my poor baby boy, oh what will we ever do without you?" as she rocked him back and forth in her arms. She told me to go get Papa, that he was likely at the temple site.

I ran the two miles to the site as fast as I could, and by the time I found Papa, I couldn't breathe. Papa took one look at my tear-stained face and my rapid breathing and asked, "Is it Swain?" All I could do was nod my head. The two of us got on Papa's horse and took off for home. I tried to tell him what had happened that morning, but I'm not sure if anything I said made sense.

This little boy had been the light that kept us going, because despite all our troubles, he was happy and cheerful and always saw the good in everyone. He was so full of love and goodness, that I guess Heavenly Father could not leave him on this wicked earth one more day.

When we got home, Mama was still holding Swain and weeping softly. Papa took him from her, kissed him tenderly, and then laid him out on the table. "Ezra," Mama said, "run over to the Rigdons and get Lucy. She needs to be here with us."

I didn't run. I dragged my feet, not wanting to be the bearer of more bad news. I wanted to run away. I wanted to go back to the times when we were all together and happy. I didn't think I could ever be happy again.

When I broke the news to Lucy, the whole Rigdon family was all over us. President Rigdon came home with us, and after expressing his sorrow over the loss of Swain, offered to give the funeral eulogy. My father readily accepted the offer.

People came from all over town bringing food and wanting to know what they could do to help. Later that evening, we went over to the cemetery and picked out a plot for Swain's final resting place near Lovina's babies. Some of the men in town got together and dug the grave.

The following day, May 13, 1838, rather than being the day the cornerstones would be laid, was Swain's funeral. President Rigdon took the stand. Several people told me later that they settled down in their seats, preparing for a long ordeal. President Rigdon was well-known for his long speeches. He had spoken at the dedication of the Kirtland Temple for two-and-a-half hours. He was a good speaker and could usually hold the congregation's attention for a long time. But this day, for the first time ever that I know of, Sidney Rigdon was at a loss for words.

"My dear brothers and sisters," he began. Then he paused for what seemed like an hour. He kept trying to speak, but the words would not come. Finally, he continued, "We are gathered here today to pay a special kind of tribute to a special kind of person." His voice broke, something unusual for the stoic Mr. Rigdon. Then he pulled it together as he made us all understand just how special my brother was. "We have all been through a trying ordeal, having to move here to Far West from the persecution that beset us in our beloved Kirtland, Ohio. We have had to leave homes, farms, businesses, and of course, our beautiful temple, to come here and start over. It seems wrong somehow that we must start again from nothing to get back to where we were in Kirtland. But here we are, trying to smile through it all as we begin once more. It has been a difficult thing.

"Now, what effect do you think that all of this, the same journey from Kirtland, this starting over in a strange place, has had on Joseph Swain, this young man who could not understand what was happening? He, like many of the rest of us, left behind everything that he knew and was familiar with, but he could not understand why.

"The journey took its toll on his fragile little body, as it did on many of us. The trails were full of rocks and potholes which made the ride very uncomfortable. It was sometimes very hot, and sometimes very cold. We did not eat the food we were accustomed to eating or do the daily tasks we were used to doing. Instead, we were faced with hardships of different kinds.

"It has been a difficult time for all of us, but it has been especially difficult for someone like Swain Williams who had the added hardship of an imperfect body, and a mind that could not comprehend why all of this had to happen. And yet, he knew that his family was with him, and the security of that family was all that mattered to him. We can, brothers and sisters, take a lesson from him." Sidney's voice was gaining strength. "No matter how unfamiliar the territory may be, no matter what the trials are, no matter how we wish things could remain the same, there is one thing that makes everything all right, and that is the presence of our family. Maybe you are thinking, 'but I don't have a family here with me.' Well, my dear brothers and sisters, you are all members of the family of God. Place your faith in Him, as this little man placed his faith in his family. We can always find our security in God's love for us. Let us use this little life of Joseph Swain Williams as a light to our feet in finding the faith that we need to start anew here in Far West. His little body may have been broken by the journey, but his spirit was not.

"We bury him today with heavy hearts, but only for a little while. For shortly, we will rejoice again with him. He will be whole and well and will be able to communicate as he never could here on earth. And what a story he will have to tell! My dearest Brother Frederick," at these words, Sidney had to stop as he stifled a sob. "And my Sister Rebecca," after taking a deep breath, he went on, "of course, you are going to miss his presence because Swain Williams was a person in whom there was no guile. He fairly shone with the Light of Christ. Most of you in attendance today do not know this, because the Williamses are very private people. But with permission from my Brother Frederick, I relate it to you here. At the dedication of the Kirtland temple, Joseph Swain Williams had the privilege of seeing the Savior. He, of all people, saw our Christ! It is true there were others who had this rarefied privilege that day, but why did Jesus Christ choose to reveal himself to Swain? I think I know the answer. It was because Swain was pure before him, and the Savior could not help himself. I know of no person who was ever hurt by Joseph Swain Williams. Quite the opposite, everyone who met him was uplifted by his cheerfulness and love.

"Yes, we will all miss the presence of this remarkably loving person who was given the challenge of inhabiting a broken body and mind. None of us knows the pains he suffered, although many of us were witness to the taunts and jeers of people who were not so kind. Swain Williams was one of those individuals who came to earth not to be tested, but to test us. Yes, of course he had his own struggles, but his bigger mission was to help us see ourselves in him.

"Each of us needs to ask himself these questions: How did I treat this special Child of God? Did I treat him like a brother, or did I look down on him because of his disability? Did I love him despite his problems, or did I join in with those who called him demeaning names, and even threw sticks and rocks at him? Did I act as the Savior would have acted, loving him unconditionally, or did I ignore him, hoping he would just go away?

"One thing I know for sure," Sidney's voice cracked, and he could no longer control his emotions. "One thing I know for sure," he sobbed, "is that he is happy now, whole and safe, waiting for the day that he will be reunited with his earthly family in the Kingdom of God in Heaven. I pray that we may all learn the lessons taught by

Joseph Swain Williams. Whenever you think of him, think of his Christlike love. Think of his desire to make everyone happy. Think of how you should treat others, no matter the circumstances. Every one of us is a child of God. Let us treat each other as such, and surely God will bless us."

Taking a deep breath to give himself a few seconds to regain self-control, he went on. "And now my dear Frederick and Rebecca, Lovina and Burr, Lucy and Ezra, I want you to know how very much I love you, and I think I speak for everyone here. You are stalwarts of the Gospel of Jesus Christ, and people we can all look up to and emulate. I say these things, leaving my blessing upon you all, in the name of Jesus Christ, Amen."

At the end of Sidney's uncharacteristically short sermon, Andrew and Daniel's father, Reynolds Cahoon, stood and talked for a few minutes. He spoke directly to our family, reassuring us of God's love for us, as proven by allowing us to have Swain in our family. He told us that the day would come when we would have the blessed assurance of being able to have him with us forever. And he reminded us of how Swain is now perfect, in a perfect spirit body, able to think and walk and talk normally. When he ended his talk, we tried to sing "Jesus, Lover of My Soul," but everyone was so full of emotions and love for my little big brother that it didn't sound too good. We didn't have an organ, or any other kind of instrumental accompaniment, just our voices. So, when they gave out, like they did this day, we just waited for the closing prayer, which was given by our family's very good friend, Heber C. Kimball.

During the next few weeks, I didn't know what to do with myself. I didn't want to be with my friends, but I didn't want to be alone, either. I continued to stay close to my father and help him in any way I could. Neither one of us had much to say. One night after I had been with Father to treat the ill child of a family across town, he let the horse pull the buggy slowly home. We had to pass by the cemetery on the way to our house. So that evening, Father stopped the buggy, and we got down and stood near Swain's grave. Father put his arms around me, and I lay my head on his chest, and we just let out all our sadness through the tears that came freely from our eyes.

We stood that way for a long time before we got back in the buggy and rode silently and slowly on home.

Out of respect for my father and for Swain himself, the laying of the temple cornerstones was postponed indefinitely. In fact, the ceremony never really happened, not the way it had been planned. The persecutions began to rain down on us to the point that once again, we had to look for a new home.

CHAPTER THIRTY-THREE

OGDEN, UTAH 1905

Shepherd's Pie

Fred stopped writing and looked up at his father. "I can see why this has been hard for you, Papa. You have never told me the details of Swain's death before. It must have been incredibly difficult."

Ezra hung his head and said, "Even after all these years, I long to see his sweet face and watch him try to be just like me. Now, it is I who tries to be just like him. Joe, you once asked me when life became easy. I will just say this. It wasn't 1838, nor 1839, not even 1840. It was not 1841, and especially not 1842, '43, '44, not until … not for a long, long time."

"Well, you have it easy now, Grandpa. You have my father and me to take care of you. Plus, Grandma, of course."

"Yes, Joseph, it makes dying easier, you are right. But it also makes it harder," said Ezra.

Joseph's face went red when he realized that he had made reference to another very difficult time, one that no one wanted to acknowledge.

"Don't worry, Joe, I know my time to go is near, and that's all right. Just think of all the people I am going to get to see, people I haven't seen for a very long time. I am looking forward to that. But I will miss you. And Grandma. And your father, and my other children. Yes, it can't be helped. It is life. We come to earth; we leave earth. It's the way it is."

Joseph couldn't help feeling badly over the mistake, and Ezra's attempt to make it all better just seemed to add to his discomfort.

"Let's change the subject," said Fred. "What else was going on in Missouri that made things so hard."

"I'll tell you, Fred, but right now, I don't think I can go on for a few minutes," said his father.

"Then you don't have to, Papa," Fred replied, caressing his father's hand as he held it gently.

Ezra sighed deeply and said, "I do have to, Son. These are things you and your children must know. In fact, there are lessons here for everyone to learn. Can I rest for a little while before we go on, though?"

"Of course, Papa. Just let us know when you're ready."

Fred helped Ezra lie down in the bed and covered him with the big comforter. It was cold and snowy outside on this January day, so Fred thought the comforter would feel good to his frail father.

When Fred and Joseph left Ezra's room, they found Henrietta fixing lunch. "You boys wash up," she said. "I have made shepherd's pie for lunch."

When Joseph came back into the kitchen, he asked, "What is shepherd's pie, Grandma? I've never heard of it."

"If you were a shepherd out on a hillside in the cold with a bunch of sheep, what warm meal might you make for lunch?"

"Hmmm," he said. "Let me think a minute." After a lengthy pause, he went on. "I guess I would be able to put some vegetables in a pot and cook them over the fire."

"Great idea. Exactly what vegetables would you use?"

"I guess I would use carrots, celery, mushrooms, turnips, and squash. Oh, and potatoes. Those are all vegetables that could be easily carried up the hillside and would keep quite well, right, Grandma?"

"I think you are right on target."

"What kind of meat would you put in it?"

"You could always use shepherds. It is shepherd pie, you know," she laughed at her own absurdity.

"Oh, Grandma, please tell me you haven't turned to cannibalism!"

"Haven't you heard that if you get hungry enough …"

"Mother!" Fred interjected. "I was really looking forward to enjoying this meal but now …"

"Oh, really, Son. You know I didn't mean it."

"Sometimes I wonder," he murmured *sotto voce*.

"What was that?"

"Oh nothing, Mother. Just clearing my throat."

Joseph, turning the topic back to the stew, said, "Well, I would have all those sheep around me. Could I put some mutton in there?"

"I suppose that would work well enough. I would like that better than shepherd."

Joseph and his grandmother laughed again, but Fred just rolled his eyes at the two of them. "It seems a little freakish to cook the very animal you were trying to tend, though, Grandma."

"Yes, I suppose it does, but they were bound to be eaten by someone, so I guess it might as well be you."

"I never thought of it that way."

She dished up three nice bowls full of shepherd's pie and put them on the table. "See what you think of this, Joe."

He looked at the fluffy white mashed potatoes on the top of the soup and suddenly felt his tummy growl. And it smelled so good. "Joe, will you offer a blessing on our food?"

The three Williamses held hands as they bowed their heads, and Joe thanked the Lord for all that they had been given, for the love that his grandparents showed daily to him and his father, and for the delicious food that regularly appeared on the table, the result of Henrietta's careful preparation.

"How was the Doctor today, Fred?" asked Henrietta. "I suppose he is napping now."

"He was worn-out from talking, Mama. He wanted to rest. I tried to tell him that he doesn't have to tell us this part of the story, but he says he does have to."

"Yes, he has told me the same things," she said. "Let's let him rest as long as he wants to before he picks the story up again, though."

"That's fine with me, Mama."

"Oh, Grandma. This shepherd must have really known how to cook. Did you learn this recipe when you were a shepherd?"

They all laughed at the assumption he had made, then she said, "Yes, Joe, I was a shepherd for a while, but I was afraid someone would make pie out of me, so I left that business."

Joseph looked at his father who secretly waggled his finger, indicating that she was pulling his leg once again, and they both burst out laughing. It was all Joseph could do to keep from spraying the pie all over the kitchen.

"Well, don't lose that recipe, Grandma," he said after swallowing the food in his mouth. "This is delicious!" And they laughed again. "It has all the ingredients in it that I guessed, right, Grandma?"

"Yes, even the mutton."

⬩

It was weeks before Ezra once more wanted to talk. February had come and gone, and March was halfway over. Spring was on its way. Ezra had spent a good deal of time resting, but this day, he was rummaging through the old papers and documents left by his father. When Henrietta came into his room, he told her to call the boys; he was ready to go on.

"Oh, Doctor," she said. "Are you sure? There is no big hurry, is there?"

"My dear love. Yes, there is a hurry. I don't know how much longer I'll be here. I keep thinking I see my father at the foot of the bed, beckoning to me. I keep telling him I have to finish his story, and so he leaves, but then he comes back a few days later."

Henrietta picked up his hand, kissed it, and held it to her face. "All right, then, Doctor, I will call the boys. But you know I'm right here if you need me."

"How do you think I make it through these days, my dear? Knowing you are right here, that's how."

She rearranged the pillows behind his back so that he was more comfortable and put the bolster under his knees. As she went to leave, he caught her arm, and she turned around. He just looked at her for several minutes and gave her arm a gentle squeeze.

She leaned over and kissed the top of his head where his silver-white hair still grew quite thick and beautiful, then she called for Fred and Joseph. Once they had assumed their accustomed places, Ezra asked Fred, "Now where were we, Son?"

"We were discussing life in Far West, Missouri, Father."

Ezra heaved a deep, heavy sigh. "Oh yes," he said. "These were not the happiest times of our lives, so have patience with me."

"We will, Grandpa, don't worry," assured Joseph.

"All right then. It was a messy time, and quite frankly, a time I don't think about that often, so I'll do the best I can."

CHAPTER THIRTY-FOUR

ABOUT MISSOURI 1838

All-out War

Ezra got a faraway look in his eye, then he went on to explain. "Inherent with telling you the rest of the story is knowing my father's shortcomings. He had flaws that led to misunderstandings, and I want to point out to you what happened because of them during the troubles in Missouri.

"First of all, he was faithful to Joseph Smith to a fault. That is not to say that they saw everything eye to eye, you already know that. But when Frederick accepted the Gospel of Jesus Christ, he also accepted the fact that Joseph Smith was a true prophet of God. He never forgot that and never denied it. So even after he was no longer in the First Presidency, Father helped Joseph in any way that he could. When Joseph asked him to do whatever he could to get the Church's money out of the Gilbert store, he set about to do just that, no matter what it took. When he was asked to go back to Kirtland and see if there was anything of value left by the Church that could be sold to help out financially, Father did that, too. When Joseph asked him to try to locate a safe place for the Saints to move to from Missouri, he did his best to find one."

"Do you consider that a flaw, Papa? I would consider that to be great strength of character," said Fred.

"Yes, I agree, Son, but remember, your grandfather was a quiet man who kept his business to himself. The problem was that when all these troubles went down in Far West and other parts of Missouri,

Dr. Williams was nowhere to be found. And what would be the natural thing for people to think about that?"

"I suppose they might have thought that he had abandoned the Saints and rode off to find some other place to live," said Joseph.

"Perhaps they thought he had turned on his family as well," added Fred.

"Yes," the old man continued. "I think you are right. Now I'll tell you what was happening in Far West.

"That summer of 1838 after Swain passed away saw relations deteriorate rapidly between the Saints and the Missourians. It started to look like there could be all-out war between us and them. At first, the thoughts of real war were exciting to fourteen-year-old me. I saw myself on horseback, flying through enemy territory, vanquishing the foe, wielding a sword that never missed its target. I defended all the Saints by defeating every enemy and became a true hero.

"Reality was much different.

"When the Saints initially went to settle in northern Missouri, the people already living there welcomed us. We settled in two sparsely populated counties, Daviess and Caldwell, which is where Far West was located, counties that had been designated for the Mormons to inhabit, and as long as we left them alone, they would leave us alone. But when the Saints began to prosper, the Missourians changed their tune. Suddenly, our people were not welcome there or anywhere else in Missouri. You see, with prosperity came power, and the Missouri citizens became jealous and greedy. They desired to take advantage of the improvements we had made in the land. They wanted control of the healthy and beautiful crops we had worked so hard to raise. But the thing that really got them worked up was the fear that the Saints would soon outnumber the original citizens of those counties. The people feared losing political control, and one thing they did not want to lose was the status of Missouri as a slave state. They knew the Latter-day Saints were against slavery, and if we had control of the vote, Missouri would lose that coveted status. Yes, as so often happens with hatred, fear is at the bottom of it, fear and misunderstanding."

"I didn't know Missouri was a slave state, Grandpa. Did you ever have a slave?"

"No, Joe. None of us did. The idea of owning another human being was so foreign to our way of thinking that it just couldn't have happened. That practice is beyond abominable, and it is a stain on our country that it ever existed. Unfortunately, that is not how most of the people in Missouri felt at that time.

"Soon they started trying to find things to hold against us or to incriminate us in any way. Assumptions began to be made that were not based in fact, and lies were told and rumors were started that the citizens wanted to believe. It's a funny thing, but people always hold on to the best, or should I say, the worst rumors. If something is said that people want to believe, or that is shocking, or that proves their point, right or wrong, they will pass it on, even if there is no basis in fact. It's a human cycle as old as history. We all tend to want to be the first one to tell our neighbors some shocking thing. And let's face it: who wants to take the time to research the truth when such lies are so convenient and tantalizing?

"The hatred began to grow, and once it started, it grew at an alarming rate. It came as no big surprise that later that year, the Missourians had decided there was only one thing to do, and that was to drive the Mormons from the state. All of us. False reports about the deluded and malicious Latter-day Saints started to spread everywhere."

"How could anyone believe that you were deluded and malicious, Papa?"

"For one thing, Son, they did not know me personally, or anyone else, for that matter. They didn't want to know us. If they had, they would have had to decide or realize that we were not the people we had been made out to be."

Joseph sighed. "How sad for them."

"On August 6, Election day, our men had to travel thirty-one miles north to Gallatin, a nearby town, to be able to vote, which they felt they must do or give up and move out. When they got there, they found a crowd all riled up by lies that had been told to them about the Saints, things like, the Mormons are horse thieves, liars, and counterfeiters, and they continued to mock our beliefs in the most unrighteous ways imaginable. Some of the men in the crowd were filled with whiskey, so it didn't take much for a fight to break out. It got pretty nasty, and men were seriously injured on both sides.

"Our men, including Joseph Smith, who had come to help straighten things out between us and them, found a justice of the peace who also happened to be a newly elected judge named Adam Black. The judge helped them write an agreement of peace which was signed the next day, preserving each other's rights and 'delivering offenders up to be dealt with according to law and justice.' But what our men didn't know was that Judge Black was also a committed anti-Mormon.

"The Missourians, now our sworn enemies, continued making exaggerated and outlandish claims, saying that Joseph Smith and others had organized an army of five hundred men and had threatened death to all the old settlers and citizens of Daviess County. Judge Black claimed one hundred and fifty-four Mormons had threatened him with death unless he signed the peace agreement that he himself had helped them write just a few days before. We hardly knew what to think, being the object of so many lies. But Joseph, true to his calling as a prophet, stood tall and said, 'There is great excitement at present among the Missourians, who are seeking an occasion against us. They are continually chafing us, and provoking us to anger, if possible, one sign of threatening after another, but we do not fear them, for the Lord God, the Eternal Father, is our God, and Jesus… is our strength and confidence.'"

"Thank goodness for the Prophet," said Joseph. "He must have been the person that kept you going."

"Yes, of course, we were thankful for him and his promising words. But we soon had a new problem to face. Our people in Far West and other places were starving, including my own family. The mobs had cut off our ability to move in and out of the town, so we had no way to buy the goods that we needed. They also took much of the food that we had worked so hard to store for the winter, and we soon found ourselves in a predicament. We didn't know what else to do but to ride to Gallatin to rob a store, fulfilling the complaint against us of being thieves, but it was do that or starve to death. I think we saw it as payment for all the food and other things they had taken from us.

"We took as much food as we could from the Gallatin store and off we rode to Adam-ondi-Ahman, where many people from surrounding communities had fled, and where the starvation was the worst. Soon it became all-out war."

"*We*, Papa?" asked Fred. "Were you in on it?

"Yes, I was, Son. I was not yet fifteen, but I could not see my family go hungry one more day, and Father, who was still away on business on behalf of the Prophet, had told me that I had to stand up and be the man. So, I rode with those determined to bring back food for everyone.

"Which brings up point number two: Father, in the deepest parts of his soul, was a healer, a doctor, a person sworn to relieve the suffering of others. As such, he was not of a mind to refuse anyone medical help on the grounds of political persuasion. In other words, he was as likely to treat Oliver Cowdery or Judge Black as he was to treat Joseph Smith. And he did treat all those men, plus others, whether they be Saints, dissenters, or Missourians. During much of the time he spent away from us, he was treating people who needed him. A two-week journey could easily turn into two months if he found people that needed the relief and healing he could give them. And if he was administering to people who were not members of the Church, it also gave him the opportunity to preach the gospel to them.

"It is easy to imagine that some of the Saints would see his caring for people other than members of the Church as him not fully supporting Church leadership, even though they had all been treated by my father and were very grateful for his help. Some people could not accept the fact that he would treat the illnesses and injuries of the enemy."

"It sounds to me like something that Jesus would do," said Fred.

"I agree with you, Son." Ezra seemed temporarily lost in thoughts again. Then he sighed another deep sigh and went on. "Now, here is something I have never been able to figure out. Amidst all of this and to this day, I have been unable to find any proof of Father being a dissenter. But there is record of his being rebaptized in August of 1838, during this whole mess with Gallatin, which seems a little strange, don't you think?"

"Maybe he wanted to repent of negative thoughts and attitudes and asked to be rebaptized to show how strongly he felt about it, and how penitent he really was," said Fred.

"It's not something that would happen in these times, but at that time, it was certainly a possibility, and something that had been known to occur. But again, there is no written record of his thoughts or actions, and the testimonies that we have found in eyewitness accounts of the time are confusing and contradictory. But this much we know: of the five revelations Joseph Smith received on July 8, 1838, the only one that was not included in the Doctrine and Covenants was directed at W. W. Phelps and F. G. Williams. It says, *in consequence of their transgressions, their former standing has been taken away from them, and now, if they will be saved, let them be ordained as Elders in my Church to preach my Gospel ...*"[51]

"What was his transgression, Grandpa?"

"Well, that is a problem in and of itself because no one seems to know, and I have been unable to find record of it. But I think it is safe to say that whatever the transgression was, large or small, he took care of it, repented, and came back into full fellowship with the Church in short order. W. W. Phelps followed suit. But the question is, how did the membership of the Church view these two men at this time?"

"I see where you are going with this, Papa. Everything he did seemed to turn the Saints against him, even though he was trying his best to do what was right," said Fred.

"Yes, now you are getting the picture. If he had stood up for himself and told everyone what he was doing and why he was gone, as one or two others had done, things may have turned out differently. And I think he thought by being rebaptized he had put all of that behind him, he would be straight with the Lord and with Joseph, and his friends would accept and trust him once again. They then would know that whatever it was that had caused his problems had been resolved, and the Lord himself had accepted him back in full fellowship. But that wasn't what happened."

"Oh no," said Joseph. "More trouble?"

"I'm afraid so, Joe. The Prophet had asked Father if he would go back to Kirtland and see if there was any property or goods belonging to the Church that he could claim and possibly sell to help the financial situation in Missouri. This took him away from our family and the Church in Missouri again, just as the problems there were becoming very serious. Some people saw it as him once more leaving the Church in times of trouble. No one knew that Joseph was the one who had sent him away. And there was nothing left in Kirtland anyway. As soon as the Saints left the town, the local people swarmed on whatever was left of value like wasps to a picnic, and everything was long gone.

"Meanwhile, the Prophet had written to Missouri Governor Boggs asking for help in defending us against the mobs, but the letter was never answered. Joseph felt things closing in on him, and he didn't know where to turn. I got the feeling that there were even times when he thought God had forsaken us. Later, when Joseph found out that the Saints were starving and suffering all kinds of hardships all throughout Daviess and Caldwell Counties, he decided to appeal once again to the governor for help. This time, he did receive Boggs' reply, but how disappointed he and all the other leaders were when they read that Boggs relegated the situation to a 'quarrel' which he said was between the Mormons and the citizens, and he would let them fight it out. All hope of help or relief from the government was lost when Joseph read this. The Saints had no choice but to abandon their homes in small settlements like DeWitt and other places, where several people had already died from ill treatment and extreme privations and join those of us in the bigger towns. As Willard Richards, a recently ordained member of the Quorum of the Twelve, put it, 'A dreadful spirit reigns in the breasts of those who are opposed to this Church. They are above law and beneath whatever is laudable. Their leading object seems to be to get all the property of the Church for little or nothing and drive the Saints out of this place.'

"When the Missourians saw their success in the smaller Latter-day Saint settlements and realized no retribution was coming from the government, the mobs marched toward the bigger settlements, burning houses, driving off livestock, and scattering many families. Joseph turned to General David Atchison of the Missouri state militia, for advice. Atchison had been a lawyer for the Saints during the

Jackson County problems and was still friendly to the Church. He urged Boggs to visit the scene of the trouble, but the governor was never willing to hear the Saints' side of the story. Instead, he chose to believe the inflammatory anti-Mormon reports, lies, and rumors.

"Guerrilla warfare raged between Mormons and anti-Mormons for two days. The anti-Mormons often set fire to their own haystacks and property and then blamed it on the Saints, spreading rumors that the Mormons were either stealing or destroying all the property of their neighbors. Members of the Church were being hemmed in on all sides, and, having no food or other supplies, we foraged for whatever we could in order to stay alive."

CHAPTER THIRTY-FIVE

Ogden, Utah 1905

Making Tacos

Ezra stopped speaking, visibly shaken at the memory of this difficult time.

Henrietta had come to the bedroom door off and on all morning to check on him. It was apparent that she was worried about what reliving all this intense history would do to her man. She took this chance to bring him a fresh glass of water.

"Oh, my angel, you must have been reading my mind," he said. He took the glass and drank it down greedily.

"I think it is about time for lunch, boys. Can you give me just a few minutes to put it on the table?" she said.

"Is there anything I can help you with, Mother?"

"Well, now that you mention it, maybe I could use a hand."

Fred followed his mother into the kitchen, leaving Joseph in the bedroom with his grandfather.

"What do you have planned, Mama?" asked Fred when they arrived in the kitchen.

"Honestly, I haven't thought of anything. I do have a pork roast all cooked, but absolutely nothing to go with it."

"Well, what if I make something today, something we might eat in Mexico?"

"Will I like it?" she asked with a little trepidation. "I mean, it won't burn my gullet, will it? I've heard about the food in Mexico."

"I don't have any way to get hot sauce, Mama, so no chance of it burning your gullet," he said with a wink.

"All right then, what do you need?"

"I need flour, grease, vegetables, cheese, and that pork roast." His mother started pulling things out of cupboards, a few things out of the ice box, and then she went to the root cellar and brought back a few vegetables.

"How did you get the tomatoes to last this long, Mama?"

"It's a trick," she said, eyes sparkling. "I take the green tomatoes that we pick in the fall, put them in newspaper-lined boxes, and then use them as they ripen. I put the boxes up on a board floor in the root cellar, so they don't touch the ground. Your father made it for that very purpose several years ago. It is nice and cool there in the cellar, but it is deep enough in the ground that it usually doesn't freeze the vegetables during the winter. I cover the whole bunch of boxes with a heavy old quilt or burlap bags just to be sure they don't freeze, but yet they still stay very cool. I keep onions the same way and usually have enough onions to last until the start of summer. I only have a few tomatoes left, but they are edible."

"Hmmm," understanding dawned on him. "I've wondered where you kept getting those vegetables."

"Yes, there are still a lot of potatoes, winter squash, and other veg-etables down there. I know we can buy a lot of things at the market, but they often don't have the things I want, especially in the winter, and anyway, I prefer to have that store right here where I can get at things easily."

"You're a pretty smart Mama," he gave her a quick hug and a peck on the cheek.

He took the flour, mixed it with a little salt and grease, and started making tortillas out of it. He rolled them thin with Henrietta's roll-ing pin. "We have a small version of a rolling pin in Mexico that we can use to roll the tortillas out right in our hands. Amanda and Nancy are both very good at it. I'm much clumsier, especially with this big rolling pin. Mama, would you mind dicing the tomatoes and onions into small pieces?"

"I can do that."

Fred continued with the meal by pulling the roast apart into shreds and warming it all up. He mixed the chopped onions and tomatoes together.

"Mama, do you have a pepper down in your magic store?"

"No, but I have some dried ones up here in the cupboard."

She pulled a jar down, opened the lid, and pulled out a few dried up-looking things that may have once been green. "Will these work?"

Fred took one and bit it, surprised at the piquant flavor. "Yes, indeed. That is perfect."

"Here, let me soak them a minute or two. They will turn right back into the way they were when we dried them last year."

When the peppers were restored, not quite to their former condition but good enough, he chopped them up and put them in with the tomatoes and onions while his mother grated the cheese.

"We call this *pico de gallo*, Mama. It isn't hot, but it will bring out the flavor of the tacos."

He handed her a small bowlful of the sauce, then heated some grease in the big cast iron skillet, and cooked the tortillas, one at a time, on both sides. He stacked them up on a plate, then with his mother's help, put everything on the dining room table.

"Son, will you see if the Doctor would like to come in here for lunch today?"

"Sure will, Mama."

As he approached Ezra's bedroom, he could hear his father and his son laughing hysterically. Fred stopped outside the bedroom door to listen in for a minute. He heard Ezra say, "Joe, did you hear about the man who sold his horse so he could buy a buggy?"

He heard Joseph laughing at the joke, then he said, "Grandpa, did you hear about the guy who sold his favorite chair so he could buy some nice pillows for it?" Hysterical laughing.

"Hey, Joe, did you hear about the…"

"All right you two," Fred interrupted.

Ezra winked at Joseph, and said, "Looks like we have to go eat, Grandson. Are you hungry?"

"I'm always hungry, Grandpa, I am a growing boy."

They both laughed again, although Fred found nothing funny in the statement.

"Then let's get going," answered Ezra.

"Do you want to come to the table today, Papa?" asked Fred.

"I do, if you and Joe will help me."

Thrilled at this, they lifted Ezra into the wheelchair and rolled him to the table.

After the blessing was said on the food, Henrietta asked, "How do we eat this stuff, Fred?"

"Just take a tortilla, Mama, and fill it full of meat and a little cheese, like this, and add a spoonful or two of the *pico de gallo*." He put his own taco together. "Roll it like this and eat it like this." He lifted the luscious food to his mouth and took a big bite. "Mmmm, that reminds me of home."

Henrietta tried to make hers as Fred had made his. When she lifted it to her mouth, half of the filling dropped out onto her plate. "Now what do I do, Son?

Her blank expression made Fred laugh.

"Just stuff it back in like this." He helped her reassemble her taco. "Now take a big bite."

She took a big bite, chewed it, then Henrietta of Boston, who never talked with her mouth full, said what sounded like, "*Mmmm, oooh, lis is gool, Fleth.*"

"Is that sauce stuff hot, Fred?" asked Ezra.

"No, it is just flavorful. If I were in Mexico, I could add some things to it to make it very hot, right, Son?" He looked at Joseph, who gave a little snort at the thought of his grandparents biting into real hot sauce and dropped some of the food out of his mouth.

He was clearly embarrassed and didn't know what to do but laugh again, which made Ezra laugh, too. Soon Fred had joined in, and finally giving into the merriment, Henrietta laughed as well. It somehow got funnier and funnier, until the laughter had played itself out.

Fred said, "Don't worry about going to pieces, Joe. We still love you. Tacos sometimes go to pieces, and we still love them."

This set off another round of laughter, until Ezra said, "These tacos are pretty good, Fred, but when do we get the pie and whipped cream?"

This time it was Henrietta's turn to roll her eyes.

CHAPTER THIRTY-SIX

ABOUT MISSOURI, 1838–1839

Losing Far West, Finding Quincy

After lunch, the boys put Ezra in his bed, and he was soon asleep. He slept for about an hour when he woke up with a start and called for Fred and Joe.

The boy ran into his grandfather's room. "What is it, Grandpa?"

"We need to finish this story. Get your father right now."

"I will, Grandpa. Will you be all right?"

"Yes," said Ezra. "Now hurry."

Within five minutes, Fred and Joe were back in Ezra's room.

Fred asked with concern, "What is it, Father?"

"I keep seeing it, Son. I can't make it stop. Please, let me tell you the rest now or I will never be able to sleep."

"What is it that you are seeing, Papa?"

"I see the atrocities that were perpetrated upon us, over and over and over again. I feel the hunger, and the anger, and…"

"All right, Papa, we will get it down on paper, then you can forget it forever." Fred hurriedly gathered the journal and the pen, and Joseph quickly pulled up his chair into his usual place.

"I don't think it will be that easy, but I'll try."

"All right," Fred said again. "Tell us whatever you need to tell us." He stroked his father's hand, in an effort to calm him down.

"Where were we, Fred?" his father asked.

"You had given us reasons why your father was having a hard time."

"That's right." Then without missing a beat, "Here is reason number three. When Father returned from Kirtland after having no success in reclaiming any property, he was reminded by the Prophet that he needed to recommence work on settling the affairs of the Sidney Gilbert store and get the Church's money out of it that was so desperately needed. This work took him from Far West to Liberty, thirty miles away in the unfriendly Clay County. Again, many of our neighbors wondered why Father was not there with us when we had such great need, and why had he gone into enemy territory. I have to be honest: I needed him, too.

"Inexplicably, two members of the Quorum of the Twelve Apostles, Thomas B. Marsh and Orson Hyde, two stalwarts in the leadership of the Church, chose this moment to desert the cause, and to actually join the enemy at Richmond.[52] Of course, this persuaded the anti-Mormons to believe that they were in the right. But the Prophet said that Thomas B. Marsh had fallen, lied, and sworn falsely, and was ready to take the lives of his best friends. Then he added, *He who exalteth himself, God will abase.*[53] These men left us at the worst possible time, a time we needed their physical strength as well as their spiritual strength. What we didn't need was for them to join the dissenters. We had enough going against us as it was.

"We had been warned that the militia was planning assaults on Caldwell County settlements, including Far West. The Prophet had told the Saints still living in the surrounding smaller villages to come to Far West for protection. We helped those who came the very best we could. That last week of October, mobs were everywhere. This time, in addition to burning houses and crops, they rustled cattle, took prisoners, and threatened the Saints with death if they didn't leave the state.

General Atchison tried again to get the governor to come to the area and see for himself what was going on, but Boggs still refused to come, having heard quite a different story. He was told that the entire Missouri militia was massacred, and the Mormons were planning to sack and burn Richmond. This was the perfect excuse he needed to order all-out war against the Saints. Then he did the unthinkable. He issued the famous order that said, *The Mormons must be treated as enemies and must be exterminated or driven from the state, if necessary for the public good. Their outrages are beyond all description.*[54]

"It was now legal to kill any member of the Church on sight. Public opinion and hatred were so strong against the Saints that even the ones who knew this was all based on lies would not stand up for the truth. Boggs' extermination order was the result of popular will. Everyone wanted us dead."

"Grandpa, how did you live through it? How did you ever escape the mobs?" Joe was visibly shaken by all of this, and tears leaked down his cheeks.

"We relied on God to get us through, Son. Sometimes when your backs are to the wall, so to speak, you find strength and tenacity above and beyond anything you thought you might be able to withstand. That is what happened to us then."

Fred took hold of the Doctor's hand and held it tight. "Father, are you sure you want to continue?"

He looked at Fred. "I'm all right, Son. I'm all right. Can you put that other pillow behind my back, though? I feel like I'm slipping down."

Joseph quickly grabbed the pillow and helped his father situate it behind his grandfather's back.

Ezra took a deep breath and continued with his story. "Two big battles took place this last week of October. The first one has come to be called The Battle of Crooked River. It took place not too many miles from where we were living. It was a bloody battle, and one that I was personally involved with. I am going to spare you the details, but I will say this. Several men on each side were wounded, one of them being an apostle, Elder David Patten. He was taken to a nearby home where he passed away a few hours later. Several others of the brethren passed away also as a result of their wounds. Some others were severely and permanently injured."

"Papa, were you involved in the militia? Were you actually in danger during that battle? Weren't you still just fifteen?"

"Yes, I was nearly fifteen, close to your age, Joe, and yes, I was involved."

Fred seemed unable to believe this. "What were you doing there?"

"I just couldn't sit still and do nothing, so I rode with the men to

Crooked River. I was captured myself and was threatened with death."

"No, Grandpa, how did you ever get away from them?" Joe bemoaned, his throat thickening.

"One of the mobsters took me by the coat collars and literally lifted me off my feet and into the air. It choaked me until I couldn't breathe, and I knew my face was turning red. I have to admit, I thought my time had come and I would not live through it. So, I prayed. I begged the Lord to save my life so that I could help my family get out of this place. I prayed harder and more sincerely than I had ever prayed in my life.

"One of the officers said, 'You better leave the kid alone. It may be hard to justify killing him.' Whereupon the man who held me said, 'nits breed lice,' as if my life held as much value as a louse.[55] To this day, I don't know why he didn't kill me, but for some reason, he let me go. He shoved me hard to the ground, kicked me in the side, stepped right on my chest, and then took off, going I know not where, although I can think of a few places I was hoping he would go."

"That must have been terrifying, Papa. I've never heard you talk about that before."

Ezra's head hung down as he said, "It's something I would rather forget."

Then looking Fred in the eye, he said, "It was terrifying, but I was oddly calm, willing to give my life for the truth. That's what it felt like I was doing."

Ezra sat still for a moment, as if trying to put into words what came next. "You probably remember hearing about the massacre at Haun's Mill, right?"

"I have, Papa, but I don't remember the details."

"Again, I do not want to get into the details but will just say that this battle was worse than Crooked River, and only about twenty-five miles east of our home in Far West. The Saints living there were mercilessly attacked by a mob that was determined to carry out Boggs' extermination order. Many people were killed as the Missourians attacked the town. Those who lived through it got out of town any way they could."

"Were you involved in that battle, Grandpa?"

"No, I had made my way home to Far West." Ezra took a drink of the water Henrietta had left for him, then continued. "Those of us in Far West began preparing for attacks as well. Since Governor Boggs issued his extermination order, the mobs were more aggressive, knowing that they would not be prosecuted for committing murder on members of the Church. Can you imagine how that affected our sense of security?"

"No, Papa, I can't even imagine."

"One night a few days later, I had ridden out on the prairie to gather the stock when I saw General Lucas of the Missouri Militia approach Far West with his army of thirty-five hundred men at about sundown. I rode back into Far West as fast as I could and sounded the alarm, but the mobs continued to gather. I helped the men of Far West barricade the city with anything we could find—wagons, timber, furniture, anything big enough to help hold them out, but it was of no use. By the next day, the anti-Mormon militia outnumbered us by about five to one. That evening, General Lucas sent a flag of truce to the Saints.

"Colonel Hinkle, the highest-ranking Mormon militia officer in the county, had secretly agreed to Lucas's demands which were, one, certain leaders would surrender for trial and punishment; two, the Saints' property would be confiscated to pay for damages; and three, the rest of us would surrender our arms and leave the state. What a mess we were in. But it got worse."

"How could it get any worse, Papa? Your property would be gone, your weapons were taken from you, and you had nowhere to go."

"We were starving to death. I don't know if there is a document somewhere stating the number of Saints who lost their lives at this time because of starvation, exposure to the elements, or outright murder, but many died. I have looked through Father's papers a few times hoping to find such a document but have never found one. I saw the situation for myself, though, and feared for all of us."

"Who were the certain leaders that were punished, Grandpa?"

"I was just getting to that, Joe. Colonel Hinkle convinced Joseph Smith, Hyrum Smith, Sidney Rigdon, and a few other Church leaders that General Lucas wanted to talk to them in a peace conference.

Can you imagine their surprise when Hinkle turned them over to Lucas as prisoners? He told Lucas, 'These are the prisoners I agreed to deliver up.' What a betrayal!

"The General rode up to them without a word and ordered his guards to surround them. They were marched into the enemy camp surrounded by thousands of rough looking men, many dressed and painted like Indian warriors. They all began to yell as if they had pulled off one of the greatest victories in history, and they kept it up all night.

"Those of us in Far West were terrified that they had already murdered the Prophet. We prayed all night for the safety of all these leaders, while they spent the night lying on the ground in a cold rain, listening to the constant mockery and vulgarity of their guards, who swore the most dreadful oaths, taunting the Prophet, demanding miracles and signs from him. They blasphemed God and mocked the Savior. I'm sure it was nearly intolerable for those men of God to listen to the evil ravings and carryings-on of these hate-possessed men. It makes me sick to think about it." Ezra had to stop to wipe his eyes, then he continued, but with wavering voice.

"In a secret, illegal court-martial held during the night—" he gulped great draughts of air— "the prisoners were sentenced to be executed the next morning in the public square of Far West."

Tears were now freely coursing down his face. "General Alexander Doniphan received the order to carry out the execution which he refused to do." Ezra raised his voice, nearly yelling. "He told Lucas, 'It is cold-blooded murder. I will not obey your order. My brigade shall march for Liberty tomorrow morning at 8:00, and if you execute these men, I will hold you responsible before an earthly tribunal, so help me God.'"

Ezra looked down at his hands as he went on in a softer voice. "Lucas lost his nerve, and our prayers were answered."

Joseph rubbed his grandfather's back as far as he could reach, then smoothed his hair back several times. Fred likewise took hold of his father's hand and rubbed his arm.

"Father—"

"No, Fred, I can't stop. Just bear with me."

Upon a silent sign from his father, Joseph ran to Henrietta, asking for her to come into the room. She brought another glass of water, and he took a grateful swallow or two.

"Mother," said Fred, "would you like to sit here with us for a while?"

"Yes, I think I would."

Fred went to find a chair for her, and bringing it in, placed it close to the head of the bed, across from Joseph.

Finally able to continue, Ezra said, "That next morning, November 1, as the traitor George Hinkle marched the Mormon troops out of Far West, the Missouri militia entered the city and vandalized the town, plundered valuable possessions, raped some of the women, and forced the leading elders at bayonet point to sign promises to pay the expenses of the militia. Many prominent men of the Church were arrested and taken as prisoners to Richmond.

Henrietta, who had taken his hand in hers, gently lifted it to her lips and kissed it.

"And where was your father while all this was going on?"

"He had been working so hard on the Gilbert estate issues. He filed the inventory of the store goods and made a list of the deeds to the real estate belonging to Gilbert & Whitney, trying to sort out whose was whose. He was at court earlier in October, but when all-out war broke out with the Missourians, and when he heard that Joseph and the others were taken to be killed, he took off for Far West as fast as he could. As soon as he got home, he commenced taking care of the wounded and helping us figure out how to get out of Missouri. We knew we had to leave the state, but we had no idea where to go. Some people wanted to go back to Kirtland, but most of us knew that would be just as bad as it was in Far West.

"Meanwhile, the Missourians' plan was to take their prisoners the fifty-seven miles to Independence for public display and trial. Thinking they might not come back alive, Joseph and the others begged to see their families one last time. When they returned to Far West on November 2 to say their goodbyes, Joseph found Emma and the children in tears because they thought he had already been shot. Although relieved to see him still alive, they were also sorrowful over him having to leave them again.

"Emma, sobbing, held onto him as long as she could, and the

children clung to him and would not let go until the guards thrust them away with their swords. This same scene was repeated at the homes of the other prisoners."

Henrietta rubbed the back of the Doctor's head and across his shoulders, hoping to relieve a little of the stress she could see that he was feeling.

"As they started on their strange and terrible march, Joseph spoke hope to his companions. He told them, 'Be of good cheer, brethren; the word of the Lord came to me last night that our lives should be given us, and that whatever we may suffer during this captivity, not one of our lives should be taken.'"[56]

"Oh, Grandpa, that is so great," Joe was obviously encouraged by this news.

"Well, yes and no, Joe."

"What do you mean, Papa?" asked Fred.

"First of all, we had not heard Joseph give this prophecy, so we believed the Missourians would do with them as they said they would. After our leaders were marched out of Far West, the commanding officer for the Missourians, General John B. Clark, ordered us all to stay in the city, which is what we had been doing anyway, as the mobs would not let us leave. But our food supplies were gone, and with no way to buy more, we were getting pretty hungry. We lived on parched corn for quite a while."

"Parched corn, Grandpa? I don't even know what that is."

"Well, let me tell you about parched corn. These days many people are calling it popcorn, but it takes a special kind of corn to pop into those fluffy white kernels you see in the stores. None of us had popcorn, just regular corn kernels. We would put the dried kernels in a pan with a little oil, and when it was heated, it would make a little pop. The heat and oil opened the kernels and softened them so we could chew them. If you had happened to store black, red, or purple corn, then parching it made it taste pretty good, especially if you had a little salt on hand, but most of us had stored white or yellow ears. White kernels were bland, and yellow ones had a bad after-taste. The Williamses were lucky enough to have stored some of all colors. Papa was often paid with food for his medical services, so when he brought ears of corn home, no matter the color, that is what we would dry. But when you get hungry enough, anything tastes good. Right, Joe?"

"I guess so, Grandpa. Everything usually tastes good to me."

"Oh yes, you are a growing boy. I remember that. But you can get sick of anything, too, if that is the only thing you have to eat—with the possible exception of whipped cream."

Ezra looked over at his wife and actually smiled as he brought up his favorite food. "Parched corn is also very hard on a person's digestive system." He held his stomach at the thought, mimicking the pain and distress everyone in Far West had experienced at some time.

"So, back to General Clark," he said, suddenly serious. "A few days later on, during the first week of November, he indicated to us that he would not force us out of the state during the winter. Nice of him, eh? Then he added, for his lenity—that means being gentle—he said we were indebted to his clemency—that means forgiveness or compassion. Can you imagine after everything the Missourians had put us through that this tyrant claimed we owed him for his kindness? He then told us that we should not even think of staying there long enough to plant crops, or to let the thought enter our heads that our leaders might be delivered, or that we would ever see their faces again. He said, their doom is sealed.[98] Although we continued to pray multiple times a day for their release, we had no earthly reason not to believe General Clark."

"But you had a heavenly reason, right, Grandpa?" Joe said hopefully.

"Yes, we did, and we continued to cling to the mercy of our Heavenly Father."

Henrietta gave him another sip of the water. "One fairly positive thing happened at this time, though. All the Saints from Adam-ondi-Ahman, those who had been living there for some time as well as those who had fled there for safety, were granted permission to come to Far West until spring. Already overcrowded for taking in Saints from the smaller villages nearby, we made room for them in any way we could, and we shared our parched corn with them. You would think that having more people added to the burdens we were already shouldering, trying to find places for them to stay and food for them to eat, would make us unhappy, frustrated, or even depressed, but it had the opposite effect. Being together like that strengthened our resolve to see this thing through, and we relied on each other to have faith that we were on the Lord's side, and He would protect and deliver us. Somehow or other, we always came up with something to eat and places to sleep, and we made it a few months longer. During this time, we all made what plans we could to leave this hellhole, as we came to think of it, as soon as we could."

"It is sad to think that this place where you thought you would be safe had turned into such a horrible place, Papa. I find it hard to imagine how bad it must have been."

"Son, let me tell you this. I am trying my hardest to tell this story as I saw it, but I have to minimize the horror of the whole situation," said Ezra. "I don't want to traumatize you or Joe too much by emphasizing just how awful it was. But I will add this one little thing. By the time we left Missouri, we were all very thin. My mother and my sisters … Everyone!" At this admission, Ezra gave a little involuntary sob and wiped his eyes.

"Even you, Grandpa?"

"Yes, Joe, even me. It's hard to stay fat on a diet of parched corn." He gave what sounded like a little fake laugh. "But we lived through it, or most of us did."

"People died, Grandpa? Anyone you knew personally?"

"Yes, I knew several people who died, but the one I guess you could say was closest to us was Lovina's third baby. They named him George Washington Riggs, and buried him near his brother and sister, and Uncle Swain. It always seemed strange to me that they named him after perhaps the most patriotic of all the early American patriots, the father of our free country, as they called him, and there we were, anything but free. But that was characteristic of the optimism we had even in these times of great trouble."

Fred sighed and shook his head. "I can only imagine how hard that was on your sister. We lost a lot of babies, but we always had at least one other child to hold in our arms. But to lose three in a row without the benefit of a living child must have been almost more than that little mother could stand."

"It was very hard, Son, but it was almost impossible to carry a child to term on a diet of parched corn. It was also hard on my mother to lose three grandchildren like that. I think she started to wonder if she would ever have grandchildren."

"What about the Prophet? What did they do with him?"

"We soon learned the fate of Joseph and his fellow prisoners. They were, indeed, marched the fifty-one miles to Independence where they were placed on public display. They were tied up in the town square where everyone could point the finger of scorn, as the Book of Mormon puts it, and mock them. Some people called them names, spat on them, and some even threw rocks. The prisoners were helpless to defend themselves, and no one stood up for them.

"After that, they were transferred to Richmond, some thirty-five miles away to the northeast. There they were chained together and put under guard in an old vacant house for more than two weeks. Can you even imagine how uncomfortable that must have been? It was very cold, they had nothing to cover themselves against the elements, and no bathroom privileges."

Joe wrinkled his nose. "That must have smelled terrible."

"Yes, and their food was horrible, also. Maybe even worse than parched corn." Ezra sighed deeply before continuing. Henrietta clung to his hand. "I told you this was not going to be pleasant," he reminded them.

"We can take it like men, right, Joe?" asked Fred.

"I think so, Dad," came his less-than-persuasive reply.

Ezra went on. "About the middle of November, they were put on trial for thirteen days under the direction of Judge Austin A. King. Dissenters from the truthfulness of the gospel bitterly accused the Prophet of being responsible for the wrongs done to them. But when the prisoners submitted a list of defense witnesses who could speak to the truth on their behalf, the witnesses were jailed or driven from the county. The attorney for the prisoners, Alexander Doniphan, although not a member of the Church but who was solidly on the side of our leaders, said, 'if a cohort of angels were to come down, and declare we were innocent, it would all be the same; for he, Judge King, had determined from the beginning to cast us into prison.'

"Parley P. Pratt had developed a great habit of keeping a diary, and luckily for us, his son, Parley Jr., took many of the writings from his diary and other sources, and put them into book form. It is called, appropriately enough, the Autobiography of Parley Parker Pratt. It was printed about twenty years after Parley died. I was able to obtain a copy of it, and I want one of you to read from it, please. I marked the passage."

"I'll be happy to read it, Papa." Fred took the book, opened it to the bookmark, and started reading the marked passage:

> For two horrible weeks, the prisoners were abused by the guards. One November night the brethren listened for several hours to obscene jests, the horrid oaths, the dreadful blasphemies and filthy language as the guards rehearsed the atrocities they had inflicted on the Saints. Parley P. Pratt lay next to the Prophet and listened until he could scarcely refrain from rising … and rebuking the guards. Suddenly, Joseph Smith rose to his feet, shackled and unarmed, and spoke in a voice of thunder:
>
> *SILENCE, ye fiends of the infernal pit. In the name of Jesus Christ I rebuke you, and command you to be still; I will not live another minute and hear such language. Cease such talk, or you or I die THIS INSTANT!*
>
> He ceased to speak. He stood erect in terrible majesty. Chained and without a weapon; calm, unruffled and dignified as an angel, he looked upon the quailing guards, whose weapons were lowered or dropped to the ground; whose knees smote together, and who, shrinking into a corner, or crouching at his feet, begged his pardon, and remained quiet till a change of guards.[57]

No one said anything for several moments until Fred spoke up. "What a picture that paints, Papa."

"It gives me the chills," said Joe.

His grandfather said, "It reinforces my testimony of Joseph Smith every time I read it."

"So, then what happened, Grandpa?"

"About the first of December at the end of the so-called trial, Judge King bound Joseph and the five others and ordered them placed in Liberty Jail, twenty-nine miles back west of Richmond. Ha! Have you ever heard of such a ridiculous name as Liberty Jail? It makes one of them, what do you call them when the two words of a title are opposites? Fred, do you remember?"

"No, I can't think of the word right off. Joe, do you know what he means?"

"I don't, Dad."

"It's an oxymoron," volunteered Henrietta without having to think about it.

"That's it," said Ezra. Then as an aside to Joseph, he said, "I knew I married a smart woman!" He leaned his head toward her and she patted his cheek.

"The jail in Liberty was really a dungeon. It was the lower floor of a two-story stone edifice, measuring fourteen by fourteen-and-a-half feet on the inside, with small, barred windows and little heat. A hole in the floor was the only access to the lower level, where a man could not stand upright. Here they stayed for four cold winter months, where they suffered from cold, filthy conditions, smoke inhalation, loneliness, and filthy food. Perhaps worst of all, they were not able to help the Saints, who were once again forced to pack up everything and move to another place.

"The good news somehow came to us that the Governor of Illinois said we could move there. We jumped at the chance, especially since the Missourians had moved the deadline for our removal from the state up to the end of February. And so, the great migration began again. Eastward we went as quickly as we could, in a steady line for several weeks. As people packed what belongings were left to them, they left the terror of Missouri. Wagon by wagon we came to the great Mississippi River. Somehow, Father had obtained a wagon, as ours had been destroyed by the mobs, and since he had been away through some of that war, he had retained his horse, so we were in better shape than many families. We helped as many people as we could, and I was able to drive a wagon for a recently widowed sister who had no one else to help her.

"When my family arrived at the Mississippi River on the eastern border of Missouri, we saw that it was full of floating ice, which made it impossible to cross.

"So, there we sat on the western shore of the river, gazing across to the city of Quincy, Illinois, and freedom, wondering if someone from the mobs would come up behind us at any moment and shoot us, as it was still legal to murder a Mormon on sight in Missouri. We were cold, hungry, and in need of shelter. As I sat there, I thought about the Prophet, Hyrum, and the others, incarcerated in that dungeon, and wondered if we were the lucky ones, miserable as we were.

"Somehow, the people in Quincy, Illinois, who knew of our plot, helped us across the river. We had to wait until nighttime when it froze solid enough to walk on, then as many of us as possible would walk or run across the river to Quincy before the ice broke up again in the morning. Those who weren't able to cross at that time had to wait for the river to freeze over again the next night. Eventually, we all made it across. And so it went for many nights.

"The citizens of Quincy did everything in their power to help us. I don't know how they did it, but they fed us, and food never tasted so good. They helped us make shelters out of our wagons in the city park, right in the middle of town. That is where we stayed until better accommodations were found, and somehow, we stayed warm. Well, at least we didn't freeze. Many of the Quincians took our people right into their homes. Many of us were given jobs. They gathered warm clothing for us, and blankets. They cared for all of us to the best of their ability. And the really crazy thing was that the Saints outnumbered the Quincians by at least double. It was a long, cold winter, but we made it through. I don't know what we ever would have done without the help of those people of Quincy."

Ezra stopped and asked, "What time is it, Fred?"

"Oh, I don't have my watch in my pocket, Papa, but it must be about 5:00."

"I think I've come to a place where I can stop for a while. Are you all right with that? I'm worn-out today."

"Of course, Papa."

"I'll go and warm you up a nice bowl of soup, Doctor," said Henrietta in her most cheerful voice, "then you can eat and snuggle down in the bed until morning."

"That sounds wonderful, Henny."

She left, with Joe tagging after her, but returned in a few minutes with a warm bowl of chicken soup and a thick slice of homemade bread and butter to eat with it. Joe came behind her with a glass of buttermilk.

"How does this look, Grandpa?"

"Perfect, Joe. Why don't you and your father get some just like it?"

***

Joe had thought that Ezra would want to get right back to the story the next day, but he slept most of that day. In fact, March had turned into April before the old man once more called his son and grandson to his side.

"We're here, Grandpa," Joe announced as he pulled his chair up to the head of the bed in his accustomed position.

"Where's your father?" Ezra asked.

Just then, Fred came into the room. "Here I am, Papa." He got the pen and journal and also pulled up his chair into his usual place.

"I've missed hearing you tell the story, Grandpa," said Joe. "It makes me happy that you are ready to go on."

"You may not be by the time I am finished," he said, "and today is the day I will finish."

Joe looked at his father, who said, "Well, we have heard a lot of hard things, Papa. I think we are up to hearing the end of it."

Giving one of his huge sighs, his father asked the accustomed question, "Where were we, Son?"

"You were telling us about the people of Quincy, and how they treated you so kindly."

"Oh, that's right," he said. He just sat quietly for a few minutes, seeming to gather his thoughts before going on. "I don't know how we would have made it if they had not rescued us."

CHAPTER THIRTY-SEVEN

QUINCY, ILLINOIS 1839

Another Sad Day... Through Ezra's Eyes

As soon as we could organize ourselves again, we started meeting together in wards on Sundays and sometimes on other days. We were all willing to work to ease the burden on the citizens of Quincy, and to do whatever else we needed to create a normal life again.

Just when things seemed to be going better for him, and as soon as he had helped us get settled in Quincy, Father was summoned back to Missouri to settle things with the Gilbert estate. It seemed like a never-ending battle, but progress was being made. So, he rode off to the west, meeting many members of the Church who were still moving east. I'm pretty sure they must have wondered what business would take him back to Missouri, and despite him treating many of them right there on the trail for a number of illnesses and broken bones, some assumed he was deserting the Church.

Finally, after months of hard work and long horse rides in all kinds of weather, on March 15, 1839, he made an affidavit before the Clay County Court in Liberty and which was published in the *Western Star* newspaper, announcing the sale of the real estate properties of the Gilbert estate. When the properties sold, the money from the sales would go directly into an account for the Church, and he would have recaptured some of the money that the Church had invested in the store. This would be such a financial boon to the Church, and it came at a very crucial time.

Two days later, he made his way to Liberty Jail in hopes of telling the Prophet the good news himself. As he asked the jailer to see the prisoners, he spoke as loud as he could, mentioning that he had some good news for them, in case he would not be allowed to see them. It came as no surprise that he was not allowed, but he hoped that the prisoners, locked in their dungeon, heard at least some of what he was saying, or at least somehow knew that he had been there wanting to see them.

Then the bomb exploded.

On March 17, 1839, the very same day Father had gone to tell Joseph the good news in Liberty Jail, a tribunal was held in Quincy where a number of men were excommunicated, including Apostle Thomas B. Marsh, W. W. Phelps, for the second time, Reed Peck, John Corrill, Burr Riggs, my brother-in-law… and my father, Dr. Frederick G. Williams.

Father, still in Missouri, knew nothing of this, and obviously could not defend himself when it happened. No one thought to ask my mother where her husband was or when he would be back, or what he was doing. If they had, she could have told them he was doing Joseph's bidding, and to at least wait until he was back, so they could talk to him about what was going on. It seems they just lumped him in with all those others, and especially because of Burr, who had become dependent on alcohol and who became mean when he got drunk, that apparently those who made up the list of men to be excommunicated assumed that Father was in sympathy with him, and by extension, other men on that list.

About a month later, I figured Father would be arriving at any time, so I kept my eye on those who disembarked in Quincy. Finally, I recognized him from far off and ran to him as fast as I could. I helped him get his horse and belongings off the boat, and then walked with him to the house where we were living. When Mother and Lucy saw us, they ran and threw their arms around Father and would not stop hugging and kissing him.

When we went inside our little house, Mother dissolved into tears. "Rebecca, what is wrong?" he asked her. "I'm here now, and I settled the Gilbert case. Let's be happy!"

"Oh, Frederick, I have the hardest news to tell you that I have ever had. I can't even force myself to say the words."

With great concern on his face and in his voice, Father looked at Mother and said, "What is it, love? Is it Lovina? The rest of us are here, so it must be her."

"No, no, it is not Lovina," she said. Finally, she raised her tear-streaked face to him and said, "Frederick, you have been excommunicated from the Church."

"What?" he gasped, slightly shaking his head in disbelief. "D-d-did I hear you right?" he stammered. "Did you say I have been excommunicated?" I could see the pain twist his face as he tried to make sense of what he had just heard. It was like he crumpled into himself.

"Yes, Frederick. I could not believe it when I heard."

"What on earth for? I thought I had straightened out any wrongdoing and was in good standing?"

"That is what we all thought, too, but your name was read along with many dissenters, including Burr." Father staggered over to the table and put both hands on the top of it. He leaned into it as if he had not the power to stand up straight of his own accord. I watched the tears roll down his face and drop onto the tabletop. He stayed like that for several minutes, unable to move or speak.

I felt like I could not stay there and watch my father grieve. I wanted to turn and run as fast as I could and find a secret place where I could scream and cry and shake my fist at heaven until God himself told me why this had happened. But I stayed there by my father, willing this whole situation to go away and for things to be better somehow. Finally, he asked, "Is Joseph in town?"

"Yes, Frederick, he has been here for about a month."

"And he knows about this, I suppose?"

"He does now, but he was not here when it happened, either, or I am sure he would have put a stop to it, Frederick."

"Then I just have one question for him." He couldn't speak for what seemed like a long time, as he leaned there, trying to get control of himself, with his lips and chin quivering and the tears still hitting the table. Finally, he spoke in a soft but distinct voice, "When can I come back?"

That is all he said. *When can I come back?*

He had every reason to be bitter, to turn his back on this community that he had loved and had tried so hard to serve, on the Prophet he had spent his time serving in every way he was asked. He could have said, "Pack up your things, family, we are getting out of here," as so many others had done. But he didn't. And I wondered then as I wonder now, of all the men who had been excommunicated in the last few years, did anyone else ask that question? Perhaps there was someone, but I don't know who. Everyone that I know of left the Church and ran away. Some came back later, but most did not ever return.

As soon as he had time to get his things put away and get cleaned up, he went to find Joseph Smith. When he found him, he asked the Prophet the same question, "When can I come back?"

Joseph said, "I just have two questions for you, my friend. Have you dissented from your belief in Christ or your belief that I am a Prophet?"

"You know I have not, Joseph. You know I was doing your bidding while I was away. I have never dissented, not for a minute. I have as great a belief in Christ as I have always had, maybe even more so now, and likewise of you as the Prophet of the Restoration. I am not perfect, Joseph, you know that, but I am trying so hard. I thought I was on firm footing, and now I find I am not."

Joseph put his arms around my father and hugged him close. He said, "At the very next conference of the Church, I will read your name back into the membership myself. I don't know why this happened. I was not here to defend you, and you weren't here to defend yourself. So many people have been excommunicated lately, that when your name came up, it seems that assumptions were made in error, and no one gave it a second thought, especially since you had been gone so long. That is not right, but we will make it right."

"Did you know that I came to see you in the jail just two days after the Gilbert case was settled?" he asked. "I came to give you the good news myself, but the jailer would not let me see you."

"The case is settled?" the Prophet almost yelled. "Did you get us anything out of the estate, Frederick?"

"Yes," Father said, and proceeded to give him the details of the whole affair.

"Oh, what great news, my friend! You have made a miracle happen," said Joseph. He put both arms around Father, and the two of them laughed with joy until the laughter turned to tears. Joseph cried with Father until they both got control of their emotions enough that my father could go home.

He came home with a feeling of peace, and we all had a pretty good night's rest. But as the days went by, I could tell that he felt strange. It was hard for him when he was released from the First Presidency a few years before, but Joseph had made sure to make him still feel a part of things and to give him things to do. But now because he was no longer a member of the Church, he couldn't even do that. His sadness was palpable.

He set up his doctor's office in Quincy and soon had a large practice again. During the ten months we lived in Quincy, Father treated at least fifteen hundred and fifty-seven patients.

With such a large practice, I started helping him more and more, especially in compounding the medications, but I was also dedicated to becoming a doctor myself and wanted to learn all that I could from him. I followed him around, like I always had, but now I watched every move he made, asking many questions, going with him on rounds, assisting him with patients in the office, and trying to learn everything about being a physician that I possibly could.

When looking at it from one side, it seemed that Father was free. He no longer had the heavy weight he carried as a counselor to the Prophet, nor was he ever again Joseph's scribe. He did not have to hold court as justice of the peace, nor render judgment. The Kirtland Safety Society and all that went with it was in the past, and he was free from the huge weight of settling the affairs of Algernon Sidney Gilbert, the thing that had taken up so much of his time while we were living in Far West.

But on the other hand, he missed the sustaining influence of the Holy Ghost and his association with his brethren in the leadership of the Church. He missed the close friendship with the Prophet, his friend and confidant. He not only felt that great void in his life, but I knew it made him sick to think he no longer felt worthy of the trust of the Church membership in general, despite the Prophet being quick to readmit him to membership. He had given everything to the Church, to the Prophet, and to the Lord, and now he just sort of didn't know who he was. Thankfully, he had all those patients to care for which gave him the means to care for his family.

CHAPTER THIRTY-EIGHT

OGDEN, UTAH 1905

Nobody's Perfect

"What do you think, Papa?" asked Fred. "I mean, what do you really think? Are you sure he never dissented from the Church? How do you know for sure that he wasn't in league with some of those who had dissented? I mean, he was away for long stretches of time. He could have been doing anything."

"I have never claimed that my father was perfect, or that he didn't need to repent. But then, wasn't it Paul who said, are we not all sinners? Who among us, if called before the Lord on judgment day, could claim to be perfect? You, Fred? Joe, what about you?"

Both of them shook their heads in the negative. "I certainly know it couldn't be me," he continued. "But if Father said that he had never lost his belief in the Prophet or his testimony of the Savior and His Church, then I believe him. I've said it before, and I'll say it again: I never knew my father to lie or even stretch the truth. If he had been guilty, he would have owned up to it, as he had when he asked to be rebaptized a few years before.

"But just to prove a point, I will tell you about two documents I found among his papers that give a couple of other reasons why I believe he was telling the truth. First, in early 1839 in Quincy, when a dissenter who had some sort of business with Brother Anson Call came to his door and asked Anson to come to a meeting the dissenters had organized, Brother Call went, just to hear them out. He made a list of all the dissenters in attendance that night, including

Lyman Cowdery, W. W. Phelps, David Whitmer, William McLellin, Burr Riggs, my brother-in-law, and many other apostates. They wanted Anson to swear out against the Prophet, and say that he, Brother Call, did bad things because *Joe* told him to. Anson said he had done nothing that wasn't by his own free will and would not join their ranks. But the reason I bring this up is because he did not list Father as one of the dissenters. Surely, someone who had been in the First Presidency who was there to bear testimony against the Prophet would have been mentioned, as that would be heavy ammunition against Joseph."[58]

Fred seemed to be pondering that information. "That makes sense, Papa."

"I agree, Son. Secondly, in a letter to the Church written from Liberty Jail, Joseph noted that the Saints had *waded through an ocean of tribulation and mean abuse, practiced upon us by the ill-bred and ignorant,* and then went on to list men who had inflicted these things upon us, high ranking members of the Church. Among the names were George Hinkle, the militia leader who betrayed them, John Corrill, W. W. Phelps, Samson Avard, Reed Peck, John Cleminson, William E. McLellin, John Whitmer, David Whitmer, Oliver Cowdery, Martin Harris, and Thomas B. Marsh. These are all men who worked closely with the Prophet, and I am sure you recognize many of these names; all the three witnesses to the Book of Mormon are among them. This must have been a heartbreaking list for Joseph to write. But conspicuously missing from the list is Frederick G. Williams.[59] Surely, someone as close to Joseph as Frederick was, the man for whom Joseph named a son, the man that Joseph turned to whenever something needed to be done because he knew it would get done, and done well, surely, if he had been a dissenter, he would have been among the names mentioned, right along with Oliver, Martin, and David Whitmer. And please don't forget that my father went to see Joseph in Liberty Jail the very day of his excommunication. It doesn't seem plausible for him to go see the Prophet to take him good news if he were a dissenter, right?"

"Then why do you think they excommunicated him?" asked Fred.

"I wish I knew, but I don't. The reason given by Elder Brigham

Young, then the President of the Quorum of the Twelve Apostles, as to why the whole list of those men were excommunicated that day was because they 'left us in the time of our perils, persecutions and dangers, and were acting against the interests of the Church.' He really did not know what my father was doing, and the one who knew, Joseph Smith, was still in Liberty Jail and would not escape until April."

"Wait, Grandpa. They escaped?"

"Oh yes, they did, Grandson."

"Did someone pass tools to them so they could cut their way out of the jail and then spur their horses on as fast as they could go?" asked Joe, his face hopeful that something so exciting had ensued.

Fred and Ezra couldn't help but chuckle at Joseph's heroic imaginings.

"That was what all of us young boys would have hoped for, but the truth was much less exciting than that. During the first week of April 1839, Joseph and the others were finally released from Liberty Jail and were to be taken to a hearing before a judge. The men who had charge of them knew they would never receive a fair trial in the state of Missouri, and so they determined to let the prisoners go. They were just let go, just like that."

"You mean, they just set them free, no fighting, no great escape or anything?" asked Joe, clearly disappointed.

"That's right, Grandson, just like that. Joseph and the others, now free, were able to make their way to Quincy by the end of the month and were reunited with their families and friends."

"Did they shoot anybody on their way to Quincy?" asked Joseph, hopefully.

"Not only did they not shoot anyone, but no one shot them. No gunfire was exchanged. However, the law that Mormons could legally be murdered was still in force, so I suppose they were very happy to get across the Mississippi River and out of Missouri."

"Oh, that is a great story, though."

"Yes, it is, and all the better because it was true," said Ezra.

"So, then what happened, Grandpa?"

"We moved to Nauvoo."

CHAPTER THIRTY-NINE

NAUVOO, ILLINOIS 1840–1842

Resolutions...Through Ezra's Eyes

The Prophet had been looking at the abandoned city of Commerce, Illinois, just forty miles north of Quincy, as a place for the Saints to live. It was swampy, but he knew that it could be drained, and the town could become a beautiful place. When someone found that the land was for sale, the Church was able to buy it, thanks in part to the money they received from the sale of the Sidney Gilbert estate that Father had worked so hard to acquire.

Finally on April 8, 1840, a whole year after his excommunication, my father stood before a conference held in the new city of Nauvoo. "I'm sorry," he said, "for my conduct while in Missouri that made you all believe I had left you in your time of peril. I ask your forgiveness, and I am determined to do the will of God in the future."

He was presented to those in attendance by President Hyrum Smith, and it was unanimously resolved that he be forgiven and be received into the fellowship of the Church. I knew it was a relief to him to have his priesthood back, and his respect in the community restored. It appears that his excommunication was based on outdated information and probably motivated by association with Burr Riggs. None of the other men who were excommunicated the same day as Father ever returned to the Church except W. W. Phelps, who came back right away, and Thomas B. Marsh and Martin Harris, much later in life. But even though he came back and was readmitted at the earliest possible date, my father was just never quite the same. Instead of jumping to the side of the Prophet as I'm pretty sure he wanted to, Father seemed to hold back and let others play that role. Instead of having confidence in himself, he seemed to feel inferior, like he didn't really belong and didn't want to push himself on others.

We lived in Nauvoo until early 1842 when we moved back to Quincy. My sister Lovina was expecting again, and when she started having troubles this time as well, Father thought that he might be able to help her. He didn't want her to have to add another child to the three precious babies she had already lost while we lived in Far West. If he could help her through this, she might be able to deliver his first living grandchild.

Burr had taken up the profession of pharmacist in Quincy, locating and processing all kinds of herbs and other remedies for doctors to use in their practices. I was only eighteen at the time, but I figured if it would help my dad with his doctoring, I would join Burr in providing him with the medicines he needed, and besides, I needed to learn more about the remedies myself if I were ever to become a competent physician.

Papa had become distrustful of Burr because he was drinking an awful lot. Burr never came back into the Church and had reverted to some of his old tricks. It was something Papa could never understand, how so many men who were once so strong in their faith, so close to the Lord and to Joseph, could just suddenly one day turn into enemies. It even happened to Oliver Cowdery, for heaven's sake, who had been with Joseph through miracle after miracle. It broke my father's heart to see all this happening, and to be powerless to help.

But something was not quite right. Papa did not have the same zest for life as he had once had. He started talking about how old he was, but goodness, he was only fifty-four years old. I'm way past that age, and I just barely got old. Something told me it wasn't the years that had made him old, but the disassociation from the leadership of the Church, the loss of trust that people had in him, his appearing to others to be something he never was, which was an enemy to Joseph and to God. I watched it drain the life right out of him and his health began to deteriorate. Joseph wanted him in a leadership role, as did many of the Church leaders and even many of the members of the

Church in general, but Papa could not take a leadership position over the part of the people whom he felt did not trust him. I admire him for that.

That summer of 1842, Papa wanted to go to Nauvoo, and he asked if I would take him. He had developed a cough that just didn't seem to let up, and he didn't want to go alone. He said he preferred my company, and anyway, I could help him if anything went wrong during the two-day trip. I hooked the horse up to our little buggy and drove my father into the beautiful city, the place of refuge and safety. As we came around the bend in the river and could see the beginnings of the temple overlooking the city, Papa sat up straighter than he had for a long time. He marveled at the size of the building, and its location on the brow of a hill. I have to tell you that he wept as he looked at it; for any number of reasons, he wept.

We went to find Joseph, and when we found him, of course we were invited to stay with his family in the mansion house. It really wasn't a mansion, not by today's standards, or any other day, but it was a nice place that could accommodate many people at one time.

I tried to stay out of Father's talks with the Prophet, because I knew he had to unburden his soul and may not want eighteen-year-old me in on everything. I took a lot of walks and visited a lot of friends from my Kirtland and Missouri days. I found William Kimball first. He lived just down the hill from the temple site. When I knocked on the door of the beautiful Kimball home, William opened it. It was so good to see him, and even though we had stayed in touch through the years, we threw our arms around each other in a brotherly hug. He then invited me into the house, and there, to my amazement, was Horace Whitney.

"Horace, what are you doing here?" I asked as we embraced as old friends.

Horace was beaming when he told me, "I am courting William's sister Helen. You know I've had my eye on her for a long time, ever since we were kids in Kirtland."

"How could I forget that, Horace. I am happy for you."

Just then, Helen came down the stairs and gave me a welcoming hug. The four of us sat for a long while discussing old times. We had a lot to talk about, and it was good for me. We talked about the miracle that was Quincy, how those people had taken in thousands of Latter-day Saints when we had no other place to go during the winter of 1839. We had all been through that ordeal, coming east out of Missouri as fast as we could in the freezing winter.

"Do you remember," said Helen, "how cold it was, sitting there on the banks of the Mississippi River, and wondering what was going to happen to us?"

"How could any of us forget that, Helen. I remember being so hungry, probably the hungriest I've ever been."

"I remember worrying if some Missourians would come up behind us and kill us before we could somehow get across that river," asserted William.

"And yet we all made it through, and here we are in this beautiful city, building a beautiful temple," said Horace.

We continued talking about Quincy, and how those people helped us any way they could. Many of them took us right into their homes, fed us, clothed us, and gave us jobs. How I grew to love that town. I know that is the reason that town grew and prospered and became beautiful. Another town nearby, also on the Mississippi River, did not fare so well. Its people treated us poorly, and it is said that some of the people who later murdered the Prophet and his brother came from there. It has shriveled up to nothing. At least, that is my observation.

Father and I stayed in Nauvoo for about three days, and then I prepared to take him the forty miles home to Quincy. When I went to get him, I found him and Joseph at the temple site. Joseph was telling him marvelous things, and Papa was lapping it all up. They told me to follow them with the buggy because they wanted to walk to the edge of town together. As we approached the River Road that led to Quincy, right there on the shore of the Mississippi River, the two of them stopped, and Joseph put his arm around my father. I pulled the buggy up beside them and heard the Prophet say, "Frederick, I hate to see you leave. You are going home to die."

Papa responded with, "I am already a dead man, dear friend."

My father had given up.

They embraced, and I could see Joseph whisper something in

Papa's ear. It brought tears to his eyes, and they embraced for the last time on this earth. I helped Papa into the buggy, and off we went, Papa turning to see Nauvoo and Joseph one last time.

About five miles into our return trip to Quincy, I got up the courage to ask Papa what Joseph had whispered to him. He looked at me with a strange look, a longing for a time past. "I won't be far behind you," said my father. "That is what he said to me." And time proved him right.

That was the summer of 1842, and my father's health steadily declined for the next few months. By the end of the summer, he rarely left the house. It was hard to get him to talk or take interest in anything.

But then in September, a couple of joyful things happened. On the 9th, Lovina was delivered of a healthy baby girl who they named Adeline. Oh, she was a beautiful baby. My parents were overcome with joy. Papa was able to sit up and hold that baby on his lap. He caressed her and held her close to his heart, and she seemed to respond to his love.

Then on September 18, Lucy was married to Nathan Pinkham, an entrepreneur in Quincy, and a good man. With a lot of help from Mother and me, Papa was able to go to the wedding. His good friend, Apostle Heber C. Kimball, performed the ceremony, and four other apostles who were Father's dear friends were there as well. He loved being around these men, his dearest friends, and he seemed to thrive on it. Things seemed to be looking up.

Lucy and Nathan lived nearby and came to visit often. Lucy was a great help to Lovina by taking care of the baby so her sister could rest. She rubbed Lovey's feet and legs and back and brought her the good and nourishing food to eat that Mother had prepared. Nathan sat by Papa and tried to encourage him to be strong. He talked about the baby and how she would grow into a beautiful woman someday, and surely Father would want to see her be married to a fine man. He said, one fine day not too far distant, he and Lucy would have beautiful children that would want to know their grandfather, also.

With so much help and attention, Lovina regained her strength quickly after the rather difficult delivery. And we all doted on little Adeline; Mama, Papa, Lucy, even Nathan had fallen in love with her as I had, but my mother especially could not get enough of that baby. Every little grimace, burp, or bubble she would make was cause for celebration, it seemed. Father always perked up at the mere sight of "his girls," his wife, his daughters, and his first living grandchild.

"Ezra," Mother confided in me, "Adeline just might be the medicine that the doctor needs to help him turn the corner and regain his desire to live."

But by the first of October, it was quite apparent that my father, despite our love, attention, and admonishment that we needed him here on earth, was not going to make it. Every day saw him sinking lower and lower into that dark abyss, with fewer and fewer trips to the surface for the life-giving air. Although I was not a doctor yet, my years of helping my father with his patients had taught me a lot, and just looking at him then, I could tell he didn't have much time left on earth. It is a look I would come to recognize very well in the coming years.

There had been a branch of the Church in Quincy since the time the Saints first came in 1839 because many church members had stayed there rather than go to Nauvoo. They had found good jobs, good homes, and good friends, so they just stayed. During our time in Quincy, our family faithfully attended the branch services every week. When Father started to miss meetings, many members asked about him, and when they heard that he was very ill, many dropped by almost daily to see how he was doing, and to try to give him the love and support that he so badly needed. One Sunday night, however, the person knocking on the door was not from our branch, but was the Prophet's brother, Hyrum Smith. When I opened the door and Mother saw who it was, she rushed to greet him.

"Oh, Brother Hyrum." My mother found it hard to control her emotions. "How good it is to see you. I know Frederick will be happy as well. I will go tell him you are here."

I asked Brother Hyrum to take off his coat and hat and sit down. He said, "I have come to talk to Frederick about things that have been pressing on my mind for some time. Do you think he is up to talking with me?"

Just then, Mother came back into the room and beckoned to him.

"Frederick is most eager to see you, Hyrum. You, of all people, are the one who can soothe his mind at this time. Please, come and sit by his side."

With me tagging along as I had done so many times in the past, Hyrum Smith went into my father's bedroom and sat down. He took hold of Father's hand, and held it with much tenderness, and began to pour out his love for Dr. Frederick G. Williams.

"Frederick, I know your time is precious, and I don't want to stay long, but there are a few things I must say. First, I love you, my brother." Hyrum choked up as the tears welled up in his eyes. I saw Father squeeze his hand. "Second, I never wanted to take your place in the First Presidency. That is rightfully your place, not mine. I raised my hand in support of you, not against you."

"No, Hyrum—you are definitely supposed—to be in that office—at this time," my father replied. He spoke slowly in short phrases, with great laboring breaths. "Yes, I miss—that association with you—all so much that my heart aches—with desire to be with you—but I know when—the Lord has other plans—and in this case—this is how it should be."

"You are a quiet man, Frederick, and perhaps your biggest problem in this life has been not sticking up for yourself. But I know the real Frederick. I know your loving and giving nature. I know that you would do anything for any one of your brethren or their families." At this, Hyrum's grip on my father's hand tightened as Father stifled a sob. "And I believe with all my heart you would never have turned on Joseph, not for more than a fleeting thought at the most."

"In that—you are right—brother," Father said even more quietly and slowly.

Hyrum continued, "Thirdly, I bring you the love of Joseph, and all of us who have known and loved you all these years. Some mistakes were made on all our parts, but I leave it to the Lord to sort them out, and in the end, all will be made right."

"What a comforting—thing you tell me—I want to face—my Savior with a clear—conscience and have—spent many days—repenting of all—my wrong doings in—anticipation of—that meeting."

Father's voice was getting weaker and softer, and his breathing was coming in ragged gulps and closer intervals, as though he could not get enough oxygen. I could barely hear or understand him.

"I am not the prophet, and I am certainly not God, but from my point of view, you are going to be able to do that very thing. I have no worries for your soul, Frederick. You are where you are supposed to be. We will all miss you, as we already have missed you. And I know your family will be so sad to see you go. But you will be preparing the way for all of us. You will be there to greet us with that loving way of yours, your quiet strength, and your sense of justice. Those are Christlike characteristics, dear friend, and you are possessed of them. I love you with all my heart."

And Hyrum put his big strong arms around my frail father and hugged him to his heart for a long time, as though this action could say the things his words could not. He brushed my father's hair out of his face and kissed him on the cheek. Then, wishing us all a good evening, he left.

I sat by my father that whole night. He was able to talk to me a little off and on throughout the night. He was able to tell me that he felt forgiven of his sins, and that he knew he would be with Swain and his parents, and the Savior himself. He was looking forward to that.

Early in the morning, Mother came into his room. Even though he instantly perked up at the sound of her voice, she could tell his time was at hand.

She sat down by him and put her head down on his chest and cried, "Don't leave me, Freddy, please don't leave me."

She turned to me and said, "Do something, Ezra. Don't let him go!" But of course, I was helpless to do anything but cry with her for him. She turned her head toward him and looked deeply into his eyes, as if she were trying to see into his soul. Then my father did a most miraculous thing. With the last bit of strength that he had in his tired, worn-out body, he raised his head up off his pillow and kissed my mother good-bye. Then his head sank back on the pillow, and he died.

I saw a tear escape his eye, and I gently wiped it away. My hero, my rock, my idle was gone from this earth too soon. Nearly nineteen-year-old me still needed him, and truth be told, I still need him today. But those nineteen years had to be enough. I took the lessons I learned from this great, great man, and patterned my life after his, as he had, to the best of his mortal ability, patterned his life after the Savior whom he loved so much.

CHAPTER FORTY

Ogden, Utah 1905

Farewell to Ogden

Ezra was unable to speak for several minutes.

Finally, Fred said, "Papa, my heart hurts for you. I have had my father here for all of my fifty-three years, and I thank God for every one of them. I can't imagine what I would have done if I had lost you when I was nineteen."

"You would have been fine because your father taught you to be the man that you are long ago." Henrietta had come in several minutes earlier when she could see that Ezra was in an emotional knot.

Fred bowed his head. "You are right, Mama. But I'm still glad I didn't lose him early."

"It is not the ideal situation to lose your father early on in life. I lost my father early, Son. And my mother, too. I agree that you are lucky to have both of us."

Things started to turn into a crying fest there for a few minutes, until Ezra said, "That is the story I brought you up here to tell you."

"Wait, Grandpa, are you saying you are done?"

"What more would you want to hear, Joe?"

"I don't know. More. You can't be through with it already," Joe whined.

"What do you mean I can't be through already? It has taken me nearly a year to tell you all of this."

"Well, what did you do next?"

Ezra sighed his deep sigh, and said, "All right, but there isn't that much more to tell.

"My father died on October 10, 1842. True to his word, Joseph soon followed Frederick in death. Less than two years later, the Prophet Joseph Smith and his brother Hyrum were martyred in Carthage Jail, just forty-three miles from Quincy. The temple in Nauvoo was never completely finished, as the hoped-for peace and safety there never fully materialized. The familiar hatred raised its ugly head again in the beautiful city, and the Saints were once again driven out, this time to a location far away in the west, to this very place where we are today.

"After my father's death, I continued to follow the pattern he had cut for me and pursued the practice of medicine. By the time we left Quincy, Lovina had given birth to another baby girl, Lucy, named for my sister Lucy who had sadly passed away a year after the martyrdom on July 26, 1845. She died after having given birth to a baby girl, Ellen, who did not survive, either."

"That is so sad, Papa."

"Lucy and I had always been close. It broke my heart when she passed away."

"And so, you had to leave the temple in Nauvoo before it was completed, Grandpa?"

"Yes, Joe. It was nearly finished by the time it became obvious that we had to move again, but even unfinished, it was a great blessing to the Saints. Before Joseph was martyred, he had revealed temple ordinances that could seal couples and families together forever, not just for this life. As soon as one floor of the temple was finished, it was dedicated so those ordinances could be performed, but the Saints were only able to use it for a few months before they were run out of Nauvoo. Everyone wanted the temple blessings before they left for the west. Many days the temple operated day and night so more people could receive them before leaving."

"Were you able to get your temple blessings, Grandpa?"

"Well, Mother and I had decided to move to St. Louis after Lucy's death. Many of the Saints from around the eastern United States were headed there to outfit themselves before heading west, and doctors were sorely needed. Luckily for me, there were a couple of very good physicians in St. Louis who took me on as an apprentice so I could complete my medical education.

"Most of the saints who came to St. Louis went on up the river to Nauvoo to receive their temple blessings before heading west. My mother and I knew that we needed those blessings, too, so in February of 1847, the two of us headed back upriver and received those special ordinances there in the unfinished temple, and Mother was sealed to my father for all eternity. That was a pretty good feeling."

"Why didn't you just stay in Nauvoo and head west from there, Papa?"

"Maybe we should have, Son, but I needed to finish my apprenticeship. Besides, the need for physicians in St. Louis was so great that I went back down there, hoping I could help. As it turns out, I was very grateful that I did."

"I bet I know why, Grandpa." Joe stole a glance at his grandmother.

"You do, huh? Well, tell us all, then, Joe."

He laughed a little in triumph. "That's where you met Grandma."

Ezra looked at his wife, and she looked at him, and a knowing smile passed between them.

"How did you know that, Joe?"

Henrietta winked at her grandson. "Because I told him all about it."

"You stinker. You stole my thunder, did you?"

"I can't remember what happened next, though, Granddad. So, what happened next?"

"Sadly, my sister Lovina passed away that same year, in November of 1847. Nathan and his mother took Lovey's two baby girls, Adeline and Lucy, and raised them. Their father, Burr Riggs, had become so dependent on alcohol that Lovina could no longer live with him, and he did not have the ability to raise the girls after her death. I've lost track of what became of the girls, but I have faith that somewhere down the line, someone in our family will find them or their children."[60]

"I hope so, Papa."

"Now, it's time for lunch," announced Henrietta, and everyone agreed. "Joe, could you come help me get a few things ready?"

"You bet I will, Grandma," said the boy, and he and Henrietta left the room.

Fred stood and stepped closer to Ezra. He took hold of his father's hand and said, "Thank you, Papa, for telling us all of this. I know much of it was not easy. But I want you to know, I love you for it. You have always been and always will be my hero."

He leaned over into his father's arms and the two of them hugged, silently communicating their love for one another. "Do you want to come into the dining room, Papa?"

"No, I think I'll stay in here this time, Son."

A few minutes later, Joe came into the room with a tray of food for his grandfather. Fred put the bed table across Ezra's lap, and Joe set the tray on it. Ezra inhaled the smell of the homemade bread and chicken noodle soup. "Mmmm," he said. "That smells so good, Joe. Thank you."

Joe left the room, and Ezra again turned his eyes to his son. "Would you mind helping me eat today, Fred? I'm feeling a little fatigued and am afraid I'll make a mess."

"Of course I will, Papa."

◆

That night as Fred and Joseph were preparing for bed, Fred said, "It's about time we head for home, Son."

"Nooooo, not yet, Dad."

"Your mother misses you, and we have almost a year's worth of work waiting for us. And I know you miss your horse."

Joseph heaved a big sigh of resignation as they crawled into bed and turned out the oil lamp. Joe lay still and silent in the dark for several minutes before saying, "Dad, I've been trying to hear God's voice."

"Have you succeeded?" asked his father.

"I don't know for sure, but I think so."

"Tell me about it."

"When I pray, I stop to listen like you told me to, and I often hear words come into my mind. They might be God's words to me, but I'm not sure. Maybe I'm making them up."

"Do you follow what the words tell you?"

"Usually."

"And what happens?"

"Good things."

"And if you don't do what the words tell you to do, what then?"

"I wish I would have."

"Well, Son, this is what I have learned. Like you, when I pray, I listen for whatever comes into my mind first. I have learned to rely on that being the voice of my Heavenly Father. That's the usual way he talks to me. But I have also had strange dreams that seem to have a message from him, or sometimes someone says something that sticks in my mind, something I can't forget, and I often ask in my prayers if that was him trying to tell me something through someone else."

"And what does he say?"

"He lets me know if it is from him by that warm tingling feeling that starts at my head and sort of moves on down my whole body. There are many ways to hear his voice, and I think he talks to each of us in the way that we can best understand. I once knew a girl who heard his voice through music. She was a good musician, and so it was easy for her to hear it that way."

"Maybe he will someday answer me while riding my horse."

"I don't doubt that, Son. You keep listening for him, and he will let you know the best way for you to communicate with him. Then have faith in the answer. He promised us that he would communicate with us, so we have to trust that he does."

"All right, Dad, I will do that."

They were both silent for several minutes until Joe said, "Grandpa is a great man, isn't he, Dad."

"Yes, he is."

"And his father was a great man, too, wasn't he."

"Yes, I suppose he was indeed, Son."

"And the Prophet Joseph, he really was a prophet, wasn't he, Dad."

"Yes, I truly believe he was."

He lay on his back staring up into the darkness. "Dad," he paused a moment before continuing. "Thank you for naming me Joseph Frederick after two great men. But Dad…"

This time he paused so long that Fred started to think he had gone to sleep.

Finally, he said in a low, shaky voice, "Dad, I think I am named for three great men."

"Really, Son? Who is the third?"

"You, Dad. You are the one I have learned the most from." Joseph was glad the room was dark because the tears were escaping from his eyes and rolling down into his ears. "Grandpa has taught me so much since we have been here, but everything I learn from him makes me realize how lucky I am to be your son. You are the one who has taught me how to be a man."

Joseph could hear his father swallow hard a few times before he said, "Thank you, Son. I love you very much."

"I love you, too, Dad."

Fred and Joseph were ready to leave for Mexico the following week. They had helped Henrietta get everything cleaned up around the house and in the barnyard. The garden was plowed and ready to plant, there was plenty of feed for the horses, chickens, and cow set up in nearby barrels, so she didn't have to carry anything heavy very far. Henrietta busily fixed and packed as much food as she could for them to eat on the way home.

"Will you be all right, Mama? I hate to leave you like this."

"I'll be fine," she told them, as they fussed around her. "Tom Budge promised he would bring Thomas and Louis by once a week to help me with whatever I need them to do. And I have good neighbors who won't let us starve."

"That is comforting, Mother, but I still worry about you."

"Oh posh. We'll be fine. We've made it this far. I suppose we can make it a bit further."

That last night before they left, the three Williamses gathered around their patriarch's bed, and took turns recalling things they had learned from one another, and to thank Ezra for persevering through the difficult story he had told them.

"I just have one question for you, Papa. Was it all worth it, all the things you went through?"

Ezra moved his eyes from side to side as if he might be trying to decide what to say. "My dear son, grandson, and of course, my Henrietta," he finally said, looking at each one of them in turn, "what we went through was very hard. We lost loved ones, we were run out of three states, we were treated by the mobs as less than human, we lost every material possession we had, we worked hard, sometimes on very little food and with tired and broken bodies. We did very hard things to the point that many of us wondered if we could go on. But if I were asked to turn around and do it all again, knowing what I know now, I would not hesitate to do it, and with a happy heart. Look at what we have gained. Can you name some blessing that you have because we were willing to do what we did?"

"We have each other," said Joe without a hesitation.

"We live in comfortable circumstances without the real threat of having someone take it from us," added Fred.

"We know we will have our families forever, and not just for this mortal sojourn," said Henrietta. "I know I will always have you." She looked at Ezra and then kissed his hand.

"And my dad and I as well, Grandma."

"That's right, Joe. You, your father, and all the other members of your family, as well as all the rest of our big family. And we will have our baby boys back," she added.

"What would you add, Papa?"

"I would add my gratitude to my father for not giving up and leaving the Restored Church when it would have been easy to do so. Had he left, it is very likely that none of us would be here in this room today bearing testimony of the truthfulness of the Gospel of Jesus Christ, for the knowledge that Christ lives and loves us, and that he will come again. That is worth it all."

They all nodded in agreement.

"And what a good example Father set for others, for everyone and anyone who may think they have a good reason to leave," he continued.

"There is never a good enough reason to leave the truth. Where would you go?" asked Henrietta.

"If you remember one thing from what I have told you boys, remember this. We are all imperfect. I am, you are, my father was, and although he came close by the end of his life, the Prophet Joseph Smith was not perfect, nor is our prophet today. There is only One who is perfect, and that is Jesus Christ. Let him be your exemplar. He will never let you down."

———◆———

The next morning, their neighbor, Brother Black, pulled up with his buggy into the yard. He had consented to drive Joseph and his father to the train station. Joe had found himself wishing that Brother Black would be late, but he was there exactly on time. Joe had slipped into Ezra's room earlier, but his grandfather was still asleep, so he kissed his head, and turned to leave the room when he heard Ezra say, "Never forget, Joe. Never forget."

"I—I love you Grandpa," he said from the doorway, then he left the room, grabbed his hat, and ran outside where his father and grandmother stood with their arms around each other.

Fred had everything loaded in Brother Black's buggy, and after kissing and hugging his mother one last time, he climbed in.

Joseph looked at his grandmother, who was holding her arms open to him, and he collapsed into her. "I don't want to leave you," he said, as she caressed his cheek and smoothed the hair out of his eyes.

"Now, Joe, you are going to come see me every year when you are old enough to travel alone, remember?"

"I will, Grandma, I promise." He gave her a kiss on the cheek, put his hat on his head, climbed into the back of the buggy, and they started on their way.

As they left the yard, Joe turned around to see Henrietta waving her arms and throwing him kisses. He held his hat up high and waved back.

A Word from Dr. Frederick G. Williams III,
Historian, Researcher and Expert on the life of
FREDERICK G. WILLIAMS

Prior to joining the Church, Frederick Granger Williams had become a successful doctor with an established practice and bright future. He had held an elected civil office for four years before moving to Kirtland, owned land, was relatively wealthy and highly respected.

He entered the Church in his mature years, forsaking all these material things, vigorously engaging in the Church's activities, whatever they were. Although his testimony and love of the gospel and for Joseph Smith caused him to be persecuted and driven from his home, and in time cost him all that he owned and broke his health, it was only within the Church that he rose to his greatest heights. He became a justice of the peace, the editor of a newspaper, the president of a bank, a trustee of a school, and a member of the Presidency of the Church. His was the privilege of being equal in holding the keys of the kingdom with Joseph and Sidney. He participated in many glorious spiritual experiences, culminating with the dedication of the Kirtland Temple where his was the great privilege of seeing the Savior Himself.

He lost his position of leadership and eventually even his membership in the Church. But whatever his personal weaknesses, he had the strength of character to maintain his loyalty to the Prophet and return humbly to the Church when it would have been so easy to have disintegrated in bitterness.

I am grateful that he did.

Dr. Frederick G. Williams III

"An Angel or Rather the Savior" at the Kirtland Temple Dedication: The Vision of Frederick G. Williams, BYU Studies Quarterly, Vol 56, Iss. 1 (2017)

Whatever Happened to ...

Rebecca Swain Williams

Rebecca was the only wife of a member of the original First Presidency, including Oliver Cowdery, to come West with the Saints. She came with her son Ezra, daughter-in-law Henrietta, and granddaughter Lucy. She lived out her life with Ezra and his family, moving to Smithfield with them in 1860, where she passed away a year later, 1861, at the age of 63. She is buried in the Smithfield Cemetery beside three of her little grandsons. There is no evidence of her ever seeing her granddaughters, Adeline and Lucy, again after leaving for the West.

Ezra Granger Williams

Ezra and family entered the Salt Lake Valley on Sunday morning, October 28, 1849. Their wagon boxes were turned on their sides facing west, and draped with canvas. This is where they lived the first winter in the valley. Ezra built them a house the next spring. In 1850 he was appointed the first Surgeon General of the Territory of Utah. He traveled as escort with Brigham Young to Iron County in 1852. In 1855 he served a mission in the White Mountains in Southern Utah. Later he served in the Elk Mountains and then in the Sandwich Islands. In 1860 he moved his family to Smithfield where his mother and three sons are buried. Later he moved to Ogden where he lived until his death in 1905, at age eighty-one, just a few months after his son Frederick returned to Mexico.

He treated thousands of people during his time as a doctor, including many Indians, some of whom became his friends.

Excerpts from his obituary: As a physician, they (the speakers) stated, he was always kind to the poor, giving his services gratis, to hundreds of that class … the example he had set before the people and his family was always of the highest type and deserving of emulation. The family … were assured that he would receive a crown of glory in mansions above because of his faithfulness to the laws and commandments of God. (*The Weekly Sun*, Ogden Utah 8/8/1905)

Henrietta Elizabeth Crombie Williams

Henrietta stood by her husband through his life without getting much recognition for herself. She was often left alone to raise the children when Ezra was away on Church business, or acting in his capacity as a doctor and surgeon. She suffered hardships after leaving Boston and a huge fortune, but in her journal she states more than once that none of that mattered because they were going to Zion. After Ezra's death in 1905, Henrietta went to live with her son Ezra Henry Granger Williams in east Ogden until her death in 1922, at age 94. She is buried by her husband and son John Albert in the Ogden City Cemetery.

Frederick Granger Williams II

Fred was a colonizer, horse breeder, farmer, rancher, blacksmith and medical practitioner. He loved to sing, play the violin and organ, and write poetry and stories. In addition to the five boys he and his wife Amanda Burns lost in infancy, Fred and his wife Nancy Clement lost three baby girls. Fred returned from his parents' house in Ogden, Utah, to his families in Mexico around April of 1905.

Excerpt from his obituary: Mr. Williams was riding on a load of baled hay when one of the hooks gave way and allowed him to fall. The rear wheel of the wagon passed over his head and neck. He died before a doctor could reach him. He went to Arizona on a mission in 1875–76, and later went to Mexico with Bishop Winslow Farr. He was driven out in 1912 by the Mexican revolutionaries and took up a dry farm near Tucson. Mr. Williams was the father of twenty-three children (*The Ogden Standard*, Thursday Evening, January 24, 1918).

Joseph Frederick Williams

When Joe was eleven years old, he started hauling lumber for the Phillip Hurst Mills through the mountains, by himself. Joe married Sara Jane "Jennie" Spencer in 1908. Three children were born to them, two girls and a boy. The oldest, named Jennie after her mother, was the only child to live to adulthood. Hazel lived 7 months; her brother Joseph Maylan lived eleven months.

During the Mexican Revolution, he saw a lot of destruction around him. In 1916, he went with the first troops to New Mexico where, on the day that his wife Jennie died, he was captured and sent by the Carbonistas to Ciudad Juarez. He was there sentenced to be shot at daybreak, but miraculously, his life was saved by the efforts of General John J. Pershing.

He later married Evelena Spencer, who bore him nine children, three of whom died in infancy—two boys and one girl. Joe served five missions for the Church, including Chihuahua, Mexico in 1919, and the Spanish American Mission (with wife Evelena) in 1964. Joe died on 11 Dec 1975 in Arco Idaho at the age of 87.

Please see more information, many photos, and more stories about these people and other topics on my website, where additional copies of the book can be purchased: **sherriefarrdunford.com**.

ENDNOTES

Abbreviations:

FGW3 on Dr. FGW: Dr. Frederick G. Williams III, *Dr. Frederick G. Williams, Counselor to the Prophet Joseph Smith,* BYU Studies, Provo Utah. This book is available on Amazon Kindle and on the Deseret Book e-book app. It contains the most comprehensive information on President Williams, and is quoted liberally here. Because it was published by BYU Studies, every fact in it had to be vetted before it could be printed, and is therefore very reliable. Please refer to it for any questions you may have about President Williams.

D&C: Doctrine and Covenants, the Church of Jesus Christ of Latter-day Saints

BofM: Book of Mormon, the Church of Jesus Christ of Latter-day Saints

PofGP: Pearl of Great Price, the Church of Jesus Christ of Latter-day Saints

1. FGW3 on Dr. FGW p. 40
2. FGW3 on Dr. FGW p. 93, *Dr. Frederick G. Williams: The Fifth and Oldest Member of the 1830–1831 Mission to the Lamanites,* by Dr. Frederick G. Williams III, p. 63
3. FGW3 on Dr. FGW p. 126
4. D&C 32:2-3
5. FGW3 on Dr. FGW p. 102
6. FGW3 on Dr. FGW p. 122
7. FGW3 on Dr. FGW p. 126-127
8. D&C 1:19, 23
9. See *Primary 5: Doctrine and Covenants and Church History,* Lesson 21, Joseph Smith is tarred and feathered, p. 111. churchofjesuschrist.org
10. The Facsimile Edition of the Revelation Books 1 and 2 of the *Joseph Smith Papers* (which are essentially the original scribal record books for the Book of Commandments and the Doctrine and Covenants), the original scribe for D&C 76 in record book 1 is John Whitmer; in record book 2 the original scribes for D&C 76 are Frederick G. Williams and Joseph Smith.
11. D&C 76:22-24
12. Primary 5 lesson 21 (see note 9) p. 111
13. See heading to D&C 81

14. *Joseph Smith Papers*, Letterbook 1:1-6.

15. *Joseph Smith's new translation of the Bible: Original Manuscripts* by Faulring, Jackson and Matthews

16. FGW3 on Dr. FGW p. 192

17. BofM: Mormon 9:21

18. D&C 93:1

19. D&C 93:20

20. D&C 93:41-42

21. D&C 93:44

22. D&C 93:47

23. D&C 93:50

24. D&C 93:51-53

25. It appears that President Williams did take the Lord's directive to heart and began to be more intentional about teaching his family truth and light. His family was the only one out of the original First Presidency that stayed true to the faith, left with the Saints in the great westward migration of 1847 and the years after to help establish Zion "in the tops of the mountains."

26. FGW3 on Dr. FGW, p. 201, and History of the Church 1:444

27. So much is written on Zion's Camp that is easily accessible on the Church's website, churchofjesuschrist.org, and by many other well-qualified historians. For more specific information on President Williams' involvement, see Chapter 11 of FGW3 on Dr. FGW. See also *The Acceptable Offering of Zion's Camp* by Matthew C. Godfrey, in Revelations in Context

28. FGW3 on Dr. FGW, p. 262

29. FGW3 on Dr. FGW, p. 266 and History of the Church 2:114

30. See FGW3 on Dr. FGW, Chapter 21 starting on p. 437

31. As recorded in D&C 90:6-7.

32. See FGW3 on Dr. FGW, Chapter 13 starting on p. 288 for more information on the School of the Prophets.

33. See D&C 89 for the full Word of Wisdom

34. D&C 88:79-80, paraphrased.

35. See PofGP Moses 7:21 and D&C 38:4.

36. See FGW3 on Dr. FGW, p. 223-246 for an in-depth treatise on these poems, including further discussion of how they relate to Enoch, and also on how many of the early hymns of the restoration were mis-attributed or had no attribution at all.

37. *Truman Osborn Angell (1810-1887) Autobiography*, pp. 14–15, Church History Library, Salt Lake City Utah.

38. See FGW3 on Dr. FGW, pp. 392-397.

39. See FGW3 on Dr. FGW, p.527, also *History of the Church* 1:444.

40. Horace Whitney later married Helen Mar Kimball.

41. "The Spirit of God," LDS Hymns #2.

42. *"An Angel or Rather the Savior" at the Kirtland Temple Dedication*, by Frederick G. Williams, BYU Studies Quarterly 56, no. 1 [2017].

43. The Kirtland Safety Society only lasted seven months, but those months created a mess that will likely never be understood on this side of the veil. My attempt to present it here is an effort to simplify a very complicated situation. Much is written on the subject on the Church website, churchofjesuschirst.org, and by many other well-qualified historians. Also see FGW3 on Dr. FGW, pp. 455–490 for further information on F. G. Williams' involvement, the many trials to which he was subpoenaed because of it, and on the quarrel between him and Joseph Smith (page 479 ff). Ezra G. Williams was with his father the day the quarrel occurred as quoted on p. 481, and describes it in his personal journal entitled "Memories of My Life." A note of interest: Years later, all the records of the KSS were found in Columbus, Ohio, the state capitol, and after having an auditor go through them, it was found that there was no wrongdoing by anyone connected with the bank.

44. See D&C 64:21.

45. Sylvester Stoddard, Microfilm, positive, included in entry "Mormon Manuscript Collection."

46. From Shakespeare's *MacBeth*, Act IV scene I

47. This is my grandmother's real authentic chili sauce recipe.

48. See *History of the Church*, 3:14

49. Oliver came back to the Church after ten years, long after Joseph had died, and humbly submitted himself for rebaptism in October 1848 in Kanesville, Iowa, and only months before he himself passed away. (*Oliver's Joseph*, Chapter One, by Richard L. Bushman, in *Days Never to be Forgotten*)

50. Martin Harris, like Oliver Cowdery, eventually returned to membership in the Church, but not until he was 83 years old, however, David Whitmer never returned to membership in the church. Despite their disaffection, none of these men ever denied his testimony of the Book of Mormon, or of an angel showing the plates to the three of them, and allowing them to be handled.

51. See FGW3 on Dr. FGW, p. 547.

52. See *History of the Church*, 3:167

53. See *History of the Church*, 3:167. Marsh was excommunicated in March of 1839, and Hyde was suspended from his office in May of that year until he met with the General Conference of the Church and explained his actions. After repenting, Elder Hyde was reinstated fairly soon, but Brother Marsh did not return to the Church until 1857, after having gone through much misery.

54. See *Lilburn W. Boggs, Executive Order to John B. Clark*, Oct. 27, 1838, Missouri State Archives, sos.mo.gov. See also FGW3 on Dr. FGW, p. 558.

55. *Memories of My Life*, personal journal of Dr. Ezra G. Williams.

56. Pratt, Parley P., Jr., *Autobiography of Parley P. Pratt*, p. 164.

57. Pratt, Parley P., Jr., *Autobiography of Parley P. Pratt*, pp. 179-180.

58. See FGW3 on Dr. FGW, p. 566

59. See FGW3 on Dr. FGW, p. 568

60. Some of Lovina's descendants were found in 1998, and have attended Williams family reunions in recent years.

www.ingramcontent.com/pod-product-compliance
Lightning Source LLC
Chambersburg PA
CBHW020349010826
48973CB00005B/1338

9 798889 454067